Where There's A Will

Mary Malone

POOLBEG

This novel is entirely a work of fiction. The names, characters and incidents portrayed in it are the work of the author's imagination. Any resemblance to actual persons, living or dead, events or localities is entirely coincidental.

Published 2013
by Poolbeg Press Ltd.
123 Grange Hill, Baldoyle,
Dublin 13, Ireland
Email: poolbeg@poolbeg.com

© Mary Malone 2013

The moral right of the author has been asserted.

1

Copyright for typesetting, layout, design, ebook
© Poolbeg Press Ltd.

A catalogue record for this book is available from the British Library.

ISBN 978-1-84223-490-7

All rights reserved. No part of this publication may be reproduced or transmitted in any form or by any means, electronic or mechanical, including photography, recording, or any information storage or retrieval system, without permission in writing from the publisher. The book is sold subject to the condition that it shall not, by way of trade or otherwise, be lent, resold or otherwise circulated without the publisher's prior consent in any form of binding or cover other than that in which it is published and without a similar condition, including this condition, being imposed on the subsequent purchaser.

Typeset by Patricia Hope in Sabon 10.75/14.6

Printed and bound by CPI Group (UK) Ltd, Croydon, CR0 4YY

www.poolbeg.com

About the Author

Mary Malone lives in Templemartin, Bandon, Co Cork with her husband Pat and sons David and Mark. As well as being a novelist and freelance journalist, she works fulltime in the Central Statistics Office.

Where There's A Will is her fifth novel.

For more information, please email mary@marymalone.ie or visit her website, **www.marymalone.ie**.

Also by Mary Malone

Love Match
All You Need Is Love
Never Tear Us Apart
Love Is The Reason

Acknowledgements

Where There's A Will has been fermenting for over two years, originating as a ten-minute class assignment before taking wings and developing into a novel. Sincere thanks, Bernadette Leach, for setting us the task of writing about 'The Street' and sparking the idea for this story.

Huge thanks to Paula Campbell and the Poolbeg team for their support, patience and understanding – and for granting me extra time to reach The End!

'The End' for an author is only the beginning for Poolbeg's magnificent editor, Gaye Shortland. Your patience was well tested on this one, Gaye, and *Where There's A Will* has benefited from your expert insight and knowledge, particularly in the minefield of inheritance! Your dedication to this story has been unbelievable. Thank you.

As with my previous novels, I struggled with the direction *Where There's A Will* was taking me. Needing an honest writer's opinion, author Mary O'Sullivan was (as ever) delighted to help. Thanks for your honesty and time, Mary. God knows where the poor characters would have ended up without your input!

Sincere thanks to numerous relations, friends and work colleagues who enquire if 'the book will be out soon'! Your nudges of encouragement keep me at the keyboard and play a huge part in getting a story from my head to the bookshops!

And speaking of bookshops, I'm looking forward to visiting as many around the country as I can. Huge thanks for your support – and of course for an eye-level spot on the shelf!

And finally, my heartfelt thanks (and apologies!) to my family. To Pat, David and Mark for putting up with my anti-social writing habits. I'm often in the room but generally in another world, regularly putting writing before other commitments and annoyingly pleading for an endless supply of coffee and chocolate. Thanks, lads.

Thanks to my mother for turning a blind eye when I produced the laptop on our weekend breaks to Kerry and also for her relentless advertising ability as she spreads the news about her daughter's latest offering to the world of books.

Finally to my brother, Barry, and sister-in-law, Miriam. I'd like to dedicate this book to you both for endless support and true friendship. With only the two of us in the family, Barry has suffered a lifetime of having me as a sister. Yet I've heard he won't have a word said against me – if what you say is true, Miriam! And as testament to his sibling loyalty, he actually reads my books! Thanks, Bar.

With love to Barry & Miriam

Chapter 1

Inheritance. The word held promise as it bounced around Kieran Dulhooly's mind. Being named as a beneficiary was a first for him. What had Aunt Polly bequeathed to him? *Bequeath* – such an old-fashioned and stuffy term, now he thought about it – not a word he'd ever had cause to use. Until now.

He twisted his wristwatch around to see the time. Forty minutes he'd been waiting in the solicitor's open-plan reception area on the second floor of the modern building on Lapp's Quay in Cork city. So much for telling me this meeting wouldn't take long, he thought, flicking idly through the morning paper, the print blurring out of focus as his concentration drifted.

Receiving a telephone call from Fitzgerald & Partners the previous afternoon had come as a shock to say the least. If the call hadn't come through on his parents' landline, he'd have assumed it was one of his wayward friends playing a practical joke and might well have ignored the instruction to attend the reading of his Aunt Polly's will. But his father's serious expression as he handed him the receiver had indicated that it was not a joking matter. What Kieran found particularly puzzling was the fact his father, as Polly's next of kin, hadn't been called to the reading too. But knowing little about these situations, he'd assumed it was all part of the legal process.

"She probably left me that rickety train set I spent hours playing with as a kid," he had commented to his father who'd remained within earshot.

But despite his outward cynicism, Kieran had found it impossible to ignore the instant warmth spreading through him. It felt good to be remembered by someone he'd held so dear, even if he hadn't always shown her how much he cared. Memories of long summers spent with Aunt Polly came flooding back. Endless days of undisturbed fun in her end-of-terrace house on Pier Road, Schull, in West Cork. No disapproval or constant correction from parents. No silent stares or stern frowns when Kieran lapsed into his over-imaginative world. And, best of all, no strict regime about chores and bedtime. Aunt Polly's was the epitome of freedom, a place where he could be his true self without apology.

His mother, Marian, had immediately hurried to the phone when he'd explained about the will reading. "I need to call your sisters and see if they have been contacted," she'd announced. "It's only fair that all three of you should be included. And what about you, Frank? Of all people, you should be there." She'd turned to her husband, expecting enlightenment from him, her eyes narrowing when he'd shrugged his shoulders, displaying an indifference that irritated his wife.

"What would I need an inheritance for? Don't I pay

enough to Revenue without adding inheritance tax to that? Polly never made a secret of her plans to pass it on to the next generation." His tone was grave, the recent loss of his sister weighing heavily on him, a degree of guilt that he hadn't brought her to stay with him for her final days mixed with his grief. Instead she'd spent the final few weeks of her life in the nursing home. But realistically, the animosity between his wife and sister had dispelled any chance of him ever inviting her to stay in their lavish Ballydehob home.

The sound of muffled conversation snapped Kieran back to the present. Glancing up from his newspaper, he saw several suited employees approach. Afternoon tea break must be over, he mused, watching with idle interest as each in turn collected folders and documents from the pretty raven-haired receptionist before proceeding along the corridor to their respective offices.

Kieran shuddered in disgust at the thought of spending day after day working in an office environment. Being cooped up in an air-conditioned room for seven hours at a stretch was unimaginable, even with the odd break for court appearances.

Ten years before, his parents hadn't hidden their fury when he'd explained his abhorrence of confinement. Since then the college qualification that had cost thousands of euro in extra tuition and repeated semesters lay unused. Bumming his way around Europe, America, Australia and Canada instead, surviving on casual employment and never worrying about tomorrow, Kieran let his gap year extend to almost a decade, visiting home only a few times in that period. And now, in his early thirties, life was equally precarious and tomorrow still didn't feature in his calendar.

"Kieran Dulhooly?"

"Yes," he responded, rolling up his newspaper and shoving it under his arm as he jumped to his feet.

"Ms Jacobs is ready for you now."

He smothered a smile as the receptionist's eyes travelled the length of his long lean body.

Running a hand over his stubble, he enjoyed her open admiration. His attention was drawn to her fire-engine-red nail polish, a stark contrast to the crisp white fitted shirt that emphasised her shapely curves. Allowing himself a brief fantasy about the red nails scrawling his tanned back, he ignored her fluttering eyelashes and parted lips, focusing his attention on the purpose of his visit instead.

"Eh, where can I find Ms Jacobs?" He glanced around him. From where he stood, he could see a number of doors leading to individual offices along the brightly lit corridor.

"Second door on the left," she directed, resuming her professionalism and pointing the way. "You'll see Ms Jacobs' nameplate on the door."

Kieran gave a gentle knock before entering the bright office.

"Mr Dulhooly, thank you for coming in at such short notice," said the solicitor, her tone polite but curt. She stood up to welcome him, walking around her desk and shaking his hand. She gestured towards the chrome-and-leather chairs at the nearby round meeting-table. "Please take a seat."

"Thank you, Ms Jacobs." He chose a seat facing the window, watching her as she gathered some printed papers from her desk and came to sit opposite him.

"Tea? Coffee?"

This came as something of a surprise. He'd been expecting a strictly business approach. "Ah, there's no need. Thanks all the same." Kieran waited for her to continue, his eyes drawn to the view of the city's dockland, the activity on the water a sharp reminder of Schull and the panoramic view he'd enjoyed from the bedroom Aunt Polly had devoted to him in Pier Road.

He was aware of the solicitor flicking through documents, a fresh bout of anticipation rising inside him. Without intending to, he held his breath, surprised by the loud thumping of his heart. Now the moment of truth had arrived, he couldn't deny his unexpected excitement at the possibility of receiving something of value.

She pushed her glasses onto the bridge of her nose, fixing her short dark hair behind her ears to reveal sapphire studs, the gesture instantly softening her look. Unlocking her briefcase, she removed a slim yellow file and placed it on the table between them. Then she got to her feet again and closed the Venetian blinds on the large window facing into the corridor. In that flick of her wrist, she shut out the rest of the office, making the reason for their meeting seem more serious.

Kieran let out the breath he'd been holding. "Surely there are more people attending, Ms Jacobs?"

He shuffled in his chair, self-conscious and out of his depth. Had he asked a stupid question, he wondered. After all, the extent of his will-reading knowledge was confined to bits of information snatched from television programmes. His mother's insistence that Dad, Beth and Charlotte would have to be included too had made perfect sense but then she'd discovered that they weren't. Perhaps the solicitor would be contacting them at a later date? Thinking about it now, he was surprised his father hadn't enlightened him a little considering his years working in courtrooms. On the other hand, he hadn't pressed his father for information – to tell the truth, he'd felt awkward about the whole thing.

"No, just you today." The solicitor's even tone gave nothing away.

Made sense to be dealt with individually, Kieran supposed. And it guaranteed confidentiality. At least then, if the train set was his only acquisition, he wouldn't be a laughing stock. But somehow it didn't satisfy his curiosity and he made a final attempt to find out more. "There *are* other beneficiaries, Ms Jacobs?" he said, rephrasing his question.

"Please call me Olivia," she prompted, her gentle laughter lightening the mood.

He fiddled with the rip in his jeans, picking at the frayed material, aware that yet again she'd evaded his question.

"I'll get directly to business then, shall I?"

He wished she would. "Please."

"*This is the last will and testament of Pauline Digby . . .*"

Kieran's concentration drifted, daring to hope that Polly had left him enough to buy that Yamaha motorbike he'd had his eye on for a while now. South America would be his next trip with a bit of luck and maybe from there he'd venture on to . . .

"Kieran, are you with me?" Olivia removed her glasses and waited for his full attention. "This is the most important bit coming up now."

He felt like a naughty child being reprimanded by a stern teacher, and blushed as he met her eye.

"*I do give and bequeath to my nephew, Kieran Dulhooly,*

all my personal effects and tangible personal property, including my home at Number 5 Pier Road, Schull, Co Cork and any cash on hand and in bank accounts in my own name . . ."

Olivia paused. She watched Kieran's facial expression change, green eyes opening wide in initial shock, cheeks flushing seconds later as he contemplated the enormity of her announcement. She'd witnessed the instance of disbelief and shock on numerous occasions. It never ceased to intrigue.

"Looks like you were her favourite, Kieran?"

His voice croaked. "My God! Are you for real?" His normal easy-going disposition vanished, his words coming out in a rush. "How much is Number 5 worth? Have you any idea? And her bank accounts?" If he were anywhere other than a solicitor's office, he'd be on his feet and punching the air. Or, even better, he'd be turning somersaults into the nearest pub and ordering a stiff one from the top shelf! But he put his celebrations on hold and maintained his composure.

Olivia put up a hand, bringing an air of caution to proceedings. "I don't have a recent valuation of the property as yet, Kieran, but you must know that despite the current depression Schull retains its sought-after and desirable status. At a guess, the house could well be in the three-hundred-thousand region, if not more. And I see from my records that Pauline's savings are sizeable, close on €100,000."

Kieran's mind was in overdrive, his imagination leaping to the surface. Over a quarter of a million? Actually nearer to half a million! Had he heard correctly? A weight he hadn't realised he'd been carrying lifted from his shoulders. He'd be free to do as he wished, would be able to buy a few cheap apartments so he could spend his time living in different cities at various times of the year. He'd indulge in his desired lifestyle – wandering between favourite destinations, not worrying too much about a well-paying job. He rubbed his sweaty palms on his jeans, a flurry of unaccustomed nervousness rippling through him. Aunt Polly had presented him with the gift of freedom, exactly as she'd done years before.

"How do I . . . what happens now . . . what should I –"

Olivia raised a hand again, cutting him off mid-sentence.

Kieran recognised her hesitancy, narrowing his eyes as he waited for her next announcement, his gut instinct yelling that something was amiss.

"There's a clause, Kieran. Something that may dampen your excitement and delay your plans a little."

"Too good to be true, it had to be," he mumbled, dropping his elbows from the table and slouching back into the uncomfortable chair. Despondency nudged against his enthusiasm. "Are there debts outstanding or something?"

"Nothing like that," Olivia hurried to assure him, remembering Pauline's devilish grin and the way her wise eyes had crinkled at the corners when she'd sat in that very office and listed her wishes. Her throaty chuckle had echoed around the room as she'd added the crucial stipulation to her nephew's inheritance, accurately anticipating his reaction.

"What then?" Kieran tapped his fingers repeatedly on the chrome arms, craving a relaxant – alcohol, weed, anything to help him relax – as he waited for her to continue.

The solicitor fixed her glasses yet again before reading

once more from the document she held in her hand. "Your aunt's final wishes stipulate that Number 5 Pier Road, Schull, must be your prime residence for a minimum of twelve months before ownership is transferred –"

"What! Is she, I mean, *was* she crazy?"

Olivia ignored his question. Pauline Digby had predicted this outburst. It was uncanny how well she appeared to know this young man.

"It also stipulates that both her bank accounts are locked down for the same duration. Withdrawals are to be prohibited. The funds have already been transferred to a high-yield account."

His eyes opened wider, his heart sinking with every detail. Twelve months. Was she out of her mind?

Olivia continued reading. "She is, on the other hand, allowing you to spend any cash remaining in her house –"

"Big of her!" Kieran muttered ungraciously, overcome by guilt the moment the words had left his lips.

"It may sound unfair now but if you fulfil your aunt's wishes – and a year isn't a long time – full title and rightful ownership will be signed over to you. A substantial gain on your part."

Kieran didn't agree. "A year! It may as well be forever!" Live in the one spot for a whole year? In Ireland? A mere six miles from his family home in Ballydehob? The idea was outrageous. Kieran wasn't sure he could. In fact, he was positive he couldn't do it. What a cruel joke! Aunt Polly had certainly had the last laugh.

Olivia continued. "Polly collected her pension from the Post Office on a three-monthly basis." She paused a moment and flicked through her files, finding what she was looking for and reading the details to him. "I've a letter here giving you authority to go and collect what's due in the Post Office. As it stands there are ten weeks of payment waiting for you – a total of about €2,300 – so you will have something to tide you over until you find your feet in Schull – should you agree to the terms and conditions Polly laid down."

Kieran nodded. "And if I don't abide by these *terms and conditions*?" It was both a rebuke and a question. The slight note of sarcasm in his tone was a deliberate attempt to mask the hurt he felt inside.

"If you reject this offer, you'll be disinherited. The entire estate will be divided equally between Pauline's two nieces, Beth and Charlotte – your sisters, I believe?" She placed her silver pen on the file cover and waited for his response.

"What a load of baloney! Just my sisters. What about Dad? He's been excluded entirely?" Kieran found it difficult to believe that Polly hadn't left her brother anything. Their close, easy relationship had been evident, something Kieran couldn't say he had emulated with his own sisters.

"He's not mentioned in this document," Olivia confirmed, withholding the confidential information Pauline had shared. She had explained to Olivia that her reason for not naming Frank in her will was one she'd discussed and agreed with her brother years before. After he had assured her that his Ballydehob home was more than enough for him and he had no desire to inherit her house, Polly had given her situation a lot of thought and decided that her 'worldly goods', as she'd laughingly referred to them, would go to the younger generation but preferably to Kieran who had genuinely cared for her and filled a huge void in her life at a time she had needed it most. Her distinct intention was to look after the *one* who'd been kind to her over the years, the *one* who hadn't dismissed her as the whacky childless aunt, the only *one* who wouldn't be like a vulture waiting for her to die so he could benefit from her spoils.

He stood up from the chair and took his newspaper from the table, disgust and disappointment emanating from every pore.

"A wasted journey for me, Olivia. And a wasted appointment for you. Nice to meet you all the same. Will I tell my sisters to get in touch?"

Olivia shook her head. "Take a bit of time to consider what's on offer. I promised your aunt I'd do my best to coax you around. I also gave her my word that I wouldn't rush your decision."

"Wasting your time. It's done and dusted as far as I'm concerned."

"I'll give you time to consider, nevertheless. I did promise your aunt."

"No. There's no point. I won't come again."

Olivia let out a sigh and pushed the document towards him, pointing at the end of the page. "I need your signature here, confirming firstly that you accept and understand the conditions associated with this inheritance and secondly that you're happy to waive any rights you have to the property."

Kieran felt defeated. Forcing him to settle down wasn't a crime on Aunt Polly's part. But it hurt that she'd put him in this position. Why had she bothered teasing him? Exclusion would have been kinder. Hell, the rickety train set would have been a precious gift by comparison.

Olivia's silver pen cold in his hand, he scanned the

document, the sight of Polly's signature bringing a lump to his throat. Her large looped letters, though evidently written with an unsteady hand, were instantly recognisable. As a child, he'd sat watching her pen letters, amazed by the care she took with each word, her pride in producing a neat script evident. He made a mark on the page – almost got as far as writing the first letter in his name – but her legible loops stared mockingly at him, penetrating his resolve, daring him to defy her offer. He dropped the pen, watching as it rolled across the glass table.

Olivia's eyes were on Kieran. "Think things over a while. It's a lot to take in. Your aunt would have been disappointed if you refused her challenge without due consideration."

Kieran rubbed a hand across his forehead, feeling the beginning of a headache taking hold. "Is that what she called it? A challenge?"

The pen rolled from the edge of the table. Olivia let it drop into the palm of her hand. "In a manner of speaking," she confirmed. "She also mentioned your interest in the sea, the endless hours you'd spent watching the activity on the water before finally getting involved . . ."

The room closed in around him, his throat constricting as the powerful magnitude of past memories threatened to choke him. He strode to the door and pulled it open with more force than he intended, needing to escape the confines of the office and the intensity of the solicitor's probing expression to get his thoughts in order. It felt as though Polly was speaking directly to him through Olivia. He grimaced as his headache pinched a little tighter.

An intuitive Olivia grabbed the opportunity to stall his final decision. "Take a while – a few weeks if you need them – to think things through properly. Weigh up your options. I'll wait for your instruction before proceeding any further. But I strongly advise you to accept her offer – you'll be surprised how quickly a year will fly by."

Kieran's newspaper was twisted into a tight roll. "It's unlikely I'll change my mind but I may as well sleep on it at least."

Olivia took a tiny brown envelope from her briefcase and came to the door. She took a set of keys from it and handed them to him. "In case you decide to take a look around the house."

"Thanks," he muttered, giving a half salute before walking away from her.

As he retraced his steps to the lift doors, the receptionist was on her feet and tidying her desk. Her admiring glances and long red nails had lost their appeal, the two-storey, three-bedroom house on Pier Road filling up his mind and emptying his heart as he hurried to leave the building, shoving the keys into the inside zip pocket of his jacket.

Chapter 2

"Any update from Kieran?" Marian Dulhooly asked Frank when she returned from her afternoon walk.

"Not a word. He's probably gadding about the city in my Merc," Frank grumbled without looking up from his paper, unable to mask his disapproval of his only son's wayward existence.

But that wasn't the only reason he was cranky. The teeniest part of him, buried deep inside, was envious of Kieran's joie de vivre and careless attitude to life. There were times, more frequently since he'd gone into semi-retirement, when Frank wished he had the guts to dispel caution and act irresponsibly instead of always following the expected route. His serious career choice had put further emphasis on taking responsibility over personal preference.

"I think I'll give him a call," he said.

Marian looked at the clock on the mantel. "I was hoping that for once he'd get in touch with us of his own accord! Honestly, he never thinks of anyone but himself."

Watching the window for the sight of the car pulling into the driveway, the afternoon had crawled by. Perplexed that her daughters still hadn't been invited to the will reading, she was more anxious than ever to find out what Polly had left her son. She was unable to relax and had taken a longer walking circuit than usual in the hope there would be some definite news on her return. She hated being kept in the dark and, no less than when Polly was alive, her blood boiled at the thought of her sister-in-law having power over her family.

"The solicitor would hardly delay him this long. He must know the outcome by now." She hovered near Frank's chair, fiddling with her sapphire engagement ring while her husband dialled Kieran's number.

"Went straight to voicemail." Frank dropped his reading glasses onto the bridge of his nose and turned to look at his wife. "Probably celebrating somewhere. He'll arrive when it suits him and not a moment sooner. Until then, all we can do is sit tight and wait."

The details of his sister's will had never been of great interest to him while she was alive and, despite his working in the judicial system for years, progressing to judge by the end of his career, she had never come to him for advice. But – and he wouldn't be admitting as much to Marian – he had taken it for granted that she'd treat all of his children equally, seeing as they were her only nieces and nephew. Yet there was a nagging doubt inside him. Kieran had undoubtedly been Polly's favourite – that had never been up for debate. But surely with him being out of the country for a number of years that was immaterial now? Not in the mood for yet another tirade from his wife, Frank kept his suspicions to himself.

With a sigh he returned to reading the newspaper, hoping that Polly's will wouldn't cause any major upset in the house. If it did, no doubt he'd be the one acting as mediator as per usual.

Beth paced the drawing room in her partially restored Goleen farmhouse, a ten-minute drive from Schull. Marian had promised to contact her with an update as soon as she'd heard from Kieran – but so far nothing.

Relying so much on being a beneficiary in Polly's will, Beth's patience was wearing thin and her resolve to remain patient disintegrating. She couldn't believe Kieran had been the only one called to the reading. What was going on?

"We'll probably be contacted in turn," she'd told her mother confidently the previous day, listening for the phone to ring for the remainder of the afternoon, its silence deafening. And now, though eaten up with curiosity, pride wouldn't allow her to lift the phone and enquire how the reading had gone. But the more time passed, the more she felt she was playing a very bad game of chess – a skill her husband had tried but failed to teach her.

Looking at the room around her, she imagined how she'd like it to be: high ornate ceiling replastered and painted, a crystal chandelier glistening in the centre and casting bright light on linen-coloured walls, with magnificent drapes framing the arched windows and breathing colour into the magnificent room. But her transformation plan was little more than a dream now, the reality of affording it slipping further from her grasp each day.

She could still remember her excitement when she

secured the early 20th century property at an auction almost a year before, a purchase made very much on a whim. Looking back on it now, she cringed at her naïvety and she'd had plenty of time to regret her spontaneity.

Not only had she paid over the odds for the supposed 'magnificent structure' and adjoining land, but, assuming the land could be separated from the dwelling, she'd neglected to research the possibility of reselling the twelve acres as a separate entity, believing the auctioneer's sales pitch that it was an option. And so she'd bought it on the premise of relinquishing the land and using the cash to refurbish the house.

Glancing through the window now, she stared at the magnificent expanse of lush grass, empty fields stretching into the distance. Her hopes had been raised on a few occasions but any reasonable offer had become tied up in knots because of the historical ring fort existing on the property. Chasing potential sales, she'd plunged deeper in debt securing archaeological reports and council permissions.

Apparently the adjoining fields could only be sold as a separate lot with an assortment of ridiculous terms and conditions – something buyers were unprepared to accept. Securing planning permission and selling individual sites was another failed venture, leaving her with a very costly and debt-laden ornament on her hands. Eventually she'd stopped trying and had instructed the auctioneers to remove the *For Sale* sign.

Aunt Polly's death had come at a perfect time – at least as far as Beth was concerned. Her head had spun on hearing the news. And though she'd never wished her aunt harm, the prospect of inheritance had been a godsend. She'd been praying for a miracle, preferably in the form of a lotto win or something equally instantaneous, to get her out of financial difficulty! But in the absence of miracles, the expected proceeds of Aunt Polly's will were keeping her sane.

Moving through the funeral days on autopilot and playing the role of dutiful niece at the reception, she listened to tales from those who knew Polly best and was struck by her scant knowledge of her aunt's colourful life. She'd been extremely popular with the locals, her warm friendly welcome something they'd all enjoyed.

As the last of the crowd left the Baltimore Inn at the top of Schull's main street on the evening of Polly's burial, Beth had barely acknowledged the array of relations and neighbours. She'd stood at the corner of the bar deep in thought. Mentally, she was planning a strategy on how best to stretch the gains from her inheritance once it came through. The farmhouse required an amount of work, a mixture of priority and cosmetic that Beth knew about and probably a whole lot more in the line of structural work that she couldn't possibly identify.

In the taxi home that evening, she undid the buttons of her double-breasted blazer, relaxing her formal attire and feeling an overwhelming calm descend upon her. Yes, the windfall due to come her way couldn't have been better timed. Leaning back against the headrest, she looked forward to a sound sleep that night, the first she'd had in quite some time.

Now, remembering her short-lived mood of relief and optimism, Beth peeled a fake nail from her index finger, absently chewing on her cuticle until the disgusting taste of glue brought her to her senses.

"*Ugh!*" she said, spitting to rid her mouth of the

horrible taste. Why on earth was she resorting to biting her nails? Things were pathetic enough without ten stubby fingernails to add to the list! She'd go over to her mum's to find out what the hell was going on.

Running up the stairs to change out of her comfortable but grubby leisure suit, she stopped on the landing and listened to Carl's snoring coming from the master bedroom. Her husband was working night shifts in an electronics factory and for the most part was oblivious and unsympathetic to how frustrated she was with the state of the house and their bank balance.

"Bloody moron," she mumbled, passing his bedroom door. "How the hell can he sleep soundly, despite everything going on?"

Another horrible few days behind them, hours of silence after a blinding row where he had shouted obscenities at her and she'd huffed and puffed and reacted to every accusation that came her way, her final argument being a tirade that he take some responsibility and find somebody to sort out their faulty plumbing.

Glancing at the bare ring-finger on her left hand, she realised it had been quite some time since Carl had behaved like anything remotely resembling a husband and even longer since she'd felt she merited the title of wife. Meeting him in Paris while she was on a six-month college-placement programme, her course work and assignments had become a poor substitute for his sultry charm and obsession with giddy adventure. Falling in love with a dilapidated old building in Goleen – not to mention borrowing beyond their means and moving into it in its current state of disrepair – had been as detrimental as giving her heart to Carl eight years before.

Pronounce you man and wife: the words rushed into her head at a similar pace to that of their hurried wedding ceremony. Twelve minutes in total, she remembered, from the officiator's *"We are gathered here today to join this man and woman"* to *"You may kiss the bride"*.

She flicked absently through the wardrobe looking for something to wear, cringing at the memory of her return home to her parents' house. Announcing her double-status of college dropout and newlywed had gone down like a lead balloon. Denying her parents – her mother in particular – the opportunity to throw a flamboyant reception in West Cork was a source of great disappointment but nowhere near as horrifying as the news Beth had married a man with few prospects. Carl's status had been the furthest thing from Beth's mind when their eyes locked on first meeting, the intensity of their physical attraction unlike anything she'd ever experienced previously. Enraptured by his spell, his passion for speed and risk transported her to a level of excitement that almost scared her.

It was difficult to recall her time in Paris without reliving the vibrancy and life bubbling inside her as she'd careered from one adventure to the next with Carl, a sharp contrast to the drab reflection staring back at her now. She pulled at her long, brown hair. Dull and lifeless, a mirror of her innermost feelings, the gleam of Paris long gone. And not only for her. Carl's exuberance had also faded.

Brought up in Paris by Irish parents, his French tan had faded in the Irish climate, his muscular physique – one of his many appealing attributes – gradually disappearing in the absence of rigid weight-training and weekly games of rugby.

Deciding she was being ridiculous worrying about exclusion from the will, she put on a pale grey knitted dress with matching opaque tights and pulled her hair into a casual up-style, letting loose tendrils fall onto her cheeks.

"Much better," she mumbled when she looked in the mirror for a second time. She smeared her lips with gloss and highlighted her cheekbones with blusher.

Driving through Schull on her way to her parents' home a short while later, she gave a wave as she passed the cemetery where Aunt Polly was buried, hoping that soon she'd have reason to stop and offer a prayer of gratitude.

Chapter 3

Jess stared into the open grave, holding the thorny stems of two black roses in one hand.

She watched the black petals and green stems sail through the air before landing on the solid oak casket. Watching the falling rain staining the wood grain and pieces of loose earth landing on the brass nameplate, relief washed over her. Once the nearby mound of earth was shovelled back into the hole in the ground, the solid oak casket with ivory satin lining would never be seen again. And neither would the cold body of her mother lying inside.

Much later, Jess pushed open the door of Number 4, Pier Road, with her stiletto-heeled boot, trying not to wake a sleeping Greg. He was heavy and awkward to carry, his weight cramping her tired arms. When she'd collected him from his friend's house after the funeral, he'd snuggled into her and closed his eyes, exhausted after a hectic day. Henry and Pru, her only sibling and busybody sister-in-law, had been very put out because she wouldn't let them accompany her inside.

But Jess didn't care. She needed time alone. To think. To grieve. To forgive – an unlikely outcome. To figure out a simple way to explain to her five-year-old boy that from now on it would just be the two of them. It would be very different.

With Greg curled up comfortably on the ancient armchair, Jess took a moment to stare at him, trailing her finger across his soft cheek, his vulnerability causing her breath to catch in her throat. Taking the old plaid rug that was normally used for picnics and makeshift tents from the back of the chair, she tucked it in around his shoulders to keep him warm. Before leaving him, she planted a gentle peck on his forehead. His skin was warm. Unlike her icy body.

She'd found it impossible to warm up for days. Not since . . . but she halted her thoughts mid-stream, refusing to let her mind dwell on the past. Her body trembled, her shoulders were hunching forward and her fingers and toes were like blocks of ice. Despite the harsh rain, it wasn't cold outside *and* the central heating was turned up full in the house. Still nothing helped ease the chill.

As she left the sitting room, she switched on a lamp in the corner of the room, pulling the door behind her but ensuring it was ever so slightly ajar. Though it was still light, she didn't want Greg to be afraid when he woke up. He hated darkness. And he hated shut doors.

Swaying backward and forward on the rocking chair in the kitchen, a last glimmer of April daylight shining through the sash window, Jess wrapped her hands around a mug of strong coffee and listened to the wind howling outside. She let out a long sigh of relief. Alone. At last. She was determined to look forward. Not back. It had been a long three days. But now she needed to unravel her thoughts so that she could get things straight. She needed to work things through and make decisions for her and Greg's future, regardless of Henry and Pru. She'd welcomed their advice and suggestions, her troubled mind confused and finding it difficult to process even the simplest of decisions. Perhaps she and Greg should get away as Henry had suggested – even for a short while. Pier Road was filled with an assortment of memories, yet escaping them wasn't as easy as jetting off to foreign shores, not until they ceased to dominate her mind.

Fixing the soft velour cushion behind her back, she savoured the opportunity to think, daring to hope that everything would turn out all right in time. But her peace was short-lived and brought to an abrupt end. A loud bang startled her, bringing her back to the present with a sudden jolt.

"What the – !" she shouted in the empty kitchen, jumping from the chair in fright, the contents of her cup spilling all over her. Spluttering and coughing as her coffee went against her breath, she wiped her stained jumper with her fingers, sucking on the back of her hand to ease the sting from the hot liquid. She held her breath a moment, peering through the window and listening intently. One thing for sure, it had been outside. For that at least she was grateful.

It must have been a dog knocking over the bins, she decided eventually, her heartbeat returning to normal. She sat into her chair in time to hear another loud bang followed by yet another. This time the noise seemed nearer.

Oh hell, she thought, what's going on? Sounds like it's coming from next door – from *inside* Number 5. Who the hell is prowling around inside the house?

She could feel the hairs stand on the back of her neck as she heard yet another bang.

A few weeks before, Polly Digby had telephoned Jess and asked her to call next door for a chat. Neighbours for years, Jess respected the old lady and was sorry to hear she was moving into a nursing home and wouldn't be returning home. The house had been empty since. This was the first time there had been any disturbance.

Jumping to her feet, Jess flicked a nearby switch, flooding the kitchen with bright light. She ran to the hallway, gave a cursory check to make sure Greg was still asleep, and took the stairs two steps at a time, stumbling as she reached the top, her hand reaching for the banister to steady herself. She hurried into Greg's bedroom at the back of the house, careful to shut the door behind her to prevent her silhouette being seen from outside. Peering into the next door's back garden, she waited for her eyes to adjust to the darkness, trying to see if she could make out any physical presence or activity. But as well as being too dark to see, the overgrown hedging obstructed her view of next door.

Leaning her forehead against the cold window pane, she found it difficult to ignore the whispers of paranoia in her head or the all-too-familiar taste of fear in her mouth, despite the fact she hadn't heard any more noises from Number 5. Her breath fogged the glass, the wind continuing to gust outside, the rain easing off. Waste of time standing here in the dark, she thought, opening the door and allowing the landing light to filter into Greg's room. But she'd only made it halfway down the stairs when she heard yet another thud and this time there was no mistaking it was coming from the vacated house next door. "And I thought life was about to get easier," she muttered, hurrying to check on Greg once more.

Relieved to see he hadn't been disturbed, she dithered over what she should do, her mind springing into action at the sound of yet another bang. Catching sight of her white face in the hall mirror, she picked up the phone to call for help.

Chapter 4

Kieran stretched out on the unfamiliar leather corner couch, resting his arms behind his head and savouring the pleasure he was receiving from the Fitzgerald & Partners receptionist. Flinching slightly as her nails dug into the flesh on his lean stomach, he quickly moved his arms and dragged his fingers through her hair before pulling her face to his and letting their lips meet once more, their tongues exploring and teasing. Her surprise attention was a timely distraction, a delaying mechanism, an opportunity to stall his decision-making.

Leaving Olivia's office in a blur of mixed emotions – confusion and vulnerability top of the list – he was anxious to get out of the building as fast as possible. Hearing hurried footsteps behind, he'd been surprised when the receptionist called his name and asked him to hold the lift.

He nodded his acknowledgement as the lift began its descent. "Come here often?" he deadpanned.

The attractive girl brought a hand to her face, smirking at his old-fashioned chat-up line. "Just about five days every week," she answered cheekily. "Your meeting cut short?"

"Ah, there wasn't any more to be said." Kieran's eyes were drawn yet again to her scarlet nails. He was overcome by a neediness he barely recognised, a desperate desire to dissipate the effects Polly's will was having on him. "Fancy going for a drink?" he asked, surprising himself as much as her. Indulging in mindless chatter and hopefully a little more with the raven-haired beauty might help him put the notion of setting down roots out of his fuddled mind. "Or a bite to eat?" he added, realising the blatant presumption in his initial question.

"Don't you want to know my name first?" She arched a perfectly shaped eyebrow just as the lift came to a stop and the doors slid open. Together they stepped onto the marble floor of the public area, the frisson in the air between them diffusing and replaced with an awkward silence.

But Kieran had his mind set on extending their meeting, determined to see (and touch) more of the sexy vixen standing close to him. "It's Amy, isn't it?" Luckily he'd taken a fleeting glance at the nameplate on her desk, his subconscious obviously memorising the detail, useful now as it turned out.

"Yes!" She was clearly impressed that he'd taken the trouble to remember her name.

"So? Are you going to accept my invitation?"

Amy nodded and giggled. "Okay, why not! There's a nice bistro not too far from here. They serve a great early bird."

Not quite what Kieran had in mind. He'd hoped they'd skip main course, mellow over a few drinks and get straight to dessert but he wasn't in a position to argue. Following her into the street outside, he let her lead the way.

Evening traffic was building in Cork city, noise levels high as they walked past the Clarion Hotel and crossed the street to the South Mall.

"Well, hello, Kieran!"

Surprised to bump into his uncle, Kieran had little choice but to stop and chat.

"Seth, this is Amy, eh, a friend of mine," he introduced them. "Amy, this is my Uncle Seth."

"Pleased to meet you," Amy said politely.

"And you too," Seth drooled.

His appreciation of the attractive young girl was a bit too obvious for Kieran's liking and Amy was looking a bit uncomfortable too.

Kieran made his excuses and moved on as quickly as possible. His bachelor uncle was something of a bad boy – in many respects.

Granted, Amy was guaranteed to have an effect on any man. Deliberately allowing her to walk a pace ahead of him for a moment, he admired her shapely figure, his desire intensifying. Neither had made a secret of their attraction, both playing the same coy game of cat and mouse. But not for too long more as far as Kieran was concerned.

Eating together was fun, the chemistry rising between them, their fingers touching as they reached for the salt at the same time, his long legs leaning against hers underneath the small table, his jeans rubbing against her bare skin. Her cheeks flushed, her wineglass emptying faster, the grin on her face broadening. She wanted him and he knew it. He wanted her and her determination to make him wait was fighting a losing battle with her body's hunger. Appetites satisfied, their food barely tasted, they made a hasty exit from the restaurant, hurried along the streets and surrendered to the inevitable as soon as they'd entered her apartment.

Chapter 5

Jess's heart thumped as she walked closely behind her brother, Henry. She cowered near the boundary hedge separating the back gardens of Number 4 and Number 5, her torch clutched firmly in her hand, the cold wind penetrating her light clothing. Her sister-in-law, Pru, had offered to keep an eye on Greg who had slept soundly throughout the disturbance. Pru hadn't been in any rush to investigate the intrusion. Jess hadn't commented, only too aware that her brother would immediately jump to his wife's defence. Though he was only three years older than Jess, she'd always looked upon him as much older. Since he'd married Pru, who did her best to deny she was a couple of years older than Henry, Jess thought her brother was even more serious than he'd been before. A typical sombre accountant, she thought, visualising him crouched over his desk in the Bandon accountancy office where he aspired to make partner.

Though the banging had subsided, Jess couldn't rest until she knew for sure that she and Greg were safe. She hadn't thought beyond securing that knowledge, had no idea what approach they'd take if there were intruders next door, and was literally taking one step at a time.

Inhaling deeply and standing up straighter, she told herself it was probably her imagination and reprimanded herself for being silly. She continued to trail Henry into the lane that ran behind the houses and through the open gate next door. Damn, she thought, why is the gate open? It had definitely been closed earlier in the day when she'd put the recycling bin into the lane for collection.

Treading carefully in the neighbour's garden, she noticed the overgrown grass, shrubs and hedging and the pieces of withered copper beech that blew around what used to be a tidy lawn.

"At least the shed's still locked," she whispered to Henry, flicking on the torch and shining the beam on the strong padlock. "No evidence it was tampered with either."

"Good," her brother responded, continuing ahead of her towards the back of the house.

Moving as near Henry as she could, Jess bit her lip. She couldn't help wondering if noises had come from the house on any other occasion. Would she have heard them? Or would she have dismissed them, too busy keeping things on an even keel in Number 4 to concern herself with anything else? Could it be that the silence in her own house tonight was amplifying everything going on around her? Jess couldn't be sure.

As brother and sister neared the back door, she slowed her pace right down, convinced something had moved in the shadows. Or was it merely debris blowing around in the grass? Glancing around, her eyes more accustomed to the dark now, her pounding heart increased tempo.

"Henry, did you see something over there?" she whispered.

"Will you relax?" Henry snapped.

She flashed the torch around once more, relieved to see the door and windows were still intact.

"No broken windows here at least, Henry," she said to her brother.

"But we should probably check the front and side of the house as well," he shot back.

"Great! Thanks for the comforting words," she replied, suspecting her brother was as nervous as she but reluctant to admit it.

"You definitely heard banging?"

Jess sensed her brother's irritation. "Yes. Definitely." She put extra emphasis on her response, needing him to take her seriously and wondering why he didn't pay her the attention he gave to his wife. Then again, she reasoned, ignoring somebody like Pru wouldn't be an option even for the toughest of men.

"And it wasn't just the wind?"

"No!" Now Jess sounded exasperated.

Henry took the torch from his sister, flashing it along the path at the back of the house, shining it on an upended recycling bin and turning to look at her. "I think we've found the root of the banging," he said aloud.

But Jess wasn't so sure. "How can an upturned bin continue to bang?"

"The lid? An animal stepping on it, making it clatter?"

"Hardly!" She flashed the torch around again and unable to find any other explanation gave more consideration to his suggestion. "Is that all you think it was? Really?"

"It's possible."

Feeling a little foolish for panicking now, she wondered if she should have bothered alerting Henry in the first place. But she couldn't have left little Greg unsupervised while she risked coming to check the place on her own. Her very first evening living alone and she'd had to call for help. I'll have to get used to managing solo, she thought, taking the torch from Henry as he kicked the spilled contents of the bin into the corner.

Though she'd had years without anyone special to turn to, Jess had never lived without another adult. And even then she'd experienced intense loneliness, forcing her to believe that living with the wrong person could be as miserable as being alone, a contradiction in itself considering the vibrancy her son's presence brought to the house. Little Greg chatted from the moment he opened his eyes each morning, his facial expressions dancing with bright-eyed enthusiasm. By the time he fell into a sound sleep each evening, she'd answered a million questions, trying to explain the simplest of things to his inquisitive mind. Thinking about him sleeping in Number 4, stretched innocently on the recliner chair with a plaid blanket tucked tightly around him made Jess eager to return to him.

"But you said you heard a noise from inside?" Henry asked then, having a sudden change of heart and looking around him, listening for a moment.

But aside from the wind that had started to abate, everything seemed still, no evidence at all to back up her claim.

Jess shrugged, suddenly doubting what she'd heard earlier. "I suppose it could have been the lid of the bin. I'm not quite as certain now to be honest. I shouldn't have annoyed you with this."

"You were right to call me. And don't hesitate if you feel the need again . . ." His voice trailed off and he rubbed his sister's arm in a rare display of affection. "Things seem okay now though. Are you happy to leave it at that?"

"I suppose it could have been overreaction on my part," she admitted, placing a hand on the back-door handle to check it was locked, her back stiffening when it yielded at her touch. "It's not locked, Henry," she said in surprise. "In fact it didn't seem to be even closed properly!" The solid wood door swung open.

Henry came and stood beside her. "Shine the torch on it."

She did as she was told and flashed the torch on the open doorway and along the doorframe.

"I don't think it's any great mystery – just that somebody has left and forgotten to lock it." He pulled it closed and pushed it open a few times. "Being an old door the clasp probably wasn't strong enough to hold it against the wind. That's more than likely the noise you heard."

To test his theory further, he pushed it back and they listened as it banged against the jamb.

Jess nodded her head. "Definitely similar," she confirmed.

"Mystery solved then," Henry said, pulling it closed one last time and ensuring it clasped into place.

Turning to leave by the back gate once more, she swallowed nervously, her concerns returning with a vengeance. Living next door to a vacant house was one thing but an unlocked empty house was an even scarier prospect. She knew she wouldn't relax, would jump at every sound and imagine all sorts in the still of night. Her mind went into overdrive in the early hours, playing its cruellest tricks.

"Henry, I'll have to report it and get it sorted as soon as possible. Otherwise I'll turn into a nervous wreck."

"Report it to the Gardaí?" Henry quizzed.

"Polly left me the number of her solicitor in case of an emergency. I can give her a call and let her pass on the message to the family."

He let out a heavy sigh, wishing he could do more to protect Jess and Greg. But relations between her and Pru were tense and mediating wasn't Henry's strong point – he preferred to sidestep the issue wherever possible. Pru would undoubtedly turn this latest event into an opportunity to manipulate his sister and take advantage of her vulnerability. She'd droned on and on as they'd driven to Pier Road, barking abuse at him when she realised he wasn't listening.

"Henry! I'll call the solicitor then?" Jess was still waiting for an answer.

"That makes sense, I suppose. You go back inside and I'll give a quick check around the front," he said, watching his sister anxiously as she returned to Number 4. She'd been through a tough time. He'd hoped the funeral would bring an end to her anxiety but seeing her on edge again this evening, he wasn't very confident.

"Where's Henry? And what on earth's going on?" Pru demanded as soon as Jess stepped inside. "Why can't you take my advice and –"

"Mummy!"

A sleepy Greg appeared in the kitchen, rubbing his eyes and raising his arms to his mother.

"Shh, sweetheart," Jess soothed her son, lifting him up and inhaling his warm scent.

Unimpressed at being ignored, Pru persisted. "Is all in order next door or were we dragged here on a fool's errand? You should move –"

"The back door was left unlocked," Jess interrupted, tightening her hold on a confused Greg. He wasn't accustomed to seeing his aunt twice in one year, never mind twice in one day!

"And?"

"And the wind caused it to bang," Henry answered his wife's question, entering the house and rubbing his hands together to instil some heat into his body. "It's bitter out there. Is it okay if I make a coffee before we leave, Jess?"

"Help yourself," she replied, balancing Greg on her hip and going to make her phone call. She winced as Pru's cackling laughter and unkind words followed her into the hallway. God damn her, she's sneering at me, Jess thought, taking a slip of paper from the hall table and punching the numbers into the handset, cursing when the connection went straight to voicemail.

"I'd like to leave a message about Number 5 Pier Road," she began, choosing her words carefully so as not to trivialise her report. She needed to be sure it was taken seriously, needed to bring months of sleepless nights to an end.

Kieran lay on his side, naked, his tan emphasised by the multi-coloured globe light rotating slowly overhead. Mellow and satisfied, he wasn't in any great rush anywhere, yet respected his companion enough not to take anything for granted.

"Care to go for that drink now, Amy?" he suggested, his finger trailing inside her thigh, his eyes taking in the contours of her face. She was arrestingly beautiful, even with smudged mascara and unkempt hair.

Amy slowly opened her eyes and sat up on the couch beside him, reaching to the floor to retrieve her discarded clothing. Leaving her white lace bra aside, she slipped her arms into her shirt, fastening the tiny pearl buttons with precision and tantalising Kieran deliberately as she strained the light material across her pert breasts, her nipples erect and protruding. Pulling her pencil skirt along her calves, she wiggled and writhed and raised her bum from the couch until it fitted perfectly over her slim hips, leaning forward to allow Kieran zip it closed for her.

The magnetic charge lingering between them intensified once more, her intentional teasing having the desired effect. He undid some of the buttons she'd just tied on her shirt, his fingers clumsy and demanding. Dropping his face to her breasts, he sucked on one nipple, then the other, his hand reaching under her skirt, his desire more profound now she'd deliberately left off her underwear. She was a tease. And he loved it. He was an experienced lover. And she was savouring his every touch.

As their climax approached its peak, his phone shrilled to life, its irritating tone breaking the spell between them and making it difficult to concentrate.

"Damn thing," he muttered in annoyance, reaching out an arm to the nearby coffee table and pressing blindly at buttons to silence it, infuriated when it recommenced its incessant ringing a moment later, succeeding eventually in deflating the mood.

"Just answer the damn thing," she whispered in his ear, biting on his lobe.

He grabbed the phone and barked "Hello!" His

longing intensified as Amy's tongue explored his body, his desire increasing with every second.

"Olivia who . . .?" He pulled himself into an upright position. "Oh, that Olivia!" He glanced at Amy, shrugging his shoulders in confusion.

Her eyes widened, her arms crossing her body. She chewed on her lower lip, a very different action from the seductive nibbling on his earlobe a moment before.

Reading her mind, he shook his head and grabbed her hand in reassurance. The call had nothing to do with Amy seducing a Fitzgerald & Partners' client.

"I see," he said into the phone, his expression grave. "Right. Thanks. I suppose I should get down there."

As he disconnected the call, he noticed another missed call – this one from his father. He'd been ignoring his calls, his tryst with Amy giving him the distraction he needed to stop thinking for a few hours. I'd better let the folks know what went on, he thought, and gave Amy's hand another reassuring squeeze before reaching for his clothes.

"How come Olivia's making calls at this hour?" he asked. "Is she ever off duty?"

Amy shook her head. "Seldom. The other partners think she's a workaholic. She takes files home, transfers her office line to her mobile, is always in work mode. I take it there's something up?"

"You know the house I've inherited?"

Amy nodded.

"Olivia received a message from some neighbour about an unlocked door and some disturbance that needs to be checked out," he explained.

Regardless of the decision he had yet to make, he was

filled with a sense that Number 5 Pier Road was reaching out to him in its own peculiar way and decided it was time to answer that call. The thoughts of unwanted intruders rifling through Polly's belongings was disconcerting.

"Olivia wasn't too alarmist but I should probably check it out."

"I suppose," a disappointed Amy agreed, tying her shirt buttons once more as he got to his feet and began to dress.

Kieran was thinking of Aunt Polly. With her six feet under the ground, he was next in line for responsibility – at least until he waived all rights to the property. And regardless of his head continuing to argue in favour of a long-distance ticket away from the country he grew up in, his compassion and love for his aunt was nestling itself into every rational argument he could think of.

Giving Amy a hurried apology and one final lingering kiss, he left her apartment with even more haste than he'd entered it, fuelled by a different hunger and passion, one that might not be sated with the same enjoyable indulgence but needed to be addressed all the same.

Chapter 6

"Mum, can I have another drink? My throat hurts."

Jess opened her arms wide and pulled her son into a bear hug. She'd taken him up to his room and changed him into his pyjamas as soon as Henry and Pru left. Tucking him into bed, she'd read him two stories but he still hadn't fallen asleep and this was his second trip downstairs on the pretence of being thirsty.

"Milk?" she offered.

He pulled from her embrace and tilted his head, his dark eyes appealing. "Coke?"

Though it was difficult to say no to that pleading expression of his (he had it perfected to a fine art and knew exactly how to wangle his own way from his guilt-ridden mother), Jess didn't relish a sleepless night with Greg bouncing from room to room and full of artificial energy. And particularly not tonight when she craved hours of oblivion that would block out the crazy thoughts careering inside her head.

"Juice?" she offered as a compromise, arching an eyebrow.

"Mum, please? Just today? A small drop? Please?" His lower lip protruded.

Too weary to argue, Jess went to the larder press and took out a half-full Coke bottle. She tipped a tiny measure into Greg's glass, diluting it with a generous amount of red lemonade, hoping it would reduce the caffeine effects. She watched the liquids blend, reminded of the nightcap her mother had insisted on having every evening at nine o'clock. There was hell to pay if either the shot or the mineral weren't to her exact liking!

Greg tugged at her cardigan. "Mum! I'm thirsty!"

She placed his drink on the table and watched his chubby hands encircle the glass before he took a noisy gulp. "Small sips," she advised gently, ruffling his hair and vowing to get him into a proper routine for the first time in his five years. It wasn't that she hadn't tried in the past. But her son's bedtime, diet and school attendance – like a lot of other things in her life – had been outside her full control. Uninvited and unwelcome interference had challenged every decision, Jess crumbling under intense pressure, her opinion obliterated.

Chapter 7

Grateful he'd accepted his father's offer of his Mercedes to travel to the city that afternoon, Kieran made the sixty-mile trip to Schull, happy to leave the traffic lights behind in favour of the quiet roads of West Cork. Passing through Ballydehob he careered beyond the turn-off to his parents' home, delaying the inevitable barrage of questions they'd undoubtedly launch about the reading of the will. Instead he sent a hurried text to his father.

Polly left me number 5. Have to stay there a year. Tk ltr.

That'll give him and Mum something to mull over for a while, he thought, unable to resist a smile as he tossed his phone onto the passenger seat. He loved his parents. Of course he did. It went without saying. But they had never – and probably would never – understand or accept that he wasn't one for following what was, in their eyes at least, considered conventional.

Parking on the quiet road right outside the house, he stepped out of the car and jumped in shock as an overfed marmalade cat shot right past him, glancing against his leg and hissing in annoyance. His escape to freedom reminded Kieran of himself and his face broke into a wry smile. In a way, he'd been doing something similar for the last ten years, only his leaps involved continents and not doorsteps. Hearing the cat crooning in annoyance across the road, he realised another difference. The tabby had obviously marked his territory, with clear intention to return as soon as the coast was clear. Kieran, on the other hand, had never been one to look back, the attraction of the route ahead focusing his desire on new and exciting adventures, keeping him moving in one direction only – forward.

The road was quiet, little activity around, lights on in most of the houses around him, making him wonder who lived there now. He unlocked the front door of Number 5 Pier Road with the keys he'd received from Olivia. Flicking the switch in the hallway, the house remained in darkness. Nothing, not even a fizz from the bulb. Dead as a doornail – just like Aunt Polly, he thought, a lump sticking in his throat as he passed by the sitting room and walked straight to the kitchen, the room where he and his aunt had savoured numerous meals while she'd invariably made him laugh with one of her many tales. 'An ease to her pain' was how her expected death had been described. So many times he'd heard it whispered at the funeral, every reminder making him flinch inside, the description so unlike the vibrant aunt he'd adored.

Trying the switch in the kitchen, he smiled when the fluorescent light flickered to life and cast its light into the narrow hallway, outlining the framed family photos, holy pictures and Polly's treasured holy-water font.

But even if there had been complete darkness, Kieran

would have had little difficulty in finding his way around the familiar geography of the house he'd escaped to on every possible occasion, a sanctuary in comparison to the tension of home. Accustomed to creeping in at all hours of the morning, way past his curfew and unknown – or so he'd believed – to his sleeping aunt, the teenage Kieran had perfected late homecomings, never once mistaking his step or causing the squeaking fifth stair to screech. And now, with the intervening years falling away, it felt like only yesterday since his last visit, the scent of lavender the only thing missing to complete the memory. Her favourite perfume, Polly had often been guilty of overkill, lining drawers with scented paper and filling glass bowls with an abundance of potpourri! He couldn't say he'd appreciated it while it was there but he missed it now it was gone.

Walking back down the hallway, he dipped his finger into the holy-water font. It was dry, a first that he could recall, obviously after evaporating in her absence.

"Stay safe on those surfboards," Polly had instructed every time he'd left the house, dipping her finger in the font and sprinkling water after him as he'd rushed out the door to meet his friends.

The years he'd been absent from Aunt Polly's life nagged at his conscience. Staying away hadn't been deliberate, merely a natural fallout from his wandering. One year turned into two, one destination leading him to another, regular letters diminishing to birthday and Christmas cards, his carefree lifestyle seldom lending itself to wasting (as he'd considered it then) cash on a trip home. He didn't see the point in beating himself up about it now. But he did regret ignoring his sister Beth's words when she'd emailed him the news that the doctors didn't expect Aunt

Polly to survive pneumonia. He had missed out on the chance to say goodbye and had nobody to blame but himself.

He'd presumed Beth was overreacting – nothing unusual with his dramatic younger sister Beth. Baby of the family, she'd always been prone to exaggeration, sailing through life with her head firmly in the sand – or the clouds – depending on which way you looked at the situation.

Shaking off the memory, Kieran put the door key in his pocket and made his way through to the kitchen once more, struck by the room's iciness. But the house lying vacant for the last while wasn't the only reason for the chilled room. Polly had constantly complained.

"Even with the oven and the gas fire on, this kitchen would freeze your butt off! Years ago I should have swapped the rooms around and put the kitchen out front. Those houses on the far side don't know how lucky they are with sunny kitchens!"

But despite her complaints, he couldn't recall a time he'd ever felt cold there and, thinking about it now, he realised how much he had taken her warm welcome and cosy home for granted, never considering that a day would come when her smile wouldn't greet him when he arrived.

Used to the privacy his parents lived in, Kieran had teased her incessantly, accusing her of nosiness as she whiled away the days watching folk coming and going to and from the pier. Her deck chair was a permanent feature outside the front door, faded from the sun but put outside each year as soon as the first rays of sunshine peeped through the clouds. Little went unnoticed by Polly's sharp eye and attentive ear: the developments on the pier, the introduction of the sailing school, blossoming romances and collapsing relationships.

Moving into Number 5 Pier Road as a bride, she'd watched Schull grow, evolving from a sleepy fishing village to a thriving coastal town. Fishermen cast their nets before dawn, seldom returning before dark and often working through the night when the yield was high. She, like many other wives, watched through the window with bated breath, beseeching and making silent deals with the ocean to return their men. Schull was Polly's town, her home, a home she generously shared with her young nephew, turning it into one of the happiest and most memorable periods in Kieran Dulhooly's life.

Flicking on the outside light – surprised when it actually worked and brought the garden to life – he tried the handle of the door, unsurprised after the solicitor's call to find it unlocked. His eyes adjusting to the light, he took in the unruly condition of the garden, gasping in disgust at the mess. Overgrown shrubbery, unkempt grass, litter on the path and that was as much as he could make out. He guessed daylight would tell a worse tale. He cursed under his breath. A sense of protectiveness sprang into being. He could imagine Polly's reaction if she could see how dishevelled the place had become. She'd taken pride in her gardening efforts and each year experimented with new bulbs, adding them into the border that ran the length of the footpath leading from the back door. She seldom paid heed to what she was setting and was excited by the surprise when they burst into life, bringing colour to what she termed her "patch of paradise".

Kieran's instincts took over, his desire to get the place

restored to his aunt's standards overpowering. Regardless of any personal decisions he'd make, he'd ensure her attachment to her home wouldn't be forgotten. Why hadn't his father come to tidy it? He couldn't understand why he left Number 5 become so neglected. Aunt Polly had only been in the nursing home a few weeks. The place had obviously been neglected even before that, particularly if her mobility had failed like Olivia had described. The impression he'd been given was that they were forever around checking on Polly. Hell, he'd been made to feel like a heel for staying away for so long but he was beginning to wonder now whether the others had been much more attentive even though they lived a few short miles away – apart from Charlotte in Canada, of course.

I didn't get to say goodbye, he thought. Well, perhaps I can put some time and effort into tidying the place up instead – my way of showing a little gratitude at last. But first he'd like to thank whoever contacted his solicitor and show his appreciation to them too.

Glancing over the hedge and noticing a light in the kitchen next door, he decided it was probably the best place to start. Neighbours here, at least from what he remembered, had always watched out for each other. Going back inside, he made sure the back door was locked this time, checking it a few times before turning off the lights and leaving by the front door. The unmistakeable smell of salty sea air was a welcome familiarity. He stood staring at the sea for a few minutes before walking up to the front door of Number 4 and pressing on the brass bell-push. It would be nice to thank them for their concern and also let word filter through that somebody was watching out for it.

He waited with curiosity to see who answered the

burgundy door. Even in the faded light from the street-lamp, the gloss paintwork gleamed brightly, a stark contrast to the faded varnish next door. The door opened a fraction and an attractive dark-haired girl peered out from behind a safety chain.

A moment passed as they eyed each other, a brief few seconds where they stared at each other in disbelief. And then, like fireworks exploding into the sky, both of their faces broke into shy smiles.

Kieran shook his head and wondered if he was dreaming – either that or he was having an *Alice in Wonderland* moment and slipping down a great ravine into the heady days of his teens. His face flushed. Jess! The effect her presence had on him hadn't changed. His inner excitement had always heightened in her company, the world a brighter place when she was around. He couldn't help staring, trying to figure out why she seemed different when her features were exactly the same as he remembered. What had changed exactly?

"Jess? It's been a while!"

"Kieran Dulhooly?" She looked bewildered. "It *is* you! What a sight for sore eyes! I hadn't heard you'd come home!" She opened her eyes wider and shook her head in disbelief.

He jerked his head towards the house next door. "I'm home over a week now, came back for Aunt Polly's funeral."

Jess released the catch on the door. "I'm so sorry about that, Kieran. I sympathised with your family at the removal but couldn't make the burial unfortunately." The words caught in her throat. What valid excuse could she offer for not attending her next-door neighbour's burial? What would sound plausible? Anything but the cold candid truth that she'd been preoccupied with morbid thoughts of her own . . .

"The last I heard about you was that you'd landed in Tasmania," she said instead, shaking off her dark thoughts and opening the door fully. "Step inside. That wind is biting."

"Living here with your parents?" he enquired as he came in.

"Both gone," she explained without elaborating.

"Oh, I'm sorry," he sympathised. "I didn't realise."

She nodded. "Have you time for a cuppa?"

"Okay – thanks. Hey, I thought you'd be long gone from here, imagined you'd be wearing your archaeologist hat, digging up bones and making life awkward for anyone threatening to disturb the past."

Following Jess inside, Kieran missed the wave of regret that registered on her face at the mention of the career she'd walked away from, a sacrifice she'd been forced to make in difficult circumstances.

"Speaking of careers," she said, deftly changing the subject and leading him through to the kitchen, "whatever happened to your hard-earned degree?"

"Don't mention the war," he laughed. "That's still a very thorny subject with my parents." He looked around him. The house, a modernised version of Polly's, seemed totally different. But his interest in the improved décor paled in comparison to his open appreciation of the new and improved Jess.

After the first few moments between Kieran and Jess, the awkwardness disappeared and, sitting at her kitchen table, they slipped into easy conversation.

Jess discreetly assessed her thirty-one-year-old guest. They had a lot in common, born in the same year – a few weeks between their birthdays – and sharing the Aries astrology sign. Listening to Kieran chat about Polly's demise, she watched how his green eyes crinkled under the bright kitchen light. His complexion seemed darker, she thought, no doubt from numerous seasons living in the intense Australian heat. Taking his hand to sympathise about Polly, his skin had felt rough in her grasp. Worked outdoors, she presumed.

She was embarrassed when she realised it was her phone call to the solicitor that had brought Kieran rushing down to Schull and she apologised profusely. He waved her apologies away, explaining that he needed to come down to check out Polly's house anyway.

Bestirring herself at last to make the tea, Jess threw a quick glance at her reflection in the mirror she'd strategically placed on the wall in an attempt to create an illusion of more space in the compact room. Spotting a smudge of mascara underneath her lashes, she licked the tip of her finger and, as discreetly as possible with a trembling hand, she wiped it clean.

Kieran watched her as she moved about the kitchen, admiring her petite figure as she stretched to an overhead press to get a tin of biscuits.

"I can't believe you're living here again," he commented.

"Well, here I am," she said, throwing him a grave glance that he couldn't interpret.

His eyes following her every move, he noticed she was much thinner than he remembered. Shapely in a very sexy way, he decided, feeling a sudden pang of guilt about the brisk way he'd abandoned Amy earlier. Poor Amy, he thought. Although he suspected she'd taken the same thing from their meeting as he had – good company and great no-strings-attached sex. No doubt, regardless of his decision on Number 5, their paths would cross again and whether they'd have another liaison or not would remain to be seen. He'd contact her, maybe even meet her and buy her lunch to apologise. She wasn't the first girl he'd run out on in such a hasty fashion but she hadn't deserved to be insulted either. He wasn't proud of his behaviour but running into Jess – the new and improved Jess who was very different from the tomboy he remembered – had to be fate (or maybe Aunt Polly) intervening in his plans. "*Meant to be*," she'd have said. A ghost of a smile flashed across Kieran's face as he imagined her peering at him over the rims of her bifocals. Letting go the memory, he focused his attention on his hostess instead.

"Milk and sugar?" she asked.

"Just milk, please, and can you leave the teabag in the cup? I like it strong."

Jess put two mugs of piping hot tea and a jug of milk on the table, then took a plate of hazelnut cookies and coconut mallows from the counter and placed them before him. She sat down opposite him at the table and nudged the milk towards him.

"But seriously, Kieran," she insisted again, "I feel like such a fool now. That bloody banging scared the daylights out of me! And if I'm honest, now that your aunt has passed away, living next door to an empty house feels a bit creepy."

"Nothing new there," he said, a grin breaking across his face. "Being alone in the dark always freaked you out."

Her face went bright red, vivid memories of her teenage years rushing to her mind. Mortified that he had such a clear memory of what seemed an age ago – and wasn't afraid to tease her about it – she dropped her gaze and focused on her tea mug.

"Seriously, forcing me to Aunt Polly's house has done me a great favour," he said. "Have you seen the state of the outside? The garden is a dump! It's no wonder you're uncomfortable. I'll get it cleared up. I'll make it look lived-in again."

"Oh, don't worry," she said hurriedly.

"Polly will come back from the dead if something's not done about it right away. You know she loves her home . . . I mean she used to . . ."

Not for the first time in recent days, Kieran had halted mid-sentence. He found it difficult to believe that Polly was dead, the anchor she'd represented in his life something he'd never forget.

Dunking a biscuit in his tea, he watched Jess with interest. Her restlessness unsettled him. He hoped it wasn't his presence that was making her jumpy. Their connection had always been special, mutual understanding getting them through the best and worst of moments. They'd known each other for years, albeit with a break of almost a decade apart from his occasional visit home, so why would she be uncomfortable around him? No doubt, if he was going to spend a bit of time tidying up next door, he'd find out soon enough.

"Enough about the mess next door. Tell me what you've been up to?" Jess asked, draining her tea and getting up for a refill.

"You mean this week since I've got back?"

"I mean your travels. How far did you get? What was it like? How many countries – continents even, did you visit?"

Kieran pondered on her questions a second, wondering how to concentrate the last ten years into a few brief answers. The person he'd been when he'd stood on the steps of the plane in Cork Airport as he departed for that very first trip bore no resemblance to the man he was now.

Reading his mind, she simplified things. "In general, I mean, what was it like to have so much freedom? How did you survive? Make ends meet?"

"I'm guessing similar to when you took off for Cambridge on your Indiana Jones escapade. Nobody to answer to, get to be your own boss, make decisions without worrying about anyone's opinion, grabbing enough work wherever it was going . . ."

Kieran's words washed over Jess, her mind drifting back. Cambridge had been nothing like the paradise he was describing. Apart from immersing herself into the "Indiana Jones escapade" as he'd teasingly referred to it, her expectations of college life had been swiftly dashed. Arriving on scholarship from an unknown Irish community school had set her apart from the outset, the majority of students hailing from private education and lavish wealthy backgrounds. "Swot," the others in her year whispered as she filed into the study hall while they skipped lectures and scarpered to the nearest off-licence, sneering at her conscientious-study attitude. She'd worked hard right through term, often falling asleep at the little desk in her room. Failing and taking repeats wasn't an option, at least not for Jess, who was dependent on retaining scholarship status.

"Earth calling Jess," Kieran teased. "One mention of Cambridge and you go all doe-eyed! That good, eh?"

"College life is similar the world over I'm sure," she responded lightly, "but hey, I was expected to turn up for class every day *and* I lived in supervised student quarters so I wouldn't be too sure that our travels were that similar."

"Ha! Supervised? I can just imagine. Ye probably gave those deans hell!"

"Whatever happened to George Roly?" she asked, changing the subject. "Didn't you two leave the country together?" She'd got to know George when he'd stayed in Number 5 on occasion, hanging out with Kieran, her and the others, surfing and canoeing for hours on end, sitting around bonfires late into the night and early morning, sipping cans of beer and laughing and joking without a care in the world.

Kieran nodded, remembering his buddy from school and what a disaster their initial adventure turned out to be. "Wise old saying – if you want to know me come live with me. Suffice to say, we weren't compatible, not by a long shot!"

"Lovers' tiff then," she laughed, her face reddening as the words left her lips, her embarrassment forgotten when Greg arrived into the kitchen, rubbing his eyes and looking very hard in Kieran's direction.

"Sweetheart, you should be fast asleep!" said Jess.

The little boy came and climbed on her lap, his eyes never leaving Kieran's face.

"Who's that man, Mum? Why is he here?" He pointed at their guest.

"Greg, don't be rude!" Jess looked apologetically at Kieran, noticing the look of bemusement on his face and realising that she hadn't mentioned her son to him. No need to explain now. Greg had taken that decision out of her hands.

Kieran was indeed bemused. He had somehow assumed, because she hadn't said otherwise, that there wasn't a man in her life. Apparently there was – and not just this little one on her lap.

"Er . . . sorry . . . I thought you were still . . . unattached," he said, trying to be delicate but needing to know.

"I am," she said, giving him a level look.

He waited for her to go on.

"Gregory," she said instead, giving the little boy his full title, "this is Kieran Dulhooly, my friend from years ago. We've known each other from when we were only a little bit older than you are now. You remember Polly from next door?"

Greg nodded enthusiastically, his lower lip protruding. "She always gave me jellies. She's in Heaven now."

Jess smiled at his innocent acceptance of the next world, wishing she shared his pragmatism. "Every time she saw you, no matter what time of the day or evening! Well, Polly was Kieran's aunty and every school holiday he came to stay with her."

Kieran put his hand out, pulling it back again when Greg ignored it and pushed his head into his mother's chest. He hadn't had much experience with young children but he could remember what it was like to be a young boy and feel threatened.

"Hi, Greg," he said. "Bet your mum never told you about the time we borrowed a rowing boat at midnight –"

Jess was quick to interrupt. "I don't think he needs to hear about that particular adventure!"

Kieran laughed, winking at the young boy. "Maybe another time then. I see you're a United supporter?"

Greg nodded vigorously, his eyes widening. He sat up straighter in his mother's lap, took a cookie from the plate and began to nibble all around the edge.

"And wrestling, what about that? You watch the WWF?"

Greg was genuinely impressed that this man, whoever he was, seemed to know so much about him. It went over his head that his themed pyjamas and slippers were a giveaway.

Jess watched the interaction between them, relieved that her son had taken to her old friend.

"Mum doesn't like me watching it. Says they're stupid." He turned his head and met his mother's eye. "You do, Mum!"

Jess didn't deny her abhorrence of her son's favourite programmes. "I keep telling you, Greg. They're only acting."

"They're not, shur they're not?" This time he turned his attention to Kieran.

"Of course not! But women don't understand wrestling, not like us guys." He stood to leave. "I'd better be going now before I get myself in trouble," he laughed.

"Are you going to be calling again?" Greg asked.

"That depends on whether your mum invites me again," Kieran said, directing his response more at Jess than the little boy. "Maybe we could watch WWF?"

"If you're planning on sticking around a while I don't see why not," Jess laughed. "Come on, Greg, let's see our guest out." She put her son on the floor and got to her feet. They followed Kieran to the front door, Greg eager for him to call again and Jess equally anticipating his company and choosing to ignore the warning bells ringing in her ears.

"Well, actually," Kieran said, turning to her as they reached the door, "I'm trying to come to terms with the idea of moving back here."

"Moving back?" What did he mean exactly?

"Polly left me the house," he explained.

"Oh! Wow! That's big."

"I'll probably stay with my parents a few more nights until I get it cleaned up a bit. And the idea of living in one spot hasn't quite taken hold as yet. I have a lot to think about."

"Even so, it'd be nice to freshen the place up while you're mulling over your decision and I'm sure the cleaning required is nothing hot water and detergent won't fix. Give me a shout if you need a hand."

"I might hold you to that," he laughed.

"She obviously thought very highly of you," Jess said. "What a great gift all the same!"

He shrugged indifferently, hiding the pride he felt inside. "Hmm, if I want to put down roots, I suppose."

"But you could come and go?"

"No. I have to live here for a year before I get rightful ownership."

Jess glanced at Kieran before asking her next question, unable to suppress momentary delight at the thought of having him living next door, their old friendship rekindled, and someone she knew and trusted on the other side of the hedge instead of him being an absentee landlord. But her delight was quickly replaced by a cloud of doubt. Would Kieran living next door complicate her life even further?

"So you may be back for good?" she asked. "To settle down like a proper grown-up?"

"Coming back for the funeral was only supposed to be a flying visit, pay my respects, do my duty and leave . . ."

"And now?"

He shrugged. Pier Road definitely drew him in. His adventures on the continents had been terrific, one blending with another, the length of time he'd been spending in locations lengthening, his hunger to move on waning slightly. What harm would it do to let Schull be another on his map? A coastal town with a definite tourist feel wouldn't be the worst place to hang about for a while. Providing the family don't drive me cuckoo, he thought.

Jess spoke again. "What an opportunity! And at our age too! Play your cards right and you're set up for life now."

"But live in one place for a year?" he repeated, giving a shudder and shaking his head, still very unconvinced. "Doesn't feel like my kind of thing."

Jess was equally adamant, letting her heart lead her mind. The idea of him living next door was taking hold. "Fifty-two weeks, 365 days, you will get out the other side." Wait and see, she thought privately. She knew that no matter how bad things seemed, nothing stopped the passing of time.

Kieran went outside and stood on the footpath, inhaling the sea air, his love for the place rushing back. He swivelled around to face Jess. She had Greg in her arms again, balancing him on her hip and planting soft kisses on his cheek. The bright sensor light shone on them. Silhouetted in the doorway, the pair looked vulnerable.

For the first time that Kieran could remember, the display of neediness didn't unnerve him or make him want to turn and run as fast and far as possible. Quite the opposite – the young mother and son made staying around a little longer a much more attractive prospect.

And as he opened his mouth to reassure Jess he'd be in the vicinity for a while – to get the place tidied if nothing else and ensure it was looked after properly and not left unlocked as he'd found it this evening – he noticed Greg's eyes widen dramatically. Kieran watched the young chap clutch his mother's shirt tightly. He strained to hear the words he was uttering, barely catching his loud whisper in the still night.

"Daddy! See, Mum, he's there again!"

Kieran followed Greg's gaze but the road behind him was empty. He turned back to Jess, puzzled.

But Jess had disappeared. In the couple of seconds it had taken him to turn around, she'd retreated into the house and closed the door. The last sounds Kieran heard before leaving her garden were shooting bolts being snapped into place. He couldn't help wondering if she was locking both of them in or locking somebody else out?

Returning to Number 5, Kieran went up the stairs and into his old bedroom. Flicking the light switch, the room lit up. Layers of dust covered the furniture and every surface in the room. Visually, nothing much had changed. Moving further into the room, he unlocked the wardrobe and peered inside. A few jackets hung on the rail, *his* jackets he realised, checking the pockets and exploring further. He moved toward the window seat and sat with his back to the glass.

His thoughts flew back to Jess and her son and the incident on the road outside. Greg's father must be a local, he mused – but not living with them it seemed, if he was to judge by the boy's reaction on seeing him. And Jess had said she was unattached. But why had the man suddenly disappeared like that? Was it because he'd seen him, Kieran, at Jess's door? And Jess's speedy departure added another layer of mystery. Something was seriously amiss between them. Had they married, he wondered. It hadn't dawned on him to enquire when she'd introduced her little son. No doubt I'll find out in time, he thought, his curiosity definitely piqued but instinct warning him to wait until Jess decided to share the details with him.

He gazed around the room. The furniture hadn't been moved as much as an inch in all the years – a single bed under the Velux, the oversized wardrobe in the corner and a matching dressing table facing the bed. His reflection was barely visible through the layer of dust on the mirror. How he'd hated that mirror on the mornings he'd been hung over, bloodshot eyes and a pale green complexion staring back at him. Mostly Aunt Polly pretended not to notice apart from the few occasions when he'd pushed it too far and she'd threatened to call his father to come and collect him. But she never followed through and invariably she'd forgiven him by lunchtime.

Spotting an ancient photo album sitting on the dressing table, he wiped the plastic covers with his sleeve and studied each one. A mixed-up selection, they brought a smile to his face, several photos taken from an upstairs window as she captured him and his friends in a variety of poses. A loose photo – obviously from a different time – had been left inside the back cover. He grinned at the image of himself and Jess laughing, Jess looking as though she was about to fall off the crossbar of his bike and his arm outstretched to catch her.

Polly must have been bored, he thought, imagining her clicking away to her heart's content and then wondering how she ran out of film! Laughing as he left the album where he'd found it, he remembered numerous occasions she'd been snapping him and the lads – and sometimes Jess too – only to discover there was no film in the camera! And it was obvious she watched a lot more than she'd let on to him. Such a great loss, he thought with a pang.

He turned to look outside, his breath fogging the grimy window pane. Clearing a patch with his elbow, he looked toward the water in the distance, glad there were no houses directly across from Number 5, the unobstructed view magnificent on a bright sunny day. Things were quiet now, very little movement apart from a fishing boat coming to shore. Hearing the muffled sound of a door closing through the bedroom wall, he thought of Jess and Greg again, his eyes still following the mooring boat.

Not knowing why exactly, apart from the bond they'd shared a decade before, Kieran's interest in Jess's life was more than fleeting. Questions floated around his head. Did Greg's father contribute to the unease he'd sensed in his old friend? Had she been through a bad relationship? Perhaps the father wanted custody of the child now or something awful like that.

In a flash, Kieran's mind was made up. He'd accept Polly's challenge. He'd stick around and rekindle his relationship with Schull and its inhabitants. A year would be manageable – even for him, plenty of time to travel afterwards if he so desired. And after that, if that were his decision, he could make a respectable rental income from Number 5 if he found it impossible to stay. What's the worst that can happen, he thought, his green eyes following the lights of the fishing boat until it veered around the headland and disappeared from sight.

Chapter 8

Kieran's text had shocked his parents and sister. Marian and Beth were still digesting the fact he had inherited the Schull property. Frank had gone to bed to ease his splitting headache.

"Beth, love, please sit down!" Marian pleaded with her irate daughter.

"I can't, Mum. How can I relax after what's happened?" She stared at the floor, eyes downcast, lower lip wobbling, very close to tears.

Marian chewed on her lower lip, her daughter's distress worrying, how to find a solution and a way out of her financial difficulties more worrying still.

"I must make you a hair appointment and get something done with those split ends," she tried, stalling for time and making a futile attempt to distract her daughter.

Beth's head shot up. "Mum! My hair is the least of my worries. It's not as if I'm going anywhere important to show off a new hairdo! Don't you get it? If I don't do something soon, I'll barely be able to afford shampoo, never mind a visit to a salon!" She fiddled with the fruit bowl, arranging and rearranging red apples, kiwis and overripe bananas.

"Sweetheart, please calm down. I know you're surprised about the inheritance but –"

"Surprised?" Beth shook her head. "I'm shocked, disgusted, any number of things. But surprised isn't one of them! What am I going to do?" She looked at her mother, huge eyes pleading, fingers pulling anxiously at the ends of her hair until it came undone and fell around her pinched face. "What's going to become of me? Polly's will was my last chance, Mum, my only chance!"

Marian took a deep breath, struggling to maintain composure. One of them hyperventilating was enough. Into the bargain, she worried that if she began a tirade on the subject of Polly's will, she wouldn't be able to stop. And whatever hope she had of helping her daughter, keeping Frank on side was crucial. Criticising Polly would get his back up, make him dig his heels in and support the decision his sister had made. And though he'd gone to bed already, she didn't trust that her words wouldn't carry up to the room overhead. She had made that mistake many times over and wasn't about to do it again.

"Should I approach Kieran, Mum?"

"I wish he'd come home and tell us exactly what the will entailed. His text was brief – there must be more than that to it – some smaller bequests. She must have left something to your father after all."

"Smaller bequests? That won't help me, Mum."

"I know, love." Marian bit her lip.

"Maybe he isn't going to stay the year?" Beth pushed

the fruit bowl away from her, the bananas now resting evenly on the apples with the kiwis clustered on top.

"He's hardly going to walk away, though, is he? And you know how he idolised Polly." Marian took a bottle of sparkling water from the fridge and filled two glasses, handing one to Beth. Kieran's loyalty to Polly could be enough to make him stay the twelve months, maybe even get a job and act responsibly for a change, she thought. At any other time she would have been thrilled to see her son was settling down. It was what she and Frank had been nagging him to do for years. But Polly's meddling, how she was orchestrating Kieran's decisions, infuriated her. Sighing, she tightened her grip on the glass and brought it to her lips as a familiar knot of resentment lodged in her throat.

Damn you to Hell, Polly Digby, she uttered silently, her daughter's anguish pulling at her heart. You've done this on purpose, upsetting my girls and driving a wedge between them and their brother. And I'm not allowing you to get away with it – not again and not any more. My three children deserve equal treatment and I'm going to see they get it – in spite of and to spite you and your intentions.

"I have been trying to get my hours back with the airline, Mum," Beth interrupted her thoughts, "but with the reduction in domestic flights and Michael O'Leary cutting every corner he can think of in Ryanair, I've had no success so far. I should never have walked away from it in the first place."

The income statement her employers had given her had secured the damn mortgage that was crippling them now. Her modest redundancy payment had barely put a dent in the cost of installing an electric shower and upgrading the bathroom. She had assumed – wrongly as it turned out –

that she'd pick up another job easily and now she was suffocating with enormous debt and long days and nights with nothing to do except despair about the situation she'd found herself in. What a disaster!

"What about Carl? Has he tried getting a second job or perhaps looking around for something that's better paid?" Marian enquired.

"He says being on shift work makes it too awkward to commit to anything else." Beth shrugged her shoulders.

Her mother bit her lip, deciding it best to change the subject or she was liable to ridicule her son-in-law. "What pressure are the banks putting on you? Are you meeting your monthly outgoings?"

Beth nodded. "Barely. And that's only the mortgage interest and nothing off the loan itself. Every day I expect a letter from them saying we have to pay more. I don't know what we'll do then."

"Pity you can't hand back the keys," Marian said.

"If only it were that simple. I could fly out to see Charlotte and try out Canada for a while."

"Is that what Carl wants too?" Marian's question was loaded.

Beth shrugged again. "It's not going to happen so there's never been any point in asking. Charlotte's so far away, isn't she, Mum?"

Marian nodded, her blonde highlights glistening under the spotlight. "I don't suppose she's ready to come back?"

"Nowhere near – she's getting on with things but I often wonder if it's only because she's in a strange continent thousands of miles away. Everything looks different when you're away and responsibilities to home are non-existent."

"You're thinking of your time in France?"

"Yes. Eight years ago now. I was a different person then, with different priorities and definitely an obscured vision."

Her thoughts drifted to sun-filled days hugging the seat of Carl's rented convertible when she should have been observing researchers in a university laboratory. Realising too late that she had cast away a once-in-a-lifetime offer for exciting science ventures would remain the single biggest regret of her life. Instead, she'd huddled against the breeze, heart racing in her chest as he'd accelerated faster and faster and transported them from the non-stop buzz of the city to the wide open space on the outskirts, coasting through rolling hillside and miles and miles of open plains. His impromptu decisions and extravagance took her breath away, his natural charm and joie de vivre proving irresistible. She was putty in his hands. The college boys she'd dated back home paled into insignificance, their boyish pranks and all-night parties seeming pathetic and childish by comparison. Her planned six months in the French city extended indefinitely, a period where her studies went by the wayside and eventually life in the fast lane caught up with the young couple. Her regret at not completing her Science degree had gnawed inside her for years. Autumn after autumn she'd contemplated registering as a mature student. But the course had evolved and the exams she'd already taken (and passed) were worthless now. She'd need to start from scratch again.

Imagining a world of lab coats, test tubes and explosive experiments brought a rush of blood to her head, the memory of dissecting, analysing and researching filling her with a hunger to return. But her fear of failure held her back, Carl's disinterest an additional factor. Finding excuses to miss enrolment dates had been easy, her confidence diminishing with each passing year.

Marian sensed her daughter's regret and sympathised. With the benefit of hindsight she could see what a wasted emotion it was, dwelling on what could have been instead of focusing and making the best of what lay ahead. But she didn't voice this to Beth, not now when desperation rested so heavily on her daughter's young shoulders.

"Every experience becomes part of who we are, love," she said. "What's going on now is merely a passing phase in your life."

"I wish it would hurry up and pass me by then."

Her attempt at a smile melted Marian's heart. There had to be a way to alter the will. Kieran wouldn't lose out. He'd get a fair entitlement.

Placing the palms of her hands on Beth's cheeks, she met her gaze. "I'm going to do everything in my power to have that will overturned. I'm not standing for this farce. You're all entitled to an equal share."

"And Kieran?"

"He'll get a third, as will you and your sister. It's the fairest, it's the decision your aunt should have made in the first place. I'm sure he'll understand."

"Oh, Mum, I don't think . . ." Beth pulled at her hair again.

"Beth, it's not like you have any other choice. You said so yourself." Marian struggled to keep her tone even, lowering her voice so Frank wouldn't hear. "What will happen if we don't do this? You'll lose your house, lose your credit rating and still owe the banks a fortune."

Beth gulped, unable to find a response. Her mother was speaking the truth. Without the inheritance, she and

Carl hadn't any chance of surviving financial doom. As for surviving marital doom, she wouldn't bet on that either. She'd been the one to keep a roof over their heads in Paris, getting a part-time waitressing job out of necessity and slogging long days and nights. She took whatever pleasure she could between shifts and joined him on some of his ridiculous escapades – it was either that or sit alone in their tiny studio apartment. Carl would follow his dream. Regardless.

"Live on the edge while we're young, babe – lots of years ahead to be sensible and do what's expected . . . *trés boring*," was his stock answer to the practical suggestions she'd put his way. And while his life-was-for-living attitude seemed perfectly acceptable in the bright lights of the most romantic city in the world, there had come an unforeseeable moment when it had all come crashing around them. Carl's idea of *trés boring* gave living on the edge a whole new perspective.

"Beth?" Marian's interruption saved her from reliving the horrific ordeal. "What do you think?"

"What's involved?" she conceded. "I suppose there's no harm in finding out what would need to be done . . . just in case . . ."

Marian drew her daughter into her arms, her lips shaping into a grimace at the prospect of contesting Polly's will. With a bit of luck, Number 5 will be sold and a new family will take it over, she thought. Then it mightn't be such a constant reminder of Kieran choosing to spend every possible hour in that end-of-terrace with his quirky aunt instead of being at home with her, Frank and the girls. She pressed her lips against her daughter's cheek, steely determination taking a tight grip inside her.

Chapter 9

In Toronto city, Charlotte Dulhooly was face-down on a massage table, Giovanni's hands pressing into the hollow between her shoulder blades. Arms stretched in front of her, she clutched the frame of the plinth while the Italian masseuse increased the pressure on her spine. Moments later, her tight grasp relaxed as his kneading fingers trailed to the outward extremity of her back, close – sensationally close – to her full breasts. A familiar tingle of desire rippled through her body, his touch feather-light on her skin and she was instantly transported between reality and fantasy, between what he was actually doing and the climactic heights they were about to reach together in her imagination.

She struggled to keep still, refusing the temptation to open her body for him or shudder in orgasm and betray the pleasure she received during her weekly hour-long sessions in the massage parlour on Yonge Street in downtown Toronto.

Six months had passed since she'd discovered the expensive treatment centre quite – and literally – by accident. Aching from a slip on an icy footpath during her first winter in Canada, Charlotte had learned a valuable lesson about altering her style to include clumpy (and ugly in her opinion) footwear as a means of keeping upright in the snow. Her first few weeks in a new country hadn't been easy. She'd disembarked at Toronto's Pearson Airport filled with battered self-esteem and little confidence, her decision to leave Ireland one of urgent necessity. Settling into a new job and coping with extreme climate conditions had been tough, but with determination and persistence (not to mention a new wardrobe filled with the most fashionable thermals she could find and an array of colourful padded ski jackets), she'd adjusted and survived, time serving to dilute some of her embedded knots of tension and push the disturbing circumstances leading to her departure from home to the back of her mind.

Following her fall on the ice, the nagging ache in her upper body persisted long after she'd ended up on the flat of her back on Bloor Street West as she hurried to her job in the HSBC Bank Canada. Finding it particularly painful following a stressful afternoon at a boardroom meeting with disgruntled lawyers, Charlotte had run out of painkillers and anti-inflammatories and was paying yet another visit to the late-night pharmacy when she noticed a masseuse advertisement in the window. **'Specialises in new manipulation technique to ease backache and muscular discomfort'** flashed in bold print from the eye-catching notice.

Whipping her iPhone from her purse, Charlotte tapped in the phone number and connected the call.

"When would you like an appointment?" she was asked after she'd explained her ailment.

"Right now," she replied, absently rubbing the base of her spine to ease her discomfort.

To her disappointment, but not surprise, it was a few days before they were able to fit her in – a promising sign that their business was thriving, she thought in retrospect.

And now, six months on, she no longer needed the therapy to ease her back. But she continued her visits, savouring the feel of Giovanni's expert hands exploring her soft, smooth skin every week.

Her impromptu move to Canada had lived up to all of Charlotte's expectations, surpassing them in certain aspects. Toronto's sprawling city offered space, independence and safety. Yielding now to Giovanni's expert touch, she guessed her life would be the envy of others: living in a spacious apartment in an exciting city, a few minutes' walk from her well-paying job in a thriving investment bank and working with dependable colleagues who were ready to celebrate lucrative deals as the occasions arose.

"Turn over, Charlotte."

Giovanni's soft Italian lilt was a timely interruption. She smothered a devilish grin and obeyed his instruction, rolling onto her back while he held the soft white towel aloft. Close to perfection, she thought, her nipples tingling as his fingers trailed her skin. If only I could transpose some of this temporary magic into the rest of my life, she thought, her smile fading as Philip Lord's threatening grimace forced its way into her consciousness as her masseuse traced the jagged scar on her chest. Will I ever banish my attacker from memory, she wondered, fighting against the familiar feelings of despair and forcing herself to relax, keeping her eyes tightly shut, a deliberate decision on her behalf to regain the gentle momentum in her daydream. Managing to banish bad memories, not wanting anything other than Giovanni's touch and voice to cut in on her thoughts, she drifted into fantasy once more.

While he moved his hands in circular movements on her thighs, Charlotte's imagination was shifting into a higher gear, progressing into overdrive. It took all her willpower to stay still as she felt the sensation of his fingers – still damp from the massage oil. She licked her lips, the roof of her mouth dry as he took her right foot in his hands and pressed her heel against his waistband, kneading each toe in succession.

But, as ever, she maintained stringent self-control. Keeping her sexual release strictly under wraps was part of the scintillating excitement. Her private and very intimate affair with Giovanni – so private that even *he* didn't know about it – was untarnished by expectation, jealousy or justification. He was her masseuse, she his client. Any move from that would destroy the magic. By Charlotte's estimation, the relationship was as near perfect as she could hope to achieve.

"I'll leave you to relax a while before getting dressed." Giovanni's soothing voice brought a natural end to her pleasure, leaving her relaxed and satisfied in the afterglow of her precious sixty minutes.

As the door closed behind Giovanni, she reluctantly let go of her fantasy and opened her eyes. She allowed a few moments for her eyesight to adjust to the soft lighting before reaching for her purse and turning her phone back on. Reality prevailed. Several beeps later, she scrolled through her text messages, quickly scanning the numerous business ones to ensure nothing required immediate attention. Seeing a message from her mother, she raised an eyebrow. Marian Dulhooly detested text-messaging, preferring direct conversation – lengthy phone calls usually.

Skipping over a few others to open her mother's message, Charlotte sat upright on the plinth and swung her feet over the side as she read the brief text, smiling at her mother's letter format and perfect grammar – no text shortcuts for Mum!

But the content was intriguing, her suggestion jaw-dropping.

"No way," she muttered under her breath, a vision of Aunt Polly coming to mind. They'd never really gelled, Polly forever criticising her love of books and pushing her out into the fresh air.

"Who'd have thought she'd be so damn conniving?" Charlotte muttered now, amused more than annoyed at her aunt's final wishes. She reread the text to be sure she'd interpreted it correctly.

Charlotte, I thought you should know that Polly left everything to Kieran in her will, providing he lives in the house for a year and leaves her multiple bank accounts untouched until then. Beth needs your support to contest this ludicrous decision. It should have been divided equally and not designed to break up our family.

Charlotte snorted. As if Polly was breaking up a tight unit!

Contact home to discuss what can be done. Mum.

Mulling her mother's words and instructions over in her mind as she dressed in a khaki green jumpsuit and long over-the-knee brown-leather boots, Charlotte perfected her lip-liner and added a smear of gloss plumper, refraining from smacking her lips together to allow the plumper to take effect. Next, she outlined her large green eyes – a constant reminder of her striking resemblance to her father and brother – with dark-brown kohl pencil, smudging a little beneath her lower lid to accentuate a sultry look. Freeing her hair from its ponytail, she turned her head upside down and ran her fingers through it to add volume, part of the preparation for the final stage of the game she played on these visits. Leaving Giovanni's massage parlour with a little swagger of her hips and her head held high, she sensed his dark smouldering eyes on her body. Silly, she knew, to pay it too much attention. Considering he has seen me without my clothes on, there's little left to his imagination, she thought . . . but she loved the way his eyes followed her until the door snapped shut. The perfect conclusion – enough to keep her going for the seven intervening days until her next appointment.

Sipping a whiskey and soda in her Harbour Square apartment before bed that evening, she stared at the light-filled view over Lake Ontario, her thoughts returning to the request in her mother's text. She still hadn't responded. Contest the will? Why? To what avail? Last thing she needed was the headache of a messy legal battle – particularly against her only brother! She sympathised with her sister. That went without saying. Working in a bank, she witnessed plenty of money-related stress. But surely Beth had other options?

From her twenty-first-floor residence, she watched the late-evening roller-bladers weaving around other pedestrians. Smiling at her mother's choice of words in the message, Charlotte didn't need any graphic explanation for her instructions. This wasn't about denying Kieran the chance of putting down roots. It was a last-ditch endeavour to get one over on Polly one final time. Polly Digby and her sister-in-law, Marian Dulhooly, had been arch enemies long, long before Marian married her brother, Frank Dulhooly.

Chapter 10

Beth stirred her cappuccino, licked the spoon and dropped it on the table beside her unread newspaper. She sipped the frothy liquid from her cup. She had wasted an entire morning in the grant section of Cork County Council and, before making the 100-kilometre trip back to Goleen, she'd decided to treat herself to a decent coffee.

Her day had started badly. Reading the note Carl had left on the kitchen table had ruined her appetite and been the main cause of her missing breakfast and chipping her favourite rose-petal mug when it smacked against the ceramic Belfast sink. "Blast and damn!" she'd screamed, her voice echoing in the empty house. Her former Ryanair colleagues had given her the mug for one of her birthdays, insisting she drink the Chablis they'd poured into it once their last passenger had disembarked.

"Whatever possessed me to leave that job?" she muttered under her breath, massaging her temples with her index fingers to ease her thumping headache.

"Would you like a menu?"

Beth shook her head and smiled at the smart young waiter who approached her table. Not unless you want me to pay by washing dishes, she felt like saying. His smart appearance reminded her of the Council guys she'd tried and failed to impress.

Justifying the country-home potential for her farmhouse hadn't impressed the grant department. They'd actually laughed aloud when she'd outlined her plans to combine a lucrative guesthouse business with a retreat for writers and artists. Admittedly her business proposal lacked a definite income guarantee but surely it was at least worth consideration?

"The market is there," she'd insisted, relieved she'd had the good sense to leave her jacket on as she felt the material of her shirt sticking to her skin. She could imagine the rings of underarm perspiration on the white polyester. "Our changing climate is encouraging people to holiday at home –"

"In their own homes or a cottage by the coast with ample amenities," the council employee had insisted. He wasn't for turning. "Not in a farmhouse in the middle of nowhere where there isn't even a decent cab service or playground for children. What do you propose to offer bored toddlers and teenagers in your country home? I'm sorry but it's a 'no' from us on this occasion."

A lump rose in Beth's throat. She felt like crying and knew she was out of her depth. She didn't have the business-speak required to outwit them. "What if I reduced the amount being requested?"

"It's low priority. Council funds are depleting and only crucial and guaranteed projects are afforded grants these days. And your financial projections lack evidence-based figures. Maybe if things improve or if you conducted a three-month trial and resubmitted your business plan we could bring it to the board but as it stands I'm afraid there's no point in proceeding."

"Can I offer you a top-up?"

The waiter was hovering near Beth's table again, a coffee pot in his hand this time.

She shrugged and accepted the coffee refill, disregarding the fact that it wasn't topped with smooth white froth or sprinkled chocolate. "Thank you," she said. In the line of a tip for the pleasant waiter, her gracious smile was as much as she could offer.

A drop of milk spilt onto her royal-blue skirt. She took a napkin from the table and dabbed it dry. As she searched her handbag for her car keys, Carl's note came to hand, the sheet of notepaper crumpled in a tight ball. It took careful handling to uncurl it without ripping it. She smoothed it on the table, her husband's scribbled words every bit as infuriating as they'd been earlier but this time minus the surprise. She presumed his use of capitals was deliberate. She took a gulp of coffee and reread the note.

ED WANTS US BOTH TO VISIT TONIGHT. BE READY TO LEAVE AT 7.45.

Beth pushed back her chair, leaving the crumpled page right-side-up on the polished table beside her empty cup. Even if somebody bothered to read the two brief sentences, their meaning would be insignificant. The threatening undercurrent in Carl's message was designed specifically for her, playing on her sympathies and daring her to refuse. Who did he bloody well think he was? From now on, she decided, I'll visit Ed on my terms instead of being forced to accompany Carl and support his ridiculous pretence that all is well between us. And furthermore, she thought, as she left the restaurant and walked towards the car park, I'll be doing it out of respect and sympathy for Ed, not to appease Carl.

Chapter 11

Marian Dulhooly sat in the gazebo in the centre of her large back garden, blowing smoke rings into the air, disgusted with herself for giving into her addiction so easily. The self-control she had exercised in quitting the deathly habit two years before had begun to unravel the moment Kieran returned in Frank's Mercedes and told them about the details of Polly's will.

"I've decided to give it a go," he'd told his parents after he'd given them a full account, arms folded across his chest, his gaze moving from one to the other as he waited for a response. "I'm going to move into Number 5 and give staying there for a year a decent shot."

"Polly would be pleased, Kieran," his father said, patting his son on the shoulder and nodding his head in approval. "Did it come as a complete shock or had she ever hinted at her plans?"

"Shock doesn't begin to describe my reaction," Kieran answered honestly. "She hasn't made it too easy for me though. I've never heard of anyone having to live in a place for a year before getting rightful ownership. Have you?"

Frank smiled. "The number of years I've spent in a courtroom, son, I've heard it all before. And some of it made the hair stand on the back of my neck! What Polly's requesting is mild by comparison."

"You're quiet, Mum. In fact, you look a bit shocked. Everything okay?" Kieran turned to his mother.

Sitting ramrod straight, her expression was difficult to read. It wasn't like her to hold back her opinion.

Marian merely nodded. "I guess it's a good opportunity for you but it would have been fairer if Beth and Charlotte were included too." She eyed her son, trying to gauge his reaction to this admission.

"Might have been but Polly had other ideas."

"Even so . . ."

"Ah Mum, if either of the girls had got the whole lot, I'd be happy for them. I'd wish them well and get on with my life. Any food going? I'm starving."

Marian had painted a smile on her face, her stomach sinking. In typical Kieran-style, he'd moved on quickly. His dismissal had left little room for argument. But it wouldn't stop her making another attempt. It would have to be spelt out for him. First she needed to speak to Charlotte and make sure she was on side. Until she'd managed to convince her eldest daughter to go along with it, she wouldn't say any more about it to Kieran. There didn't seem much point.

"I can throw on a mixed grill if you like. There's some homemade brown bread to go with it?" she'd offered instead.

"Sounds great. With real butter too! Thanks, Mum."

Over a week had passed since then and Marian was still waiting for Charlotte to make the time to talk to her in detail about things. Her attempts so far had been cut short for one reason or another and, with the time difference and her busy work schedule, Marian hadn't been able to do anything about it. Although she had a sneaky suspicion that her daughter was avoiding her and the thorny subject of inheritance. She took a last drag of her cigarette and stubbed it out on the ground with the heel of her boot.

"How was your game, Frank?" she croaked when she went back inside. She broke into a fit of coughing, her throat tightening once she opened her mouth to speak.

"Good. Yeah, I enjoyed it, got plenty of *fresh air*," he replied.

His emphasis on 'fresh air' wasn't lost on her. His disdain of her 'filthy smoking habit', as he referred to it, was an old argument in the Dulhooly household.

"Frank – about Beth? Don't you think we need to do something?"

He ran his hand across the back of his neck. "We've been over this, Marian."

"But something has to be done." It wasn't her first attempt at coaxing him to approach Polly's solicitor and suggest contesting his sister's decision.

Frank shook his head, weary from her incessant nagging. "Good God, woman, my sister was entitled to give her entire estate to the dogs' home if that's what she preferred!"

"The dogs' home would have been fairer than the choice she has made!"

"I thought you'd be delighted Kieran's staying around?"

"Of course I'm delighted. It'll be great getting to know him again."

"Well, then?" Frank searched his wife's face, hoping she was starting to see sense.

Marian pursed her lips. "Making a few changes to the will doesn't necessarily mean he'll leave again."

Frank let out a groan. "You honestly believe that?"

Marian shrugged. "I've heard stories from other families."

"Rumours," Frank muttered.

She continued as though he hadn't spoken. "If we talk to the solicitor and get a guarantee that all three of our children will get an equal share, Kieran will understand. You're Polly's brother, a nearer relation. You can dictate it."

Frank pulled his wine-coloured golfing jumper over his head, tossed it on the back of a kitchen chair and fixed his thinning hair back into place. "You don't understand the legal system at all, do you? We can't walk in to the solicitor and instruct her to rearrange Polly's inheritance to the way *you* feel it should have been done." His tone was laced with sarcasm. "Anyway, you, or Beth for that matter, haven't the right to contest the –"

"And as per usual, Frank, you've got the power but refuse to do anything with it!" she spat at him, eyes filled with anger. Deeply hurt by his condescending comment, she didn't wait for him to lord it over her with his highfalutin' legal speak. "That will be a great help to Beth! You'd rather be loyal to a dead sister than a daughter who is hanging on for her dear life!"

Beads of cold perspiration broke out on Frank's forehead. "Beth only has herself to blame. If she'd asked for advice beforehand, I'd have warned her to keep the hell away from that monstrosity of a house. It's not help she needs now, it's a miracle."

"She's our daughter, our youngest." Marian's voice caught in her throat.

Frank turned away from his wife. "Beth's a married woman with a husband who should make it his priority to provide for her."

Like you provided for us, Marian thought silently, bitterness seeping through her, old memories jumping to the fore. She couldn't deny that materialistically he'd been terrific but, when it came to giving them his time, his apparent heroism paled significantly. She couldn't help remembering the endless stream of late nights he'd worked late and the lonely weekends they'd waited patiently for him to return from golf. Sighing, she let go of her dark thoughts. It was useless revisiting ancient arguments. She doubted there was any point introducing those years as a comparison. He hadn't understood then and it was unlikely he'd understand now.

"Carl hasn't a notion of stepping up to the plate, Frank."

Frank's green eyes flashed. "So why organise a golden handshake?" he continued. "As her husband he's entitled to half if they split up. Has that not crossed your mind?"

"Couldn't Beth sign something or have the solicitor draw up some agreement that would deny him any part of it in the likely event of that happening?"

Frank sighed. "The law is tricky. Hell, I'd give Beth some of my savings if she was on her own – she'll get them anyway when I die – but there's no way I'm giving that spoilt brat an easy ride!"

"So Beth continues to suffer."

Frank's expression was grave. "And if we put money their way, what will they have learned? Either of them?"

Marian brought her hands to her face. Frank could be so obstinate at times. She tried one last time. "Please give what I'm saying some thought."

He took his jumper from the chair and folded it neatly, carrying it with him as he walked away from her. "I'm not going to change my mind, Marian." Frank was definite. "The will stands as Polly wanted it and I'd appreciate if all of you would respect that."

Marian's frustration was at an all-time high. She was tired of holding back. "What respect did Polly show us when she wrote her will?"

"Marian, I've a blinding headache. Please let it go."

"But surely you get what she was playing at? How can you be so blind?"

His face reddened. He cast around, speaking through gritted teeth. "I'm not the one who needs to have my eyes tested."

"She did it out of spite, to have one last dig at me!"

"Finally!" Frank threw his hands in the air. "We get to the truth! At last you're being honest about what's going on inside that head of yours!"

"Truth?" Marian's face flamed.

"That's what this is really about. It's not you worrying about Beth or trying to help her back on her feet. You're thinking of yourself and how you can fight against Polly one last time!"

"Damn you, Frank. You never take my side of things where Polly's concerned."

"Despite what you might think, Marian, the world doesn't revolve around you." The jumper fell from his hands. He stooped to retrieve it.

"Certainly not where you're concerned!"

"Leave things be, Marian," he looked up at her, a warning in his eyes, "this time."

"I'm not sure I can," came her reply.

"Well, you won't get my support and without it –"

"What's new? I'll get support elsewhere seeing as you've made it obvious you couldn't care less!"

Frank left the room with a thumping headache.

A furious Marian returned to the garden when he'd left, lighting up another cigarette and inhaling deeply. What gave him the right to undermine her, put his sister's wishes far and above any of hers? She'd had a lifetime of living in Polly's shadow, had never measured up to his precious sister. Taking another drag from her cigarette, she wished for the umpteenth time that she hadn't set out to trap him into marriage. What she hadn't realised in her rush for revenge was that in trapping him, she was also imprisoning herself.

And now he was leaving her no choice but to follow this through without him. A barrister in semi-retirement, he had invaluable legal knowledge and could easily sort out the mess if he wanted, which he didn't.

Flicking cigarette ash onto the grass, her thoughts turned to Kieran, her only son. Her relationship with him had become strained when Polly got her claws in him, enticing him from her, becoming his confidante and encouraging him away from his family home. Frank had turned a blind eye, particularly once he'd accepted his son wasn't going to be the fourth-generation Dulhooly to spend his professional life in the courtroom – at least not in the way his father had in mind!

Her failure to hide her animosity towards Polly became an unresolved issue between mother and son as

Kieran got older. She adored him and the growing distance between them became a great source of heartache and something she blamed entirely on her sister-in-law.

"Show some respect when you're speaking about Aunt Polly," he'd respond automatically when she'd pass a snide comment about his stay in Number 5 Pier Road, yet another male in her life going through a phase where he wouldn't have a word said against precious Polly. Frank's loyalty to Polly had remained steadfast. Even on the occasions he was present for Marian's arguments with their son, he'd rarely correct Kieran, more often than not leaving the room and opting out. And so it had continued time after time, fraying at their relationship and increasing the tension between them. Kieran's decision to travel had come as a mixture of relief and remorse to his mother, relief she wouldn't have to watch from the sidelines as he treated Polly more like a mother than he did her and remorse that she'd wasted the years when she should have been close to him, allowing her resentment for Polly to drive a wedge between them.

The garden was chilly after the warmth of the kitchen stove. She finished her cigarette and tossed the butt away, catching the first glimpse of daffodils shooting through the earth. New beginnings, she thought, crouching down to take a closer look before returning inside.

Frank was engrossed in the evening news bulletin. Still too annoyed to go and join him in the living room, Marian took the portable phone and went to her bedroom to call long distance.

Charlotte answered on the first ring.

Having exchanged pleasantries with her eldest daughter, Marian sat on the bed and listened impatiently as Charlotte filled her in on how she'd passed her weekend.

"Charlotte," she said, "have you been on to Beth since?"

She could hear Charlotte's groan on the other end of the line.

"Not this again, Mum."

Marian moved off the bed and went to stand by the window. "I know you're not completely in favour –"

"It just doesn't sit well with me at all, Mum –"

"But it's important to your sister," Marian continued as though she hadn't spoken, refusing to take 'no' for an answer again that day. "Why can't you understand how desperate she is? It's not as though she asks very often."

Charlotte's sharp tone came down the line. "And when she does, it's not like I make a habit of refusing."

Marian sighed in exasperation. She had a tougher fight on her hands than she'd expected. More defiant than her sister, a lot like her father in fact, Charlotte had an orthodox sense of fair play – even in the most horrific of situations.

"This is Polly's way of splitting you up good and proper. Favouring your brother and luring him to the easy-going lifestyle in Schull at every hand's turn – she did that to annoy me!"

"Mum, not that old nugget!"

"Any scrap of trouble he got into, I'd swear she was encouraging his little escapades, allowing him stay out as late as he wanted and seldom monitoring the company he was keeping. For years I had my suspicions that she had him calling her 'Mammy'!"

Charlotte's deep groan finally halted Marian's flow. "Dramatic, Mum, even for you," she said. "Kieran loved

Schull. He was a different person there, could suit himself, stroll down the pier, hang out at the beach all day every day. He made his life there. Once he got into the habit, he lost any allegiance he had to home. I honestly don't think it was anything malicious to get at you or anybody else. He was just a boy having fun."

"But there are only the three of you. If she had children of her own –"

"Mum! That's below the belt. Losing her husband to the sea in their first year of marriage – have you any idea how heartbreaking that was? Can you not show her a modicum of respect? Not even now? She is *dead* after all, no longer a threat."

Marian had the grace to wince at Charlotte's words, although she took umbrage that her eldest daughter considered Polly a threat to her. Huh! Threat indeed, she thought. Downright nuisance would be a better description.

"Charlotte, have you any idea what's at stake here?" She took a tissue from her jeans pocket and dusted the screen of the flat-screen TV. "Your father's denying he knows how much the place is worth but I know you're turning your back on what could make a substantial difference to the rest of your life."

"But it's not mine! It's Kieran's. He wouldn't interfere if things had worked out in my favour."

Marian grimaced. Charlotte's words echoed her brother's. "Will you call your sister, please?"

"I'll do it soon, Mum. But, honestly, from my own perspective, I'm not interested. I'm coping fine on what I earn here. I'll call Kieran and suss out his plans – he could be contemplating taking off again. Then your fussing would be needless."

Marian clutched the tissue in her hand. "But . . . eh, do you think that's a good idea? Talking to Kieran, I mean?"

"I'm not lying to my brother. If we're going ahead with this venture, he's going to hear it from me. I'm not taking the coward's way out and letting the solicitor inform him that his sisters are contesting the will. What does that say about us as a family?"

Marian resented her daughter's obstinacy but made an effort to keep her patience. "Not a word to your father though . . ."

To appease her mother, Charlotte relented – for now at least. "All right."

Mother and daughter agreed to get in contact again after Charlotte had spoken to Beth and Kieran, then both hung up at the same time, neither very pleased with the outcome of the call.

Chapter 12

"I'm disappointed Beth couldn't make it this evening," Ed commented to Carl.

Apart from the odd sigh or exclamation, there had been very little conversation since Ed and Carl had taken their places either side of the chessboard ninety minutes previously.

"Definitely next time. She was in the city today and didn't make it back on time." Carl gritted his teeth, hating lying to his brother but too proud to divulge the real reason for her absence.

In foul humour when she'd returned from her visit to the Council, her mood had worsened when he'd handed her the letter they'd received from the bank, detailing their mortgage arrears and requesting a meeting to discuss increased repayments. She'd stormed away from him, yelling and screaming as she'd pulled pots from the press and set about chopping potatoes and vegetables for their dinner – which unsurprisingly had turned out to be a tense, silent affair.

"Not to worry," Ed said.

"But she'll call to see you soon," Carl promised, seething that her stubbornness had won out. No matter what he'd said, she wouldn't budge and he'd had no choice but to make the trip to the hospice in Bantry to visit Ed alone.

"Make sure you tell her I'm looking forward to her visit. She brightens up the place with that smile of hers and she's never short of a story or two either."

Ed slid the black rook to the next available square on the chessboard, aware that Carl was assessing this movement and its consequences to the game. He was also aware of his discomfort every time he mentioned Beth and his reluctance to engage in too much conversation.

Carl's eyes narrowed at Ed's latest play, his opponent's sharpness amazing in light of his grave illness. He threw a quick glance at the older man. The whites of his eyes resembled a dull egg-yolk, his complexion a horrid grey – like that of a sky on a dreary winter's day. He'd seen healthier-looking corpses. Mistaking this man in his forty-ninth year for an octogenarian would be easily forgiven.

Sighing deeply, Carl's heart ached for a chance to relive the years he'd taken Ed's existence for granted. But how could I have known his life would be cut short, he reasoned?

Carl's thirtieth birthday being still three months away, he doubted very much Ed would be alive to share cake and champagne. Never once imagining disaster could strike twice in one family, now he lamented the years he'd refused the invitations to spend summers sailing leisurely around the south of France or joining him on his travels to all five continents in his search for the latest in couture fashion.

Ed couldn't be blamed for the distance that grew between them; the fault lay entirely with Carl. And he knew it only too well. Ed, in his usual carefree manner, had continued to issue invitations but left the decision to accept or reject with Carl, never once trying to change his mind once he'd replied.

Lowering his eyes to the chessboard once more, Carl placed index finger and thumb on one of his white rooks, dithering over the move and twirling it from side to side on the inch square. His heart wasn't in the game. A life without Ed seemed unbearable, his foundation whipped from underneath him.

Confusing round-the-clock-hired-help with quality parenting skills, Carl's parents had been more like distant relations than a proper mum and dad so Ed had stepped into the breach and replaced them as Carl's sole source of stability. As a result, he'd relied on Ed for advice and a helping hand whenever required. It had been Ed who'd taught him to field off school bullies, Ed who'd slipped the condoms in his rucksack on his first secondary school trip, Ed who'd counselled him through his first heartbreak and Ed who'd placed an arm around his nineteen-year-old shoulders and hugged him tightly when he'd broken the news of their parents' death, gently explaining that the cable car they'd travelled in had dropped thousands of feet from the Swiss Alps, killing them both instantly.

"They didn't suffer," Ed had told him, not that it made any great difference to Carl whose initial reaction to the news was one of relief.

While the world without his parents was undoubtedly changed and more financially difficult than before – at least until he reached twenty-one years of age and gained access to the vast property they'd left him – Carl's strength of personality shone through as it had failed to do in their presence. Their death had altered everything, reduced his fear of failure, permitting him to carry plans through to fruition (or not, in certain cases) without the added burden of their critical disapproval – the one thing he was guaranteed to receive. And Ed had offered stalwart support.

"I don't know if I'm ready," Carl had admitted to Ed when he was offered a coveted place on the French under-21 rugby team a short while after the accident.

"Nonsense," Ed had proclaimed.

"But what if I make a fool of myself?" he'd protested, still unsure about the responsibility he was being offered. "What if I'm the cause of losing a game?"

"You'll be part of a team," Ed had reasoned. "It's unlikely you'll be the sole cause of losing any game. Now get your butt down to training before the offer's withdrawn and thank them for the magnificent honour of playing at national level."

"Mum and Dad are probably up there waiting to haunt me," Carl had grimaced, reminding Ed how immature he could be.

"Let their influence go! Their lives have been cut short. Nobody knows what's waiting around the next corner. Grab this opportunity with both hands and let it be one less regret in your life." Ed's encouragement was limitless. And though he didn't voice it to Carl, he wondered about his parents' last thoughts. Had they had regrets?

"I'll give it a bash then," Carl had decided, securing a promise from his brother that he'd attend his first game. Moral support on the sideline would make a pleasant change.

Carl's confidence soared over time – arguably to a level of cockiness in his early twenties where he took liberty rather than opportunity and extended his brother's advice to taking every perceivable risk he could muster, leaving Ed to wonder if he'd encouraged him a little too much and succeeded in making him reckless.

Thank you, Ed, Carl said silently now as he moved the rook piece straight ahead, oblivious to the knight waiting to capture yet another of his pieces.

"Careless move – you slipped up there," Ed commented, leaning his elbows on the small table and studying the board for his next move. "Distracted?"

"Eye off the ball," Carl responded. "I don't intend making a habit of it though!" he added with a laugh.

Ed held the pawn in his hand, shifting his gaze to his brother. "You and Beth? What's going on? And don't try and fudge an answer, Carl. I may be dying but I'm not a blind fool."

Carl's expression paled at first, then turned a deep shade of guilty red. His brain whirred, the secret he'd been keeping from Ed jumping to the forefront of his mind. Frantically searching for an answer to the simple question he'd been asked, he muttered something unintelligible.

"Speak up, Carl!"

"There's nothing wrong. We're fine."

"Carl, give me a little credit at least. Spill!"

"Nothing to tell."

"Give me strength, kid brother. You forget I know you better than you know yourself."

"Speaking of strength, shouldn't you be saving yours?"

Ed shook his head. "Don't be so patronising. And evasiveness doesn't suit you, Carl."

"Sorry but look, we'll work it out . . ." His voice trailed off.

"She's a keeper – a bit neurotic at times perhaps – but a keeper all the same. You should appreciate how lucky you are, not let some trivial nonsense drive a wedge between you. Somebody like her may never come along again for you. And I know you love her . . . at least you used to."

Carl let out a long sigh, staring at the modern art adorning the pale peach walls. Ed's appreciation of art came a close second to his passion for fashion and designer clothing. The majority of his paintings – gathered over the years from a variety of galleries and exhibitions throughout the world – had been decorating the walls in his South of France chateau before his fall from grace when the chateau, paintings included, had been sold. He'd been cheered no end when Carl had managed to "rescue" a selection and arrange for them to be shipped to the hospice, never questioning how his brother had accomplished that or managed to have them released from the country. Choosing from such a large collection had been Carl's biggest problem, trying to remember the ones Ed had loved most.

"I'll rest a lot easier now having these beauts around me," Ed had declared when Carl arrived into his room one Saturday morning, the maintenance man behind him with an electric drill and some hooks. As each magnificent framed piece took its place on the wall, Ed launched into the story of where he'd purchased that particular painting or who had gifted it to him.

If only there were a life partner I could have transported to his side, Carl thought with regret. Then I'd feel my contribution was making a real difference.

Despite the many lovers in Ed's life over the years, he'd admitted to Carl there had only been one he'd have settled down with for life. But he'd messed up and taken their unique love and special connection for granted. He had assumed incorrectly that their relationship could take second place to business, be put on hold when it suited him, yet still survive. Walking into their home after an intense three-week business trip, he'd been appalled to find a brief goodbye-note on the pillow of their king-size bed and he'd never found true love since.

"Carl! Are you going to hold out on me all night? Why won't you tell me what's going on with you and Beth? It's not as if I have all the time in the world to wait!"

"That's below the belt. Anyway, it's nothing for you to worry about. We'll work it out," Carl ran a hand through his thick black hair, feeling like a rabbit in headlights. Finding an acceptable explanation – reasonable or not – would drag ancient revelations from the closet. He'd have to declare a lot more than the issues tearing his marriage apart if Ed was to fully understand the root of the problem. Although in a way they were all connected. The thoughts of sharing this confidence brought him out in a cold sweat. The tight bond they'd been sharing would be blown asunder. He couldn't bring himself to imagine Ed's disgust and disappointment – or worse still rejection. More than anything, Carl wanted his brother to have a good impression of him. Revealing his darkest hour would shatter that illusion for sure. And though he knew he was living a lie where his brother was concerned, Carl preferred it to its horrible alternative.

But he had his work cut out for him. Ed wasn't easily placated.

"What's driving you apart? That's what I need to know? Beth adored the ground you walked on when you lived in Paris – and you her in your own way, come to think of it. What's changed?"

"Ed, you need to conserve your energy. No need to fret about us and our silly arguments. We have the rest of our lives to sort it out –" Oh God, he thought, what an insensitive statement. His guilt worsened when Ed closed his eyes for a moment, his forehead creasing as a fresh bout of pain flashed through his entire body.

Carl changed the subject. "Come on, Imelda will be back later to whip your ass. Shouldn't you get a bit of shut-eye in the meantime?" One of the nurses had taken to sharing an occasional chess game with Ed, something that eased Carl's concern about his brother's shortage of visitors.

He reached across for the tablets left by Ed's bedside, handing the small container and glass of fresh water to his brother. "Take these. They'll take the edge off the pain."

Ed acquiesced, popping the pills in his mouth and washing them down with a slug of water. He flopped back in the chair.

"I won't give up until you tell me, Carl. And if I'm exhausted it's down to you and your stubborn refusal to own up to what's going on. I'm all you've got. Who's going to sort you out when I'm not around? I want to know everything has been done to help while I still have breath in my body."

Carl felt torn, knowing on one hand that his brother was playing the invalid card to force information from him, while accepting on the other hand that he was genuinely concerned about himself and Beth.

"And don't think you'll fob me off with a concoction of lies," Ed added.

"Trust me, Ed. There's nothing at all for you to worry about."

"I want to die in peace and seeing that distant look in your eye, kid brother, isn't making it easy for me. I know you. You can't hide the truth, not when it's flashing in your eyes."

Carl licked his lips, his discomfort increasing. "Ed, I'll make an effort with Beth. I'll get it sorted. Can we forget about it now, please?"

"When that haunted look leaves your face, then I'll forget it but until then . . ." His voice trailed off and he shrugged his thin shoulders.

Carl's guilt intensified. "I want to enjoy whatever time is left with you, make the best of it. Can't we let it be about us brothers? Nothing else?"

"Life isn't like that, Carl. You can't just shut out what's going on around you."

"But it's my turn to protect and support you for a change. Please let me do it my way. I thought you believed in letting me make my decisions and living by them regardless?" Carl's steady voice belied the rising emotion inside him.

Ed leaned back in his chair, the chess game forgotten. "We've come full circle, you and I. You're the strong one now, leading for both of us."

"Hardly!" Carl exclaimed.

"You underestimate your capability."

"That attitude mightn't be unfounded though," Carl interjected.

"So if you want to take me out of my misery, let fixing your marriage be the final thing I can help you with."

Pushing back his chair from the table, Carl stretched his long legs to the side, careful not to tip against the table and disturb the chess pieces.

"Beth's obsessed with the house," he began, wondering if that snippet would appease his brother's concerns. It wasn't an untruth – not entirely – just not the most significant reason behind their frayed relationship and the bad atmosphere prevailing almost all of the time now.

Ed ran a finger around his cracked lips. "I told you: don't patronise me, Carl. Not at this stage. You're making it up as you go along." He gave a weak smile, his eyes crinkling at the sides. "I'll haunt you from the other side."

Carl didn't respond for a while, his expression darkening, a lump rising in his throat. "That's not funny, Ed. You've no idea how much I'm going to miss you when . . ." This time his voice was thick with emotion, a rare display of weakness for the youngest brother.

Putting his head in his hands, Carl was torn apart with grief for the brother who sat opposite him, offering the same staunch support he'd always provided. His failing marriage gnawed inside him. His past actions had been unforgiveable but unavoidable, not that Beth was prepared to either understand or accept that. And neither would Ed if he knew the truth, no matter what dying wishes he proclaimed.

He glanced up from the table, not surprised to find his brother staring at him, a questioning and expectant look on his face as he waited for his admission. But Carl's lips were sealed on this subject. He was hiding a lot, had been for quite some time, several situations snowballing as a result of one wrong move. What a relief it would be to divulge his darkest secrets, he thought, imagining what it would be like to wake in the morning without the burden of a guilty conscience. But it wasn't to be at this late stage. He daren't risk a showdown with Ed, daren't risk his brother's disapproval so near his death, not when their relationship was stronger now than it ever had been. He couldn't bear to see his brother's belief in him collapse. Ed would not be hearing the truth – at least not from him. And that was his next big concern. How would he ensure Beth didn't squeal? He took a deep breath and improvised as best he could to put Ed's mind at ease.

"Ed, honestly, it's just that massive imposing house that's coming between us. I never really wanted it if the truth be known and Beth's obsessed with restoring it to how she thinks it should be. A pipe dream if you ask me, one we couldn't afford."

"If my business wasn't in dire straits, you know I'd help you out." Ed clenched and unclenched his fists.

"Don't, Ed," Carl warned, concern spreading over his face as hurt and humiliation spread across his brother's.

"But I was careless! How else did that bloody plagiarist steal my designs! If I got my hands on him, it's untold what I'd do. My reputation is ruined in the fashion world."

They'd been over the story so many times. Ed's business had been pushed out of the market by a more affordable label, launching identical designs on to the catwalks. Within two seasons Ed's sales went crashing through the floor. Unfamiliar with haute couture in Paris, Carl had gawped in disbelief when Ed shared the extent and speed of the damage. Maintaining the design house along with meeting a minimal payment to outstanding creditors had quickly drained Ed's limited funds, with no sign of any sales income for quite some time. Living in the belief that Carl still had an income from the family vineyard in France, he'd asked Carl to top up the monthly lodgement so as at least to keep his company afloat.

Ed closed his eyes a moment, focusing his concentration on the sharp pain slicing through his body. "At least my life assurance policy will clear the debts when I'm gone." He attempted a laugh, his face contorting as another sharp stab gripped his body. "About the only thing I'll leave behind." He looked apologetically at his brother as though he were letting him down.

"I'd rather have you here for as long as possible." Carl struggled to steady his voice. "We both would."

They finished the game in relative silence, then a victorious Ed leaned his head back on the chair and repeated his request.

"Send Beth to see me. I'd like to have a chat with her alone." He opened his eyes again, daring his brother to defy him.

"I'll slip away now," said Carl, not committing to his wife's visit. "Back in a day or so."

"I'll expect her then. Make sure you ask her – if she doesn't show up, I'll ring her myself. It's not as if I can hang around waiting!"

Ed's words followed Carl into the quiet corridor, echoing in his ears and festering in his heart long after the door had snapped shut behind him.

Chapter 13

Greeted by the aroma of hot sausage rolls and pastries in the supermarket on Schull's main street, Kieran followed the heavenly scent to the hot counter.

"A couple of sausage rolls and maybe one of those bacon and cheese thingies . . . oh, I'll have a hash brown too, please."

"Sausage rolls are four for a euro. Will I give you four?"

"May as well," Kieran smiled, his stomach already growling, the breakfast cereal he'd had earlier having failed to satisfy his appetite. He'd eaten at his parents' home on occasion over the past few days but the strained atmosphere had ruined his appetite and made his mother's fine cooking less palatable. Older and wiser supposedly – him and them – yet nothing much else had changed in the Ballydehob house from what he could see: his parents sniping at each other, pretending a normal relationship while avoiding spending much time together, the things he'd put to the back of his mind during his travels. Nothing to do with me anyway, he'd decided, as he'd repacked the few bags he'd brought home with him and asked his father to drop him to Number 5. Making Schull his home for now would allow him to be his own boss, as well as affording him the opportunity of some time to think in peace.

Earlier that morning, he'd spotted Jess hanging washing on the line. It was his first glimpse of her since her peculiar disappearing act from the doorstep. He hadn't liked to approach unannounced, preferring if their next meeting was initiated by her. He was looking forward to catching up with her again. The vibe between them had been good. He wouldn't rush her – he had the time to wait.

"I'll have a cup of tea to go as well," he said to the attractive assistant, taking the paper bag she passed across the glass counter and grabbing a few sachets of salt from the basket.

"The drinks are self-service." She pointed. "Just over there."

Watching the waves crashing on the rocks a short while later, he munched on the sausage rolls, flicking the flaking pastry from his jeans and taking in his surroundings. The footpath extending along the cliff edge was another welcome improvement and no doubt the numerous sets of steps to the waterside attracted more families these days. Biting into the cheese and ham jambon, he recalled a different time where he and his buddies jumped from the cliff edge onto the rocks, tossing their shoes down first and leaping barefoot – just for the hell of it. His face breaking into a smile, he was sorely tempted to untie his laces and repeat the teenage habit, convinced he'd get the same adrenalin rush even after all these years.

The soles of his feet were hardened from hours on the stony surfaces and rough sand back then. Summers were about messing on the beach, in and out of the water, swimming, canoeing and rowing until the sun set and it was impossible to see. Their days regularly ended with a bonfire, masses of toasted (or burnt) food and a few cans of the cheapest beer they could get their hands on.

Adults shouted at them to keep the noise down but seldom interrupted apart from that, none interested in scrambling down the uneven surface to reinforce their orders. The tiny beaches amidst the rocks were private havens for adventurous teens. There were no wetsuits, no safety areas, just the heavenly experience of freedom. And by some mysterious miracle, they had escaped serious accident, with grazes and cuts being the extent of their injuries.

As well as the beginning of his love affair with the water, Schull filled Kieran with a desire to avoid restriction. So many nights he'd remained on the beach long after the others had stumbled home, lying on his back – mellow from the effects of alcohol – as he stared at the inky sky and watched the stars and the moon slide in and out behind clouds. This was a custom he enjoyed many times in the years that followed, lying on some of the world's most magnificent beaches and staring overhead at the activity in the sky.

A sudden disturbance behind him brought him back to the present. He swallowed the last of his food, glanced at his watch and smiled. Break time at school – no other sound could equate to that of dozens of excited children. He looked behind him, taking in the familiar sight. A different generation with a similar agenda to those that came before.

Boys and girls in red jumpers, white shirts and grey trousers burst into the playground, some happy to walk around munching fruit or bars, others making straight for the basketball court and pouncing on the discarded balls on the court.

Kieran got to his feet, hurrying towards the school yard as a basketball flew over the wire and rolled down the sloping field. He stuck out a tan hiking boot and stopped the multi-coloured ball.

"Hey, I know you, I saw you before," came an accusing voice.

Kieran approached the court, bouncing the ball as he went.

"You came to visit my mum!"

The ball slipped from his hands. As he stooped to pick it up, Kieran came to eye-level with a small blond boy with soft curls dancing on the nape of his neck as he clutched the mesh wire and jumped up and down.

"You were in my house. Remember?"

Before he had a chance to respond, a crowd had gathered around the little fellow, various ages and heights, male and female, all curious about the stranger tossing back their ball.

Kieran was very grateful to hear a tumble of questions coming from the gathered friends, saving him the embarrassment of admitting that he'd forgotten the little boy's name.

"Greg, who's that man?"

"How do you know him?"

"Greg, is he your uncle or cousin or something?"

"I'm Kieran." He lifted his arm and lofted the ball over the high fence, smiling as some of the children disbanded from their huddle to chase the basketball, a few of the boys diving dramatically on top of it.

Greg remained at the wire, a serious expression on his face, looking as though he had several questions he wanted to ask.

Hearing the school bell ring signalling the end of morning break, Kieran made to leave.

"See you around, Greg," he said, raising a hand in salute.

"Are you living next door now?" the child called after him.

Kieran turned back to face him. "Sure am."

Greg's eyes widened, a few stammers leaving his lips before finally he found the words he was searching for. "Mum's not able to fix my bike. The chain's off for ages and it won't go. And the wheel's flat too. Can you fix bikes?"

Kieran nodded, hiding his amusement. "Call in with your mum – and your bike – later on and I'll see what I can do." He gave him a wave, pleased the child's serious expression had been replaced with a smile.

His step was lighter as he made his way back towards the pier, his energy revived. He could actually visualise making a life there, filling his days with activity, maybe even get a job. Am I actually thinking like a grown up for a change, he wondered? Nobody would be more surprised than himself if that was the case. Then breaking into a grin, he decided he was acting more like a lustful teenager at the thoughts of getting closer to the hot girl next door than a thirty-one-year-old man thinking of settling down.

He burst into Aunt Polly's house with renewed vigour, running in and out of every room, throwing open the windows and allowing the sunshine and fresh air to filter through the house, reminded of the number of times Polly had asked him to do the exact same thing.

"You've younger legs than me," she'd say, or "It takes a strong lad like you to win an argument with some of those rusted window catches." Of course he knew she was teasing, Polly's ability to take care of herself was never in question.

He took an honest look at the house he'd been gifted, unable to deny its charm and attraction. Even as a summer-rental property, he imagined it would be in high demand with its sea view and close proximity to the water activities in the summer months. Admittedly it would benefit from a little modernisation and a fresh coat of paint – and definitely a colour change. That would brighten the interior significantly without losing Polly's quirky old-world charm entirely. A lover of strong, bright colours bordering definitely on gaudy, she had refused to move with the times and introduce neutral shades to her surroundings, happy with her citrus-green kitchen and harvest-orange sitting room.

Kieran strolled between rooms, taking in their characteristic detail – high ceilings, sash windows and a magnificent ocean view that would be difficult to surpass. Running a hand across one of his aunt's antique dressing tables, ignoring the trail of dust and remembering her attachment to the tiny figurines sitting on top, he realised how lucky he was to have a chance of owning such a beautiful property – a house he could be proud of, a house filled with happy memories both for him and for Polly. At least he assumed his aunt had enjoyed happy days there. As a boy he hadn't paid too much heed, as an adult he hadn't been around to notice. And now it was too late to enquire.

So many questions popped into his head as he scrutinised the rooms in greater detail, opening and closing wardrobes and drawers. Spotting a bundle of notebooks, he reached to the back of the drawer and pulled them forward, realising after a quick glance that what he held in his hand was a collection of diaries, pages well-thumbed and crinkled by the looks of them. They were held together with a piece of pink knitting wool tied in a neat bow. Kieran was tempted to take a peek and read about the intervening years in his aunt's life, probably her innermost thoughts. The last time he'd visited, she'd been active and healthy, full of fun and willing to sit for hours listening to the plans he had in mind once he'd stepped on the plane to explore the world. Never once had she nagged him about the four years he'd spent in college. Neither had she tried to dispel his excitement about his decision to follow his heart and travel. Staring at the diaries for a few moments, he decided against prying. Another time perhaps but for now he had more than enough memories. Perhaps when they began to fade he'd probe a little more.

Kieran peered under the bed in the largest bedroom. Polly had used it as a type of dumping ground, a place – as she said herself – she didn't have to keep in order. And she hadn't been joking. Overflowing cardboard boxes took up most of the space, an ancient suitcase and accordion case stacked one on top of the other under the old-fashioned iron frame. Those who knew Polly best would agree that meticulous housekeeping had never been her first priority, but having a well-stocked larder and a crackling open fire were something she'd taken great pride in. As he got to his feet, Kieran dusted off his jeans and put any further investigation of the boxes on hold.

He continued to the bedroom across the landing where Polly had slept for over forty-five years. South-facing, the room was the warmest in the house. He rubbed a hand over his stubble as he mooched around to study the array of framed photographs on the wall. In all the years he'd stayed under her roof, Polly had never encouraged his being in her bedroom and he'd accepted without argument. Now she was gone, however, and her will had proved how much he'd meant to her, so he was confident she wouldn't mind him making it his own.

He stared at an old black-and-white photo of his aunt, admiring the younger version of the kind-hearted woman he remembered. She was standing against an old tree, her lips shaped in a broad grin, her shoulder-length waves swept back from her face and a smouldering look in her eyes. Kieran guessed her love was directed at the person behind the camera. He'd seldom given thought to her life as a young woman, what her dreams had consisted of or whether she'd loved. There was so much he didn't know about her. His eyes were drawn to the box of jumble peeping out from underneath the bed. Maybe sorting through her stuff would fill in the gaps, build a fuller profile of her life and help him discover the side of her he'd never given consideration.

As he glanced back at the photo he gave a gentle nod in his aunt's direction. "I'll accept your challenge, Polly. But don't go haunting me while I'm here, tied down to one place for a year," he whispered, grinning as he imagined her chuckling and rubbing the palms of her hands in victory.

Deciding to formalise the arrangements while it still seemed a good idea – and before he talked himself out of it again – he searched his phone for Fitzgerald & Partners' number, planning on dealing with two issues with one call. Despite his family's opinion that he cared little for anyone other than himself, he was concerned about Amy. He wanted to clear the air between them – and clear his conscience.

"Kieran Dulhooly speaking," he said, running a hand across his forehead when he recognised Amy's voice at the other end. No time like the present, he thought, tackling the first of his 'issues' head on. "Amy! I've been meaning to call you to apologise."

"I'm sure you have," came her curt response. "Is there something I can help you with?"

"Honestly, I want to apologise, explain why I had to run off like that."

Amy's tone lowered. "Go ahead, I'm listening."

He could hear her fingers moving across the desktop keyboard. She couldn't be too upset if she wasn't giving him her undivided attention. He couldn't deny this pinched his ego. "I needed to check things out at the house . . ." Kieran allowed his sentence to trail off, searching for the words as he went along. The spontaneous evening in her city apartment seemed a million years away now, a brief interlude between two parallel lives.

She didn't respond, wasn't making it easy for him. He couldn't say he blamed her.

"Look," he tried again, "I had a great time. It was fun . . . good fun. I'm sorry how it ended."

He let out a sigh of relief when Amy's laughter came down the line.

"I'm kidding, Kieran. Don't take yourself so seriously. I had fun too and, just so you know, I'm not in the habit of picking up clients!"

"You made an exception for me 'cos I'm irresistible," he deadpanned, picking up on her mood and following her lead. He was relieved she'd let him off the hook, had expected to do a lot more grovelling.

"I'll see you around, then," she said.

"Eh, Amy, one more thing . . ." Damn, he still had to talk to his solicitor.

"I presume you didn't call specially to speak to me. I guess you're looking for Ms Jacobs? Will I put you through?"

"If she's available, that'd be great."

He moved around Polly's room while he waited for Amy to come back on the line. The drawers stuck in the tall, narrow chest. He nudged and nudged the top one loose until finally he managed to pull it open.

"Putting you through now, Kieran."

"Thanks again, Amy. See you around."

Then Olivia's professional tone sounded in his ear. "Hello. What can I do for you?"

He wondered what his lawyer would think of the attention her receptionist was bestowing on one of her clients.

"Ms Jacobs – I mean, Olivia," he began, "I hope it's not too late but I've had a rethink about Polly's will. I've decided to give it a go."

"Oh, I'm delighted," she began.

Her words of approval were reassuring, though closely followed by a degree of caution. Kieran couldn't help smiling as he listened to her reiterate the main details.

"The terms of inheritance are specific. Live in the house for a year. And, Kieran, I must mention that proof will be required once the period has elapsed or midway if there are any people contesting the will."

"Proof? What sort of proof?" Kieran realised how ignorant he was about the legal system. Who would have thought inheritance would have been so complicated? Then again, it wasn't as though he'd needed any such information – or had any interest – before now.

"Utility bills, bank details, change of address on your documents – that sort of thing."

Kieran groaned inwardly. Paperwork! What a pain! The only document he'd ever worried about had been his passport, keeping an eye that it was up to date so he could take off whenever he felt like it. And bills – he hadn't given those any great thought! He'd need to get a job at this rate. Or collect Polly's pension that Olivia had mentioned during his first visit.

"Okay, I'll set stuff up so there'll be a year's supply of evidence. Do I need to visit your office again to sign documents or something?" Despite Amy letting him off the hook, he didn't relish bumping into her in person quite so soon. He poked through the papers in the drawer, old appliance guarantees, a few religious prayers and what looked like the leaflets contained in medical supplies. Did she throw anything away, he wondered?

"No need to travel such a distance," said Olivia. "I'm satisfied that everything has been explained in detail and you have a thorough understanding of your aunt's wishes."

"No mistaking them," Kieran commented.

Flicking through the manual for a twin-tub washing

machine, he vaguely remembered his aunt lifting laundry from the washer into what she called the 'spin-dryer'.

"I'll send the documents by registered post," Olivia went on, "and you can get a local solicitor or commissioner for oaths to witness your signature. Register them again on return."

"Oh, that'd be handy – send it to Number 5 Pier Road. It can be my first letter, an official document – proof I'm living there. I might even believe it myself!"

Olivia laughed at his admission and gave one last run through the terms and conditions, her final words a pleasant reminder. "Don't forget to collect any outstanding pension –"

"Your mention of bills reminded me of that," he admitted.

"And any cash you find in the house is yours to spend now but the bank accounts can't be touched."

"Does she have money tucked away in a mattress or somewhere I should know about? Did she specify that to you recently or was it a long time ago?" He was curious about when she had made the will. At what point had she decided he should be sole beneficiary?

"I met with your aunt before she went to the nursing home. She made the long journey to the office to review her will one last time, too independent to let me travel to Schull. The poor darling was terrified of Alzheimer's, or worse, having watched so many of her counterparts diminish once they'd left their own homes. Moving to the nursing home on a long-term basis was a terrifying but unavoidable prospect."

"You think that was truly the case? Were there no other options?" Kieran voiced a question he'd been longing to ask, though he knew he had no right. Yet he pounced on the opportunity to ask a neutral party's opinion. Polly might have confided in Olivia.

"That's not for me to judge, Kieran. I can only tell you what I saw with my own eyes. Her mobility was severely curtailed. Living alone put her at huge risk. And she was exhausted from trying to manage. I'm no medical expert but seeing her dragging herself with a walking aid from the lift to this office, taking a minute between each movement to get her breath back inspired very little confidence."

"If someone had offered to stay with her?"

Olivia's voice was gentle. "I don't think any such offer materialised. And she wouldn't hear of bringing her bed downstairs. We had a good chat the last time she asked me to visit. But in the end her stay there was short . . ."

There was a pause on the line.

Kieran's mind was a muddle, anger simmering underneath that Polly had been neglected by her family and guilt reminding him that he'd also been party to this neglect. He sat on the bed, his eyes drawn to the ancient black and white photograph on the dressing table, one of Polly with his father, cute siblings dressed in their Sunday best. Hadn't his father taken any steps to help? Or had Polly's stubborn independence led her to refuse any offer he might have made?

Olivia's voice cut in on his thoughts. "To answer your question about the money, Kieran, Polly said there was cash hidden in the house. In fact, she hinted that finding it would be quite a treasure hunt."

Kieran grinned and shook his head. "Thanks, Olivia. Looks like I've a mystery to solve." Polly's sense of humour had remained right to the end, playing games even from beyond the grave. Where on earth had she stashed this cash though, he wondered, getting to his feet once more and returning to the chest of drawers. "I can freshen up the place as I go along. Keeping an eye out for bundles of money will make me tread cautiously and think twice before tossing things in the recycling pile." He closed the top drawer and yanked open the second one. Old-fashioned underwear stared back at him, rolled in neat piles in the narrow drawer. Again, he closed this one, deciding against rifling through his aunt's ancient hose and panties. Too gross – even if there were bundles of cash lying underneath! He'd park that idea for now. At least not until it was a last resort. Polly's deviousness amused him. Her way of ensuring he didn't hire a skip and throw everything into it.

"Maybe she designed it to keep you occupied so you wouldn't be tempted to take off again?"

Olivia's enjoying this too, he thought, feeling partly amused and partly irritated. He wondered how much Polly had disclosed to the glamorous solicitor. Slightly miffed, he felt like the butt of a joke between the solicitor and his aunt. Polly, wherever she is flying her angel wings, is probably laughing her head off at how difficult she's making this for me, he thought. From nowhere, he remembered one of the things she'd regularly spouted at him: 'If it's worth having, it's worth fighting for – never give up, lad.'

"Everything's in order so?" he asked. "Do I need to send you confirmation once I have the utility bills set up?"

"Yes. You'll need to get your aunt's name taken off and new agreements set up. Photocopies of bills, account numbers, agreement with service providers – that sort of thing."

"And that's it? I just go back and live there and call you in twelve months? I don't have to do anything else?" Too simple, Kieran thought. There has to be a hitch!

"Eleven months and three weeks to be exact. Polly left instructions that I was to count in the time it took you to make up your mind."

The phone still at his ear, he stared at another photo. She was older in this one, a closer resemblance to the person he'd sat for hours chatting with. His expression softened. What had been going through her mind when she'd plotted her will? Why was it so important to her that he remained in the house for a year? He'd do his best not to let her down.

"She left another note for you. I'll include it with the documentation. Is there anything else, Kieran?"

"This is mad! I can't believe I'm agreeing to this but in for a penny and all that . . ." He laughed with Olivia about his aunt's clever insight, ending the call shortly afterwards and shaking his head in wonderment. What the hell was he letting himself in for?

A bubble of rising excitement gurgled deep in his stomach, followed closely by a nudge of apprehension. What would the next year throw his way? Living back in the nucleus of his family and an assortment of neighbours and friends he'd grown up with would take a little – or maybe a lot – of getting used to. And if he survived the year and beat Polly's challenge – after that, would he sell and run? Anybody's guess but he had to wait for eleven months and three weeks to pass before he could think about that decision.

A pounding on the front door interrupted his thoughts. Descending the stairs, he pulled opened the door to see an eager Greg and embarrassed Jess standing on his doorstep.

"He says you offered to fix his bike?" Jess blurted out, her son clutching the handlebars of his bike, her hands on his shoulders, standing behind him as though he were her shield. Her face was flushed and her eyes were darting between Kieran's face and the top of Greg's head.

Kieran nodded, his mouth drying. He hadn't expected them so soon, hadn't expected them at all if the truth were known. "I sure did. I was throwing a ball over the school wire and met himself here." He was sorry he hadn't taken the time to clean up a bit more, at least spray some air freshener to give the place a lived-in smell. Too late now, he thought, pulling the door back to allow them pass through the narrow hallway.

"See, Mum, I told you!"

Kieran laughed at the young boy's sincerity. "Wheel in your bike, Greg. I'll have a look." As he issued his invitation he realised he didn't have any tools, not unless there was a supply in the shed. He still hadn't ventured to the wooden shed at the bottom of the garden to see what was inside – junk if the shabby outside was anything to go by. It'd be worth a look, an excuse to delay Jess and her son longer, a prospect that sat well with him.

"When I was here before, I told the lady her house is like a rainbow!" Greg gawped around him, peering into the sitting room, fascinated by the array of bright colours.

"Greg, where are your manners!"

"What, Mum? It *is* like a rainbow." He pointed at the red carpet on the stairs. "Red and yellow!" He pointed at the orange walls, looking around for something pink and spotting a cushion on the sitting-room couch. "See, there's pink and I bet there's blue somewhere too!"

"Kieran, are you sure you'll want to help this cheeky little boy?"

He laughed at Greg's astute observations.

"But you promised!" Greg insisted, pulling a puncture-repair kit from his pocket and shoving it into Kieran's hands.

"Greg!"

"Leave him. He's perfectly right. Aunt Polly loved loud colours. Bet she has all seven colours of the rainbow if we checked the rooms. I hope to get around to calming the colour scheme a little but God only knows when –" He shrugged his shoulders and laughed, leading his visitors through to the kitchen.

The gingham curtains flapped in the breeze, his breakfast bowl and coffee mug sat unwashed on the draining board.

Greg's simple truth amused him. Pity that outspoken attitude changed with maturity. Life could be a lot less complicated, Kieran thought, maybe, if people spoke their minds and paid less attention to what was politically correct or socially acceptable.

"It hasn't changed a bit," Jess commented, glancing around the room where Polly had poured them endless glasses of lemonade and served homemade cookies and chunks of brown bread slathered in butter and strawberry jam. In those days, the old range was always warm, the distinct aroma of baking lingering long after they'd demolished the last cookie or slice of bread. "I'm trying to recall the last time I stood in this kitchen with you."

Kieran shook his head. "That time I came home?"

Their eyes met.

Jess swallowed hard, her gaze shifting from his handsome face, a flush warming her cheeks as yet again his words transported her back in time. "Ah, Kieran, I'm not that bad! I have popped in and out to Polly over the years. We had some great chats!"

"Thanks for that, Jess. It's good to think she had someone to keep an eye on her."

"She was a howl, great company," Jess remembered fondly. "And sharp as a button too!"

"My bike!" Greg was growing impatient, his timely demand a welcome interruption for his flustered mother.

Kieran ruffled his hair. "Sorry, mate. Wheel it through to the back garden and turn it upside down on the path outside. Think you can manage that by yourself?"

"Let me, pet." Jess hurried to do it for him.

"No, I'll do it. I'm not a girl!" He brushed away her offer of help, determined to show off how capable he was, then pushed the bike through the kitchen and out the door which Kieran had opened for him.

Kieran put a hand on Jess's elbow. "This is a job for the boys. Why don't you stick on the kettle and have a cup of coffee ready for the workers – well, maybe a glass of milk for himself there?"

"Are you banishing me to the kitchen?" Jess looked around, grabbing a tea-towel from the table and swiping it playfully at him.

Kieran ducked and took the keys from the counter. The intervening years fell away. Their deep friendship surged through the time they'd been apart. He couldn't deny how good it felt.

He opened the repair kit and peered inside. The contents wouldn't get the job done. "Let's see if Aunt Polly left any tools in the shed, Greg."

"Are we getting hammers and stuff?" Greg skipped

alongside Kieran down the garden. His eyes were bright with excitement as he watched Kieran try a few keys. "I didn't know old ladies had tools. Would they know what to do with them?"

Jess had followed them. "Honestly, Kieran. Please don't go to any trouble. I can easily put my hands on what you need next door."

"Mum! It's okay. And this is man's work. Kieran said so!"

"You'd better not hurt your mum's feelings," Kieran winked at Greg, "or we mightn't get our drinks afterwards."

The young boy giggled and shrugged his shoulders. "What if you don't have the right key? What will we do then if we can't open the shed? Will you still fix my bike?"

Jess gave up and, shrugging her shoulders, returned to the kitchen.

"Let's try this rusty old key . . . gotcha!" Kieran said, unhooking the lock and pulling back the wooden door.

The hinges squeaked as it opened out against them. He swiped at the cobwebs and stood in the entrance, gazing in amazement at the contents of his aunt's shed. It was packed to capacity, resembling a dumping ground if he'd ever seen one, everything in disarray, a disaster waiting to happen if things began to fall. Clearing it out would be at least a week's work, something to fill his time if nothing else.

Feeling Greg pushing against his legs, trying to get past him, he turned on his heel and lifted the little boy up overhead, swinging him around in the air to distract him from the contents of the shed. "It'd take hours to find tools in there, I'm afraid, not the type we're looking for anyway. We'll have to improvise."

"But what about my bike?" Greg repeated between giggles.

Kieran lowered the little boy onto the ground. "Run back inside and see if you can find two dessertspoons."

As soon as Greg had turned his back, Kieran closed the door and snapped the padlock shut. Destroying the shed and contents without even going through everything was very tempting. He couldn't imagine it held anything of value, considering the mess it was in. But Olivia's suggestion that Polly had left some sort of treasure trail of cash for him halted his train of thought. Nothing could be thrown out until it had been thoroughly searched.

Greg was looking through drawers when Kieran went back inside.

"Greg!" said Jess. "Come away from that drawer this instant."

"It's okay, Jess. I told him to get me two spoons. They should do the job. The shed's in a right mess, not a hope of finding anything in there."

Spoons found, they trooped outside again and set to work.

"We're having spag bol for tea," Jess said when the puncture was repaired, the chain links tightened and the bike fit for purpose once more. "Will you join us as a thank-you?" She turned to her son. "What do you think, Greg?"

Greg nodded as he threw his leg over the saddle and cycled unsteadily down the garden path, shrugging his shoulders and squealing in delight. He had his bike back. Dinner didn't quite hold the same importance.

"What time suits?"

"Around an hour? Would that suit?" Jess's face

flushed. She hadn't considered that he'd have other plans. Running her fingers through her hair, she smoothened it on to the nape of her neck, the short style feathering around her face and neck.

"An hour is perfect. I'll grab a bottle of wine – red or white?"

"You choose," Jess said, her face breaking into a grin.

"What's the joke, Mum?" Greg stopped the bike with the toes of his runners. Seeing his mother in such a good mood made a nice change. She might let him stay up late.

"Use your brakes, not your shoes," she responded, dodging his question. She didn't think her five-year-old would appreciate being told that Kieran made her feel warm and gooey inside! And she certainly wasn't revealing that in front of the man in question. She was confused enough herself.

Kieran leaned against the door frame, enjoying their exchange. Like Greg, he'd noticed the great big grin on her face and wondered what was behind it. Unable to resist teasing it out a little further, he probed the reason behind her smile. "You didn't answer his question. What's so funny?"

She cocked her head to the side. "Just think it's amusing that we're finally going to share a civilised drink with a very normal dinner. Makes a change from the soggy sandwiches and the metal taste of cheap and often out-of-date beer from mangy cans we normally had in each other's company."

He pointed toward the sitting room. "I can always grab the rug from the couch and meet the two of you for a picnic on the beach."

"A picnic?" Greg pulled the brakes so hard the back wheel went in the air and swung around.

Jess ignored his suggestion, unsure how to take it. Was he being flirtatious? She was struggling to interpret his signals. "Greg, you'll hurt yourself if you don't stop messing. Come on, let's go – we'll go out the side gate. Time to do some cooking. It's not really the weather for picnics yet. Maybe in another few weeks."

Greg flipped the pedals backwards, spinning them as fast as he could. "Is fixing bikes your work, Kieran? My friend's dad fixes trains. That's his job. Cool!"

"At the rate you're spinning that chain, I'm guessing I'll have a full-time job fixing your bike!" Kieran went ahead of him and opened the side gate.

"We'll see you later then," Jess said, holding the saddle of Greg's bike to prevent him from cycling too far ahead.

Waving his neighbours off, Kieran watched them go down the passageway that ran between the house and an old stone wall, then closed the gate after them and returned to the shed, pulling the door open wide and staring aghast at the mess. Travelling the world on a shoestring budget had forced him to stay in several questionable addresses, the array of rubble heaped in Polly's shed reminding him of one that had been in particularly bad repair. Rubbing his scalp, he contemplated where to start clearing out, his deliberations interrupted when he heard his name being called.

Going back into the garden, he was surprised to see his father and mother coming through the side gate. Receiving an unexpected visit from them was peculiar in itself. They seldom did anything or called to anyone without a huge announcement.

"Back door's open!" he called, snapping the padlock shut on the shed door and following them into the house.

"Can I get you a coffee?" he offered.

"No, thanks," Marian said, glancing around her and screwing up her nose. "Place smells musty, doesn't it?"

"What do you expect?" Frank reacted instantly. "It's been empty for weeks!"

Kieran sighed. And so it goes again, he thought, Mum unable to resist her snide remarks about Polly and Dad permanently on the defensive. He wished they'd get to the point of their visit and leave him get back to what he was doing. Inviting Frank out to the shed on some pretence or other was tempting but no doubt Marian would follow and pass another comment about the amount of rubble hoarded there.

"How're you settling in, Kieran? Are your feet getting itchy yet?" Marian enquired.

"It's still a bit like being on vacation to be honest, too soon to judge."

"Wouldn't it be easier on you to share the responsibility with your sisters?"

"Marian, I thought we'd agreed to butt out and mind our own business?" Frank glared at his wife, clutching the back of a kitchen chair, his knuckles white. "Kieran's a grown man, entitled to and capable of making his own decisions."

Kieran was struggling to contain his rising anger. Not once had his mother wished him well with his new venture. "Maybe you should listen to Dad. He has a point," he said through gritted teeth. "I am an adult and have managed to make decisions for the last number of years, unaided by you or anyone else."

"Yeah, but Beth . . ." Marian stammered then pursed

her lips in annoyance. She wasn't as surefooted as she'd been when she'd arrived.

Kieran turned away a moment, wondering what on earth she expected from him. "What about Beth? Nobody twisted her arm behind her back when she married Carl or bought that massive house."

Frank cleared his throat.

Kieran and Marian turned to look at him, waiting for what he had to say.

"Polly would be delighted to see you living here, son." He glared at his wife. "Marian, can't you let go whatever ridiculous notion is going on in your head and wish your son well?"

Ignoring her husband, Marian appealed to Kieran once more. "Dividing everything three ways makes more sense. You would still get a substantial amount – more than enough to fund another trip and you'd be free of the burden of taking care of the place. And your sisters would benefit too – there would be a much better sense of fair play."

Kieran gave a hollow laugh. "Anyone would think you're trying to get rid of me, Mum," he said. "When I was travelling, you spent your time nagging me to settle down and get a proper job. I wish you'd make up your mind."

"Of course I'm not trying to get rid of you! But this," she paused and waved her arm around, "playing house isn't you!"

Frank released his grip of the chair. "I'll be in the car, Marian." He turned to his son. "Do you fancy a game of golf one morning? Give us a chance to catch up properly?"

Kieran shrugged but didn't reject his father's invitation.

"I can't say I'll be much in the way of opposition but why not!"

Marian waited until her husband had left the house. "I'm sorry if I'm upsetting you, Kieran. Despite what you might think, I don't begrudge you this windfall."

"Don't make me laugh, Mum. If you don't begrudge me, why are you trying to convince me to release 'my windfall' as you put it?"

"What one of you gets, so should the other two."

He sucked in a breath, his next statement coming out in a rush. "What's really galling for you is that Polly has done things her way, Mum."

"That's not one bit fair, Kieran. Polly was entitled to her decision but she's coming between you and your sisters. That's why I'm concerned, no other reasons."

He snorted. "Don't make me laugh. Beth hasn't been exactly rushing here to find out how I'm settling in or ask me straight out if I'd prefer not to be stuck here. And Charlotte hasn't even picked up her free office phone to get in touch."

"And if they did, would it make a difference?"

"Not really. It must have been important to Polly that I live here. So I'll give it a shot. Out of respect for her." He didn't meet his mother's eye, but imagined she was furious.

"But Polly's not here any more. You've got the opportunity to make your decisions, help your sister."

"The will specifies that I live here for twelve months. And that's what I intend to do." This time he looked directly at Marian, defiance in his expression and tone. "For Polly," he repeated.

"Don't you think her demands are a simple control mechanism so she can dictate from the grave?"

"That's not what this is about. If you knew her properly, you wouldn't even suggest it."

Marian's response was barely audible. "Knew her? Nobody knew her like I did."

"Knew her? You hated her more like. Why bother denying it?"

"Hate's a very strong word."

Kieran sighed, feeling a strong sense of déjà vu and wondering why he was even engaging in this conversation with his mother. For years they'd battled the same issue, a waste of breath then and even more so now.

"Beth will have to find another way out of her current predicament," he said. "I'm not budging and neither will I undermine Polly's final wishes for her home and belongings."

"But she's your sister . . ."

"Yep, my sister who hasn't the guts to come and ask me for help, which makes me wonder, Mum, if it's you who's fixated on changing the will, not the girls. Do you stand to benefit yourself? Or is it merely out of spite for a woman you resented all your life?"

"Of course not!"

"Is that the truth?"

"Your father's revving the engine. I'd best go."

Kieran shook his head. His mother was clearly flustered and anxious to flee from their heated discussion. There wasn't a sound to be heard, the revving engine an excuse to leave seeing as she was losing the argument.

After he closed the door behind his mother he checked

the time and realised he was due next door for dinner shortly, leaving him very little time to take a shower and change his clothes. He was grateful for Jess's invitation. It made a welcome distraction following his parents' frustrating visit.

Chapter 14

Jess hummed along to the radio as she stirred the bolognese sauce into the pan of steak mince. Spaghetti bubbled in a pot. She put the tray of garlic bread in the oven, reduced the heat underneath the pans and hurried off to change.

She slipped into the paisley swing dress she had laid out on the bed earlier. The hemline sat above the knee, and when she'd teamed it with burgundy opaque tights and her matching chunky bracelet and necklace she was pleased with the look. Twirling around in front of the mirror, she grinned mischievously at her reflection, shaping her lips into a seductive pout.

Kieran's unexpected appearance on Pier Road had lifted her spirits, though having him living next door was also more than a little disconcerting and had already begun to colour the plans she'd been contemplating for her future. Surviving without any great support in recent years had become second nature. Relying on another person to any great degree was almost alien at this stage.

Henry and Pru weren't much in the way of support, her brother's fear of upsetting his wife getting in the way of him ever putting his sister or nephew first. Jess wished he'd respect her right to an opinion when Pru took it upon herself to dictate, often taking liberty and pushing ahead without even waiting for her agreement.

Pru's latest bug-bear was a serious issue, however. For Henry as well as her.

Moving closer to the mirror, she spotted a smudge of mascara under her lower lashes. Carefully wiping it away with a cotton bud, she found it difficult to push Pru and Henry from her mind. I'm as much to blame on this occasion, she thought. I gave them reason to believe their – at least Pru's – idea would work. I need to take responsibility and tell them straight that I'm not sure any more, that I've changed my mind about swapping homes with them. In the absence of a will or any form of legal document deciding on the true ownership of Number 4, brother and sister would have to agree an amicable verbal agreement. Temporarily at least.

She tossed the bud in the bin, running her mascara wand over her lashes once again, refusing to dwell on depressing thoughts, allowing giddy excitement to rise to the surface instead.

Knowing her old friend was in the vicinity made it easier for her to get out of bed in the mornings, the expectation that she might bump into him forcing her to make a greater effort with her appearance. Her thoughts were brighter, the dark cloud she'd lived under no longer as prevalent. It hadn't disappeared entirely of course. How could it? In truth it probably never would, at least not without the miracle of a time capsule where she could eliminate much of the previous few years. But she was enjoying brief interludes of glorious forgetfulness and now here she was, like any normal thirty-one-year-old, waiting for a good-looking guy to call to her house and share a pleasant evening with tasty food, good (well, hopefully) wine and – she didn't allow her imagination to think beyond that.

A mixture of anticipation, excitement and trepidation gurgling inside her, she moved away from the mirror to take her favourite boots from the wardrobe. Putting her fingers in the leather tabs she pulled them on, arching her foot and admiring her shapely leg. She knew she was in good shape, recent stress curbing her appetite and burning calories!

She hurried downstairs. The sight of the three place settings at the kitchen table warmed her heart as she breezed into the kitchen. Silly to dwell on such a tiny detail, certainly not something she felt she could admit to anyone when she'd been pretending life with Greg alone fulfilled her existence. Pretending to herself as well as anyone else who bothered to ask.

"Greg, come in and get cleaned up for dinner! Food's almost cooked and Kieran should be here shortly."

She watched her son from the front door as he cycled around the small open space to the front of the house. Life was so simple through his eyes. No yesterdays, merely the right now and of course the promise of tomorrow. He unstrapped his helmet and dropped it on the ground.

"Ten more laps, please, Mum?"

"Maybe after dinner."

"But, Mum, I want Kieran to see how fast I can go. Look, watch me, please."

Big blue eyes pleading, a serious expression on his face – she found it impossible to resist. "Once more then, let me see you." She forgot to remind him to put his helmet back on, her thoughts drifting again to the house next door and how her perspective had changed in the shortest space of time.

She heard Kieran banging his front door. Her heart fluttered, despite every doubt and concern forcing itself to be heard. Believing she was entitled to a bit of fun – long overdue, in fact – she shoved every negative and cautious thought to the back of her mind and watched Kieran approaching. Her eyes left her son as he cycled faster, showing off for their approaching guest. She missed the leg of his jeans getting stuck in the spokes of the wheel. She missed the back wheel rising high off the ground. What she couldn't miss, however, was his loud yell piercing the air.

Jess stuck to the ground, bringing a hand to her face as though in slow motion as Greg's left cheek banged against the concrete, the bike landing on top of his small frame.

Kieran was on his knees beside him, slipping his outstretched palm under the child's face, wiping away his tears and encouraging him to be brave.

Jess watched the scene unfold. Then, her feet finally moving, she rushed to her son, her heart thumping in her chest, her flutter of excitement replaced by the cold grasp of fear. "Greg – Greg! Are you okay? Kieran, is he okay?"

"He's fine, Jess. He just took a tumble."

"But he might be concussed! We should – I mean, *I* should take him to the doctor! Or should I go straight to A&E?"

Greg, still on the ground, shook his head in protestation. "I don't want to go to hospital," he blubbered through his tears. "And it's not my head! It's my leg . . . it's stuck. Look!" He pulled and pulled at the leg of his jeans, to try and release it from the spokes of the bike, but the material was well and truly caught. Kieran gently began to extricate the fabric.

"Kieran," Jess said, "careful! Greg, try and stay still, pet. Just a few more moments."

Kieran stopped tugging at the material. "What's that smell, Jess?" He sniffed the air, the strong stench of burning making him realise they had more than one crisis on their hands.

"Oh cripes, the dinner – I left the pots switched on – and the garlic bread will be cremated!"

"Run in and turn them off. I'll look after the little fellow – nearly there now anyway. Things will be a lot more serious if the house goes on fire!"

Jess ran to the cooker, wiping away the tears that flowed on her cheeks. How had everything fallen apart in an instant? Their lovely evening was ruined. She flicked off the switches. The bread was indeed cremated. The spaghetti was curdled into a congealed mess. Judging by the vile burning smell, the bolognese sauce was stuck to the base of the pot. But none of it mattered, not when Greg was lying on the ground outside. *Why can't I do anything right? Everything – everyone – I touch, something happens, good turns to evil. Is it me? It has to be. And how could I honestly expect any better luck after . . .*

"Everything okay in here?" Kieran came into the kitchen.

Tears stung her eyes, the mascara she'd applied so carefully earlier smudging under her lids. She nodded. "Where's Greg?"

"Mum," Greg hiccupped, following his hero indoors, limping into the kitchen in his underpants, "I want a drink."

"Sweetheart!" She rushed to take him in her arms, pulling back when he winced at her touch.

"Ouch! My face does hurt after all. Can I see it in the mirror? Is there blood?"

Jess examined the graze, already dreading his screams when she went to clean it. He wasn't the greatest of patients, never had been. But disinfecting would have to wait a while. She needed to settle him first, allow him a few minutes to get over the shock.

"Couldn't save the jeans, I'm afraid, Jess, but I guessed you were more concerned about his leg! He's a tough one." He crouched down to take a look at the little boy's cuts and grazes. "Aren't you, buddy? Ready for the racing circuit in another few years!"

Greg braved up a little. "I want my United tracksuit, Mum. I'm going back on my bike."

Jess shook her head. "I don't think so. Not today. I have to clean that cut on your face so it doesn't get infected. You should never have gone back up on it without your helmet."

His lips shaped in a pout. "I just forgot the helmet. It's stupid anyway. Too heavy."

Jess frowned. She wasn't allowing him to get into the habit of leaving the helmet behind. "Greg, behave now. That graze on your face is nasty. If you'd worn your helmet, I wouldn't have to clean all those cuts and you wouldn't be whinging."

"No, you're not cleaning it. It's too sore. I'm going back outside."

He turned on his heel and made to scarper down the

hallway but Kieran was at the door before him, blocking his path. He pointed at Greg's legs and tipped his chin upwards to make him look at him. "Are you heading out there in your underwear? What if some of those girls from the playground pass by? Don't want to give them an eyeful of Spiderman, now do we?"

Greg giggled, bringing his hands to his face. He'd forgotten his trousers weren't on.

Kieran tapped the child on the shoulder and gave him a wink. "I don't think the spag bol's going to reach the table this evening, do you?" he asked. "Not if the smell is anything to go by. So what do you say we head up to The Baltimore Inn for fish and chips? And maybe some of their ice cream to get over the shock. That was some fall you took. The lads at school will be dead envious if you have a black eye!"

Greg's eyes widened. He was already nodding his head. But he wasn't going to waste a chance to turn the situation around in his favour. He folded his arms across his chest. "Only if I can take my bike 'cause my leg's too sore to walk."

"I could carry you on my back," Kieran offered, glancing at Jess who was still pale from the shock.

"I'm not a baby. I want to take my bike."

Kieran's expression was serious, his eyes holding the little boy's. "If you allow your mum to clean that graze on your cheek. Deal?"

Greg raised a hand in the air to high-five Kieran. "Deal! But I want *you* to wash it. Mum doesn't like blood. It makes her pass out. When my –"

Jess grabbed his elbow, cutting him off mid-sentence. They'd had enough drama already for the evening without him divulging family stories. "Let's go up and get you washed and dressed if you're going back outside. And this time you wear your helmet! No more being silly. If I see you on that bike without your helmet again, I'll give the bike to the charity shop for another little boy." She wore her sternest expression, which when mixed with a snow-white face and wide eyes, was foreboding in itself.

"But I want Kieran to wash the cut!" Fresh tears poured down his face.

"Kieran's our guest. He has done more than enough for us already today. Let me do it, love."

"But, Mum!"

"Maybe it's bedtime. That's a nasty shock you've had. I think we'll cancel dinner."

"No. I'm not even tired and you can't make me go to bed without dinner. But –"

"But nothing," Jess insisted firmly. "If you want to go out, you have to let me clean those grazes." She turned to address Kieran. "We'll be down in ten minutes max. I'm so sorry about dinner."

"Relax. These things happen. It's not like I'm fussy. It'll be fun heading out. We'll be the talk of Schull after morning Mass at the weekend."

"Ah, but that's where you're wrong," she told him. "Schull has become very contemporary while you've been gone – it's not the land of squinting windows you remember."

"You want to bet on that?"

She ignored his last comment. "Fish and chips are on me. Otherwise we're not joining you."

Kieran shrugged and smiled. Not exactly flush with

money, as of yet anyway, the arrangement suited him perfectly. He watched her drag a reluctant Greg from the kitchen and towards the stairs. Instead of idling around for them to return, he took a dessertspoon from the table and scraped some of the spaghetti mess from the pot, careful not to scrape the enamel.

What was Greg going to say about his mother fainting around blood, he wondered? Why had Jess been so anxious to interrupt? Or was it only embarrassment? Obviously not a subject she wanted aired anyway and not top of his list of concerns either. He was far more interested in hearing a little more about how serious she'd been about Greg's father. Yet another unanswered Pier Road question. For a small – and sometimes sleepy – West Cork town, it sure had its share of skeletons.

Hearing his hosts chattering, he looked up to see Jess returning to the kitchen with a petulant Greg in tow. He held up a sparkling stainless-steel pot, all traces of congealed spaghetti scrubbed away. "The other one's fit for the bin," he told her, "but I managed to save this one."

"I'm so embarrassed, Kieran. What a disaster! I've totally ruined dinner."

"Ah, give over. The Jess I remember was a far cry from domesticated. You ran a mile from doing anything in the kitchen. No need to impress me with new and improved culinary skills."

She flicked imaginary dust from her dress, avoiding meeting his eye. His reference to their past had a ring of intimacy about it. Am I that transparent, she wondered? Impressing him was exactly what I had in mind. And look where it's got me! What must he think?

"Maybe so, but believe it or not I *am* able to rustle a

dinner together," she sighed, starting to tidy up the remainder of the mess.

Kieran's return to the neighbourhood had rekindled old memories for her. Friends – of a platonic nature for years – they had played rough and tumble with the rest of the gang, sharing an inquisitive kiss after a few cans of beer one summer's end, not realising at the time that it was a goodbye kiss of sorts. The feel of his lips on hers had stayed with her for ages after, the way she'd hurried away from him as soon as they'd pulled apart one of her biggest teenage regrets, a memory she'd played over and over in her mind for a long time after, each time her imagination conjuring a different ending to her tale. Studying Marine Engineering, in the Institute of Technology in Cork city, had kept him around for a few years longer, his summers in Schull continuing until he'd decided to set off on his travels, his degree in one hand and a rucksack in the other. Bumping into him on one of his rare visits home, she'd spent a fun evening in his company listening to tales of his exploits and envying his spirited lifestyle.

And looking at him now sitting across the table from her, she could see he hadn't changed one iota. He was still the carefree guy she remembered from years before – stronger, more mature and better looking of course – but other than that he was still fun to be around and could be relied upon to remain calm in any crisis. Watching him mess with Greg's curly hair as he held him at arm's length while her son tried to get free from his clutches, she couldn't remember a time when Kieran had lost his temper or stormed off in a huff, unlike many of the other egotistical teens they'd hung around with in the area. Easy-going by nature, he'd been a natural joker and generally one to tease the others, taking any banter directed at him and more than capable of laughing at himself.

She felt a little foolish in light of the seemingly wasted effort she'd gone to that evening. Dressing to impress – or cooking to impress for that matter – had been an obvious waste of time, the brief physical contact they'd shared the furthest thing from his mind! It was clear to see that he still saw her as the gangly teenager, his friend, someone to kill a bit of time with and nothing more.

Greg pulled free from Kieran's clutches, startling her out of her daydream and scurrying past her towards the front door. By the time she and Kieran had followed him outside he was sitting on his bike, helmet fastened and ready to go. Relieved to leave the smell of cremated food behind, she locked up the house and joined the boys.

The trio made their way to the corner of Pier Road and turned left on to Main Street, Greg pushing hard on the pedals so he didn't have to dismount on the slope. Jess and Kieran fell into an easy step as they escorted the young – and weaving – cyclist. Despite the upheaval of Greg's tumble and a wrecked dinner, the evening was surpassing Jess's expectation. It made a pleasant change from the dull existence her life had become. But the voice of conscience forced its way into her head, issued its warning loud and clear. *Don't obsess, don't allow his presence to consume or dictate every decision.* Despite Kieran's protestations that he was ready to settle down in Pier Road, his love of the wanderlust lifestyle lurked firmly underneath. What would happen when the twelve-month period was exhausted? Anybody's guess, she decided, putting her hand to the back of Greg's bicycle saddle and giving him an extra push to help him on the incline. He turned to her for a brief second and gave her a mischievous grin. His eyes were bright. He looked more elated than ever before, standing up from the saddle to push the pedals harder so he'd make it to the top of the hill without dismounting. Jess's heart soared, the magic of the moment obliterating all else.

Taking a leaf from her son's book, she focused ahead, willing the past to fade and eventually disappear and allow them the chance to breathe easy for a change. She wouldn't look too far into the future, wouldn't get carried away with how much she was enjoying Kieran's company, and would simply do her best to live one day at a time and enjoy the unexpected gift of friendship that had come her way.

Now, she thought, breaking into a jog to catch up with a very wobbly Greg, all I have to do is ignore – or at the very least control – the uncontrollable, teenage-like heat bubbling inside me every time I'm within arm's length of the man next door!

Chapter 15

Unknown to Kieran as he tucked into fish and chips, he was the main topic of conversation in a telephone call between his sisters.

"Do you think Kieran will take off again and relinquish his claim to Aunt Polly's?" Beth asked.

"I don't think he's going to give in. From what Mum says he's determined to stick it out."

"So contesting the will is my, I mean *our*, only hope of getting a share?"

Charlotte sighed. "To be honest, sis, I don't feel as strongly as you about doing that. In my opinion, it was gifted to him and tough luck on us."

"But why should he get everything? Kieran disappeared for years, barely acknowledged Polly, didn't even respond when I told him she was dying," Beth insisted.

"But the few times he was home, he spent time with her. And he was thousands of miles away, it wasn't like he could pop home whenever the notion took him," Charlotte defended her brother. "The same could be said for me, and not only since I left Ireland. I was the world's worst visitor even when I lived a couple of miles over the road. I'm not in a position to cast aspersions!"

"Your situation is different. Even Polly knew that it wasn't easy for you to make a trip home. But I spelt it out to him in black and white, told him she hadn't much time, and still he never bothered, despite how close they'd been. Yet he's the one standing to gain everything now, just because he took refuge there as a rowdy teenager. And don't tell me that was to keep her company."

"You're being unfair, Beth," Charlotte accused. "He genuinely cared. And he brightened up her life immensely. She was forever alluding to that."

"He ran wild in Schull. Remember? Staying there suited him as much as her." Beth closed her eyes as she waited for Charlotte's reply, her lengthening pause difficult to decipher. Was her sister going to acquiesce or refuse?

"Let me think about it a while longer. Maybe I should take a trip home. Time-zones and cross-Atlantic phone lines aren't the easiest way to negotiate something as intricate as this if we do decide to go ahead."

"I couldn't ask you to do that. Backing me up will be enough."

"I'm still not sure about it though. And have you thought about what's involved in contesting a will?"

"Can't say I'm very au fait to be honest. Are you?"

"Not really, but I imagine it'd take a significant amount of time and probably money too, particularly if you have to engage a solicitor to act on your behalf."

"You're really not convinced about this, are you?" Beth sighed.

Torn by the desperation in her sister's voice, Charlotte

found it difficult to refuse outright. "It wouldn't be an overnight resolution, Beth. These things take persistence and patience, lots of it."

Beth's despondency intensified. "Well, I won't be able to do it alone. Having both of us on board would make all the difference."

"Perhaps if I speak to Kieran and test the waters? Who knows what his plans are!"

"I don't know. What if –"

"I think we should talk to him – both of us – before doing anything – to see if there's another way of resolving this. For all we know he may already be thinking of leaving and then your worrying will have been in vain. It comes to us then anyway."

"I haven't the guts to broach the subject."

"But he's your brother."

"I know. But if he says 'no', that's it then, the door is closed."

Changing the subject, Charlotte enquired if Beth had given any more thought to her suggestions on making the land surrounding her house earn an income.

"I have put some work into it, whether it's up to standard or not remains to be seen. Anything's better than sitting around full of self-pity."

"Well done," her sister encouraged. "You've nothing to lose and it could surprise you and go a bit of the way towards household bills."

"I hope you're right, Charlotte."

"What have you got to lose?" Charlotte asked, their conversation a stark reminder of the difference in their lives and the reason Beth was so desperate for money.

"I suppose you're right," she conceded. "I'll have to

run it by Carl though and I'm not looking forward to that."

Charlotte struggled to remain calm, her brother-in-law's lazy attitude a major source of irritation for her. "Well, if he says 'no', ask him what he has in mind instead! Be firm."

"And you'll still think about the inheritance like you promised?"

"Of course. But I think we'd need Dad on board, seeing as he's officially her next of kin," Charlotte warned before hanging up.

Staring at the computer screen, Beth studied what she had done so far.

Charlotte will laugh at my efforts to create a website, she thought, inserting a section on location, following the instructions in her sister's email.

She bit her lower lip and stared through the window, looking critically at the panoramic view and attempting to see it from a stranger's perspective. Goleen was remotely located, a couple of hours' drive from the city and poorly serviced by public transport. Would she be relying solely on locals?

"Can't see how people are going to travel this far," she mumbled.

Time would tell, she decided, her spirits brightening as she remembered how popular the area was with tourists in the summer months. Bringing her attention back to the screen, she saved her work, relieved that she had at least made a start.

"Talking to yourself?"

Swivelling around, Beth blushed. Carl was standing

behind her, arms folded across his chest. She hadn't heard him enter the room, didn't know how long he'd been standing there.

"I don't see anyone else here, do you?" Her response was sharper than she'd intended.

His expression darkened. "It was only an observation, no need to take the head off me!"

She turned back to the computer screen, keeping her back to her husband as she took the opportunity to update him.

"Charlotte thinks we could rent out the stables and paddocks and maybe set up some sort of dirt track for quad-bikes, at least make an income from the land seeing as we can't sell it. We could rent out the barn too as a venue for events."

Unable to see his face to assess his reaction, Beth waited for a response, expecting it to be negative.

"Quad-bikes? An interesting suggestion, I suppose. Although we'd need proper course boundaries. I could try one out, to get a few ideas."

"I hadn't thought of that," Beth admitted.

"If it's not properly set up, it would be mayhem, with people crashing into each other head on. And probably suing us into the bargain!"

His enthusiasm surprised her. She'd expected indifference or objection. It was a relief he wasn't averse to the suggestion.

"What about renting the stables and maybe fencing off a few paddock areas?" she continued.

"We don't have any use for them so why not? But won't we be expected to have some sort of industrial insurance?"

Beth tensed as he moved closer, his distinctive cologne

sending an unexpected shiver down her spine. Not now, she pleaded with her body. Don't go all gooey for him, just because he's being nice to you this once. Suppressing her feelings, she tilted the screen towards him. "This is the website, a draft of the Home Page. It's still a work in progress but it's a start I suppose. What do you think?"

"Not bad for a first draft, has a decent amount of info. But it won't get any attention without photographs."

Her stomach somersaulted, his praise sending a rush of heat through her. She swallowed hard.

"I'll take a few photos in daylight tomorrow," he offered, scrolling to the next page. "Add my mobile number to the contact details if you like."

She kept her eyes on the screen and forced her mind to remain on the website. "What about the ring fort? Charlotte mentioned it as a type of tourist attraction. What do you think?"

He crouched down and pulled the keyboard towards him, adding a line of text, correcting a typo and inserting his mobile number before pressing save. "We could add a bit of history and background detail, maybe upload an audio onto the site. Visiting Americans would love it."

Beth moved her chair to put more distance between them, his proximity far too unsettling. "You're not against it so?"

"Of course not. What do you take me for?" Noticing the time on the computer screen, he got to his feet. "I'm heading to work. I'll get the photos taken for the website and then link the address on Facebook and Twitter."

"Thanks," she said. "I'll get on to some of the newspapers and see if they'll give us a mention."

"Talk to you tomorrow then."

For the first time in a while, she didn't breathe a sigh of relief when the front door banged behind him. Remaining in front of the computer for a while longer, she swivelled gently on her chair and thought about what had just happened. Had her body reacted to the scent of his aftershave? It had been so long since they'd shared a civil conversation . . . or anything else civil or intimate for that matter. Imagining him sweeping her slight frame into his strong arms, his fingers trailing every inch of her bare skin and her savouring a deep exploration of his body before he finally penetrated her, two bodies joined as one, two minds – she jumped with fright when the front door opened, her cheeks already flushed with excitement. Had he felt it too? Is that why he'd returned? Would fantasy become reality?

"Forget something?" she asked when he came in.

"Forgot to ask if you'd made the lodgements to Ed's account? I'll give him a call and let him know this month's covered. Oh, and don't forget he wants to see you."

It was as if he'd poured cold water over her, instantly dampening the flushes of pleasure she'd been experiencing, the lustful images she'd been imagining disappearing in a puff of smoke. Mortified that she'd been such a fool yet again, she turned to face him, convinced she'd imagined their short reprieve from battle.

"Have you organised a plumber?" she shot back before answering his question.

And in one fleeting moment they'd reverted to sniping at each other.

"There's a guy calling later."

His look of annoyance didn't escape her.

"And how're we going to pay for that?" she asked.

Carl gritted his teeth. "I'm doing a few jobs for him on his car in exchange." Talented under the bonnet of a car, he could work miracles on even the most complex engine. "If that project works out, it'll help us keep on top of Ed's payments."

Beth couldn't control her outburst, the intense anti-climax fuelling her anger. "Good," she muttered ungraciously.

"The lodgements?" he asked again, dark eyes boring into hers, his defiance evident.

Beth held back her tears. "I don't have anything to lodge. You'll have to tell Ed the truth, explain why the vineyard isn't bringing in an income."

Carl glanced at his watch. "I haven't time for this! I'll be late for work. I won't upset Ed, not now when his time is running out. You'll get your wish soon enough when his life assurance clears the payments."

Beth gasped, his cruel comment a sharp reminder of Ed's arrival to their home. Opening the door to find Ed on the step of their Cork city rented accommodation had been a jaw-dropping moment for Beth, particularly as Carl had always insisted that Ireland and its old wives' tales and quaint traditions would be a source of irritation for his fashion-designer, cosmopolitan brother. Paris, its culture and couture – according to Carl – coursed through the blood in Ed's veins despite Irish parentage and spending the first ten years of his life in Dublin's south side. Paris was as much a part of him as his fashion designing, the hub of the industry he adored, the location he vowed never to leave. Not realising death was already setting its trap, he'd regularly joked about his ashes being scattered throughout the greatest Parisian design centres and boutiques.

The day he'd turned up out of the blue at their home, Beth

had stammered out a distracted welcome to the visibly aged and extremely ill gentleman on her doorstep. She figured the day of his impending death and scattering of ashes might be a lot sooner than any of them could have envisaged.

"But you're quite prepared to upset *me*? Your family loyalties are selective to say the least!" She glared at her husband.

"That's rich coming from you!"

Carl's fascination with his much older brother both irritated and bemused Beth. Very often, she used this vulnerability as leverage, threatening to expose the damage Carl's serious errors of judgement had caused. If she took Ed aside and filled in the gaps of the years he and Carl had been apart, their mutual admiration might become somewhat skewed and one-sided. At least Ed would know the full extent of their financial troubles and not assume incorrectly that they were in receipt of a hefty income from France.

"You'll have to stop fabricating excuses," she said. "Ed might surprise you if you tell him the truth. I can't imagine it would matter very much to him now."

But Carl was adamant, his pride more powerful than logic. "How many more times must I tell you, Beth? It's not going to happen."

Swaying between despair and fury, she spoke through gritted teeth. "Where am I supposed to get this so-called money to lodge? I collected my unemployment money, paid a meagre amount off the electricity bill, put some food in the fridge and there's barely enough left for petrol for the week!" She shook her head. He'd been cosseted and spoilt all of his life, expecting bailout after bailout.

"Transfer some from the mortgage account if you have to," he instructed coldly, before leaving the house again.

This time Beth didn't only breathe her usual sigh of relief when the door banged behind him. She let out a high-pitched scream of frustration. Additional earnings from quad-bikes or anything else would be a mere drop in the ocean if Ed's failing business continued to drain their paltry income. Embarrassed and humiliated by the lecherous thoughts she'd been indulging in after her husband's initial departure, furious that Carl still had the ability to arouse her deepest passions, she ran up the stairs and turned on the shower, tears coursing down her cheeks as she suffered the intermittent change in water temperature, the instant fluctuation from hot to cold too close a reminder of her crashing descent from exhilaration to disappointment.

Chapter 16

Kieran yawned widely. He'd slept soundly, woken early by the sound of squawking gulls, a morning call he was regaining affinity with since his return to Pier Road. Arms behind his head, he contemplated the day ahead. He'd promised Greg he'd kick a ball with him in the park. He'd promised Jess he'd join her for lunch – she'd invited him to make up for the spoiled spaghetti bolognese and to prove that she had developed some culinary skills! At least he had cash in his wallet now he'd collected Aunt Polly's pension. He'd buy Jess a nice box of chocolates and pick up a comic for Greg.

Hearing the front gate creak, Kieran listened attentively and waited for the familiar rattling of the letterbox. At least he assumed it was the postman. Who else would be calling at this unearthly hour of the morning? He leapt out of bed when he heard something fall on the floor below, his curiosity piqued. A letter wouldn't make such a noise, he thought, it had to be something bulkier. Perhaps Aunt Polly was a mail-order fan, and this was something she'd ordered before she died. He went to investigate, his interest heightened when he saw the brown package lying on the floor.

Stooping to retrieve it, he turned it over in his hand, pressing gently against the edges, even going as far as shaking it. The small parcel felt light. A slim box wrapped in a padded envelope was the nearest he could guess. Nothing rattled – no defining scent. He smoothened out the crinkled paper as best he could, reading the printed label and wondering if it had been addressed incorrectly. It was addressed to neither him nor Polly. The packaging was ripped at the corner. The recipient's name, however, was printed in clear bold print: **John Kilmichael**. The name meant nothing to him. He'd never heard of him. Why was this guy's post being delivered to Number 5 Pier Road, care of Pauline Digby? Kieran had no idea but inexplicably it filled him with unease. He hoped this John Kilmichael person hadn't been taking his aunt for granted or using her in any way. Though he knew he had little right, he resented this stranger's intrusion on his aunt's home and privacy.

Flipping the envelope over in his hands a few times, Kieran scrutinised it more carefully, searching for a postmark, turning it this way and that – looking for a stamp or post office franking or label. But there was none. He pulled open the front door and peered up and down the street. No sign of a postman or anyone else who could have delivered it either. So as well as wanting to know who John Kilmichael was, Kieran also wondered who'd dropped it through the letterbox.

As he pondered on the delivery, the doorbell went.

"Yes," he grumbled, peering around the door, conscious

he wasn't even dressed. "Registered mail," the postman replied in a bored voice, handing him a pen and showing him where to sign.

"Thanks."

Opening the envelope, he took out a number of documents, sighing at the number of them. Included was a small brown envelope with his name on it, written in Polly's handwriting.

Just then his mobile phone rang upstairs. He dropped the John Kilmichael package into the drawer of the hall table and made for the stairs, shoving the small brown envelope into the inside pocket of the leather jacket hanging in the hallway as he went. He'd be going out later and would read it then.

If nobody turns up to claim the package, he decided, stretching across the double bed to grab his phone from the bedside locker, I'll ask Dad about this John Kilmichael when we're playing golf. He'd surely know Polly's friends and might be able to shed some light on him. Yes, he thought, he'll probably know how I can get in contact with him.

Hearing his older sister's voice on the phone came as quite a surprise. "Charlotte!"

In truth, they rarely kept in contact, their parents being the main link between them, keeping each of them informed of the other's movements. Of his two sisters, Charlotte was the one he'd always connected with best. She didn't beat about the bush, didn't hide her intentions and generally accomplished most of what she set out to do. He'd always admired her for that. Beth, on the other hand, had been spoilt and attention-seeking from the moment she'd entered the world. She was dramatic and childishly impulsive, prepared to blame unfortunate circumstance for her misdemeanours, seldom adult enough to accept responsibility and loath to admit that her poor decision-making had got her into yet another mess.

Getting the usual intro of pleasantries out of the way, Kieran mentally calculated the time difference between Ireland and Canada.

"What on earth are you doing making phone calls in the middle of the night? Is something up?"

"Ah, I couldn't sleep and I'm toying around with a trip home so readjusting my body clock won't do me any harm. But there's something I wanted to talk to you about first."

He opened his eyes wide at his sister's announcement, not only amazed that she was considering returning to Ireland but also that she was going to the trouble of telling him personally instead of letting him hear about it through their parents. That in itself was a first. Then, he supposed, he'd hardly been top of her list of priorities when he'd been halfway across the other side of the world. It wasn't as if her movements affected him very much – apart from the free accommodation she'd given him when he'd arrived unannounced on her doorstep in Toronto.

"Why are you coming back now?"

"Ah, with Aunty Polly and everything, makes you think . . ."

"But I thought you left on a one-way ticket? That you'd left for good? Wasn't that your intention?" He had a hazy memory of a long, deep and meaningful conversation they'd shared in a Toronto bar, both of them inebriated and well past caring about protecting personal pride. They'd both suffered massive hangovers the following morning, and neither took the plunge to extend the conversation into the cold and sober light of day.

She changed the subject. "From what Mum's saying you're planning on sticking around long term. You – the guy who swore hell would freeze over before he'd live in Ireland with its squinting windows and telltale culture ever again."

There was something about her tone that set off a warning bell in his head. This isn't a social call, he decided. "No doubt you've heard about the inheritance?" he said, cutting short her cat-and-mouse game.

"Mum mentioned it. And says you're settling in. It must be strange?"

Kieran pondered on her question. Could the feeling of calm that came over him as he stared at the ocean and watched how the water glistened in the sunshine be described as strange? Certainly not, anything but. "I'm going to give it a go anyway, take one day at a time. I owe Polly that much at least."

"So you *are* setting down roots – didn't you say you'd never spend more than six months at the same address?"

"Perhaps I'm maturing. At last. Who'd have thought?"

"It's a big commitment. Are you sure it's what you want?"

Ha, he thought. I know why she's calling me. It's all making sense. She's in cahoots with Mum and Beth and she's been nominated to convince me to share my gains with them. Holding his breath, he worked particularly hard not to rise to her bait and to figure out the best way to respond to her question. The years they'd been apart slipped away, taking him back to when they'd been squabbling kids in their parents' home. He recognised the defiance in her tone, visualised her bottom lip protruding and imagined the fire emanating from her green eyes. He'd watched her explode often enough, had often been the cause of her rising temper, most often deliberately. Charlotte wasn't one for holding back.

"Kieran? Are you still there?"

"Spit it out, Charlotte. Be straight with me. If you've something to say, just say it." His transcendent calm was under pressure to survive.

"It's Beth, she's at her wit's end, could do with a dig out – her rightful share – of the place."

"Rightful share? What the hell!"

"She is – I mean was – depending on it," Charlotte spelt it out. "Come on, Kieran, she's worse off than the two of us put together. And you said yourself, you're not even sure it's what you want."

"Whoa there a moment," Kieran ran a hand through his hair, inhaling sharply. As ever, somebody else's predicament had to come before his. Didn't they think he could do with a leg-up in life?

Barely out of bed an hour and already he'd had two surprises. The day was shaping up to be interesting to say the least. It might have helped if he'd had his daily breakfast of strong coffee, cereal and fruit inside him before launching into this particular argument. But that luxury would have to wait.

"Polly's choices were of her own making. They had nothing to do with me, Charlotte."

"They have now though," his sister shot back. "And you're in a position to help Beth out of a major hole. Don't you think Aunt Polly would understand? She'd trust you to make choices of your own."

He ran his hand through his hair. God but he could do

without this hassle, yet he was determined not to be railroaded.

"The fact you and Beth couldn't stand her probably had something to do with the fact she didn't leave you anything. Ring a bell, Charlotte? Rake up a few memories?" He hadn't meant to lash out but sometimes the truth was the only option and, in this case, his sisters couldn't deny the little regard they had for their aunt.

"That's not true! We respected her." His sister was indignant.

Kieran scoffed. "Both of you used every possible excuse in the book not to visit and on the odd occasion you made an exception Aunt Polly couldn't wait to see the back of your spiteful attitude. That nasty undercurrent wasn't lost on her."

"Don't know why we bothered so!"

"She knew only too well that her quirky décor and simple lifestyle was beneath your standards!"

Charlotte's gasp came down the line. "Says the perfect teenager who kept his dear old aunt awake half the night with loud music and gangs of friends, bringing them to the house even though you'd been told not to!"

Kieran laughed this time. "That's Mum's version you're spinning, Charlotte. Goes to show how little you knew. Polly loved company, always had room for an extra mouth at the table, told me to bring whoever I wanted back, that all my friends were welcome."

"Easy to say now she's gone, Kieran."

He ignored her barb. "She told me over and over to treat the place like home. Comical, really, as that was the last thing I wanted her house to be like – our home! How did you and Beth stick it?"

Charlotte muttered something under her breath, then brought the subject back to the will. "It still doesn't explain why we've been ignored in her will. We've the same relationship to her as you. How often did you visit during the last five years?"

But Kieran was on a roll. "Anytime I was home – not enough, I admit, but at least I made a genuine effort. You, on the other hand, turned your nose up at her and refused to hold a conversation she'd be interested in, snapped answers to her questions – and now you want to turn that memory around and make it sound like you were a devoted niece! Don't make me laugh!"

"You only went to Schull to get away from Mum and Dad, not to mention running wild and flirting with foreign students for the entire school holidays! I can't see it had anything much to do with a great desire to see Aunt Polly or spend some quality time with her."

Rubbing a hand across his forehead, Kieran swallowed back resentment. To think when he'd answered the phone, he'd been stupid enough to believe he had a connection with his older sister. Based on this conversation, he reckoned he had as much of a connection with Charlotte as he had with the mysterious John Kilmichael, a faceless man he'd never heard of in his life.

"Kieran, have a re-think about the inheritance. We'll put it on the market. The area is still very popular. We all know you'd prefer to be riding the highways or sailing the high seas without a care in the world. Keeping your feet in one spot for twelve months is neither who you are nor who you want to be . . ."

"Eleven," Kieran muttered. He winked at the framed photo of Aunt Polly on the dressing table. She seemed to be looking right at him, willing him to do her bidding and not be diverted from course.

"Sorry? Excuse me?" Charlotte asked.

"Not even eleven months left to be precise," he determined. "Good few weeks gone already. The twelve-month period started the day of the funeral."

"You're counting the weeks! That says enough."

"And I've never been as ready to settle down in one spot as I am now if you want to know the truth. So you can fly home, hire the best solicitor you can and contest the will, do whatever the hell you want, Charlotte, but I won't be breaking the terms and conditions set down by Aunt Polly. Her dying wish has become my living goal – we'll call it my mission statement. What I'll do after the twelve months have elapsed I've no idea but for now I'm going nowhere so get used to it! And you can repeat that back to your minions."

Charlotte fell silent on the other end of the line. His little speech had floored her. She had no further argument. Her brother's voice returned on the line.

"I've got to go, Charlotte. Have a nice day – or do they say something different in Canada?"

"Kieran, don't be so bloody stubborn. At least think about it for Beth and leave me out of it," she tried one last time. "I've no interest. It's Beth who needs it."

Kieran gave a hollow laugh. "Look, I'm enjoying it all the more now I know it's driving the rest of the Dulhoolys insane."

"Selfish!" came his older sister's retort, before the line went dead. She'd broken the connection.

Long after their conversation had ended, Kieran continued to stare through the window, the sense of calmness he'd savoured long gone. Fighting against the suffocation of being cocooned in one place, he watched neighbours passing by outside, some stopping to chat and bid each other the time of day and others rushing along on some mission or other. Was this a life he wanted? Was it a life he could enjoy, knowing his family would stick their noses in his business whether he welcomed it or not? Kieran's doubts were returning, fighting for a place in his head over so many other emotions. Glancing at the photograph, he picked it up and stared at his aunt. What do you want from me, Polly, he asked silently?

Up to now, he'd been enjoying his return to Schull, feeling he actually belonged somewhere, a place he loved. Being with Jess and Greg had stirred something inside him. Life on the road – or on the run as he was sometimes accused – had been amazing, and no doubt could be again. But if he bailed on Aunt Polly's challenge now, he knew he'd live to regret it. And he'd carry the guilt of not giving it a decent shot with him. Maybe one day he'd return to that lifestyle but for now it would be put on hold.

He was well aware that his telephone conversation with his sister would be relayed to Beth and his mother. He didn't doubt he had entered into Battle Stage 1 for Number 5 Pier Road. The Dulhooly family were anything but shrinking violets. He'd be confronting them en masse, his father included he suspected. Although Charlotte hadn't mentioned him.

On my own again, it seems, Kieran sighed, his spirits lifting when he noticed Greg and Jess on the street below. He pulled open the window and leaned out, calling to them and beckoning to them to come in. Company for breakfast was exactly what he needed to take his mind off his family. It was only when Greg started pointing and mother and son burst into laughter as they stared up at him that Kieran realised that his Bart Simpson boxers were on full view – much tighter than they should be thanks to his lack of understanding of Aunt Polly's ancient washing machine!

Definitely a crazy day ahead, he thought, grabbing the nearest pair of jeans, a T-shirt and a hooded sweatshirt and pulling them on before running down the stairs to open the door to his amused guests.

Chapter 17

Charlotte was livid when she got off the phone. Livid with herself.

Prancing around her apartment, giving up any intention she had of dropping to the floor and doing her morning routine of press-ups followed by gruelling tummy crunches, she hovered near the drinks cabinet, reluctantly moving away a moment later without succumbing to the temptation of opening it. Pouring a double or treble whiskey on the rocks held so much appeal. But she didn't trust herself to stop at one and neither did she relish the probable consequences. Arriving into HSBC intoxicated and applying a fuzzy brain to the management of million and billion-dollar corporate accounts would horrify her colleagues, not to mention her clients.

Morning television did little to distract from her frustration. The smiling blonde presenter's scripted speech irritated her as she listened to her fake enthusiasm droning on about the perks of Canadian winters, emphasising the tourist advantages of ski resorts and mountain adventures.

The phone call to Kieran had gone any way but the way she'd hoped. And in truth, she only had herself to blame. I should have given it more thought, she realised, grabbing the remote control and flicking through the channels, making the smiley blonde and the snow-capped peaks disappear from the large flat screen.

Beth's desperation when they'd spoken on the phone, combined with Marian's dramatic plea to challenge Kieran's inheritance had put her under pressure. But looking back she realised she'd omitted one very important factor before dialling her brother's mobile number. She had neglected to consider her brother's feelings. She could see that now – bright and clear – when it was too late to undo their conversation.

Seething that she'd totally ignored Kieran's perspective and jumped straight to Beth's defence without giving any time or attention to his feelings, she knew that given another chance she'd handle the situation very differently.

For all my supposed business acumen and tact in the boardroom, I'd want to work on applying the same precision to personal situations. I could at least have congratulated him, shown him a bit of understanding and put out feelers about Beth's financial problems. He might have volunteered a bit of help or support that could have made a huge difference.

She pressed frantically on the buttons of the remote control to find a less irritating programme. Putting myself in his shoes for a moment would have helped me see things from all sides, she thought, flying through the channels in a blur, barely letting them set on the screen before flicking ahead again. What do I know about his life or dreams any more? He's no longer the wild teenager who'd stop at nothing to have some fun. Maturity has more than likely changed him, as it has me.

Her mind drifted back to the enjoyable few days they'd shared when he'd travelled around the east coast of Canada and stayed a few nights in her apartment. He'd been good company, had shown her tremendous support as he'd listened to her pour her heart out, never once displaying a modicum of criticism as she explained how her manipulating behaviour had put her in an impossibly dangerous situation and she'd been lucky to escape with her life.

Feeling an uneasy ripple of guilt coursing through her, Charlotte's face flushed. Had she not learned anything from the horrific experience she'd suffered literally in Philip Lord's hands? Other peoples' emotions weren't playthings. She deeply regretted her accusing words to Kieran, cringing inwardly as she remembered her nasty insinuations, the way she'd belittled his close attachment to Polly. She'd displayed no concern at all for his feelings. How could she blame him for being defensive – what other way could she have expected him to react?

She put her head in her hands and groaned. Bringing her channel-surf to a stop on a music channel, she increased the volume significantly and watched Adele performing 'Setting Fire to the Rain'.

As Charlotte's body swayed in time to the music, her mind devised a way of making things up to her brother.

She tossed the remote away from her. What a bitch I was to him, she thought. Why on earth should he turn his back on the inheritance? Why should he step back from good fortune? Would Beth? Would I? Highly unlikely. And Kieran wouldn't expect it from us.

Having come to a decision that she knew would infuriate her mother and sister, she took her exercise mat from behind the couch and dropped it on the wooden floor.

Throwing herself into her morning exercise routine with gusto, Charlotte couldn't get Kieran from her mind. Looking back on their sibling relationship she remembered how they'd adored each other in equal measure before Beth had burst into the world, bawling and screaming and demanding more attention than normally required by an infant. Four years older than Kieran – sensible and mature for her age, used to a predominantly adult world – Charlotte had assumed the role of protector the moment she'd laid eyes on her little brother. Barely bigger than her favourite doll, she'd fallen instantly in love, his arrival brightening her world and turning a shy and introvert little girl into a devoted big sister.

Content to be the apple of his big sister's eye and claim her attention as he progressed from infant to toddler, Kieran hadn't put up much objection to her incessant fussing – at least not while it suited him to have her as his personal playmate, at his beck and call for every whim. Their stints playing doctors and nurses gave them endless hours of entertainment, with him receiving pretend injections, tittering when the blunt 'syringe' tickled his soft skin. His turn at being doctor invariably involved cutting open some part of Charlotte's anatomy with a plastic knife from her doll's house. His giggles could be heard throughout the house when he ran after his patient, his chubby legs struggling to catch her, the gun and holster buckled around his waist weighing him down. And after a marathon session of cutting her open, followed by a major bandaging drama with one of Marian's clean tea-towels, he'd pull his gun from his holster, aim and fire! Charlotte, needless to say, dropped to the ground and lay completely still as any good victim would.

On the days Charlotte was in school, Kieran missed her company and waited eagerly with his mum at the school gates. He was beside himself when his adored sister emerged, seeing it as his excuse to jump out of the buggy and grab her hand so the fun would begin all over again. She never disappointed, every day bringing a new adventure, their bond tightening all the while.

Charlotte exhaled slowly as she flexed first one foot and then the other, stretching her arms and touching her toes, feeling the strain behind her knees until her legs trembled and she rolled on to her side to begin a series of leg lifts, ignoring the strain on her muscles as she remembered Beth's arrival. A little more than two months after Kieran's second birthday, she'd arrived into the world with screaming attitude and strong lungs, her presence turning the Dulhooly serenity on its head and drawing a halt to their fun-filled hours. Doubled over with colic pain, her stomach cramping, Beth wailed day and night. Her demands exhausted Marian, changing her from a caring, carefree mother to a snappy, impatient crank who was constantly exhausted. Tension built in the house, nobody escaping its wrath, tempers frazzled and arguments regularly brewing. Detesting returning to a stressful household, the number of hours Frank spent at home shrank on a continuous basis, his relationship with his children deteriorating with his increased absence. His working day lengthened, his hours on the golf course even more so. Playing a four-ball when he was supposedly working late became a regular excuse.

Struggling to cope in his absence, an embittered Marian begged the six-year-old Charlotte to take her younger sister in her lap and pay her some attention at any given opportunity, leaving her very little time to entertain Kieran.

Quickly realising that his playmate had shifted her attention to the red-faced screaming baby who'd entered their household and ruined everything, Kieran made a brief attempt to secure attention from his mother. But soon tiring of her abrupt dismissals, he gradually mastered the task of self-entertainment, content to receive the odd word of praise when the others – anyone, in fact – had a moment to notice him. The more attention Beth demanded, the less Kieran expected to receive, his independent streak a natural development in the circumstances.

Panting for breath, Charlotte took a break to get a glass of iced water, mopping the perspiration from her face with a towel before taking a long cold drink. She watched the sun making its first appearance of the morning and her stomach sank as she recognised the connection between present and past. Once more, as per her mother's instructions, she was being pushed to silence Beth's screams. Regardless.

She turned and spilled the remaining water down the sink, watching it bubble before disappearing down the plughole – a bit like her relationship with Kieran if she allowed it to disintegrate again, like it had when her baby sister came into the world. At six years of age, she'd been too young to understand the damage Beth's interference and her mother's instructions had done to her fun-filled relationship with Kieran.

Shaking out her arms and legs, she began her cool-down regime, inhaling a deep breath, stretching her arms high over her head and holding the position for a count of twenty. I'm not six any more, she thought, dropping her arms and exhaling slowly before repeating the exercise three more times. And I have a mind of my own to use as I see fit, something she'd proven to herself on numerous occasions since emigrating – or running – to Canada.

As she peeled off her lycra shorts and top, she considered calling Kieran back to apologise and explain her change of heart. But then she decided against it. The mood he'd been in, he probably wouldn't believe her anyway. Instead she stepped into the shower and allowed the power jets do their job, her body savouring the familiar tingling as the warm water bounced against her skin.

Beth and Marian wouldn't understand her change of heart so she'd play along as though she were going to support their objection to the will. Her brother deserved family support instead of the stab in the back they were planning for him. And in the absence of anyone else, she'd see he got it.

Chapter 18

A family who had lived independent lives up to the time of Polly's will reading, the Dulhoolys were more than making up for lack of contact. In an attempt to have an honest conversation with his son, Frank had collected him early that morning, taken him to Bantry for breakfast and then driven to Bantry Golf Club.

Out on the course, Frank winced as he watched Kieran's clumsy efforts.

"Try this club, might be better for you," he said.

Kieran took the second club from his father. "The fault lies with the player not the clubs, Dad," he laughed. "I haven't set foot on a golf course in years. And it shows!"

"Time to remedy that then." Frank flinched as he watched his son swing the club. "Bring your hands closer together. It's not a hurley you're swinging!"

"I'm a long way from being a pro like you, Dad! A lot of hours to clock up."

"I'll have to organise a few lessons for you."

Kieran laughed at his father's eagerness. "Are you trying

to make yourself look good, dragging me around the green behind you?" His club connected with the ball but unfortunately it veered to the right of his target, his father's sharp intake of breath speaking multitudes.

"Just thought it'd be nice to share a game now and then." Frank took his shot with ease and accuracy, following the ball with his eye until it dropped on to the green and rolled close to the hole. "And it's easier to talk without your mother constantly badgering on about the will."

"Beth hasn't approached me for help, Dad. Come to think of it, I haven't seen much of her, not since the funeral. I get the feeling she's avoiding me."

Frank took a towel from his golf bag and cleaned his club. "She's been badgering the rest of us about it instead, probably afraid you'll shoot her down if she asks. She has always been a bit spoilt, not great at making decisions."

"If she can wait until the year's up, I'll do what I can. But my hands are tied until then. They'll have to find another way to get out of their mess."

"My sentiments entirely. As for Carl – another example of her decision-making – he'd want a shake. Going around as if he hasn't a care in the world, leaving Beth to do all the worrying."

"Can't say I've seen much of him, wouldn't really know him."

"You and me both! But what I do know is enough."

Kieran followed his father along the course, admiring the magnificent grounds, the vivid green grass reminding him of his intentions to get the gardens in order at Number 5. "Talk about hitting the ball off focus," Kieran laughed, stopping to line up his next shot, holding his hands closer together as per Frank's instruction and glancing from the ball to the flag.

"Just to be clear, Marian and Beth know exactly where I stand on the situation and without me – whoa, that's not a bad shot at all, lad!" Frank said, diverting from what he'd been about to say as Kieran's shot travelled towards the hole. "A few lessons and plenty of practice and you'll be a worthy opponent in no time!"

"Don't get carried away, Dad! Beginner's luck, that's all. Give me a few hours' sailing around the coastline any day!"

"Hi, John," Frank said to one of the men in a nearby group who were waiting to tee-off.

"Oh, that reminds me," Kieran said as they moved towards the next hole. "You ever hear Polly mention a person by the name of John Kilmichael?"

Frank let go of the hold he had on his golf bag, ignoring the sound of clubs clinking against each other as it dropped on the ground, his face turning a shade of grey. "Don't tell me that bastard has been mooching around?"

Taken aback by the shocked reaction, Kieran put a hand on his father's arm, his eyes filled with concern. "Take it easy, Dad. I haven't seen him. Nobody has called. A package arrived in his name and I was wondering how to get in contact with him to pass it on. That's all."

Frank stooped to pick up his bag, stumbling slightly on his feet as he did so.

"Let me, Dad." Kieran picked up the bag for him.

"Don't encourage him around the place," Frank instructed, fiddling with the strap of the leather bag. "He's bad news. Polly should have left well enough alone."

"But who is he?" Kieran was intrigued.

There was a silence. Frank stared into space.

"Dad?"

"Let's just say, Polly took Kilmichael under her wing some time back." He stared into the distance, his eyes narrowing, a pensive look on his face. "Against my better wishes I might add."

"Took him under her wing! Where did she meet him? Were they, eh, you know?" Kieran took extra time positioning his tee, finding it difficult to verbalise his question. Imagining Polly in a relationship felt a little strange. "She hardly befriended some random stranger?" he asked finally.

"It'll be dark before we get to the eighteenth at this stage," Frank complained, misjudging his next shot entirely and cursing as the ball went into the rough area. He had sidestepped Kieran's question.

"That's all you're going to tell me?"

"Another time, son. As you can see the mere mention of him is already putting me off my game."

Kieran badgered him further, refusing to accept that the subject was closed, feeling that Frank's reluctance to talk about Kilmichael was creating far more intrigue than an explanation ever could. But his questions fell on deaf ears and Frank ignored them. Eventually his son relented and allowed him to continue with the game in peace.

"Cheers for springing for the round, Dad," he said as they drew up outside Polly's house, "and for almost letting me beat you in those last few holes!" Noticing the concern still lingering on his father's face, he nudged him with his elbow. "I enjoyed the morning. Want to come in for a drink or coffee?"

Frank shook his head. "I've a few things to get back to," he explained. "But whatever you do, Kieran, don't encourage John Kilmichael. Promise me you won't. In fact, don't even tell him she passed . . . don't tell him she's dead. Just get rid of him as quickly as you can."

"If I get to meet him, I'll keep that in mind but so far all I have is his post. But if he does come knocking, I'll be at a loss unless you tell me what the hell's going on." He got out of the car, letting the door close gently behind him.

Frank clutched the steering wheel in a tight grip, chewing on his inside lip and gazing at his sister's house. Shifting the gear lever, he put the car in first gear, his foot on the clutch so it wouldn't jump forward. After another moment's thought, he leaned across and lowered the passenger window.

"Kieran, wait!" he called, beckoning him to come back to the car window. Watching his son double back he continued to stare at Number 5, remembering his sister taking him into her confidence, and pausing a few further moments as he made up his mind about sharing her secret with Kieran.

Crouched down on his hunkers, Kieran put his head in the window to hear why his father had called him back. "Dad?" he prompted. "Was there something you wanted to tell me?"

"John Kilmichael is Polly's son. He lives in Dublin and turns up here now and again – he's a sales rep."

Kieran's mouth dropped open and he almost lost his balance at his father's announcement, regaining it before he toppled onto the concrete. Staring in disbelief at his father, their eyes met in the dimming light. Kieran knew Frank was telling the truth.

"No way! And I'm only finding out now, like this? You've got to be kidding me!"

"Do you see me laughing?" Frank asked gravely.

"But why didn't she leave the house to *him*? Her son! That precedes a nephew who hasn't visited in quite a while! But where has he been all these years? Why did you keep it a secret from me? Who else knows?"

"A story for another day, son. I enjoyed the golf – pity this had to spoil it though."

"But Dad, come on, what aren't you telling me? And who's the father?"

Frank evaded Kieran's last question. "Polly lied to John. She never told him he was her son."

"*What?* She never told him!"

"No. And neither can you."

"Me? Unlikely, seeing as I've never met him!"

"Kieran, listen to me: only you and I know about his relationship to Polly. And I'd like it to be kept that way!"

"So you've kept this from Mum too? But she must have known Polly was pregnant?"

"No. Polly took care no one did."

"But why is it such a scandal? We're no longer in the Dark Ages and Polly was one of the most liberated, broad-minded women I ever knew!" This form of underhanded behaviour didn't match the aunt he'd known and loved.

"Circumstance can lead to difficult choices, Kieran. Over forty years ago, times were very different. And so were social attitudes."

His father's words went around in his head, his confusion lingering long after Frank had pulled away from the kerb. Remembering his father's reaction to his announcement that Kilmichael's post had landed in Number 5 had been a huge eye-opener for Kieran. Exploding in such a fashion was out of character for Frank, maintaining control and keeping emotions under wraps more his usual behaviour.

Why wouldn't his father elaborate and tell him the full story? Why the big mystery? He tried to imagine what kind of relationship Polly had built with John Kilmichael. On what premise had she welcomed him into her life? Mystifying to say the least.

Entering the house, Kieran pulled open the drawer in the hall table, eyeing the package addressed to John Kilmichael and toying with the idea of opening it. He picked it up, twirling it around between his fingers. But loyalty to Polly and the freedom she'd afforded her son forced him to put it back again. His aunt had obviously placed some sort of trust in John. But what Kieran couldn't fathom was why she'd gone to the trouble of reuniting with him yet had never disclosed their blood relationship.

Pushing the drawer shut again, Kieran inhaled the faint scent of lavender as he walked upstairs, unsure if the aroma was real or imaginary, but knowing that his decision to allow the man his privacy would have met with Polly's approval and in his heart he liked to think she was showing him that.

Chapter 19

Beth pushed her legs out straight in front of her, moving the swing higher and higher and leaning her upper body backward until she could look up at the sky. She'd arranged to meet her mother in the Ballydehob playground. They hadn't wanted Frank walking in and overhearing their conversation. Her mother had explained how he'd forbidden any interference in Polly's will, so with that in mind they'd agreed to work in unison without his knowledge, relying on Charlotte to delve into the legal requirements instead. Meeting Kieran a few times, she'd chickened out of her planned confrontation, the words she'd rehearsed dying on her lips.

"How's life in Schull?" she'd asked when they'd bumped into each other in town one afternoon, her heart sinking when she noticed him carrying a bundle of DIY materials, hardly the evidence she'd wanted to see and dissolving any hope she'd retained that he'd have a change of heart and take off across the world once more. Venturing into the safer arena of small talk, she'd spent a few awkward moments with her brother before rushing away on some pretence or other.

Dropping her feet to the ground and lowering the swing to a near-stop, she swayed gently and watched the activity around her. Two sisters raced each other to the giant slide, their legs clambering up the steps, their excited laughter ringing in Beth's ears and reminding her of the fun she and her sister had enjoyed in this same playground. The equipment was less sophisticated back then of course, but the thrill of whooshing down the slide or clambering onto the old steel see-saw had been exactly the same.

Charlotte's contact had been minimal in recent days, little more than hurried emails, her marketing instructions easier said than done.

Let it go live to test the market but keep updating it. Polish, polish, polish – it has to stand out in the market place. Generate some props around the place – borrow a few horses for photos if you must. Customers need to see its potential.

Beth had responded to her suggestions with more questions, taking the opportunity in one of her emails to enquire if she'd spoken to Kieran. She must be up the walls at work, Beth decided, when there was no response, envying her sister's well-paying job and hectic life. Anxious to get things moving, she'd forwarded Charlotte a selection of photos for her opinion.

Receiving a text from Carl saying he'd uploaded photos on the computer had come as a surprise, one less task for her to do. But still it didn't alleviate the humiliation she'd felt after her ridiculous (at least by her consideration) physical reaction to his close proximity. Unpredictable lust playing its usual tricks, she'd decided, trying and failing to obliterate the delicious feelings of quivering heat floating through her body when she'd inhaled his scent as he'd crouched beside her. Dismissing it as unfulfilled hunger and refusing to acknowledge the possibility that it could be a revival of the intense attraction they'd once shared, she'd strived to keep her mind busy, only relenting to her expanding fantasy as she lay under the quilt at night time, her soft skin tingling as she allowed her imagination free rein.

"You're too big to be on a swing."

A startled Beth swung her head around, smiling when she looked into the face of a little girl – three or four years of age at most. She stood to the side of the swing, hands on hips and a petulant look on her impish face as she waited expectantly for a response from Beth.

"But my bum fits," Beth teased, inching to the left of the red plastic seat to prove it. "Want to give me a little push and then I'll get off. Promise."

"Victoria, don't be annoying the lady!" came a shout from behind the playground's wooden maze. Dragging a little boy by the arm, a visibly stressed woman appeared a brief moment later.

"I'm so sorry," she said to Beth and then turned to scold her daughter, her little boy doing his utmost to pull his hand out of her tight grasp. "Victoria, what have I told you about speaking to strangers?"

"But she's on a children's swing, Mum! Daddy says adults shouldn't be on these swings. She could break it! Then there would be nothing for the boys and girls." Her lower lip protruded, hands on hips and eyes accusing.

Beth got to her feet. "Best do what I'm told," she said, bestowing an apologetic smile on Victoria. "Your daddy's perfectly right. The swings are for little people not sad old fogies like me!" Despite the smile on her face, a deep sense of sadness seeped through her. Is that what I've become, she thought, a sad old lady – well, maybe not that old but certainly sad – who has taken to mooching around a swing in a children's playground? All I need now is a few cats crawling over me to complete the picture!

"So sorry to ruin your few minutes of relaxation," the woman said, glancing around her before asking, "Your kids are hiding around here somewhere?"

Beth shook her head, a familiar ache crossing her chest. She struggled to maintain her composure, her eyes bright with tears, her smile disappearing. Such a giveaway. Will I learn to hide the heartache?

Instantly, the other lady apologised. "Oh, I'm so sorry! I've spoken out of turn. Ignore me, I never think before opening my big gob."

"Swing now!" The little boy pulled free of his mother's grip and threw his arms over the seat of the second swing, lifting his knee and attempting to climb in a cumbersome and dangerous fashion.

"Wait!" the mother warned, grabbing him deftly and guiding him towards the toddler swing. Lifting him up, she avoided his kicking legs, eased his wriggling form into the safety seat and then breathed a visible sigh of relief. "Sorry again," she mouthed, giving her son a quick push before helping Victoria onto the swing Beth had vacated. Making sure the little girl was holding on to the chains with both hands, she gave her a push while keeping an eye on her little boy at the same time. "Peace for a few minutes," she commented.

"Your hands are full. I'll leave you to it. Here's my mum now anyway." Beth turned away from the familiar sympathy and pity in the other woman's eyes.

"Isn't she too big to be at the playground with her mummy?" she heard Victoria ask as she walked away from the swings and the young family.

What a perceptive little girl, she thought, forcing a smile on her face as she approached her mother. Funny, she couldn't remember Marian ever pushing them on the swings. Her memories were of Charlotte standing behind her, picking her up when she fell over and making everything okay again – exactly as I'm expecting her to do now, she realised.

"Beth, I'm sorry I'm late," Marian gasped as she hurried towards her daughter, air-kissing her on both cheeks as per usual. "You wouldn't believe the morning I've had."

"Nothing to worry about, I hope?"

She shook her head, eyes bright with enthusiasm. "Quite the contrary, a bit of hopeful news for a change."

Drops of rain pattered on the ground around them.

"Damn, we'll get soaked! Quick, let's run to the café," Marian squealed, taking an umbrella from her handbag and holding it over them as they made a dash for the local coffee shop. "I'll fill you in when we get there."

"Heard from Charlotte?" Beth asked, hurrying to keep up with her mother whose regular walking, tennis and golf games maintained her fitness levels, despite her smoker's cough.

"Not a word! I still don't know if she's spoken to Kieran. Although, knowing her meticulous attention to detail, she could be beavering away in the background and getting to grips with what we're taking on. She might have it all under control when she eventually surfaces."

"That reminds me, she promised to get me some info on liability insurance too."

Arriving outside the café, Marian shook the rain from her umbrella and closed it. "Insurance?" she enquired.

"Charlotte suggested I try and lease out the grounds for a variety of activities." Each time she mentioned the notion, she gained more confidence, was less fearful of the implications.

"Not a bad idea either. You should talk to your dad about that. He'd be impressed you're being proactive and I'm sure would have sound advice to offer. And maybe if he sees you're making an effort –"

The bell tinkled overhead when she pushed opened the café door, drowning out the end of her sentence, but Beth had the gist of what she was saying. Connecting with her dad on a neutral topic might make him more sympathetic. She might have a point, Beth thought, following her mother through the glass door and groaning inwardly when she noticed Carl seated at a nearby table, his head stuck in a car magazine, apparently oblivious to the world and the problems going on around him. Bitterness rose inside her and an image of the unpaid final bills thrown on the hall table instantly came to mind. But at least that was easier for her to deal with right now rather than an image of him sending shivers through her entire body. Stop! she screamed inwardly, worrying about the pathetic confused mess she was becoming. Confused emotions, inability to make decisions. Who'd believe she'd once held the coveted position of being top of the élite science group in second-year at university?

Marian turned to face her, giving her a questioning look.

"Keep going, Mum," Beth instructed, appreciating her mother's consideration but determined to retain some modicum of pride. It was about all she had left and she wasn't leaving just because *he* was there. God damn him! Didn't he know she often spent a morning there with her mum or a friend? Couldn't he have gone elsewhere?

"You get the seats, love. I'll order coffee and scones."

"Cream and jam with mine, Mum, please," Beth requested, knowing that if she didn't state her preference, her mother would arrive with low-cal spread and probably one scone between them! Marian's calorie-counting diet wouldn't fulfil Beth's desire for something wicked and, on her current budget, a treat from her mother was as near to wicked as she would get.

While her mother went to the counter and queued, Beth, needing something to prevent her from glaring in Carl's direction, checked her emails on her mobile. With surprise, she noticed a few enquiries about her new website. Tired of waiting for Charlotte to get back to her, she'd pored over the website detail time and time again (as much to keep her brain occupied as anything else) until finally she felt it included nothing incriminating and was safe to transmit to the outside world. Pressing the *publish* button to let it go live, she hadn't made any other great efforts to advertise apart from posting links to a few social-networking sites and emailing a few local heritage sites. She'd sent Carl the links but hadn't bothered to ask if he'd posted them anywhere. And he hadn't bothered to enlighten her.

Reading the emails now, she gripped her phone tightly, a mixture of excitement and anticipation flooding through her. Top marks to Charlotte for her brainwave – nothing unusual there of course! Beth had assumed her amateur website would remain under the radar but apparently not. Scanning through the enquiries with interest, she checked the email addresses and was as confident as she could be that the majority were genuine. Unbelievable, she thought, reading through them again, unable to believe the number of responses. Glancing at Carl, the teeniest part of her wanted to share the news, let him be part of it and try and work together to make it work. Reading each one in turn, she responded with a promise to forward details of prices and availability as soon as possible. A good start, she thought, smiling as she scanned the next one: **My daughter has her heart set on a barn dance for her 21st and what you're offering looks ideal.** Beth chewed her lower lip, suddenly overwhelmed and apprehensive. Attracting interested parties was easy. Providing a quality service, however, could be a completely different matter. She took a deep breath and contemplated the reality of handling the project. She'd need assistance, couldn't manage every aspect alone, the practicalities being beyond her ability.

Stealing another glance in Carl's direction, she watched him flick through his magazine and twirled her phone between her fingers. I'll have to broach the subject with him sooner rather than later, she thought. Otherwise he'll step outside the door one day and find potential clients rambling around our property! Tempted to take the cowardly route and send him a text later, she wondered about her best approach.

Her phone beeped again, another new email in her inbox, one of the photos from the site included in the message. She was warmed by the image of their Goleen residence coming to life before her.

"Nice to see you smiling for a change," Marian commented as she placed the tray on the table.

"Some enquiries about renting the stables."

"That was quick!"

"Tell me about it. Too quick – we're nowhere near organised for viewings."

"Still, it obviously has potential."

Beth agreed but still had lots of unanswered questions. She'd have to get advice. Would it be wise to allow people on the grounds for viewing before sorting out insurance? And should she have a guaranteed market before investing money? Groaning inwardly, she realised outlay would still be required to get the project up and running and, even if it turned out to be a successful venture, it would take substantial capital investment to get it off the ground. Polly's inheritance would really be the answer to all of her prayers. It would allow her keep the Goleen house and get her activities business off the ground. At a stretch, she hoped she could use it as financial support while studying again for the degree she'd walked away from years before.

Snapped out of her trance when her mother cleared her throat to get her attention, Beth poured milk into her coffee, spilling a little over the edge of the mug.

"You said 'we', Beth. Is Carl in on this project of yours?"

Beth shrugged. "If it's going ahead, he'll have to pull his weight. I'm not exactly equipped to erect fences and create dirt tracks!" She took a sip of coffee, wincing as the burning liquid stung the roof of her mouth. She reached for the milk jug once more. "You were going to tell me what delayed you?" She was happy to change the subject.

"Oh yes. Seth called as I was leaving. I've been leaving messages for him."

"Uncle Seth?" She put her phone back in her bag. "How's he keeping? Is he still seeing that fashion model?"

Marian laughed. "I never thought to ask but with his track record, it's unlikely." She picked the raisins, peel and cherries from her scone, dropping them onto the plate. "I don't know why they don't do plain baking here," she complained.

Beth smiled. She'd watched her mother decimate food for years, nothing new to the measures Marian went to reduce her calorie intake. But she ignored her complaint.

"So, Mum, has the good news you mentioned have something to do with Seth?"

"Yes." She chewed her food slowly, sipping from her mug and dabbing her lips with a serviette.

"Yeah? And?" Whatever it was, there had to be a twist. Nothing was straightforward where her uncle was concerned.

Seth was Marian's brother, the 'brains of the Brixton family' as she referred to him. He was an authority on most subjects, a tried and tested businessman in many industries. 'A gangster' was how Frank described him – no love lost between the brothers-in-law.

Over the years, Beth had overheard numerous arguments between Marian and Frank, with Marian regularly comparing Frank to Seth, making no secret of her belief that her husband paled in comparison. Though she'd never been brave enough to voice it, Beth often felt like reminding her mother that Frank was the one with the solid profession and regular income while Seth floated on the cusp of many a wave, scraping through deals by the skin of his teeth. One thing he had been born with, however, was luck and good fortune. And though there were many occasions he'd teetered on the edge – had even made the headlines with a few appalling decisions – Seth Brixton seldom failed.

Marian took a sip from her Americano, running a finger around the rim of the cup to remove her lipstick stain. Her brown eyes were intense as she brought her daughter up to date on her conversation with Seth. "I called him last week about the will. Without your father's help, this is too big for us to manage alone."

Beth's breath caught in her throat, the prospect of Seth's involvement even scarier than Marian being in charge! "I feel something illegal coming down the tracks, Mum!"

"We will only get one opportunity to turn this situation with Kieran around to *your* satisfaction . . ."

Beth groaned – really scared now. "You make it sound like I'm the only one to benefit here! Aren't you forgetting Charlotte and Kieran's shares too?"

Marian exhaled but didn't make any attempt to appease. "Of course not! But you're the one depending on it."

"But Seth? Can you honestly trust him? Aren't you worried he'll lead us down some crooked path?"

Her mother's shoulders went back, defiance in her eyes that anyone dare criticise her beloved brother. "At least he's willing to help! And Seth's discretion is unquestionable."

Her insinuation that he was offering assistance while Frank had refused wasn't lost on Beth.

"But Kieran is Seth's nephew? Have you told him *who* we're ousting?" Beth lowered her voice to a whisper, glancing around the café, paranoia increasing her awareness.

"Naturally I explained your predicament to him. And of course he understood the implications but he's still willing to help in whatever way he can."

Lifting her teaspoon, Beth stirred sugar into her coffee. Knowing Seth's approach, she suspected at best his involvement would be too heavy-handed.

Marian sensed her disapproval. "Seth sees it like any other business deal, not a split of family loyalties. And so should you!"

Beth inhaled sharply.

"What's more," Marian continued, "I've helped him out of a few tight scrapes over the years – unknown to your father I might add. He'll come good for me." Her expression softened. "And for you."

Beth felt uncomfortable at the thought of her uncle hearing about her plans to oust her brother. And to make matters worse, Marian had already alerted Kieran to that fact. And now Seth. Sighing, she relented.

"What does Seth suggest then? How much does he know about these situations?"

Marian fiddled with her teaspoon. "What he doesn't already know, he'll find out."

"But what's he going to do? What reasons can we use for overturning the will? And will they be legal?"

"Leave it with Seth. He'll find a way to make it work."

"Don't tell me he's going to fabricate a new will?"

Marian smiled at her daughter's question. She'd made the same suggestion when she'd spoken to her brother. "That would have been the simplest option, but too difficult to make it stand up in court according to Seth."

"No matter what he proposes, I'm guessing there will be an element of dishonesty attached. I'll mess the whole thing up if I have to take the stand in court!" Beth rubbed the serviette along the palms of her hands. Her mother's mention of court had scared her, the word 'perjury' flashing in neon lights before her eyes. What hope would she have of convincing a judge and jury that she'd given her aunt due care and attention while her brother swanned between continents? None, she reckoned. They'd see right through her and they wouldn't be up to much if they didn't.

Marian placed a hand over her daughter's, giving it a gentle squeeze. "Nothing so obscene or public, Beth. He's working on a couple of realistic options that he feels could work."

Beth's anxiousness escalated to fear, a cold sweat running down her spine. I haven't thought this through properly, she thought. "No, Mum," she gushed. "This is crazy, too risky. Being in debt to the banks is one thing but lying in court – and what about legal costs?" She paused for breath, eyes wild, fingers fidgeting nervously with her serviette.

"*Shh!*" Marian silenced her. "Seth will be discreet. He knows a doctor who may be persuaded to produce documents and question Polly's sanity at the time her will was written."

Beth cringed. Her mother had described this as 'nothing so obscene'? Had she heard correctly? Producing false documents and questioning Polly's sanity? Too cruel.

"Ah no, Mum. We'd never get away with that. Polly had the same GP for years. And he knows the family too. He wouldn't jeopardise his practice, risk being struck off – what would he stand to gain?"

But Marian was insistent. "Seth's going to use a geriatrician, somebody further up the hierarchal ladder than her GP. There are ways around everything."

"Ah, Mum, what about her dignity? And Dad? He'll never speak to me again!"

"He'll get over it."

Beth scrunched the serviette into a tight ball, circling it between the palms of her hands. "It's not worth this much upset."

Marian shot her daughter a defiant look. "Polly's dead and buried, in the earth as lunch for the worms. None of this will do her any harm."

Beth brought her cup to her lips, swallowing the remainder of her coffee without even tasting it. "I've changed my mind, Mum. I'm not going through with this. I'll fight the banks whatever way I can, see what business I can drum up with this new venture," she took her phone from her bag and waved it in her mother's face, "with the summer months ahead."

Marian shook her head, running a hand through her short hair. "Don't be ridiculous. Nothing's set in stone. This is just one of the options open to us, the one that Seth recommended. But he probably has a few others up his sleeve. We can go back and talk to him."

Beth raised an eyebrow, petrified her uncle had already started proceedings. "Mum, I'm happier to leave things stand. Good luck to Kieran."

The waitress came to their table, offering a coffee refill. Both women refused.

"Let's hear Seth out at least." Marian eyed her youngest daughter, wanting more than anything to erase the pain from her face and see the light return to her eyes.

Deep in thought, Beth smeared an extra blob of cream onto her scone, looking around the café. As her eyes rested on Carl, she was shocked – horrified would be a better description – to see her father taking a seat in the pew beside him. What the hell was that about?

"Mum, don't look now but Dad has joined Carl at his table. Have they been in contact recently?"

Marian totally dismissed Beth's warning and turned right around, meeting Frank's gaze head on.

"Marian, Beth," he said, giving a nod and casual wave before returning his attention to Carl. But he looked alarmed.

Beth's instincts were on red alert. Instantly uncomfortable, she looked away, wishing there was a side door out of the café so she could avoid bumping into either her husband or father. But no such luck. Unless she waited for them to leave, she'd have no option but to walk past them.

"Why are they together, Mum?" Her head ached. "Could it be something to do with Polly's house?"

"Of course not!"

"You're sure, Mum?" Beth pushed her plate away.

The enjoyment from her calorie-laden treat had been well and truly ruined. The two men in the corner booth – engrossed in what appeared to be an extremely serious conversation – had once meant so much to her, and she to them she'd believed. And now she was panicking at the thought of having to walk past them. Her relationship with Carl was probably doomed from the beginning and she wasn't sure there was any way forward for them. If anything they were living in their own private purgatory, unable to reverse out of the mess they were in or escalate forward to something better.

And then there was Frank, the father she'd idolised as a little girl.

"Earth to Beth!"

"Sorry, Mum, I was miles away."

Marian was still surveying the two men discreetly. "They could just be discussing golf?"

"Carl doesn't play," Beth replied flatly.

"Oh well, I'm sure it's nothing sinister and certainly nothing to do with the will. Your father's adamant Polly's decision stands."

Beth couldn't relax. She hadn't the heart to continue. "Can we leave now, Mum? I can't relax with Carl and Dad on the far side of the café."

Marian nodded. "Of course, if that's what you want. Why don't we just leave things to Seth and see what he comes back with?"

Beth zipped up her jacket, watching Marian fixing a bright pink scarf under the collar of her navy rain mac.

"Ready then?"

More despondent (if that was possible) than when she'd arrived, Beth followed her mother, relief coursing through her when the waitress chose that moment to serve Carl and Frank. She skirted by their table as the waitress served them toasted sandwiches. She was saved the trouble of choosing between stopping to talk or avoiding them. What it didn't save her from, however, was the snippet of conversation she overheard as she skimmed by the waitress.

"Kieran might offer some help but not a word to Beth..."

Frank's sharp tone rang in Beth's ears.

Beth's stomach churned. She didn't wait to hear any more. She hurried onto the street. Taking great big gulps of fresh air into her lungs, she waited for her heart rate to return to normal. What on earth was going on? What could her father – and maybe her brother – be discussing with Carl? I must be going mad, she thought. They barely tolerated each other. Dad refused to help me, yet he's blatantly cutting a deal with Carl and making sure I'm kept in the dark!

Hurrying to catch up with Marian, she linked her mother's arm and fell into step, her head spinning as they walked the short distance to the car park.

"Thank you for calling Seth, Mum," she said, planting an unexpected peck on her mother's cheek. "Your support means everything to me. And you're right. I should listen to what Seth suggests before making a decision."

"You're welcome, pet. But not a word to your father until this whole sorry messy is sorted out."

Marian pulled her scarf over her mouth, hiding the smile spreading across her face as she glanced upwards and imagined a ghost of Polly Digby glaring upon them from high above the overcast sky.

Chapter 20

In College Street Library in Toronto, Charlotte was busy researching *Project Kieran*, as she'd come to think of it. Sitting in front of a computer screen, totally engrossed in the world of litigation, lodging caveats and viable evidence, she was oblivious to the mêlée of students positioned in small groups at tables around the library, cramming for their upcoming exams. Trawling through large legal tomes, she'd turned to the Internet, concerned that Canadian law differed in part to the Irish legal system.

"Ten minutes to closing."

Charlotte smiled at the librarian, unable to believe two hours had passed. "No problem. I'm almost done here anyway."

"Irish?" the librarian enquired.

"That obvious?"

"To me it is anyway. My maternal grandparents come from County Wicklow. You know it?"

"Vaguely," Charlotte replied, printing the article she'd been reading. She took her page from the printer, folding it in four and slipping it into her handbag along with the others she'd printed earlier. Plenty of reading to do later, she thought. "I'm from West Cork, southern tip of the country."

"But isn't Ireland a tiny country? I thought everybody knew everybody there. That's what my grandma told us."

"In a manner of speaking," Charlotte agreed. "Wicklow's on the east coast, bordering Dublin – our capital. Ever visited?"

The twenty-something ran her fingers through her long dark hair. "Not yet, but hopefully one day. You here on vacation?"

Charlotte shook her head. "I work in HSBC."

"But you've still got family back home?"

"My parents, one brother and one sister." Surprising herself, she added, "I'm toying with the idea of returning home soon though."

"Gosh, it must be difficult to be so far away from family." The librarian tidied the tables around Charlotte as she chatted. "I see mine every day – don't think I'd survive without my daily dose of hugs! Don't you miss home?"

Charlotte felt an unexpected pang of envy for the relationship the other girl was describing. Maybe I'd have been homesick too if I had a family of huggers! But the Dulhoolys weren't demonstrative, neither in public nor in private. Slipping into her lightweight fleece – finally the temperatures were increasing and she'd happily shed one layer of clothing – an image of their West Cork home came to mind – large in size but light on atmosphere! She couldn't say she'd felt any more alone in Toronto than she'd often felt in the big rambling house in Ballydehob. Hardly surprising our history of relationships is so appalling, she thought, with our parents' constant bickering!

"Texting and emailing makes it easier," she responded eventually. "It's not like I'm waiting for letters to arrive."

"I'd bet! Not to mention Facebook and Twitter. Best way to keep in touch, I guess?"

Charlotte fussed with her handbag, her cheeks flushing. She had deliberately avoided social networking, not wanting her profile up there for all to see.

"How long do you plan on staying back home?"

She met the librarian's gaze and shuddered inside. Toronto had provided a safe haven since her fiasco with Philip Lord. "It depends . . ." she began, faltering as she searched for an explanation. Depends on so much, she thought, unwilling to voice it aloud.

"I'm sorry if I'm prying –"

"Oh no, you're not!" Charlotte realised she'd made the librarian feel uncomfortable. "Depends on how much I enjoy the visit. And whether my ghosts have been laid to rest," she added with a smile, taking lip balm from her jacket pocket and smearing it across her lips. She took a glance at her watch. After nine – too late to get a massage appointment with Giovanni. His sensual touch would have been a welcome release from the memories her conversation had stirred.

"Call in and let me know how it goes – if you decide to come back here, that is."

"I'll bring you a stick of Wicklow rock," Charlotte smiled.

The librarian frowned in confusion. "A Wicklow rock? You're allowed carry that back on the aeroplane."

"It's a candy stick," Charlotte explained, "not an actual rock from the ground!"

They spent a few more moments chatting about Ireland, Charlotte selling it proudly to the Canadian librarian.

"Maybe one day I'll come by and visit. You can advise me on where the best places are."

"Oh, you'd be so welcome. And Wicklow has the most magnificent scenery. Dublin too – it's a real cosmopolitan city. And West Cork – where I hail from – and Kerry, our nearest neighbouring county, have wonderful scenery and are renowned for giving a true Irish welcome. You'll have to sample the Irish hospitality! You won't be disappointed."

"That's what my mum says too. She's only ever been once but was blown away by its beauty. She says the grass over there is greener than anywhere else in the world. Is that true?"

Charlotte grinned. "Ireland certainly boasts the greenest grass in the world and if you can find the end of the rainbow, you'll be rewarded with a crock of gold!"

Students made their way toward the exit, the overhead announcement advising patrons that it was time to leave.

"See you again, I hope," she said, following the others to the exit door.

"I'll be too busy chasing rainbows," the librarian replied with a laugh.

On her walk home from the subway station, Charlotte's mind buzzed. Faces she'd walked away from became images in her head, confusing the bravado she'd felt recently and making her seriously question a trip home.

Am I off my head even considering going back to Ireland, she wondered? I'm seldom lonely, rarely without a number to call if I fancy a little company, and never without a credit balance in my bank account. And of course I have my weekly hour on Giovanni's plinth. But the voice in her head reminded her of how dead she felt inside? Why do I crave passion and fulfilment? Weekly visits to the massage parlour were an ideal solution in the aftermath of heartbreak, but as a long-term solution lacked real emotion and vibrant connection with another human being.

She broke into a run, clutching the handle of her bag as it bounced against her. The librarian had planted the seed of an idea in her head. Social networking might well provide the solution she was looking for. If nothing else it'd give her a squint at how her old life had progressed in her absence. And by 'old life' she meant the lavish circuit she'd indulged in, enjoying a prospering career as though it would never come to a stop . . . but, in true disaster style, she'd ignored the alarm bells, stepping into a nightmare where a one-way-ticket was her only way out.

Back in her apartment, she dropped her bag on the couch, changed into her cosiest pyjamas and dressing gown and settled in for a night's surfing on Facebook. Charlotte couldn't wait to delve into the lives of those she'd left behind. But first she needed a bogus account. Protecting her identity was essential on this occasion. Setting out on a stalking mission, the last thing she wanted was to be discovered, the new persona she'd created for herself in Toronto married with the shame she'd left behind.

Munching on a wholemeal cookie, she turned on her laptop and set about registering as a new Facebook user. Damn, she thought, reading the conditions and realising she'd need an email account as verification. Opening a second internet session, she created a fictitious email account, did the necessary to activate it and then returned to the Facebook page. By now her initial giddiness had worn off and a modicum of common sense was setting in. *No matter what I discover, what's done is done. I've left that phase of my life well and truly behind.*

"Strong coffee required before I delve into this," she said aloud, hitting the power button on the radio as she passed it. Background music – that would help hopefully. She couldn't believe how jittery she felt, unable to decide if the tremors inside her were as a result of fear, apprehension or ridiculous excitement at the thought of seeing a few familiar faces.

At last, half a cup of strong coffee inside her, as well as the six biscuits she'd munched on without thinking, she set about creating her new profile, struck by the irony of 'Someone That I Used To Know' playing on the radio, lyrics poignant in the circumstances.

Inebriated by the freedom of 'being somebody else' she pulled a name from the top of her head and typed it in. **Mia Zepo**, she entered, smiling as it appeared on screen. Mia – a cute, short, three-letter name. So much better than being lumbered with a lengthy, stuffy-sounding name like Charlotte. To be doubly sure, she put the name into a Google search engine and was relieved to find no one with that name. Good, she thought, I can't be accused of impersonation.

Choosing a predominantly Canadian profile, she enjoyed creating this new persona.

Hometown – Montreal, she decided. Taking a train up there one weekend, she'd been intrigued by its old-fashioned atmosphere with its cobblestone streets and adorably quaint shops, the beauty of Notre Dame Basilica along with the art galleries forever etched in her memory. Yes, she thought, Mia from Montreal.

Birthday – this she decided in an instant. It would definitely be summer. Having a Christmas birthday was an entire pain. Parties were non-existent and presents were generally wrapped into one with her Christmas gift.

This is fun, she thought, carried along with the freedom of reinvention.

About You – this one required a little more thought and she decided to skip it for now. She'd find out a little more about 'herself' first as she continued through the profile questions.

Sex – female, she typed in, deciding that no matter how confusing things were, she wasn't interested in a gender transformation just yet. She'd prefer to be a woman who could kick ass!

Relationship – without thinking she entered 'married' into this slot. It'd be nice to try it for a while, even as an alter ego.

Activities – another category she completed with little contemplation. Tennis, skiing, snowboarding and travelling. Skiing and snowboarding she had never attempted, but she could vouch for her love of tennis and travelling and experiencing new places was something that she only wished she could have more time to enjoy. Then again, what was stopping her? As she scrolled back to the **About You** question, she wondered about the vastness of Canada and all the places she'd promised herself she'd visit and hadn't. It's not too late yet, she decided.

Carefree and home-loving, she typed into the blank field. **Domestic goddess loves to entertain family and friends – all welcome to sample my exquisite home-cooked dishes.**

Charlotte smiled at Mia's profile. Domestic goddess couldn't have been further from the truth. She didn't even venture as far as adding water to a packet mix! Home baking where Charlotte was concerned consisted of a trip to the local delicatessen or cake shop. But Mia was of a different variety. Mia had talents of her own. She ignored the flashing icon requesting a profile picture. That would remain blank. A faceless persona – perfect to pursue Philip Lord.

Philip Lord had exploded into her life when he'd taken over as Branch Manager in the bank she'd worked for on South Mall, Cork. Recognising her potential and encouraging her to strive toward increased responsibility, on a professional level he'd been enormously influential in her life. Her career had lifted to great heights and, with his encouragement and support, she'd met increasing success every step of the way, evolving from one of the lowest paid clerks to a position equalling that of Assistant Manager. An astute Philip had deftly organised every competition and hurdle she'd jumped.

But with elation came one very prominent downside. The physical attraction was one-sided. And despite Philip's handsome good looks, his toned physique and easy charm, Charlotte despised him. The way he stood too close made her skin crawl but she hid it well. She'd looked forward to the day they'd take separate paths in the banking world, but greed made her hold out for the final few steps on the promotion ladder, a decision she'd had plenty of time to regret. Progressing to managerial if not directorship level was her ultimate ambition, her interest in anything else secondary while she was on the road to accomplishment.

Pouring a glass of her favourite white wine, she wondered about her nemesis. Unusual names were easier to find – less of them. Charlotte had barely brought her drink to her lips when Philip's face appeared on her screen, his sleazy grin exactly as she remembered. Clicking on his photograph, she held her breath while his profile appeared on screen.

She pulled the laptop on to her knees, filled with a mixture of intrigue and disgust as she read through his personal details. His single status wasn't surprising. His wife had obviously seen the light and left him to his own devices.

She clicked to view his photographs, disappointed when access was denied. He only shared with people he was connected to on Facebook. Damn, she thought, clicking to add him as a friend. "Let's see how long it will take Philip to befriend Mia!"

Needing distraction, she scanned the material she'd printed in the library, content in the knowledge that few conditions applied to Polly and the terms she'd applied to her will. The date she'd signed it was a factor but other than that, she couldn't see any major grounds for overturning her decision to leave it to Kieran, despite her specific set of terms and conditions.

Polly's ownership of the property wasn't questionable, at least as far as Charlotte knew. Questioning her mental state appeared to be the only option applicable. Dad would have a fit if Mum and Beth even tried to go down that route, Charlotte thought, glancing at the clock.

Then the phone rang. Definitely someone from home at this hour, she groaned.

"Hi, Beth," she said, sitting cross-legged on the couch.

Beth began to tell her about the responses to her website and Charlotte's thoughts drifted back to the question of the will.

"So what do you think?"

"Sorry, Beth, I didn't catch that."

"Just wondering if you'd help me with a response to the enquiries?"

"No problem. Forward them and I'll look at them while we're talking."

Opening the email account on her laptop, her Facebook page disappeared from view and her sister's correspondence appeared in the Inbox.

"Promising," she said. "I like that one wanting to hire it for a birthday party. A marquee's the solution there."

"You really think so?"

"Look, read what it says –" Charlotte's sentence caught in her throat as a pop-up message appeared on her screen. Unable to resist a peek, she changed between screens, gasping when she realised Philip Lord had accepted her request. Her body trembled, her mouth dried and her pulse raced at the base of her throat, Beth's voice going unheard on the line.

"Charlotte, are you listening to me? This is a long-distance call!"

"Sorry, Beth, I'm distracted. What is it you were asking me?"

Her sister repeated her questions and Charlotte responded as best she could, finding a logical solution to all apart from the financial issue. "Take part payment in advance if they're willing to go ahead with the booking. Asking for 60% isn't exorbitant in the current environment, getting the balance on the day of their event. That way, you won't be out of pocket for very long and will have some compensation for cancellations."

"Are you still contemplating a visit home?" Beth ventured.

Philip's eyes bored into Charlotte's – even if it was from a 15-inch screen – bringing a flood of distressing reminders, particularly those of their last meeting and the evil threats being bandied about the boardroom.

"I'll have to check if I can get time off," she improvised, "but I'll let you know. And in the meantime I'll help in whatever way I can from here."

"Okay, thanks. One last thing, Mum's been on to Seth about the will."

"Seth! How is he?" she asked. She hadn't been expecting Slimy Seth (as she'd nick-named him years before) to be dragged into this. A clever move on her mother's part but not good for Kieran, she knew. Her uncle's incredible ability to turn even the most difficult situation to his advantage could seriously endanger Kieran's right to sign on the dotted line.

She'd have to intervene, offer to mediate with Seth if there was any chance of her keeping a step ahead and cutting him off before he had the opportunity to do serious damage. God damn it, this was turning into a complicated charade, one she mightn't be able to manipulate quite as easily as she'd first believed, particularly with her devious uncle involved.

"He was full of bright ideas for Mum, although I can't say I like the sound of them, Lottie, to be honest."

"Really?" She glanced at the time. "Will I call you back, Beth? That way we can share the cost of this conversation."

"Please," Beth agreed and disconnected.

Unable to resist the temptation to check Philip's page before returning the call, Charlotte was instantly engrossed. He's still in banking, she thought, although not where we worked. Typically, his friends were mostly female. Her eyes opened wide when she recognised a few familiar names. "Damn him!" she said. Mud hadn't stuck for very long. With a sinking heart, she logged out of Mia's account, unable to put herself through any more home truths. He had come out unscathed while she had to recreate a version of herself in a brand-new country.

Draining her wineglass, she went to get a refill, standing at the window and staring at the twinkling Toronto lights, her fingers undoing the button of her pyjamas and tracing the jagged scar on her chest, tears falling on her cheeks.

"Oh shit," she said after a few minutes, running her sleeve across her cheeks.

She had almost forgotten Beth.

"About time too," was Beth's greeting when she answered on the first ring.

Instead of inventing an excuse, Charlotte picked up their conversation where they'd left it. "So, what exactly has Seth got in mind?"

Listening to an account of her uncle's proposal, she closed her eyes in dread. How the hell am I going to intercept a geriatrician's report? Would it be enough to relay her knowledge of the bogus report to the solicitor? She jotted down as many details as possible, her gaze straying to the laptop, longing to slide into Mia's life in place of her own. Looking around the pristine apartment, she tried to imagine a different lifestyle, one filled with fun and love, a family unit – like the one described by the librarian. What would it feel like? Closing her eyes she tried to imagine trading places with Mia, swapping one life for another, obliterating all else and easing into a world of nappy changes, play dates and school runs. If only it were that easy. If only.

"Has Mum said any more about it to Dad?"

"They're barely speaking. He doesn't want to know apparently."

"I'll give Seth a call for an update." The lightness in her tone belied the heaviness in her heart.

"And you'll forward a few sample responses to those emails I sent you too?"

"I'll do it straight away," Charlotte promised, then asked her sister for her uncle's number, hoping a call would lift the feelings of desperation that had settled over her.

She rang him straight away.

"Uncle Seth! Charlotte here," she said, feigning a sweetness to the old codger even though she didn't trust a word that came out of his mouth.

"Dear God, girl, aren't you on the other side of the Atlantic?"

She met his sarcasm head on. "Sure am but we have phones over here too."

"And you only thought to use it now!"

He's no fool, she thought, picking her words carefully and enquiring about his health and golf handicap in that order.

"Not on the course as much as I'd like these days. And you? Taking Toronto by storm, I'm sure?"

She laughed, genuine this time. "Making my stamp in a very small pond."

"Want to tell me why you called?"

"Mum's been hankering on about this will business. She said you're in the driving seat on our behalf."

"Setting a few things in motion. The objection has already been lodged. Waiting for a response."

"Using what grounds?"

"Sharp as ever, my young niece!"

Charlotte was impatient. "Sharper," she retorted, reminding herself to mask her eagerness to find out what was going on.

"Polly's sanity is the easiest route but to safeguard I've planted a few seeds of doubt for the solicitor in relation to ownership too. Distract her while my acquaintances work on the medical records."

She took a sharp intake of breath. He was devious. "But surely full ownership reverted to her when her husband drowned?"

"The body never turned up, conveniently making things a little more complex."

Charlotte gulped, feeling an unfamiliar rush of sympathy for her aunt, imagining her heartache as she'd waited all those years. "I'd forgotten that," she admitted. "It must have been a dreadful time for her."

"She survived! And her life turned out okay afterwards." Seth's tone was mysterious.

She could hear another phone ringing in the background. "I'll let you get that," she offered, glad of the excuse to break off. She had more than enough to think about.

Chapter 21

Jess's phone rang, the sound of the vacuum-cleaner drowning out the ring tone as she hurried through her cleaning routine to try and get it all done before collecting Greg from school. She moved from room to room in Number 4, letting the cleaner do its work sucking up dust and crumbs, bits of food that Greg dropped as he moved around the house with a lopsided plate in his hand, and so much sand that she wondered if there was any left on the beach. While she was humming a tune and remembering Greg's excitement the previous day, the ringing phone remained unheard.

She dragged the vacuum upstairs to clean her bedroom, Greg's room and the bathroom floor. She wouldn't bother with the other room – it wasn't as if it was ever used any more. Even Greg avoided it. Only the day before, when he'd returned from his trip to the beach with Kieran, running around the house with his arms stretched wide either side as he pretended to be the kite Kieran had promised to buy him, he still avoided that room, despite it being larger with plenty of 'flying space'.

She smiled as she watched the sand being swallowed into the vacuum cleaner. He'd had such fun with Kieran the previous afternoon, his eyes bright with excitement when they'd returned. He'd babbled on and on while she'd bathed him, his voice rising as he told her about the massive tunnel Kieran had helped him dig.

"I swear, Mum, Kieran thinks it could almost go down to Australia!"

"Koala bears and kangaroos will be burrowing through it in the morning then?"

"Don't be silly! We're not finished digging yet."

She moved from room to room, remembering how he'd run around the house, full of beans as though it were first thing in the morning and not nine o'clock on a school night!

But Greg's good humour had disappeared overnight. He'd been stubborn and difficult when she'd called him for breakfast, arguing and doing his utmost to skip school. Tired and irritable, he'd fought with her from the moment he'd opened his eyes.

Her thoughts turned to Kieran. She already found it impossible to ignore the excitement she felt around him. His presence made her forget about everything that had come before. Her heart soared every time he was in close proximity. Loath as she was to admit it, she was well aware that the feelings erupting inside her resembled those of a love-sick teenager.

Jess knew she was a poor substitute for a real daddy figure, had been from the time he'd reached toddler age. He was a typical boy, loving dirt and mess, seeing an adventure in every game and loving being outdoors. It frustrated him when she wouldn't allow him to explore things further – particularly when it came to worms and wriggly insects and how many he could poke out of the ground. He complained strongly when she pulled him away. No matter how hard she tried to fill that particular void in his life and be macho about things she detested, she failed miserably.

He craved male company – no doubt of that in her mind. She had seen enough evidence in the short time since Kieran had come knocking on their door. The dynamic between her and her son had changed. Oh, she knew he still adored her. She would always be his number one – that wasn't concerning her. But he'd found another adult, one who understood his maleness, appreciated the rough and tumble boys thrived upon. All to the better where little Greg was concerned. And Jess couldn't deny she agreed. But would it last? Would Kieran stick around?

She changed the attachment on the vacuum cleaner and set about getting into the difficult-to-reach places, wondering how on earth spiders managed to create so many cobwebs between her cleaning stints. She hated cleaning, hated the monotony of doing the same thing over and over and seeing very little reward – at least not once Greg returned from school and undid her hard work.

As she stooped to retrieve one of Greg's many dinosaurs from the bedroom floor, she accepted with a pang of remorse that dinosaurs of the plastic variety would be the nearest she got to uncovering history for quite some time. Looking at the grumpy face of Tyrannosaurus Rex, she couldn't help grinning. It reminded her of the scowl on her son's face as they had approached the school gates but, no matter how much she loved him, there were days she'd have given anything to be on an archaeological dig, exploring the present for evidence of the past, spending endless hours searching and trawling through earth, researching every aspect until she'd uncovered its place in history. Delving into the world of archaeology had instilled a permanent sense of anticipation, anxiety about the ruins to be uncovered yet a heart-thumping excitement at the treasures waiting to be explored.

She disconnected the vacuum cleaner and stored it in the closet on the landing, glad to see the back of it for another while.

Downstairs she popped a few ice cubes in a glass, turned on the tap and let the cold water flow over them. Filling it to the brim, she brought it to her lips and took a long refreshing drink. Her gaze strayed to the back garden, the bright sunshine inviting as she took her drink outside. She sat on the wooden seat her father had made, a wave of loneliness sweeping over her as she remembered him calling it a loveseat. How she wished he hadn't left, walked out of her life abruptly, unable to take his wife's browbeating any longer. What a difference it would make to her son's life, how he'd enjoy living with a loving and fun grandfather! She ran a hand over the seat, the wood rough in parts after a severe winter.

"You'll bring your boyfriends here," her father had teased, laughing when the young Jess had swatted his suggestion away in embarrassment.

She'd never been sure who he'd had in mind as he'd nailed and glued the pieces of wood together – not once had she seen her parents sit alongside one another in the house, never mind in the garden! Getting older and more aware of her parents' relationship, she'd seldom witnessed displays of affection, animosity being in regular supply instead.

Gazing at the array of blooming shrubs and flowering plants, she admired the legacy her father had left behind. The endless hours and patience he'd invested had resulted in lavish blooms and magnificent colour. She tried her best to keep it neat and weed-free, but her best efforts fell short of the masterpiece it had been when he'd still lived there. He'd spoken about the plants as though they were real-life people who would respond to his nurturing. And with little exception, they thrived under his expert care.

He'd taught her a certain amount and left her hungry for more, encouraging her budding interest in nature and sowing the seeds for whatever lay in store for her future. She accepted his nuggets of advice, seeing them as words of wisdom, treasuring his gentle manner and often wishing that her overbearing mother would disappear and then it would only be the two of them.

She sipped her water and pondered on her parents' relationship, one she'd never understand, but it taught her not to settle for anything less than a loving relationship. Anything else could be worked at but without love there could be nothing.

Kieran's voice drifted over the hedge, his words lost in the breeze, a flutter travelling the length of her body as she imagined his tanned arms and legs. She wished she could stop fantasising about meeting his lips with hers, her mouth drying as she imagined his tongue gently exploring her mouth. She hugged her arms around her body, the glass cold between her fingertips.

Had her parents started out with that form of lustful excitement, she wondered, pulling her feet up under her as she remembered her mother's cruel jibes at her father's love of nature, berating him with snide remarks. Jess's tolerance of her mother's nastiness had reduced with the onset of her teens. Invariably, she'd jumped to her father's defence, suffering the wrath of her mother's sharp tongue for her trouble.

"She doesn't mean it," her dad had said to Jess on numerous occasions, after she'd been severely scolded for back-answering her mother.

"Why do you defend her? She treats you like crap! Why put up with it?"

"Jess, why don't we go and have a walk on the beach? Your mother's tired, needs a rest." He'd eased the blow of his wife's cruelty time after time, doing his utmost to excuse her behaviour – and, as soon as she was out of view and earshot, winking at his daughter and restoring her confidence with his words of sincerity. As a young child she'd accepted his explanation and let go her anger and frustration towards her mother. But in her teens, particularly in the year before she'd left for college, Jess had argued more and more with her mother, refusing to accept her father's feeble attempt to excuse her time after time.

"Dad, don't even bother any more," she said to him one day as he worked in the garden. "You might be prepared to put up with her appalling put-downs, but I'm having nothing else to do with her."

"Henry's able to overlook things, why can't you?"

"She doesn't give him grief, Dad! And he has never once stood up to her."

Her father only sighed, weary from the continuous arguing between his wife and daughter.

"Soon I'll be in college, so until then I'm ignoring her. And if you have any sense you'll do the same. I pity you being stuck with her for the rest of your life. At least I can get away. What on earth possessed you to marry her in the first place?"

She'd known as soon as the words had left her mouth that she'd overstepped acceptable boundaries. Her father was old-fashioned in his thinking. This time there were no platitudes from her dad.

"Jessica, stop it! That is not how family should behave toward one another. I won't have you speak about your mother like that!"

She approached him and crouched next to him where he knelt. "I'm sorry," she said, putting her arm around him in an awkward hug. "Take a break. I'll get you something to drink. Come sit on the bench, Dad. It's such a nice day and you've worked for ages."

And there, as on so many previous occasions, they had spent treasured hours together, away from the watchful and envious eye of Jess's mother.

Inheriting her father's grave attention to detail and despite her difficulty with complex mathematics, Jess had come top of her Leaving Certificate year, gaining a coveted archaeology place in Cambridge and excited about the prospect of escaping her mother's clutches.

She remembered her joy as she'd opened her college acceptance letter. While she was excited about leaving the homestead to branch out on her own, he was suffering the grief of a parent watching his adored daughter take an important step without him at her side.

Her years in Cambridge resembled those of secondary school, with her performance each year surpassing the one that came before, her achievements acknowledged by every one of her lecturers, their interest in her academic prowess proven over and over by the number of times her name was put forward for some prime opportunities in her field. Their encouragement boosted her confidence. Her results were amazing, a deserved testament to her dedication and hard work, as well as the sacrifices she'd made to her social life. Offers came her way even before her results were officially announced, her grades guaranteed as far as her lecturers were concerned, seeing her as a credit to their college's reputation.

Clutching her coveted degree, she was on the cusp of change, her life opening like the petals of one of her father's roses, delving into pastures new (or old in her archaeological world) and exploring what she'd spent four years training and studying for at Cambridge University.

Securing several job offers – mostly in the UK, she thought long and hard before making her final choice. Opting for the archaeological route rather than anthropology, she was excited at the prospect of holding down a real job, deciding to take a trip home to Pier Road before immersing herself into her new job. The time had come to join the real world.

But she couldn't have anticipated the amount of change and challenge awaiting her, eventually witnessing her father's sudden departure from the family home the most heartbreaking of all. She'd cried bitter tears after he'd hurried from the house with little more than a change of clothes and a toothbrush in his small holdall. He'd reached breaking point, his wife's incessant insults no longer bearable.

Chapter 22

Kieran picked his way through the mess in the shed, cursing aloud as he ripped his T-shirt on a protruding nail. The place was a health hazard! He'd made several attempts to clear it out, distracted on every occasion and shutting the door again, finding the mammoth task overwhelming. Already into May, the days were long and he'd reacquainted himself with the beach, spending hours surfing the waves and chatting on the beach with some of the locals. Greg had become a regular visitor, slipping through the hedge that separated their back gardens. The little guy was inquisitive, bombarding him with questions on every subject as they passed a football to each other, using their sweatshirts as goal posts and taking turns as they lined up for a shot on scoring.

"Ouch, jeez, what the hell was that?" He cursed aloud when he stubbed his toe against the metal frame of an ancient wheelbarrow. Wearing sandals isn't very clever, he thought, bending down to rub his big toe.

He dragged the barrow through the pile of rubble.

Kieran continued clearing out, disappointed when he didn't come across anything of great interest or value. Sweat pumped through him, his T-shirt and knee-length shorts clinging to his skin as he traipsed in and out of the garden with armfuls of junk. It was so tempting to abandon the job and change into his surfing gear. The sun was making an appearance, a slight breeze in the air.

Sneezing, he moved back inside the dusty shed, determined to get through the rest of the stuff as quickly as he could. He grabbed four paint tins, a bucket of roller-sleeves and outdoor paintbrushes and, turning the barrow up once more, he threw them into it. It would make it easier to shift them when the time came. He'd contact the skip hire company and have them deliver a skip. He'd have everything ready in advance so it shouldn't be there long enough to cause too much inconvenience or raise objection by the neighbours if it attracted unwanted attention.

The mess in the garden was another day's work. Staring at it now it was impossible not to remember the hours Polly spent on her hands and knees tending to flower beds. His job had been to push the mower around, receiving a little cash from her for his trouble. It must have been tough on her seeing it like this, he thought, supposing it had been quite some time since she'd tended it herself. He'd been surviving on the money he'd collected from the Post Office, very little left of it now. Too busy lazing around he'd put minimal effort into sorting through the house, failing so far to find the cash that was supposedly lying around.

He leaned against the shed and took a proper look around, comparing the dishevelled garden to Jess's next door. Hers was one to be proud of, one that could be enjoyed. She'd already had him over for an impromptu barbeque, teasing him that eating outdoors would be a nice reminder of his time in Australia. He smiled as he remembered the evening, Greg almost ruining the meal with a bad football pass, his aim toppling over the barbeque. Luckily Kieran had managed to grab it before any damage was done. But aside from that, they'd shared a laugh, her infectious giggles on the increase after a few beers, her eyes dancing giddily as they rekindled old memories. And if Greg hadn't monopolised his company for the evening and refused to go to bed until the party was truly over and Kieran had left, who knows how it would have ended?

Looking around him, he toyed with the idea of returning the invitation. Although it'd be difficult to relax with a beer in the mess he was looking at right now – not that he considered himself exceptionally fussy – but the prospect of inviting Jess over altered his level of interest and pride. And cooking outside wasn't the only entertainment he had in mind, the stir of desire he felt in her presence becoming more prevalent with each meeting. So far he'd held back, had kept his male instincts firmly under wraps, alien behaviour for Kieran. But Jess was different. The trusting look in her eyes and her underlying sense of vulnerability made him crave her all the more, but also instilled a fierce sense of protectiveness inside him. He unscrewed the top of his water bottle and took a long slug, spluttering and choking at the unexpected boom of a man's voice in his ear.

"What the hell do you think you're doing?"

"And what gives you the right to creep around here?" a red-faced Kieran retorted, his voice breaking between bouts of coughing as he tried to get his breath back. He struggled to get his heart rate back to normal, eyeing the stranger closely.

"You're trespassing on property that doesn't belong to you!" the man said.

Kieran stared at the tall sandy-haired stranger, rage building inside him.

"And you're telling me this back garden belongs to *you*?" he replied, replacing the lid on the water bottle and tossing it on to the grass.

"No, but I am a friend of the owner."

Kieran calmed a little. A friend. What friend, he couldn't help wondering, eyeing the stranger and finding it difficult to put an age on him. Older than me for sure but probably not much over forty.

"Look, I wasn't expecting anyone to be here. I thought you were a burglar when I saw you clearing out the shed." The visitor ran a hand through his hair and fiddled with his glasses, hazel eyes curious as he waited for Kieran's response to his explanation.

"Why don't we start this conversation again," said Kieran, "with you telling me exactly who you are and why you're snooping around?"

The other man eyed him warily, nodding his head and making to extend his right hand but obviously thinking better of it. "I'm John Kilmichael, a close acquaintance of Polly's." He shoved his hands in his trouser pockets.

Kieran stared in shock, trying to absorb his uninvited guest's announcement. *John Kilmichael* – the name went around in his head, Polly's son, his cousin. The tall handsome man standing in front of him bore no resemblance to either his aunt or the ogre his father had described. 'He's bad news . . . get rid of him . . .' – he remembered Frank's words clearly. I should have pushed him for more detail, he thought, curiosity building inside him.

"Kieran Dulhooly, Polly's nephew," he offered after a short pause.

"She's mentioned you," the man said, nodding his head slowly.

Kieran noticed the muscles on his tanned arms, a man in very good shape, someone who took pride in his appearance, confident too if his stance was anything to go by and definitely attractive to the female sex.

"I can't say she's ever mentioned you to me though," Kieran threw back at him, hoping to glean some more information about his uninvited guest.

"Are you the guy who was travelling?"

"That's me."

"You're Frank's son?"

"Sure am. Have you met Dad?"

John nodded. "Once or twice. We've had a few brief conversations. Polly speaks very highly of him, has him on a pedestal so to speak."

His tone says it all, Kieran thought. It's very obvious he's not sharing that opinion! "Have you travelled far?" he asked.

John brought his gaze to the items Kieran had dumped on the grass, studying them as though they were items of great value. "I'm a sales rep, living in Dublin. Pass through now and again and always give herself a call." He jerked his head towards the house. "Hard to visit at all without getting an appetite for her home baking."

What's that supposed to mean, Kieran wondered, the response adding to his unease, his senses on high alert. How comfortable was he with Polly? Had he got his feet firmly under the table? John's familiarity irked. Why, without the truth, would a man like him want the company of a woman over twenty years his senior? It still made little sense to Kieran. A picture of his aunt's corpse came to mind. Although a good-looking woman in her day, the years had been unkind. She'd aged a lot even since his last visit home.

"How long since you've been to see her?" he asked.

"Rang the doorbell last time I was down here but no reply. Tried calling too but she wasn't answering her phone. I was hoping she'd be around today?"

Kieran shook his head. "You've missed her again, I'm afraid. But maybe I can help? I'm staying here at the moment." His last sentence was deliberate, letting John know the house wasn't vacant. No harm in sending out that message.

"Nothing in particular. I'd like to catch up with her, see how she is. I'll wait if you don't mind." He looked at Kieran expectantly. "Or I can call back in an hour or two if that's better?"

Kieran reached to the ground and picked up the water bottle, unscrewing the cap again and taking another slug, his brain whirring. If his father's warning wasn't spinning around his head, John Kilmichael would probably have been somebody he'd have chatted normally with and explained about Polly's demise. He was polite, friendly and had started out with Polly's interests at heart when he'd thought she was being burgled. He searched for a response, torn between following his gut instinct and heeding his father.

"She's away for a few days with a local group of seniors," he said, fiddling with the top of the bottle to avoid meeting John's eye, his lie prompted by the memory of a group of senior citizens he'd noticed getting on a minibus that morning.

"Really?" John shook his head, a grin on his face. "That's a bit of a turnaround. She always said she'd hate to be stuck with a gang of old fogies, mocking them in a kindly fashion, and swearing she'd be on her death bed before she'd be caught playing bingo and whist in the afternoons!"

Kieran laughed along with him, agreeing with him but not admitting it, impressed at his perception of his aunt. "Leave your number and I'll pass on the message." He'd have to talk to Frank as soon as John left. Otherwise he'd be spinning a web of lies that would be impossible to memorise.

"Polly has my number," John said, then swivelled his head around at the sound of a child's voice.

"Kieran, want a game of ball?" A small fair head appeared through the back gate.

"Sure, come on in," he invited, delighted with the interruption. Greg couldn't have timed it better.

"You'll tell her I called so?" John repeated. "Tell her I'll be looking forward to meeting up with her soon."

"As soon as she returns from this trip," Kieran stated, struck by a longing to talk to her and ask her what the hell was going on. In that moment, he'd have given anything for his aunt to make an appearance, a real one though, not a ghostly apparition! "Sorry you've had a wasted trip, John."

"Not to worry. As I said, I was in the neighbourhood." He nodded in Greg's direction. "Your opponent is keen," he commented, watching Greg placing two cracked flowerpots on the grass, obviously creating a goal space.

"Going to play for United, aren't you, Greg?" Kieran was glad of the distraction.

Greg beamed, looking around him for the football and spotting it under the hedge.

Watching John Kilmichael leave by the side entrance, his gait jerked a niggle of familiarity in Kieran's mind. Who else walks like that? Throwing their right leg out to the side a little as they walk? Who is it he reminds me of?

"Who's that man?" Greg asked, picking up a football from under the hedge, demanding his attention. "*Catch!*"

"His name is John Kilmichael but other than that I have no idea!" Although I've a feeling I'll be seeing more of him, he thought, running to grab the football before it bounced against the kitchen window. He tossed it back to Greg, laughing when it rolled between his legs. "*Goal!*"

"Not fair. I didn't know we'd started yet," Greg pouted.

"I'm so sorry, Kieran," Jess announced, her head appearing over the hedge. "Is he annoying you again?"

"Not at all, leave him. I'm due a break from cleaning!"

"If you're sure."

"Positive," Kieran assured her, meeting her smile with his as she gave him a little wave and disappeared.

Later that afternoon when Jess called Greg home for his tea, Kieran returned to clearing out the shed, going through the random selection of items with less enthusiasm than earlier, his thoughts fixed on John Kilmichael and the complicated tale he'd spun him. Resurrecting his aunt from the dead would only last so long, he thought, wiping the sweat from his forehead. A tidy shed for his day's work, a confused mind for the night ahead no doubt.

Chapter 23

Frank Dulhooly shook two tablets from the container and popped them into his mouth, following them down with a long slug of water. Staring through the kitchen window, he willed the tablets to kick into action and dull the throbbing in his head. He'd had a blazing row with Marian the previous evening, the worst they'd had in a while. His head still ached, the sharp insults they'd exchanged difficult to forget. Their marriage had always been tumultuous, neither slow at holding back, their incompatibility impossible to overcome.

Part of him regretted holding back the truth as they'd traded sharp retorts. If he'd answered her questions about his meeting with Carl honestly instead of being cagey and hesitant, he'd have had a peaceful night's sleep and not a night of restless tossing and turning. It was no surprise he'd woken up with a throbbing head!

"I'm off to meet *our* daughter," Marian snapped, entering the kitchen. "See if I can help her even if her own father is working against her."

He didn't bother to turn around and face his wife's wrath. There wasn't much point. Days would pass before she'd address him in a civil tone again. Sighing, he continued staring at the overgrown shrubbery and hedging, wishing he could channel his anger and frustration into putting shape on the garden. But failing health – not to mention the continued warnings he'd received from his cardiologist – no longer permitted him the luxury of breaking into any form of sweat. His gym regime had been seriously curtailed, the gentle programme created on his doctor's advice a paltry substitute for the stringent physical routine he had revelled in. Golf, also played at a slower pace, was as near as he got to relaxation these days. And of course he didn't need a medical professional to point out that stress was increasing his problems.

Marian knew nothing of his health issues, paying sparse attention to him or his activities – at least not that he'd noticed. Feeling particularly sorry for himself, he surmised that her only interest in him was the lifestyle he'd provided. There'll be money spent today, he mused, moving away from the window when the front door slammed behind his wife, followed by the distinctive rustle of gravel as she pulled her Range Rover away from the front door. Every row cost him dearly, her shopping fetish exacerbated by anger.

Damn woman and her unfounded accusations, he thought, still peeved by her taunts. Rubbing a hand over his temple, he failed to soothe his still-aching head. If anything it was worsening. Reaching for the receiver on the wall phone, he dialled his son-in-law's mobile number, deciding to tackle the thorny issue they'd discussed in the coffee shop. At least I'll have reason for a splitting migraine, he thought! Gritting his teeth, he inhaled deeply and barked a gruff hello when Carl's cool tones came down the line.

"Carl, I've been thinking about your proposal and I'd like to get things moving right now."

"Yeah?"

"No point waiting around."

"Oh, right?"

Frank recognised the surprise in the younger man's voice, taking pleasure in shocking him. How dare Marian accuse him of failing his daughter? His children were everything to him but that didn't mean they always had to get their own way. He wondered how she'd behave if the inheritance was coming from her side of the family. Very differently, he suspected.

"Before we take this further, I want to reiterate what we agreed."

"I thought we'd been over it enough by now," Carl returned without hesitation. How many more times, he thought, his father-in-law's insistence at repeating every detail grating on his nerves. But he wasn't in a position to check him, needing his assistance to guarantee Ed the peace of mind he deserved.

"You walk away from Beth, lock, stock and barrel."

He heard his son-in-law's sharp intake of breath, mistaking exasperation for concern. Were there still some feelings left between his daughter and Carl, he wondered? There certainly hadn't been any grand gestures of affection between them, at least not in his company and certainly not from the snippets Marian had shared with him. What he'd witnessed recently had been a disturbing reminder of his relationship with Marian, resentment festering between them, snapped words and venomous looks. Wishing more than anything he'd heeded Polly's repeated – if wasted – words of warning when she'd begged him to reconsider marrying Marian, he continued his conversation with Carl, hoping to save Beth from a similar fate, enabling her to get out while she still had the best years of her life to enjoy.

"What if Beth wants us to have another chance? Shouldn't that decision be between me and my wife?"

"Not if you want me to realise your brother's final wish."

Frank waited, unperturbed by the lengthening silence, making no effort to fill it, not a bit surprised when Carl acquiesced with little argument.

"Okay. Once everything's in place and it's literally in black and white on legal documents, I'll move out of Goleen."

Frank gritted his teeth. Carl's tone was a little too smug and spoilt for his liking. "Not just out of the house and the area, out of the country." Ireland's too small, he thought. Beth deserves a fresh start, one he'd see that she would receive.

"But –"

"That's the deal, Carl. You can return to France, or wherever the hell takes your fancy. I don't need to know your chosen location, once you're out of Beth's life."

"But what about –" he tried again.

"I'll sort it," Frank insisted, interpreting his son-in-law's concerns. Lodging enough money in a bank account to get him as far away as possible would be a small price to pay. With a bit of luck and co-operation from the right people, he'd be gone by Christmas. "I'll need documentation of the case so far, copies of whatever Ed gave the authorities, dates and times of investigative interviews and anything else you can think of."

"Should we meet to discuss it in more detail?"

"No need," Frank said. The less contact he had with his daughter's husband, the better it suited him. "I'll be in touch when I need to speak with you. And I'll pay Ed a visit too, hear the saga from the horse's mouth so to speak."

"And what do I do in the meantime?"

"Put one foot – or hand – out of line, particularly where Beth's concerned, and the deal's off."

"What if Beth wants me to stay, Frank?"

"I don't think you're in a position to throw idle threats around, Carl."

The continuous dial tone rang in Frank's ear. His son-in-law had hung up. Ignorant so-and-so, he thought, replacing the receiver and sitting down to think through his strategy.

French law was a minefield and the press there were vultures, sinking their teeth in a story and tearing at it until all life had been sucked away. This was how they had destroyed recent events in Ed's fashion house, bringing it to its knees overnight, attacking its reputation and tarnishing it beyond repair. Frank admired and appreciated Ed's depth of devotion to his business. Building it up from scratch, applying every breath and ounce of passion on it as others bestowed them upon their families, its disintegration ripped through his heart like the piercing pain of grief. Too advanced in his illness to tackle the press and judicial system, he had come to Ireland to die. Begging Carl to continue his fight and defend his company's reputation, he'd outlined his two final wishes: the first to have his name cleared and his designer label restored to its rightful place on the fashion A-list, the second to die with his brother at his side.

Frank took his mobile phone from his pocket and scrolled through the list of contacts, dithering over his best approach. Carl had neither the means nor resources to deal with such a huge task. His efforts failing miserably, he'd approached his father-in-law. Inviting me to the coffee shop to ask for help must have severely dented his pride, Frank conceded. They'd never shared a very close relationship, Frank allergic to Carl's cocky attitude and not afraid to show it. His finger still on the scroll button on his contacts list, he stopped at a name he hadn't been in touch with for a very long time – an industrial-espionage private detective.

The last he'd heard through the proverbial grapevine, Mags was divorced and working around the clock. Could she provide the key to my problems, Frank wondered, his finger hovering over the green button to dial her number. If she answered and agreed to co-operate, she could be his fast-track to the nub of the issue, saving him time wading through layers of red tape. Time being scarce for Ed, there wasn't a moment to waste. He stared at the phone, his heart rate increasing as he punched in the first few digits of Mags' number. Ridiculous at my age, he thought with a wry smile. One digit left to press, he tossed the phone onto the island unit and left the kitchen to pour a stiff brandy, ignoring doctor's orders and unconcerned that the clock still hadn't struck noon.

Olivia Jacobs pulled open the top drawer of her filing cabinet, flicking through the sections until she came upon the file for Number 5 Pier Road. She returned to her desk, opened the folder and scanned the array of documents carefully, refreshing her memory on every detail. Pauline Digby had been specific in her instructions, had anticipated a flurry of confusion over her decision and put as many safeguards in place as possible. Even at that, however, Olivia still had a process to follow and despite best-laid plans these situations invariably presented exceptional circumstances, an angle that hadn't been considered and evidence that might well be enough to rewrite history.

The recent objections wouldn't have come as a surprise to Polly. And despite anticipating as much, Olivia knew the dear old lady would still have been hurt by the insinuations. Tough as she appeared, Polly's staunch independence paramount, intuition led Olivia to believe that the older lady's hurt would cut deep if she were reading the health appraisal being issued against her now. Questioning her sanity, alluding to a long period of time where her brain's processing ability had failed gradually, would undoubtedly infuriate her.

Dialling 0 for the Reception desk, Olivia chewed on the inside of her lip, instilled with a sense of responsibility to protect her client's pride and dignity. "Amy, can you come in here a moment, please?"

Amy appeared within seconds, tottering in high heels that added at least four inches to her height, her working attire of tight-fitting white shirt and knee-length black pencil skirt impeccable as usual.

"Can you scrutinise these medical records for me, please? Compare them against the dates and conditions outlined in this geriatrician's report. Highlight the discrepancies and drop the list into me when you're finished. I'll contact the geriatrician directly once I've gathered my facts."

Amy nodded and took both listings, arching an eyebrow when she read the client's name, a vivid and fond memory of the sole beneficiary coming to mind. "Wasn't this a straightforward case?"

"You're working here long enough to know the answer to that," Olivia smiled. "Close the door on your way out, please."

Once the younger girl had disappeared, Olivia reread the second objection, this one more complex than the first. Pauline hadn't anticipated this one, she thought, frowning as she got up from her chair and took a law book from her bookshelf. At least she didn't make any mention of it to me, but then, she thought with a grim smile, there's nothing quite like inheritance to bring all sorts from the closet. It had been a while since she'd dealt with illegitimacy and the inheritance laws surrounding it. Rights had changed but she needed to brush up on her knowledge to ensure she represented her client's interest to the best of her ability. The evidence was there. Now it was her job to ensure Polly's heartfelt decision to provide her nephew with a home and a source of financial stability remained in place. Though she hated letting emotions colour professional decisions, she couldn't deny that it rankled that Polly hadn't divulged her innermost secret, considering she'd relied upon her judgement. Not the most sensible pieces of information to withhold under the circumstances, as it put her other decisions in jeopardy.

Chapter 24

In the middle of the night, Marian felt the bedroom close in around her. Her dependency on nicotine was on the increase. Seth's progress with the legal process was slow, making her anxious and jittery and unable to relax. He'd lodged the objection with Polly's solicitor, had sent Marian a copy of the letter. Reading every sentence a few times, the cruel dishonest facts filled her with serious apprehension rather than the satisfaction she'd been expecting. But the letter would already have arrived in the solicitor's office so it was too late for regrets, a time instead to remain calm and hope for the best.

Lying in bed in the dark room, unable to sleep and craving a cigarette, she was haunted by an image of a grinning Polly Dulhooly, transported back to their first meeting in Marian's uncle's hotel.

Eight years her senior, Polly held the position of kitchen supervisor in the seaside hotel. Offered a summer job by her uncle, Marian had little interest in washing dishes or waiting tables but had accepted the position to put an end to her parents' nagging.

Arriving late on her first day, Marian had refused to remove her coral lipstick or wear a net over her long fair hair, delighting in getting Polly, her supervisor, into trouble. Confident her job was safe because she was the owner's niece, she made no effort to conform to hotel rules, her unruly behaviour thwarting Polly and reducing the standards of her precious kitchen. By the end of Marian's three-month stint, Polly had got into the habit of ignoring the owner's niece, leaving Marian off the hook on many occasions and withering her with murderous looks each time they came in contact. Their mutual loathing continued from that summer in the hotel, Marian's relationship with Polly's only brother Frank the final insult.

Turning on her side, the pillowcase crinkling against her cheek, she glanced at her husband of over thirty-five years and wondered, if he hadn't been called to the bar shortly after Seth had introduced them, where she would be right now. It's unlikely she'd have married him without his professional success. Their relationship would have fizzled out if he'd been stuck in a dead-end job. But relishing a taste of the finer lifestyle became an accessory she found difficult to let go. Their courtship was short, their wedding a lavish affair, their differing relationships with Polly a continuous point of contention. Returning from their honeymoon, however, Marian was enraged to discover her brother, Seth, had taken more than a fleeting interest in her new sister-in-law at their reception. Doing everything in her power to warn him against her, she offered little sympathy when inevitably he realised their unsuitability and had confessed to Marian that he'd had enough.

Twisting and turning and finding it impossible to get into a comfortable position, Marian eventually gave up and slid out from underneath the covers so she wouldn't wake Frank. Her eyes blurred as she focused on the green digits on the digital clock and groaned inwardly when she realised it was still only 3.00 a.m. Subtracting five hours made it 10.00 p.m. in Toronto, a good time to get Charlotte at home. Taking her pale pink robe from the end of the bed, she pulled it around her and went downstairs to make a hot drink and call her daughter.

Flipping from his side onto his back as soon as Marian had left the bedroom, Frank opened his eyes. He too had lain awake for hours, mulling over his recent conversation with Carl and wishing Beth hadn't witnessed their meeting. Hurting his daughter had never been his intention, quite the opposite in fact. The hurt in her eyes, the shock that registered on her face that day in the café had stayed with him. He pulled the quilt up under his chin, a sudden chill passing over him. He sincerely hoped he was doing the right thing. In time she might appreciate and understand his reasons for excluding her. Hearing Marian's muffled voice through the floor, he presumed she was calling Toronto. Her fixation with overturning the will was consuming her, her clandestine phone calls childish in his eyes. He licked his lips, his mouth dry. But he wouldn't go to the kitchen to get a drink of water, not being in the mood for confrontation with Marian. He'd been relieved when she'd stopped trying to persuade him to get involved, her assumption that he wasn't aware of what she was doing a source of mild amusement – a bit sad too if he were honest. Rolling over on his side once more, he buried his head in the pillow and smiled. Marian was building herself up for a very big fall, an unexpected surprise, one she could have avoided if she'd heeded his words of caution. She just didn't know it yet.

Chapter 25

Carl burst into the house, beads of sweat dripping off him, his body ready to collapse. It was the first time he'd exercised in quite a while. He had run around the perimeter of their grounds, appreciating its beauty as he hadn't done previously. Planning the best quad-bike route as he'd skirted the extremities, he imagined it would be easy to get in place, separating it from the paddock area to minimise any disturbance for the horses – hypothetical as it was for now. Must be the prospect of leaving that's making me nostalgic, he thought, opening the freezer and taking out a tray of ice cubes.

Buying the place had been Beth's idea. He'd gone along with it, caring little about their increasing debt and believing the auctioneer when he'd indicated the opportunity for resale. What a joke that was, he thought, banging the plastic tray to release the ice cubes, dropping them into a glass of water and refilling the tray before putting it back in the freezer.

"There are a few people calling to look at the stables later this morning."

Carl's glass hit against his teeth, his wife's arrival startling him. Conversation had been minimal since their meeting in the coffee shop, neither of them mentioning it directly, yet the incident remaining silently between them. Remembering Frank's stern warning, he bit back his retort and struggled to maintain a pleasant manner.

"I don't have plans if you want me to show them around?" he offered.

He noticed her raise an eyebrow.

"If you like. Or we could both meet them and discuss prices."

"Did you Google the going rate?"

She nodded. "Varies but I have a ballpark. I left the list by the computer if you want to take a look."

"Are you still contemplating the bike trail?"

She nodded. "I need more info on that one but I visited two to take a look. I'm waiting for insurance companies to get back to me. Some of the quotes are astronomical."

"It'll need a few mounds of earth to add a bit of adventure," he said, rinsing his glass and leaving it on the draining board to dry. "I'll have a go at it. No harm getting a bit of it done while you're waiting. I'll fence off the ring fort or we'll have the authorities on our backs. What do you think?"

She nodded again, her surprise evident. "I guess not. Funding's the issue as usual though."

He side-stepped the issue of money. "That brook at the end of the field should be included too, would be a shame not to take full advantage. And it'd be unique, something other trails wouldn't have. I'm sure I can dream up a bit of danger, let it be optional for some of the younger ones. What about the bikes? Have you thought about supplying them? Or is it just the route we'll provide?"

"We'll be lucky to pay the insurance for now. But maybe we could stretch to buying bikes in the future?"

"Up to you," he said, feeling her eyes upon him as he turned to leave. He wouldn't be around to see it develop. The deal he was striking up with her father would make sure of that.

Their civil conversation giving her the breakthrough she'd needed to finally broach the unmentionable, she called him back.

"What were you discussing with Dad that day in the coffee shop? You two have never had that much in common?"

Carl raised an eyebrow, her accusing tone irritating. "Why don't you ask him? You probably wouldn't believe my version anyway."

So much for thinking we'd reached some sort of amicable truce, Beth thought. Wanting to find out what was going on between her father and husband had been eating her up inside. But she didn't rise to his sarcasm, continuing with more direct questions instead.

"Carl, what's going on? Did you ask him to intervene with the bank for us even though he'd refused me already?"

"No." He didn't meet her eye. She hadn't mentioned the outcome of Polly's will to him. And he hadn't asked, their fraught relationship getting in the way of most conversations they'd had recently.

"Has it something to do with Ed? Please don't expect Dad to pay his bills!"

Carl's eyes darkened. "We've been over this, Beth. I'll do whatever it takes to help my brother."

"Regardless of dragging others down with you, including us?"

He spelt the situation out to her, delivering it in a slow and even fashion as though he were speaking to a small child. "Ed is dying, Beth. For the first time in my life, he needs my help and I won't fail him."

"Our help," she corrected him. "The decisions you're making affect both of us, increasing our own debts more and more."

"Frank and I have come to an arrangement."

"I bet it's one that benefits you!"

He leaned against the doorframe, his weariness evident in his stance. "I can't refuse, not after everything Ed's done for me. I owe him. It may be the last thing I can do to put his mind at ease. Don't expect me to refuse because it's not going to happen."

Beth's frustration was at saturation point. "And what about me, Carl? Don't you think you've got an outstanding debt of your own to consider? Don't I deserve some sort of recompense?"

He ran a hand over his face. "Let it go, Beth. I did what you wanted, coming to Ireland, supporting your decision to buy this monstrosity of a house."

"You had no choice but to leave the country! You were on the run from the French police. Still are, I might add. And as for this house, you made no objection at the time. It wasn't as if I dragged you to sign on the dotted line!"

He stared at her.

She stared back, swallowing the lump that rose in her throat, knowing tears weren't too far behind.

"My brother's dying." It was as if he'd pressed rewind and they were back at the beginning of their conversation once more, neither making progress convincing the other, nobody winning the argument.

"Ed wouldn't expect us to fork out money if he knew the truth about the vineyard. Why won't you swallow your pride and open up to him? Wouldn't it make you a better person?"

The look on her husband's face withered her inside.

"He wants to see you," he announced flatly. "Alone."

She looked startled. "On my own? Why?"

Carl shoved his hands in his pockets. "He asked to see you. I'm assuming he wants to quiz you on our marriage, find out what's gone wrong between us. He knows there's something up. Ed's no fool."

She recognised the warning look in his eyes. Don't tell him, his expression said. Guard our secrets. Don't send him to the grave hating me.

"You want me to lie to him?"

"I want you to protect him from any unnecessary suffering. Why expose him any further?"

"What deal have you struck with Dad?" She didn't mince her words.

"Frank's willing to bring up the shortfall on the repayments on Ed's business, keep it afloat."

Beth shook her head. "No, you can't let him do that. Where's the point? Why not just let it go now? It's losing money every hour, becoming obsolete. It won't be anything without Ed behind it. Did you tell Dad that?"

"He's a professional, Beth. He doesn't need telling."

"He's your father-in-law. How ruthless are you?"

"That's rich coming from you!"

An indignant Beth threw her hands in the air. "What's that supposed to mean?"

"Have you forgotten what you're planning yourself? Rather underhanded stealing from your own brother, don't you think? At least I'm trying to protect my sibling!"

Her face turned bright red. She made no response. How did he know?

Carl shook his head. "Tut, tut! Not very nice to be on the receiving end of sensitive accusations, is it, Beth?"

Stunned into silence, she gawped at him.

"Didn't realise I was home when you had that long conversation with your sister?"

Beth struggled to remember. She'd taken the phone to her bedroom. He hadn't been home when she went upstairs. "Were you listening outside the door?"

"Don't be ridiculous. When Charlotte called you back, I picked up the phone downstairs, intrigued by the litany you launched at her from your end. I was interested. I decided to listen."

"You're pathetic."

"Does Frank know what his family are up to behind his back?"

"No! And there's no need to upset him either!"

"I thought not. Now I'm sure you've little objection to my dealings with him after all? Frank will maintain the balance of the repayments and try and re-launch the investigation to clear my brother's good name, Ed gets his dying wish and you keep your dirty little secret."

Holding back her tears was a severe struggle for Beth. But already humiliated enough, she managed to hold them back, attempting some form of defence to his astute observation. "Kieran will still get his share."

"You're cheating your brother. Why bother denying it? Granted, I'm hardly in a position to judge you."

And with that he turned on his heel and left, leaving

her standing in the middle of the kitchen, frustrated beyond belief, her tears finally betraying her as they rolled down her cheeks. Turning to pull a segment of kitchen paper from the roll, she was startled when his voice cut through her thoughts.

"What happened to us, Beth? What happened to those two people riding on the pinnacle of love in Paris? How have we reached a point where we can barely stand in the same room without sniping at each other?"

The colour drained from her face, her icy tone matter of fact. "You caused the death of our baby, Carl. As a couple, we've been dying ever since."

She pushed past him, her heart heaving with loss. Halfway up the stairs, she flipped around once more.

"Let Ed know I'll be in before the end of the week. There are a few things I'd like to talk to him about too."

She'd sit with her brother-in-law. She'd decide for herself if he was strong enough for the truth. Carl's dictating had gone on for long enough.

Kieran was still sleeping when he received an unexpected call from Olivia. "How are things in Number 5?" she enquired after her initial greeting. "Everything working out well for you?"

"Think so," he answered, stifling a yawn, yet suddenly on full alert. She hasn't called to enquire how I am, he thought, holding his breath while he waited for her to drop her bombshell.

"I'm afraid we have a slight hiccup. The will's being challenged."

He pulled himself into a sitting position, glancing around him, savouring the familiarity of Polly's bedroom, the room where he was enjoying waking in the mornings, opening the curtains to the magnificent view of the Atlantic spreading beyond the harbour.

"I should have known it was too good to be true. But I can't say I'm surprised. I've had a feeling something like this would happen."

What he didn't realise was that Olivia was pleasantly surprised to hear the tension in his voice. For a guy so adamant about not setting down roots when he'd attended the reading of the will, she was reassured to hear the strong element of dread in his voice at the thought of losing Number 5.

"Unfortunately, yes. But I'm lodging a counter-appeal so we will fight back. I'm not sure yet if the objections will be upheld – in the meantime I'm trying to decide on the best course of action."

"Objections? There's more than one objection?" At a guess his sisters and mother were involved but why weren't they working together?

"Yes, two separate claims."

"It's my family, isn't it? I expected that."

"Well, yes, but there's an unexpected complication . . ."

That sounded ominous. "Yes?"

"Look, Kieran, I'm sorry but I'm very pressed for time just now – I'm meeting a client in ten minutes – it's best if I ring you back later to explain about the objections. Is that okay?"

"Fine. Thanks, Olivia."

No point worrying, he decided, throwing back the quilt and getting out of bed. He'd keep up his end of the bargain and after that he could only hope for the best.

Kieran wasn't the only one in receipt of an unpleasant call that morning.

"Hello?" Jess was unprepared for the raised voice on the other end.

"Jess, it's Pru. Where the hell are you? And why didn't you answer the phone yesterday when I called to confirm?"

"Excuse me?" Damn, damn, damn, Jess thought, remembering a couple of hours too late that she'd been supposed to meet her sister-in-law that morning – and the missed calls she'd noticed the previous morning.

"Our appointment? This morning at ten – to suit you, I might add, so you'd be back in time to collect Gary."

"It's *Greg*," Jess interrupted her, refusing to allow her away with mistaking his name. Being her husband's only nephew, getting his name right surely wasn't too much to ask!

Pru railroaded ahead as if Jess hadn't spoken. "Surely you couldn't have forgotten?"

Jess closed her eyes, her heart sinking at the sound of her sister-in-law's accusing and berating tone. She'd received a text from her a few days before, inviting her to meet up for a chat – more of a demand than an invitation judging by the end result. Acquiescing to an early-morning meeting had brought an end to Pru's incessant texts but as soon as she'd pressed 'send' Jess had paid little heed to the arrangement, so distracted with Kieran she had pushed almost everything else to the back of her mind, enjoying the fun she was having and acting selfishly for a change.

"My time's precious, Jess. I've got more to be doing than sitting around cafés waiting for you to turn up. If you hadn't the manners to turn up you could at least have sent a text!"

"It's been a hectic few weeks," Jess said by way of excuse. "My head's all over the place."

"I'll give you another thirty minutes."

"It's too late now. I wouldn't be back on time to collect Greg." She crossed her fingers, hoping Pru would take no for an answer.

"It's decision time, Jess – then we can all move on with our lives."

Jess shuddered at the other's icy tones. Not for the first time, she wondered what the hell had attracted Henry to the cold and calculating Pru.

Why had she agreed to meet her? Flatly refusing her offer couldn't be done over the phone so she would have to do it face to face – but not without Henry. Despite marriage giving Pru an equal share in his worldly goods, in Jess's eyes she should mind her own business and allow brother and sister come to a decision without her interference.

"Pru, I'm not being put under this pressure! When I'm ready you'll hear from me. I have a son to consider."

"Oh, for goodness sake! Your indecisiveness is so annoying."

"We've all had quite a shock, not something I can dismiss as quickly as you it seems."

"Shock! Your mother was unwell for years. It was only a matter of time before she croaked it. Henry's anxious to get things sorted out. And he's under pressure at work so the last thing he needs is you adding to his anxiety."

As if it isn't obvious who's putting the pressure on him, Jess thought, gripping the receiver in her hand, tension building inside her. "If he's stressed, it's definitely not a good time for change."

"Are you saying you've changed your mind?"

Despite her belief the night her mother died that she'd never sleep soundly in that house again, moving out of

Number 4 was the last thing Jess wanted now. Distancing herself from Kieran and the fun he'd reintroduced to her life was a depressing prospect now she'd come to enjoy his company. Greg would be devastated. And if she was reading the signals correctly, there was the faintest glimmer that Kieran too would be disappointed!

Would she have the strength to persuade her brother and sister-in-law? It had only been a verbal agreement, not binding. Had she enough fight to demand she continue living in the family home, even though Henry's hard-earned bonus payments had funded the newly fitted kitchen and modernisation throughout – something that was topmost in Pru's argument. Their mother hadn't been afraid to demand his input.

"Your mother's wishes were specific, Jess." Pru was on a roll.

"But not legally binding!" Jess shot back. She brought a hand to the base of her throat and swallowed hard, forcing back against the rising ball of stress the mere mention of her mother brought, the metallic taste in her mouth making her want to throw up.

It was Pru she had to convince. Henry would do as he was told – or instructed. Pity he'd never shown her – or their father now she thought about it – the same level of respect and support he'd shown his mother. A true mammy's boy, he'd lapped up the attention she had showered upon him all his life, turning a blind eye to her many faults.

Why the hell didn't I check the caller ID before answering the phone, she thought with regret.

Reaching out for Henry's assistance when her mother's behaviour had finally spiralled out of control had been out of necessity, not choice. Bloody hell, I am his sister after all, she thought. Shouldn't that count for something?

Things had been so damn difficult for Jess and Greg when her mother had been alive, her physical cruelty reaching crisis point one evening, forcing Jess to run out of the house terrified, cradling her terrified son in her arms. With a small child to protect, she'd had no other option but escape the danger zone their home had become and run to someone who she'd hoped would understand. In sheer desperation, she'd called a cab and arrived on her brother's doorstep, carrying nothing apart from her cab fare in her pocket and her sleeping son in her arms.

What she hadn't factored when she'd made her midnight flit to her brother's house was that Henry could barely scratch his head without seeking his wife's seal of approval. And, unfortunately, this occasion had been no different.

"It's Mum, Henry!" she'd cried when he'd answered the door. "I was downstairs getting her medication and she took her stick to Greg. I ran when I heard him screaming. She fired a glass at me, lashing out at me with her stick when I grabbed Greg from her grasp. Poor child was frozen to the spot, terrified to move –"

"Take a breath, Jess. That doesn't sound like Mum."

"I've been trying to tell you how bad things were. But you wouldn't listen."

"But I've never seen that side of her."

Pulling the belt of his dressing gown tighter, eyes bleary from being woken out of his sleep, a concerned Henry ushered his sister and nephew inside.

"What's all the racket?" Pru arrived into the kitchen in sapphire pyjamas, the remains of a face mask on her face.

Feeling Greg's knees tighten around her hips, Jess had planted a kiss on his cheek. In different circumstances she'd have made a joke about scary Aunty Pru but not that evening.

Jess looked at Henry, willing him to ask his wife to go back to bed, to give them a few moments where she could just talk to him alone.

"Mum's been a bit troublesome," he'd explained to Pru, playing down the situation.

A bit troublesome! I've described the most horrific domestic scene and he calls it 'troublesome'! "Not quite the description I'd use," Jess spluttered, refusing to protect their mother's reputation. "'Aggressive and out of control' would be better words and even they're not apt!"

"Where is she now?" Pru looked around as though she expected the elderly woman to appear from somewhere.

Jess was flabbergasted. Pru hadn't even asked if she and Greg were okay. "She's in her room, complaining because I didn't count her tablets before taking another lash of her crutch!"

Pru tutted indifferently, showing no sympathy whatsoever.

"Henry!" Jess turned to her brother. "We've got to do something, get her into a home where qualified people can deal with her aggression. Otherwise she's going to hurt one of us."

"Getting her into a home would be at huge cost, I might add!" Pru said, aghast.

Jess felt in danger of taking a swipe at her sister-in-law. "Greg and I aren't safe with her in the house and all you can think of is cost!"

"Coffee would be great, Pru," Henry soothed, ushering

his sister and nephew into the living room, making his usual effort to diffuse the rising tension.

They sat and talked into the night, a bored Greg falling asleep after drinking a glass of milk and munching on a tasteless rice cake, his health-and-figure-conscious aunt refusing to have tasty biscuits in the house.

Pru's accusing voice over the phone brought her back to the present.

"What has changed so suddenly?" she demanded. "You were in favour of the idea when she died, even the night we dropped you back to the house after the funeral? Said it was what you wanted too!"

"I was an emotional wreck! I've had time to think and now I'm not sure it's a good time for any drastic change. It's a serious decision, Pru, one that will affect Greg's future as well as mine. I have his school to think of. I've made enough hasty and regrettable decisions –"

"You initiated this," Pru interrupted. "As for school? He's in Junior Infants, not settling into a university degree!"

"He's happy and content with his friends," Jess muttered, not expecting any understanding but mentioning it as a point of importance.

"Didn't you say Pier Road had sucked enough life from you already? Weren't you complaining that you were suffocating there?"

Not any more, she thought, staring through the window, her eyes shifting towards Number 5, gaining confidence from the support and hope Kieran had been offering her and Greg. She paced the living room, the phone still to her ear. Absentmindedly, she stared at the variety of photos hanging on the wall, some of her and Henry, an ancient one of her parents' wedding day and several of Greg's twinkling smile.

She was well aware that her greedy sister-in-law's only ambition was to acquire a desirable postal address, plans already in place on how she'd change it no doubt. And once those changes were in place, there would be no overturning their agreement – verbal or otherwise.

"Pru, if you don't mind, I'd rather discuss this with Henry." She inhaled deeply, anticipating an onslaught. "It is more *his* decision than yours. Tell him to get in touch."

"Stop hiding behind that supposed fragility of yours," were the last words Jess heard before she cut the connection.

Chapter 26

Kieran untied the pink knitting wool, releasing Polly's bundle of diaries from its tight hold. Several times he'd been tempted to take a peek through her personal memoirs but hesitated at the last moment, taking issue with invading his aunt's privacy. Today felt different. Olivia's call had been disconcerting, the knowledge that his sisters were trying to oust him from Number 5 niggling at him and instilling an urgent sense of protectiveness inside him. Chosen as her benefactor, her privacy had suddenly become his responsibility, her personal history his to protect. If the house were to be taken from him with somebody else gaining from her death, he'd like to think he'd censored her most personal items against prying eyes.

Starting over twenty years before, she'd filled a notebook for each of the earlier years, real diaries for more recent times. Opening one of the notebooks, he smiled at the innocence of her daily entries, an observation of life around her, little to interest Kieran. Skimming ahead a few years, he peered through another one, carefully peeling the pages apart and reading Polly's entries, her life appearing very mundane, a weekly bus trip to Skibbereen the highlight of her activities. He smiled at the birthday entries, all of his family included apart from his mum. No surprise there, he thought, doubting the two strong-willed women had ever exchanged a birthday gift in their lives, seeing as they could barely exchange civil conversation! House insurance renewal dates, TV licence reminders and notes dotted sporadically throughout constituted the remainder of the entries, weeks of pages completely blank apart from the date at the top of the page, obviously a quiet period in her life.

Not expecting anything of great difference in the others, he pushed the notebooks aside, turning to the more recent diaries instead, surprised when a sealed envelope fell from the bundle, a few initials written in block capitals on the outside. Prepared to find money or a legal document, he was intrigued when the contents revealed what were apparently three letters.

Taking the first one – which was undated – he unfolded the single sheet of lined writing paper, smiling at the familiarity of his aunt's handwriting.

Scanning the letter, however, her words tore at his heart, the smile leaving his lips, nostalgia replaced with a deep sympathy for the troubled woman who had penned the heart-breaking details of the loss of her loved one to the cold arms of the sea. It was written to her husband, Glen, expressing her heartbreak, her love. Loneliness emanated from every word, the smudged ink a tell-tale sign of the copious tears she'd undoubtedly shed. Pouring her heart into a letter displayed her desperation, her frantic clutch on hope. He could only assume that penning the letter was a coping mechanism for his aunt, a way of pouring out her feelings though she'd probably known in her heart that her husband was lost forever.

More apprehensive as he unfolded the second letter, he drew it closer when he realised it was far more recent, written little over five years before. *Number 5 Pier Road, Schull* in the top right-hand corner, the date underneath and then the salutation.

Dear Kieran, I hope this letter finds you well. Actually, I hope this letters finds you at all would be more appropriate with the rate you're moving address these days!

He grinned at her humour, remembering her frustration when her letters arrived to a particular spot after he'd packed his rucksack and moved on. Despite his efforts to leave a forwarding address, he knew there had been lots of post he hadn't received. Polly was one of the few who'd written to him, his mother on the odd occasion in the first year but the rest of his family relying on text and email messages.

His eyes drawn to the page, he continued to read, grinning at her description of the summer regatta.

Lots of old faces around this week as well as the usual onslaught of hopefuls and hangers-on, swanning around in beige shorts and squeaking boat shoes.

Skimming through the next few lines, his attention sparked at her mention of Jess.

Got a few glimpses of Jess next door, back permanently by the looks of it but never seems to be outdoors much, not like when you were here. Inseparable, the two of you. You should call her, she appears to be very down, browbeaten by her cranky mother no doubt. I know I should . . . Oops, there's someone at the door. I'll have to finish this later.

Turning over the page, there was nothing on the other side, her visitor obviously distracting her. The letter had remained unfinished and never posted.

Kieran frowned, puzzled as to why Polly would keep a half-finished letter to him for perhaps four years and then seal it up in an envelope as if it were of some significance.

The third one was bulkier. Unfolding the pages, this time on unlined paper and dated two years previously, he found her writing more difficult to read, a shake in her hand evident. Kieran gasped as he read the opening: *My dearest John*. The intended recipient was clearly John Kilmichael from the harrowing description of her shock pregnancy that followed. Another letter of heartache but this time to somebody who was very much alive but yet again the letter had never been sent. Flicking to the last page, she'd signed it, *Yours in regret, Polly*, after heartfelt pages of explanation behind her reason for giving him away as an infant.

Why hadn't she posted this one, he wondered, or handed it to John, revealed to him that she was his mother? His father's words came to mind. John didn't know he was her son. What a waste, it didn't make a lot of sense.

Moving through the subsequent paragraphs, he felt uncomfortable reading her disclosures. He was saddened that his aunt had been deprived of a relationship with a child she'd given away at birth, the depth of emotion in her letter testament to the fact that she'd agonised over every sentence, releasing emotions she'd never shared, leaving this earth without the pleasure of properly reuniting with her only child.

He folded the letter, returning it with the others to the envelope, aware that it posed a problem. Did Polly expect him to deliver the letter to John? She knew – or fervently hoped – he would be going through her things, intended him to find it. So what then had she expected him to do with it? Yet, according to his father, she had been adamant that John should not know. But now she was dead . . . perhaps that changed everything. It was a dilemma.

With a heavy heart, he took a brief look at the more recent diaries, noticing a series of red X's accompanied by the letter 'J' dotted sporadically throughout the last two years of his aunt's life. He assumed these had something to do with John, marking the days perhaps when she'd received visits from him. About to retie the bundle and put them back where he'd found them, he changed his mind and flicked back a few more years, the absence of any 'J' obvious. But if John didn't know the truth, how had they made their initial contact? He found the point where she had first begun to record the 'J's, but there was no mention there of how John had come into her life.

He picked up the last diary, swiftly glancing at some of the last entries, saddened by the words she'd written about her impending stay in the nursing home, accepting independent living was no longer an option. *It's time to say goodbye to Pier Road and be taken care of*, she'd scribbled, adding a few more similar sentiments in some of the date segments.

Picking up another diary he spotted his own name and examined it more closely.

Damn, Kieran's letter returned. Another 'not known at this address', an omen no doubt to mind my own business.

Mind her own business about what, he wondered, flicking the diary closed to check the year. Same year as the half-written letter he'd found. An omen to give up writing him letters seeing as he'd seldom bothered to respond? No, he thought, that didn't make any sense, didn't connect with her thinking she should mind her own business. Had she been about to encourage him to return home? His guilt increasing at the lack of effort he'd made to keep in contact, he bundled the diaries and notebooks together, knotting the pink knitting wool around them again. He pushed them back in the drawer, disappointed he hadn't found more answers yet reluctant to pry any further for now.

In dire need of fresh air and distraction to let go of the memory of Polly's despair, he checked his watch. Plenty of time before Greg's out of school, he thought, deciding to pay a visit next door and invite Jess for a walk. He realised he knew so little of Jess's life since she'd left for college, their meetings sporadic in the intervening years. There was still so much they needed to catch up on and an hour without Greg in their company would give them an opportunity to talk and fill in the gaps. Polly's indication that Jess had been unhappy was fuelling his curiosity. Probably something as simple as hitting a downer after her few years in a posh college, he thought, or breaking up with one of the posh English guys she'd studied with. Imagining her with other guys, he splashed some of his favourite cologne on his skin and eyed himself critically in the mirror, wondering how he'd measure up against her ex-boyfriends – including Greg's father, whoever he was. So far she hadn't mentioned having any significant other in her life – in fact, she had denied it that first night. Nor had he noticed any man paying a visit. But that wasn't enough to assume she wasn't seeing anybody and certainly not enough to presume she'd agree to go on a proper date with him.

She's not going to look twice at me, he thought, unless

I improve my pathetic wardrobe of clothes! He'd left his limited amount of personal belongings in the house he'd been sharing with a few other lads, expecting to return on the same airline ticket.

Pulling a plaid shirt over his T-shirt, he walked away from the evidence of his aunt's regrets in life, his spirits lifting as he approached Number 4, every moment precious now he was no longer guaranteed a permanent address in Schull. Amazing how much more desirable Number 5 seemed when there was a risk he could lose it.

Frank Dulhooly was at home alone, his day already ruined by a pressurising call from his son-in-law. Carl had telephoned to see if he'd received the limited documentation he'd dropped through the letterbox, badgering him on the lack of progress.

"Yes, I've received it and I've gone through it," Frank had said, his patience wearing very thin with his son-in-law. "But there's no concrete evidence there. I'll have to speak to Ed and get more exact detail."

"But I'm not sure he's strong enough to be tackled like that."

"Well, it's the only way I can get international investigators to take this seriously."

"Don't wear him out," Carl had ordered ungraciously.

"I've already explained that this won't resolve itself overnight, Carl," Frank had responded gruffly, the younger man's brazen attitude adding to his irritation.

"Frank, we're fighting the clock here as you know."

"Well, stop wasting my time and let me get on with it!" His tone had been less than civil as he'd brought their brief telephone conversation to a close.

Researching his best approach and talking to a few legal counterparts, he'd compiled a list of worthy contacts who were in the strongest position to pressurise the French authorities to upscale the investigation and escalate the efforts being made to identify the culprit – or culprits (these guys rarely worked alone) – responsible for stealing, copying and reproducing Ed's designs.

"Fraud has practically forced his company out of business, not to mention shattering a reputation he'd spent years building," he'd explained over and over to his contacts, appealing to their better nature to help him find a loophole to get the case reopened. A difficult investigation but not impossible, he believed.

He stared at the computer screen, his document still blank. He was finding it difficult to decide on an appropriately effective opening sentence, the lack of definite results from his phone calls forcing him to expand his network of contacts.

Composing an email with the intention of issuing a collective request to a number of European lawyers was no mean feat, particularly when he was demanding a fitting response in the shortest time possible, relying totally on good will between nationalities. No longer a fresh case in Paris, already pushed well down the to-do lists by French police, he'd have to provide a powerful reason to have the case prioritised.

Frank swivelled in the leather office chair, the blank screen mocking him. He turned towards the window, gazing at green fields stretching for miles. Over the years, he'd repositioned his desk on numerous occasions, sometimes needing the view as a distraction, forcing him to take a break from the files he'd brought home. But then there were other times when the view was a distraction, his conscience pricking him because he wasn't outside playing with his children, accompanying Marian on a walk or tending to the garden. On those occasions, he'd turned his back on the view – and his family – and focused intently on the cases at hand, locking himself away for hours at a time until eventually Marian and the children had stopped asking for his company.

Apart from a few extra houses dotting the horizon, the West Cork landscape had changed little with the passing of time. Unlike me, he thought – the drive and ambition he'd enjoyed as a younger man had noticeably faded, forcing him to analyse the price he was paying for a fulfilling career. He'd chosen work over family, had let precious years pass when he could have been part of their fun and strife and watched them grow. And now, he thought, turning around to face the blank computer screen once more, I'm snatching occasional games of golf with a son I hardly know and resorting to underhand trade-offs to secure a daughter's future and demonstrate concern. Painfully aware of the silence in the house, he punched an opening greeting into the document.

Feeling more assured about his reasons for negotiating with Carl, he punched in a few more lines, words passing from his mind to the screen, the professional side of his brain overruling emotion and getting the job done. He stopped typing, reading over his draft, pleased with the message it conveyed. Fingers on the keyboard once more, he added a word of sincere thanks, typed his name and credentials and sent the email. European support would help him widen the net and broaden the investigation. He had already made several phone calls, speaking to contacts he hoped would act on his behalf. With multiple investigative teams working across borders, word should spread quickly, speeding up the process and exerting additional pressure on keeping the case open. Clearing Ed's reputation while he was still alive was paramount, a higher priority than financial retribution. Acquiring public acknowledgement and an apology from the international press would be a start. Convincing the fashion world to reintroduce his labels to the podiums during London, Paris and New York fashion weeks and market them as the élite brand they'd always been would be a magnificent result, a result Frank knew wouldn't come without a bit of good fortune and a lot of effort on his behalf. But ridding their lives of Carl, particularly Beth's, would make the exercise and risk worthwhile.

Relieved his request was already winging its way around the world, he took his mobile phone from the desk and idly flicked through the contacts, stopping once again when he reached Mags. Ignoring his reservations and the gnawing apprehension building inside, he pressed the green button. His heart leapt as the call connected, sinking once more in the space of ten seconds when it went straight to voicemail. Leaving an official message, he spoke slowly and clearly, listing his contact details and asking her to get in touch, careful not to make reference to their past acquaintance.

Chapter 27

"God damn you, Pru," Jess muttered in the empty house, dabbing her face with a damp tissue and cursing her sister-in-law for dragging up distressing memories.

"Speaking to me?"

Jumping in fright, she turned around. She had neither heard nor seen Kieran arriving through the back door. She noticed the shock on his face as he watched her dry her tears.

"Are you okay?" he asked, his eyes filled with concern as they held hers. "It's not Greg, is it?"

Jess shook her head, tossing the damp tissue in the bin. "I had an argument with my bitch of a sister-in-law on the phone earlier today. Another one!"

"Another sister-in-law?" He looked confused.

"No," she smiled through her tears. "Only one sister-in-law – one too many at that. Another argument."

"Families!" he commented.

"Can I get you a drink?" Jess took a bottle of 7UP from the fridge and poured herself a generous amount, waiting for Kieran's response before filling a glass for him.

He nodded, delaying his proposed invitation for a walk. "A drink would be great. Thanks."

"Let's sit down."

He sat at the kitchen table and she sat opposite him. She leaned her elbows on the table and sipped at her mineral. The time had come where she needed to share her troubles with somebody other than Henry and Pru and, in all the years she'd known Kieran, she'd never heard him judge anyone, happy to live his life his way and allow others to make their own choices. Shifting in her chair, her knee accidently knocked against the table and almost caused his drink to spill. Putting her hand out in apology, her fingertips touched his bare arm, his skin soft to her touch, the burning desire to entwine her fingers in his and mould her body against his taut frame scaring her with its intensity. Unaccustomed to such strong feelings, she jumped up from the chair, not trusting herself in her current emotional state to resist the strong temptation to kiss him.

"More 7UP?"

"No more for me, thanks." He paused. "I thought you wanted to talk," he then said, his voice soothing.

Leaning against the counter, she launched into an account of her conversation with Pru, barely stopping to draw breath as she explained the pressure she felt under to move out of Number 4 and take up residence in Henry's modest bungalow instead. Her facial expressions alternating between distress and fury, she vented her feelings, laying more blame on her sister-in-law than on her brother.

"I don't think Henry cares. Living in Clonakilty suits him, makes his commute to work easier. I can't imagine he'll enjoy the Schull to Bandon commute in the dark winter mornings. But Pru's greed and ridiculous obsession with status was her only concern. I can imagine her boasting about taking up residence in Schull."

"But Pier Road houses aren't exactly mansions. I'm not sure I get her obsession?"

"You've been away too long, Kieran," she said, her gaze holding his for the briefest moment. "Schull has been a very sought-after address, particularly before the property bubble burst."

"Better than Clonakilty?"

Jess nodded. "Wait until the height of summer. You'll notice the élite clientele who spend their weekends here, their luxury cars filling the streets."

"Oh, I'd no idea we were living in such a desirable location, with houses still fetching a reasonably attractive selling price considering the economic climate," he said, putting on a posh accent and laughing. "That must be why my family have lodged an objection to Polly's will."

"You're joking?" Jess's mouth dropped open. "I can't believe they'd undermine Polly's decision like that."

"Well, believe it."

"But aren't you devastated?" She raised an eyebrow, the news adding to her depression.

He shrugged. "It's not what I want but there's not a whole lot I can do about it, not yet anyway."

"How can you be so calm?"

"It hasn't happened yet," he pointed out. "No guarantee their efforts will be successful. Just have to wait and see."

"I wish I could be quite so confident where Pru and Henry are concerned," she sighed.

Some instinct made him ask, "Is there anything else troubling you, Jess?"

"Living here with my mother hasn't been easy and

Pru's playing on that now to get me out, making it sound like a new address – her address in particular – is going to clear my memory with a wave of a magic wand."

"How long since your mother passed away, Jess?" His recollection of Jess's mother was relatively vague. He now couldn't imagine he'd spent so much time next door yet never held a proper conversation with her.

"The same week as Polly but we had a private funeral. It was too tough what with –" Her sentence trailed off, her eyes downcast.

"Had she made a will?" At least Polly had the good sense to make one, he thought, even if it is causing bother.

Jess shrugged. "No. My mother was a law unto herself," she admitted. "Never did anything in her life to help others. She was self-obsessed, thought only of herself."

The comment in Polly's letter mirrored Jess's statement. "How did she get on with my aunt?" he asked out of curiosity.

"Polly was far too kind and polite for the likes of my mother," came her mumbled reply. "Mum insulted everyone who came her way so after a while it was no surprise that very few bothered even saying 'hello'. Although, come to think of it, Polly surprisingly continued to smile and issue a greeting."

"And your dad? Did he pass away too?"

Jess gulped, looking directly at Kieran, a tear rolling down each cheek, sliding unchecked down her chin before dropping onto her top. She came and sat beside him, consoled when he covered her hand with his, holding it in a loose grip. She didn't pull away, savouring the feel of his skin on hers, their first proper contact since his return.

"Dad's not dead – at least not that I know of. He left

one weekend around six years ago, walked out on us, couldn't stick my mother a moment longer. God knows but he'd put up with her antagonism for long enough."

Jess went to take another sip of her drink but knocked the glass over, the liquid spilling onto the table. She hated pulling her hand from beneath his but had no choice. "Damn!" She hurried to get a cloth, rushing back to clean up the mess before it dripped onto the floor. "I'm not normally this clumsy," she explained, silently accepting that she was more accident-prone in his company.

She returned the cloth to the sink and then came back to her seat, pleased when he slipped his hand over hers once more.

"Do you remember him? Dad, I mean?" she asked through fresh tears.

Kieran thought for a moment, deciding he'd been living in some form of bubble for all those summers. He'd taken very little notice of anyone's parents back when they were teenagers, least of all his own. "Vaguely," he responded, not wanting to offend.

"Wait there while I get a photo. I should have one close to hand. Maybe it will jog your memory."

Kieran heard her footstep overhead, guessing by the muffled banging noises coming through the floor that she was searching through drawers, sliding them open and closed in quick succession. Silence resumed upstairs and, when she reappeared in the kitchen, she held a disk in her hand.

"Best I could find," she explained, "the last recording I made of him, the Christmas before I graduated from Cambridge."

"Okay," Kieran said, bemused she wanted him to sit

through a home movie but willing to watch if that's what would help.

"Come on, there's a DVD player in the living room."

Flopping on to the floor in front of the TV, Jess pushed in the DVD and pressed play. Kieran remained standing, taking in the freshly plastered walls, polished wood floor, modern leather furniture and flat-screen television, giving him an idea of how much potential the Pier Road houses had. And it's obvious Pru's thinking along the same lines, he thought, not to mention my own family!

Distracted by the amateur home movie, his face broke into a grin as he watched a younger Jess gadding about on the TV screen, the scene transporting him back in time. Her eyes sparkled – he'd forgotten how expressive she'd been, the giddy antics she'd enjoyed. He looked from her on-screen image to where she was sitting cross-legged on the floor now. They could have been two different people. On screen, long dark curls swung to her waist, a direct contrast to the funky pixie cut she sported now.

Emotion stirred inside him, her current vulnerability stark and appealing. Putting his own concerns to the back of his mind, he went and knelt on the floor beside her, contemplating placing an arm around her shoulders. Only a few hand breadths between them, he inhaled her scent, inching even nearer to her, supposedly to get a better view of the TV screen, overcome with an overwhelming urge to kiss her on the lips. Feeling the distinct stirrings of desire, he was on the verge of cupping her chin and tilting her face to his when she jumped to her feet and pressed pause on the remote control, freezing the screen. Damn, he thought, kicking himself for his indecisiveness. The opportunity to taste her lips had passed.

"There, Kieran, that's him, that's Dad." She searched his face for recognition.

Kieran slowly got to his feet, not trusting himself to remain in such close proximity, his interest in kissing the beautiful, fragile woman standing inches away from him delaying the reaction she was expecting from him. Getting his emotions in check, he shoved his hands in his pockets and nodded, staring at the middle-aged man on the screen and trying to force a little enthusiasm into his response.

"Oh yes," he lied. "I do remember him now. Have you had much contact with him over the years?"

Shaking her head, Jess pressed the stop button, the screen going black once more. She flopped onto the patterned rug, closing her eyes for a brief moment, making Kieran suspect she was fighting back a fresh bout of tears. "Not a word in over five years."

Then, making no eye contact with Kieran, she described her intense heartache on the unforgettable day when, after yet another degrading showdown with his wife, her father had walked out the door wearing his Sunday sports jacket and trousers and taking nothing whatsoever with him from the house.

"I'd heard the expression of leaving with nothing but the clothes on your back but I'd never imagined it'd happen in my house . . . but, actually, I'm wrong . . . he took a photo album I'd given him the previous Christmas, a snapshot of my years in Cambridge mixed with a trail of ancestral ruins we'd visited over the various semesters."

"Things must have been pretty nasty for him to up sticks and take off?"

She nodded slowly. "By that time my mother's grinding and criticising was incessant. Morning till night, it never let up. Anytime he dared to defend himself, she lashed out with cruel insults, breaking his spirit time after time until the man could genuinely take no more."

"What about money? How did he manage after he'd left?"

She shrugged. "Whatever cash he had in his wallet on the day was as much as he took with him. Other than that, he has never once made a withdrawal from a bank, Post Office or Credit Union account."

"Doesn't sound like he wanted to be found?" Kieran didn't like to pry about his profession or whether they'd been financially well off, but Jess's father must have found work somewhere. How else would he have survived? Assuming of course that he had survived . . . He banished the thought as soon as it entered his head, going to sit on the leather couch, Jess staring at him, teary eyes filled with sadness. Looking at her sitting on the mat, she reminded him of a lost puppy, her vulnerability intensifying his urge to reach out and take her in his arms. Struggling to hide the effect she was having on him, he crossed one knee over the other and tried to combat his desire, doubting she'd appreciate any romantic advances in the middle of pouring her heart out.

She pulled her knees up, resting her chin on them and nodding her head in agreement. "You're dead right. He didn't want to be found. I hoped he'd come back after Greg was born, just to see us if nothing else, say hello to his grandson and leave again if he had to. But there was nothing, not a birthday or Christmas card, phone call or visit. I was devastated but never dared mentioned it to Mum." She shrugged her shoulders.

"What was her reaction to his departure?"

"Acted as though he'd never existed. Refused to talk about him or try and locate him."

"Perhaps he tried to contact her and she never told you?"

"Well, if that's true, he didn't try hard enough! He played the victim, allowing Mum to win, turning his back on his daughter, son and grandson, treating us as though we'd done something wrong." Her hurt was masked in bitterness.

Kieran could see why she'd feel like that. "It's impossible to read another person's mind, even those we feel we know well."

Jess stared into space. "I've wondered about suicide and other stuff but I keep telling myself he'd have been identified and we'd have been notified if his body had been found."

"You would think so." Kieran gave a shudder. "Would your mother have been spiteful enough to hide correspondence that came from him?"

She rubbed an imaginary mark on the knee of her jeans. "Who knows? Anything's possible. But I doubt it – I would normally be the one collecting the post from the door."

"But why didn't you leave too? Go with him?" The notion made a lot of sense to Kieran.

"He left so suddenly," she said. "There wasn't time to think. I was confused by raging hormones and tied up in a series of gynaecology appointments."

"You should have at least left your mother's house when you were so unhappy. I don't know why you didn't."

"I was having a baby on my own, Kieran," she shot back, diverting her gaze away from him. "Running away wasn't an option." Her tone was sharper than she'd intended, her heart hardening in defence. It's so easy for him sitting there suggesting that I could have managed in a dingy flat or apartment with an infant, she thought. He wouldn't say that if he'd walked the floors at all hours of the night with a baby with colic!

The absence of any other form of support with Greg had left her vulnerable. Instead of moving away from her mother as she'd intended, circumstance had forced her to remain, leaving her trapped in her childhood home with a bitter mother who wouldn't know a normal conversation if it jumped up and bit her on the backside! But useless and abusive as she'd been, at least she remembered to put on loads of washing and ensure Greg had an endless supply of clean clothes, something Jess wasn't sure she'd have been capable of coping with in the first months of motherhood. Her mother had been healthier then, more independent, and not as immobilised as she'd been when she'd died.

"I didn't mean to offend you, Jess, but to me staying sounds more difficult," Kieran clarified.

"Look, my father never asked me to go with him. My mother, tough as she was, at least gave me a roof over my head and kept food in the fridge, the main two commodities I needed in the first few months of Greg's life."

"And did you try and get work? I remember how much you'd looked forward to a career."

With a wistful expression, she shook her head. "Coming back home after my degree was a huge mistake – it sapped my energy and my initiative. My mother demanded all my attention. Then, eventually, finding out I was pregnant knocked my confidence and I talked myself out of applying for positions, believing a pregnant inexperienced applicant wouldn't even be considered."

"And since he was born?"

Again she shook her head. "Wasn't to be. Mum's health – you'd swear she planned it – deteriorated. Time just drifted by, my confidence disappearing with sleepless nights and repeated nappy changes. Suffering the loneliness of being without my own father, I tried my best to be mother and father to Greg."

"And as he got older?"

If only it had been so simple, she thought with a sigh, his questions nothing she hadn't asked herself over the years. "I lost my nerve, hadn't the guts to be completely alone with a small child in a strange town without a proper means of supporting him. And Mum threatened to cut me off without a cent if I left Pier Road. Scraping by on benefits, trying to cover rent and utilities and food and clothes, wasn't exactly the upbringing I had in mind for Greg. And I was no match for my mother's manipulative tricks." What she'd left unsaid was that she had never given up hope on her father walking through the door, alive and well, breezing back into her life as though he'd slipped out to the shop for milk and bread.

A comfortable silence settled between them, Kieran the first to break it when he got to his feet.

"Come on, Jess," he said, holding out a hand to her. There was still plenty of time before Greg was due to be collected from school. "We could do with a walk and some fresh air."

"I must look a sight," she said, slipping her hand in his and staggering slightly when he pulled her to her feet, clutching his arm to steady herself.

Staring at her intently, he thought she had never looked more beautiful, her eyes bright and shining with unshed tears, her lips quivering, her cheeks slightly flushed. It took great willpower not to wrap his arms around her tiny frame and pull her head into his chest, encouraging her to cry and cry until she had no tears left, kissing her soft lips until they were numb, replacing her pain with in-depth pleasure.

"What about Greg's father, Jess? Couldn't he have offered help?"

She pulled her hand from his, shaking her head in response.

He mentally kicked himself for his insensitivity, the spell breaking between them. "None of my business," he apologised. "Forget I even asked that question."

"You've listened to enough of my moans for one day," she said. "And that walk sounds like the therapy I need after a stressful morning. Give me a few minutes to freshen up and then I'll join you outside."

Conversation was minimal as they strolled along the pier, both deep in thought as they inhaled the salty air and enjoyed the peaceful atmosphere.

"The *craic* we had here," he commented as they watched a few lads push a fishing boat into the water.

"Don't remind me," she said with a smile. "If my mother knew half the things we got up to, she'd never have let me outside the door!"

"You had as much freedom as the rest of us if memory serves me right."

"Suited her not to have a bored teenager under her feet."

The sun made an appearance from behind the clouds.

"I haven't told Greg the truth about his real dad," she said evenly, turning her face to the sun and closing her eyes, savouring the delicious feel of heat on her skin.

"I suppose he's none the wiser at his age. Would he even question it?"

She pursed her lips. "Every little boy wants a dad he can turn into a hero, someone he can aspire to be when he grows up," she replied, her voice tinged with sadness.

"Never looked at it like that. So the dad's not around?"

"I've created a story for him about a sailor sailing the high seas in an enormous ship."

"And he's never questioned the length of time he's been away?"

The sun disappeared behind dark clouds. Jess opened her eyes once more, turning to face Kieran. "His concept of time isn't great and thankfully he's easily distracted. So far at least."

Kieran recalled the distant look in Greg's eye as he'd stared beyond him that first night he'd visited Jess's house. He hadn't taken too much notice of the water activity at the time, but thinking back on it now there must have been a ship's lights visible in the distance. Could that be what had made him whisper "Daddy"? The innocence of youth, he thought, and the lengths some mothers will go to protect their children. But if he was right, if Greg had just been looking at a distant ship that night, his own assumption that the father was a local man was unsound. In fact, it was probably someone from college that she'd rather forget. Perhaps that's why she'd returned to Schull so suddenly. Then he remembered how she had so abruptly disappeared inside her front door that night and he wondered again.

But all that didn't matter. A day might arrive when she felt like sharing and he'd be happy to listen if she chose him as her confidant but for now he was happy to provide a shoulder of support and friendship to help her through the awkwardness with Henry and Pru. How their relationship would progress was anybody's guess.

"That imaginary sailor's a cool story for Greg," he offered kindly.

"I'm not trying to be coy," she explained, "but some things are best left as they are, this being one of them, I believe."

She looked at him long and hard, expecting disgust or disapproval in his expression, a trace of pity for how irresponsible she'd been, hugely relieved and grateful when he didn't register any of these emotions. Without uttering another word, she clasped his hand and mouthed a silent 'thank you'.

"Your story, your business," he repeated, putting his other arm around her shoulders and pulling her to him, stronger evidence of his understanding than any words could be.

"Come on, lady, it's almost school time. Your son will be waiting to sail home."

They laughed together, the atmosphere between them lightening in an instant.

Reaching the school gate as the children ran out, bags on their backs and smiles on their faces, Kieran and Jess both opened their arms when Greg came running towards them.

"Are you here to collect me?" Greg's eyes lit up as he ran straight into Kieran's arms, barely acknowledging his mum.

"What about my kiss?" she exclaimed, dropping her arms by her side.

"I'm too old for kisses," he said indignant.

"You tell her, kid," Kieran teased, winking at Jess over the boy's head. "Why do mothers love to embarrass their sons?"

Greg shook his school bag off his shoulders and handed it to Kieran. "Will we go to the park now?"

"After you've eaten your lunch," Kieran promised, pleasantly surprised when Greg slipped his small hand into his as they stepped outside the gate and onto the footpath.

Jess took her son's other hand and they swung him high in the air between them, his squeals a source of interest and envy to the other children, encouraging him to swing higher and higher, continuing for the short distance to Pier Road.

"Can we go to the park in five minutes? I'll eat lunch as fast as I can," Greg pleaded as they arrived at their houses, all too soon for the little boy who'd have happily continued kicking his feet in the air. "Kieran, can we?"

But Kieran wasn't heeding his small companion, his attention turning to the man sitting on his front wall.

"John!" he called, catching his guest unawares.

John Kilmichael had been looking in the other direction, Kieran's arrival taking him by surprise. He got to his feet, shoving his hands in his pockets.

"Hello there. Kieran, isn't it?"

"That's right. These are my friends and neighbours, Jess and Greg."

"I'm sorry, I was miles away, never noticed you approach. Polly's not answering," he commented, jerking his head towards Number 5.

Greg screwed up his face in concentration, staring at the man, taking in his sensible jumper and trousers and polished black leather shoes. Then he piped up after a moment: "I met you before in Kieran's garden."

"Good detective work," John said, smiling. "Nothing much slips past you!"

"We're going to the park," Greg told him, pushing his chest out.

Jess's phone rang at that moment and she moved away from them to answer it.

Damn, Kieran thought. He needed to get John away from Jess and Greg. And soon.

"Greg, I'll give you a call as soon as I can. Wait for Mum next door like a good boy."

But Greg wasn't budging. "You promised."

"Is there something I can help you with?" Kieran asked John, feeling perspiration rolling down his back.

"I was concerned when Polly hadn't called, thought I'd pay another visit seeing as I wasn't too far away. You did pass on my message?"

"Of course but she's been a bit under the weather." Kieran's response sounded flippant, even to his own ears. He glanced at Jess, relieved she was still engrossed in her call.

Explaining Polly's continued absence would be difficult. John's contact had been regular before she'd been taken into the home. As the thought went around his head, he wondered why Polly hadn't informed him she wouldn't be around. He could have visited the nursing home. It wasn't as though it was a surprise decision. And combining her diary entries and her instructions to Olivia, she'd had time to make arrangements, wasn't shifted suddenly or unexpectedly. So why had she excluded John? Or had she simply run out of time before managing to contact him?

"Kieran, Greg and I should go. We can catch up later." Jess's return cut in on his thoughts.

"But, Mum! We're going to the park!" a petulant Greg insisted.

"Please don't let me delay you if you've got plans," John apologised, pushing up the sleeves of his navy lambswool jumper as the sun made a pleasant appearance.

Kieran groaned inwardly, wishing the other man was unpleasant and difficult. Lying to him would be easier then. *How on earth did I allow my father to tie me up in knots with this man?* Other than that one conversation on the golf course, he hadn't taken any opportunity to discuss the subject with Frank, reluctant to upset him and waiting for him to offer further information.

But how the hell can I keep pawning him off if he turns up like this, he wondered, struggling to think of something to say? *Concoct another load of lies? Or make a sneaky call to Dad for advice or permission? I'm a bit old for that now*, he thought, staring at John openly, trying once more and failing to see any resemblance between him and Polly. He wasn't convinced. Could his father possibly be mistaken?

Life had been so straightforward before this, nobody to worry about or take responsibility for, nobody but himself. Sighing, he took his house keys from his pocket and made to go inside.

"Jess, I'll catch up with you later," he said.

"But you said we'd play football, Kieran! Didn't he, Mum?" Greg looked up at his mum, reluctant to return home without Kieran in case he was denied his coveted trip to the park.

"Is Polly up to visitors?" John asked.

"Polly's in Heaven with my nana," Greg piped up in a very matter-of-fact voice.

Kieran and Jess exchanged a swift look, John standing between them, tallest of the trio, looking from one to the other, waiting for somebody to explain Greg's announcement.

Thinking about it later, Kieran would realise that the child's statement could have been explained as confusion, misinterpretation or merely a story concocted by an adult to placate a child's inquisitiveness. But the deathly silence that followed ended any opportunity for subterfuge, the shocking truth registering on Jess and Kieran's faces, instantly giving the game away.

Unexpected drops of rain began to fall, a vivid rainbow sweeping across the sky overhead.

"Let's get inside," said Kieran. "John, step in out of the rain. Jess and Greg, you too."

Walking through the hallway Kieran contemplated giving John the package, but then thought better of it, realising it'd look suspicious if he happened to have it sitting in a drawer, yet had made no attempt to contact him. Greg's announcement needed explaining first. He'd see about the package afterwards.

"Kieran?" John was the first to speak when they stood in the kitchen.

Kieran let Greg's school bag slide from his shoulder onto the chair, stalling for time. "Greg, there's an old hurley and sliotar in the garden if you want to play with them while the adults chat."

"But it's raining!"

"Sorry! I wasn't thinking."

"We should go home for lunch, Greg," Jess decided, preferring to leave Kieran alone with his visitor, confused about what was happening and terrified Greg would make an already awkward situation much worse.

"No, Mum, I want to play with this!" Greg had spotted the cuckoo clock on the wall and pushed the hands around, rubbing his hands in glee when it made the wooden bird come out of its perch and chime *"Cuckoo! cuckoo! cuckoo!'*.

I should never have lied to John in the first place, Kieran thought, cursing his father for putting him in the situation. He doubted he'd get out of the fix he was in without resorting to something close to the truth.

"Kids are gas, aren't they?" he said.

"Can be at times. Although they've been known to make more sense than adults at other times!"

Ouch, Kieran thought. "Care to take a seat?"

John shook his head and eyed him squarely. "Only that I've seen the photographs, I'd be seriously concerned about your viability as her nephew. What the hell's going on here? And what is the truth? Is Polly dead or alive?"

"No need to get hostile," Kieran warned, disliking his abrasive tone and recalling his father's dislike of the man who seemed to loom over him.

"Answer my question then. Where's Polly? Has she disappeared off the face of the earth?"

"I told you already," Greg piped up again. "She's in Heaven. Didn't you hear me the first time?" This time the young boy swung around to face John, aware that his declaration was gaining him attention for some reason and playing to its strengths. "Do you know anyone in Heaven?"

"I'd like to think so," John responded. "When did Polly go there?"

Jess intervened at this point, glaring at John, unimpressed that he was resorting to quizzing Greg. "Seriously, we must leave. Grab your bag, Greg. Kieran will call over when he's ready to go to the park. Won't you, Kieran?"

"Shouldn't be too long, mate," he promised, tossing the little guy's hair and gaining a laugh for his trouble, his eyes swiftly meeting Jess's.

"See you later so," she said. "Nice to meet you, John. Let's go, Greg."

Accompanying them to the door, Kieran closed his eyes and shook his head when Jess eyed him curiously. "I'll explain later," he whispered, closely followed by, "if I can!"

He let them out and returned to the kitchen.

"Actually," he said, meeting John's gaze head on, "Greg was telling the truth. Polly has passed away."

"Since my last visit here?"

It was tempting to lie again but he resisted, knowing the date of somebody's death was freely available on the Internet to anyone who cared to check.

He shook his head. "A short while before that."

John stared at him, perplexed, the colour draining from his face. "But why lie? I'm sure the whole of Schull were at the funeral? Why hide it from me?"

Kieran sighed, still fumbling for an answer or an acceptable reason when his mobile rang. Glancing at the screen, he realised it was Olivia. Great timing, he thought, more bad news!

"Excuse me," he said, "this is important. Back in a moment."

He went into the living room to take the call, closing

the door behind him, beyond caring whether he could trust Kilmichael alone in the kitchen or not. And he figured his guest was probably beginning to feel the exact same way about him – and with good reason. Yet he doubted he was ready to leave just yet.

"Olivia, how are you?" he asked, flopping into the armchair and waiting for the next chapter in the saga that Number 5 had become.

"Kieran, I must apologise for not getting back to you before now. I just didn't get a chance. Right – you remember I told you there were two separate claims submitted?"

"Yes?"

"One is, as you rightly suspected, from family members citing their claim to an equal share."

"On what grounds?"

"I've received two geriatric assessments, one dated before and another dated after I witnessed her will, supposedly verifying memory slippage and traces of onset dementia."

Kieran inhaled sharply. Inconsiderate, selfish bastards, he thought, horrified his own flesh and blood were capable of such a low act against Polly. He'd rather hand them the keys and walk away than allow that case continued. He clenched his fists tightly.

"My mother and sisters?" He wanted clarification.

"Both sisters were named in the original letter but I have only one signature," Olivia declared.

Probably Beth slow to commit as usual, he thought, Charlotte the more professional of the two and unlikely to drag her heels in any situation.

"Hang on a minute, Olivia," he said then, suddenly nervous that his conversation might possibly be overheard by John.

Taking the stairs two steps at a time, he went up to his bedroom and closed the door, forgetting in his haste to enquire which sister's signature was present on the document.

"Had Polly been attending the geriatrician?" he asked, sitting on the bed. "Or is this the first you've heard of it?"

"Other than the documentation in front of me," Olivia said, "I've got nothing to go on. I'm waiting on hospital records but these things often take time. And, regardless, I'm obliged to follow through even though I'm positive they're wasting their time."

"But didn't you mention that it'd go to my sisters if I broke the terms and conditions?"

"A different scenario entirely, Kieran. Objections of this sort can only come from the deceased's next of kin and, though the girls have lodged a written petition in the hope of overturning the will, I'm happy to tell you that it's a definite non-runner."

Knowing little about these matters, Kieran was confused. "But aren't we next of kin as well as Dad? She didn't have any children so surely Beth and Charlotte can make their claim on the place?" The words stuck in his throat, the man downstairs in the kitchen testament to the facts being otherwise.

"With your father – Polly's brother – still alive, overturning the will would revert full right of inheritance to him."

And that'd explain why Frank hadn't been too bothered about Marian's threats. He knew she'd be wasting her time unless they managed to get me out. Is it naïve to assume Dad has no part in this, he wondered, finding it difficult to believe his father would ever show such disrespect for Polly.

"So I continue living here in the meantime as though none of this has happened?" he asked. "Or will I be thrown out until it's resolved?"

"Not at all, you must stay. It's very important you do," she clarified. "Now, the second objection is more complex and unexpected. It's something that was news to me unfortunately. It has put me at an instant disadvantage, particularly when Polly's not around to clarify the situation."

Recognising uncertainty in Olivia's tone, Kieran got to his feet again, going to stand by the window. The rain had stopped. He smiled as the secondary-school students passed down the road in various groups, messing and teasing, belting each other with school bags and letting off steam after a day's confinement in a classroom. Olivia's voice jolted him back to the present, her words ringing loudly in his ears.

"John Kilmichael is the name on your second objection," she told him. "Ever heard of him?"

Struck by the irony of the situation, he grimaced. "Heard of him? He happens to be less than twenty feet away from me right this moment. He's standing in the kitchen demanding to know if Polly's dead or alive, yet you're telling me he has already contested her will?" More than anything, Kieran hated being made a fool of. And unless he was seriously mistaken, he was being taken for a mug by the man who'd hovered over him demanding answers moments before. Now who was being secretive and devious? Now who was playing silly games?

"He's known to the family then?" Her surprise was evident.

"My dad met him on a few brief occasions. And he's called twice since I've moved in."

"I have a detailed statement here in front of me where he's declaring himself as Polly's official next of kin."

"Her son?"

"You knew?" Again, Olivia sounded surprised.

"Dad told me. But, according to his version, John wasn't privy to this information. He doesn't know he's Polly's son."

"Somebody's lying to you, Kieran," she said, stating the obvious.

"And it can only be one of two people," he seethed, an image of his father's uncharacteristic reaction rushing to mind, followed in close succession by the accusatory tone of John Kilmichael a short while before. "Have you concrete evidence that he's her son by any chance?"

"I've requested it but am still waiting, I'm afraid."

"And there's nothing I can offer to do to help. I've no idea where he was brought up or by whom. I'm guessing this would matter?" Kieran forced himself to contemplate the options, the reality of John Kilmichael disappearing quietly from their lives unlikely.

"Yes, very much so. New rules have been implemented to protect the rights of children born out of wedlock. Each case has to be analysed on individual merit, other factors impacting too."

"Such as?" Kieran turned his back on the schoolchildren, staring at the mantelpiece ornaments instead, smiling wryly at the headless ballerina, unable to believe Polly had left the pink china doll sitting there after he'd knocked it to the ground and decapitated it.

Using a whole tube of Super Glue, he'd stuck the torso back together, her head in smithereens, cast around the fire grate and beyond repair. 'We've our very own Humpty

Dumpty,' he'd laughed with Polly when he'd handed his aunt her ornament, relieved when her eyes crinkled and her lips shaped into a mischievous grin. 'That's the last time I'll get you to do the dusting!' she'd said, her feigned stern look followed by a hearty laugh. That was one of the things he'd loved most about her, her ability to accept imperfection in others.

Olivia explained some of the consequences. "If Polly had her son adopted, the situation would be different and his right to inheritance would then be from his adopted parents, anything he'd receive from Polly needing to be specified on the will. It's a complicated affair to be honest and I'll need to establish all the facts before making a proper assessment or decide how best to challenge this counter claim."

"Have you met him yet?" Kieran asked out of curiosity.

"No. But I've set up an appointment for later in the week. Correspondence so far has been by post."

"Thanks, Olivia." Armed with that nugget of information, he ended the call and immediately dialled his father's number. If Polly had wanted John to benefit, she'd have put a procedure in place.

"I think you need to get to Number 5 now, Dad. Kilmichael's here and knows a lot more than he's letting on. He's claiming to have an entitlement to inherit as Polly's next of kin."

There was a brief silence, then Frank said curtly, "Be with you in two minutes. As it happens, I'm just driving up the main street."

When Kieran returned to the kitchen, John was sipping a glass of water and staring at one of Polly's many wall photos.

"Making yourself at home?" Kieran snapped, startling him.

"You asked me to wait while you took the call. The glass was on the draining board. It's not like I was prying in the presses or anything!"

No longer in the mood to placate the other man or be taken in by him, Kieran came straight to the point. "That was my solicitor, Olivia Jacobs. But then I think you're already acquainted?"

"Olivia Jacobs – no – I don't know any Olivia Jacobs. Why do you think I do?" He rinsed the glass and replaced it on the draining board.

"Cut the innocence. Olivia just confirmed that you've lodged an objection to Polly's will."

John's eyes narrowed. "So she is really dead! I wasn't sure if you were telling the truth."

"Hardly a joking matter," Kieran deadpanned.

John ran a hand over his clean-shaven face, confusion etched on it. "But what would give me the right to stake a claim to your aunt's inheritance? I don't follow."

"Yes, Kieran, perhaps you'd enlighten us by responding." Frank's face was black as thunder, a steely warning in his green eyes as he walked in the back door in time to catch John's final question.

Looking from his father to John and back again, Kieran's head thumped. "Your name is definitely John Kilmichael?"

"Yes."

Frank continued to glare at his son. "Kieran, for God's sake! Quit pussyfooting around. What the hell are you on about? Why should a stranger have any such rights?"

"You've met John here before, Dad? Yes?"

His father nodded but didn't speak.

"Olivia has the documentation in her office," Kieran said. "And," he added with vengeance, stabbing a finger in John's direction, "she's meeting with *him* later in the week."

"First I heard of it," John retorted.

"You've obviously got your facts wrong, Kieran," Frank spat, the veins in his temples throbbing. He looked like he was about to explode.

"Were you adopted?" Kieran blurted out. He was tired of secrets and undercurrents, preferring everything to be thrown out in the open, the only way he believed issues could be resolved.

"That is none of your business," John responded evenly.

"It's very much my business if you're trying to get me out of this house!" he shot back. "And Dad's business too."

Frank scowled at his son, his mouth opening and closing but no words coming out. He threw his hands in the air, disgusted with his son's behaviour after he'd specifically asked him to keep his mouth shut.

But Kieran wasn't about to be silenced. His tirade of unanswered questions continued.

"Care to tell me where you were born and who raised you?"

John was visibly taken back by his onslaught. "I might reconsider seeing that solicitor this week after all," he announced. "I could do with harassment advice! What did you say her name was? Olivia something or other?"

Kieran shoved his hands in his pockets. "Finally we get the truth."

John ignored him. "There should be a package here with my name on it – something I ordered – it would have been delivered by the company. If you know where it is, I'll take it and be out of your hair."

"And why was it delivered here?" Kieran didn't see any point in denying the package had arrived.

"It's something Polly asked me to order but, seeing as she's not here, I'll take it with me."

A shiver ran over Kieran's body, a vivid image of his aunt coming to mind, forcing him to rethink his attack on the other man. He had been welcomed into the house by Polly after all. Frank had testified as much. John probably didn't deserve the animosity he'd been shown but it was too late now for recriminations. The damage had already been done.

"I'll show you out, shall I?" Kieran led the way into the hallway where he pulled open the drawer in the hall table and took out the package, handing it to John. Then he opened the front door and gave a curt nod as John passed him.

"Kieran," John began, stepping outside the house and pausing a moment. He ran a finger around the outer edge of the rectangular package, pursing his lips as though contemplating what he was about to say. He looked at Polly's nephew, the young man's cold expression changing his mind on what he'd been about to share. Now wasn't the time. "I'll be off so."

"See you, John." Kieran banged the door closed and leaned his forehead against it. He still had to face his father's wrath. Bringing a hand up and releasing the catch on the door once more, he was tempted to step into the sunshine and walk and walk, letting fate decide his destination, forfeiting ordinary life and its tedious issues for the freedom of travel and a nomadic lifestyle.

His father's booming voice came down the hallway.

"Kieran, what on earth was that all about? I specifically asked you not to tell him anything!" He stepped into the hall.

"Are we going to the park now?" Greg's innocent plea followed closely behind, his indignant face appearing at Frank's side.

"Greg, get back here this instant!" Jess scolded her son from the kitchen doorway, the tiny hallway already crowded. "I told you Kieran had visitors!"

Groaning inwardly, Kieran turned to face them. Fate's intervention was already at work, Pier Road and its issues calling on him to stay.

Frank had swivelled around at the sound of Jess's voice, embarrassed his accusation had been overheard.

"Hello," Jess smiled, making a discreet grab for Greg's arm and trying to coax him to her. "I'm sorry he's barged in. Without permission, I can assure you!"

"Dad, this is Jess," Kieran introduced them, welcoming the distraction and the opportunity to delay an explanation that he didn't have for his father as yet. "And this impatient little guy is Greg. I'd promised him a trip to the park but John's visit delayed things."

"Nice to meet you," Frank said, turning to follow Jess into the kitchen. "We've met before, I'm sure," he commented, stumbling a little as Greg dashed around him.

"Greg!" She pulled him by the arm. "Will you be careful? Apologise to Mr Dulhooly."

"Sorry," Greg said chirpily, jiggling his bum, unable to stand steady.

"Call me Frank, please, Jess."

"I was often chatting to Polly when you pulled up outside, Frank." Jess brought Greg to stand in front of her, holding him by the shoulders, much to his dislike.

Frank studied the little boy and his young mother for a moment, glancing at Kieran and back to the duo again. "I couldn't have it on my conscience to delay a trip to the park any longer. He looks like he's about to burst!"

"No, don't be silly," Jess insisted. "Tomorrow's another day. Apologies again for barging in unannounced."

"No, Mum!"

"Greg," Jess took his hand firmly in hers, "what have I told you about bad manners? We're interrupting Kieran and his dad. Now come on, you've got homework to do."

"Too nice a day to waste indoors," Frank offered kindly.

Kieran watched their exchange with interest, surprised at his father's understanding of Greg's impatience. He'd have expected him to encourage them away, thought he'd be gunning for an explanation about John.

"Join us for a kick around in the park, Dad?" he invited on impulse.

Greg's eyes widened. "Yeah, we could take turns in goal. Cool! Two out field instead of only one."

Frank cleared his throat, a blush of embarrassment flushing his cheeks, replacing the fury from earlier. "I'd only slow you down. Too long since I've kicked a ball." He glanced surreptitiously at his son.

Kieran registered the unspoken message in his eyes, a fleeting wave of regret for the father-and-son moments that had passed them by for a variety of reasons. Instantly the mood changed between them.

"Payback for disgracing me on the golf course," Kieran said, the determination in his tone leaving little room for argument. "And as for you, Greg, I'll beat your socks off if it's me against you out field!"

"Are you sure?" Jess enquired, her son still imprisoned by her tight hold of him.

Kieran glanced at Frank and then at Greg. "Positive. You're welcome to come and watch me taking these guys down," he laughed.

"Think I'll pass on that pleasure." She turned to face Frank. "I can get this munchkin home if you'd prefer?"

"Plenty of time for talking later," he responded. "Doesn't necessarily resolve things anyway."

"Jess, we'll catch up with you in a moment." Kieran was anxious to clear the air with Frank so it didn't put a damper on their afternoon.

"Come on, Greg. Let's wait for them outside."

"Dad," Kieran said as soon as his neighbours had left, "I know you're annoyed but there wasn't any point in carrying on a charade after Greg letting it slip to John that Polly has passed away."

"Oh! So that's what happened," said Frank, his anger evaporating. "But what's this about the will?"

"Olivia was quite specific on the phone. That's why I called you to come over. She told me John Kilmichael had put in an objection. He denies it but she had it in writing on her desk. He must know Polly was his mother. What other reason would he have to object?"

Frank shook his head. "But Polly was adamant she hadn't told him. Right up to the moment she died. And, though it broke her heart, she cut all contact once she entered the nursing home, too distraught to keep up the pretence that he was no more than a friend, unable to deal with the situation under such emotional circumstances."

"What a troubled mind!" Kieran uttered with a long sigh. "I wonder what she would have done if he had turned up and found her before she died, though? In fact, from what he said, he probably did come here while she was in the nursing home. Anyone could have told him where she was, had he asked. What would she have done then, I wonder? I guess we'll never know." He thought again of the outpouring of emotion in the letter upstairs that she had written to John, and wondered again what she had intended him to do with it. But then something else struck him. "John was so convincing, letting on he thought she was alive. He really was. None of it adds up."

"He's clearly a better actor than we're giving him credit for," Frank said, remembering the other man's indignation. "Unless he has only been throwing us off the scent, trying to catch us unawares."

"His meeting with Olivia is only a few days away," Kieran said. "We'll know the outcome soon enough. Until then there's nothing we can do about it."

"Best go and play ball then, let off some steam." Frank smiled at his son.

Kieran grinned, deliberately omitting the remaining detail from Olivia's phone call. His father had enough on his mind without the added burden of his daughters making an attempt at slandering Polly's memory, stripping her of her dignity by questioning her sanity. And while Olivia had been confident their objection was rather misguided with Frank being her next of kin, Kieran knew his father would be extremely hurt on Polly's behalf.

A short while after the men's exchange, Jess stood at her front gate and watched in disbelief as the trio tapped a football up the road, the men taking hold of Greg's hands as they took a right turn on to Main Street and towards the park. Tears sprang to her eyes as she went into her house. Feeling foolish at her ridiculous display of emotion, she brushed them away. But an overwhelming warmth spread through her, remembering Greg, his delight obvious as he'd skipped up the road between the two men, his afternoon enriched by the simplest of outings, a taste of the normality he'd been denied until now.

Chapter 28

Beth waited with trepidation for the first of their potential clients to arrive in Goleen. Butterflies in her stomach, she checked her appearance for the umpteenth time, trying to get the correct balance between professional and welcoming. She'd changed her outfit three times already and yet was sorely tempted to dash upstairs and change into black trousers and matching jacket, the first outfit she'd put on that morning. The ringing doorbell halted her in her tracks. It was too late to worry about her khaki combats and flat desert boots making the wrong impression, time instead to reveal the promise of the Goleen land to interested clients.

"I'll get it," Carl grumbled, surprising her by running down the stairs.

Relations between them appalling since her accusation about him killing their baby, they'd worked silently and separately on their divided responsibilities. Carving out an earthen adventure trail and fencing off some grazing paddocks had kept Carl busy between shifts at the factory. He'd also visited a circuit of activity centres throughout the county. Impressed by one in particular, he recognised a potential to expand beyond quad bikes to utilise the trail to its full potential. He'd sullenly suggested to Beth that they open it for BMX and trail bikes too.

"There's a market for that sort of thing too, resources are lacking in this neck of the woods. No harm adding it to the marketing and insurance paraphernalia as you're at it."

"No reason why not," she agreed, secretly impressed and adding it to her lengthening to-do list of responding to enquiries and negotiating public-liability insurance estimates.

Inhaling sharply while Carl greeted their group of potential clients and one or two investment types, she painted a smile on her face and welcomed them into the kitchen, grateful for the burst of strong sunshine warming the large room. Eyeing them warily, Beth watched as Carl made easy conversation, noticing how the three females fell into easy chatter with him while the five men seemed to take more notice of the magnificent view through the window, eager to get on with things from what Beth could gather.

Small talk and refreshments out of the way, the group settled down to business, Carl's enthusiasm surprising his wife yet again.

"We'll take you outside shortly," he said. "You'll obviously want to see things first hand but I've also put a slide show together to whet your appetite on what it could be."

Beth frowned in confusion – she hadn't realised he'd organised some preparatory shots. "Will I get the laptop for you?" she asked.

"No need," he said, taking a memory stick from his

pocket and sticking it into the port on the television set. "We can show it here."

They all settled down and watched with avid interest. Beth was hugely relieved that all the comments were positive.

"The ring fort is a great asset," one of the men announced, his eyes never leaving the screen. "Kids will love that, adults too."

"And it's made me wonder too about giving riding lessons here instead of just offering stable facilities," another potential investor said when the short presentation came to an end.

"Still needs a bit of editing and it's only a first attempt," Carl said dismissively.

But Beth recognised a sense of pride in his comment. And deservedly so, she thought, impressed and grateful for his input.

"I'd like to work out a safe way of incorporating the small river at the end of the far field but I haven't quite figured it out yet," Carl was saying, pulling on a jacket. "Mightn't be suited for anyone under twelve but from what I've seen we'll need a separate – and obviously safer – track for them anyway. Easier to supervise too."

Happy to allow him take the lead, Beth cleared the empty mugs from the table, grabbed a mint-green mac from the coat-stand and followed the group outside, confident that some if not all would instil both life and income to their Goleen residence. Hurrying to catch up with the others, she cringed as their string of questions began. Carl's words went over her head, his easy chatter about the ring fort history lost on her as she contemplated their visitors' concerns, each one a potential financial outlay, an increasing amount of money they didn't have, yet essentials that would have to be in place before her Goleen Activity Centre could be brought to life.

Carl led the group into the barn.

"I see you've set up the barn party-style," one of the women commented, flopping on to a straw bale and glancing around.

Beth entered the barn, glancing around at the disarray of straw bales placed precariously around. "Teenager heaven," she said, remembering the request to hold a 21st birthday party.

"Although they'd have to be supervised. Imagine the damage a stray cigarette butt could do?"

Beth nodded at the lady who'd pointed out the potential hazard, something that genuinely hadn't crossed her mind. "Looks like it'll be a full-time job at this rate," she said, masking her growing concerns behind a broad smile.

One day at a time, she thought, concentrating only on the group of people joining her and Carl on their tour of the fields and refusing to entertain the doubts fighting for space in her mind. Are we biting off more than we can chew, she wondered.

"When do you hope to be up and running?" asked one of the group.

Carl turned to Beth for the first time since they'd left the house. "I'll let you answer that question, Beth."

"As soon as the insurance is in place." She struggled to keep the uncertainty out of her tone. "Although I'm guessing we'll need a Health and Safety inspection before that'll happen so I'll keep you up to date on progress if that's okay."

Looking from one of the group to the other, she

wondered if they'd have anything to do with the venture if they knew meeting the hefty insurance premium was dependent on Seth's intervention to overturn her aunt's will and uproot her own brother from his new home.

Chapter 29

Charlotte rambled through the Eaton Centre stores in downtown Toronto, lugging items around department stores and discarding them on rails before getting to the till, unable to focus on even the simplest of tasks. Her mind wavering between fantasy and reality, her history with Philip Lord was consuming her since he'd accepted her pseudo Facebook friend request, distracting her working day and disturbing her sleep at night. Mia Zepo's Facebook profile was expanding. Philip Lord had been in touch, intensifying Charlotte's hatred for the man who had sabotaged her reputation. Receiving email notifications to let her know when Philip Lord's status had been updated, she jumped each time her phone beeped, often abandoning important tasks to take a peek. Reading and rereading Facebook posts, she sometimes got so carried away that she forgot she was replying under the guise of a happily married woman with a couple of kids and a giant husky dog who slept at the foot of her bed!

Several postings later, Mia and Philip's relationship

was moving into dangerous territory. Public wall posts were replaced by intimate private messages and instant chat at all hours of the day and night, leaving Charlotte disgruntled and confused, despising the obsession that had begun to take hold and regretting tapping into his life yet again.

Temperatures were high – even by Toronto's summer standards. After a frustrating twenty minutes rifling through her wardrobe that morning, Charlotte had grabbed her credit card and set out to replenish her collection of summer outfits, putting her phone on silent to avoid the temptation to check any alerts.

"Are you okay there, madam?"

Charlotte looked up startled, taking a moment to figure out why the sales assistant was bothering her. Realisation dawned, however, as she remembered the variety of items draped over her arm and saw she was headed in the direction of the Exit doors. Up ahead, the security guard was also scrutinising her with his beady eyes, waiting to pounce no doubt once she crossed a particular invisible line.

That's all I need, she thought, to get arrested for shoplifting! I suppose they have a job to do but still, she thought, do I honestly look like somebody who's about to attempt to run past a six foot six tank for the sake of a few flimsy summer dresses?

"Just making up my mind on a few things," she said hurriedly, bestowing an innocent smile on the assistant and indicating the mixture of colourful summer dresses she'd picked up on her wander around the ladies' department. These look more like something Mia would wear, she decided, wondering how much it would be to buy a wig, change her style and slip into another woman's life.

"There's an extra 10% off for today only," the assistant said.

Charlotte feigned enthusiasm. "I haven't quite decided yet but I'll bear that in mind."

Assured that the tall lithe brunette wasn't about to leave the building with a collection of this season's dresses draped over her arm, the assistant moved away from Charlotte, leaving her to continue browsing.

Eventually Charlotte abandoned all the items she had been carrying. On the verge of leaving the store, planning on smiling at the burly security guard on her way out the door, she made a sudden U-turn when she spotted a stunning sequinned dress on a mannequin. Scanning nearby rails for an identical one, she couldn't find a replicate of the exquisite bronze number with a high neckline. That short hemline would show off my long legs to perfection, she thought, looking around for the assistant.

"Excuse me, I'm wondering if you have that bronze mini in my size?"

"Let me check for you, madam," said the assistant, making for the counter, Charlotte in her wake. "It's new to our party-line, arrived in-store last night and already selling well – created by an up and coming Paris designer who's breaking into the Canadian industry. So popular already, on every magazine and bill board. Have you noticed the label?"

I don't need the lowdown on every detail, Charlotte thought ungratefully, bored by the assistant's sale pitch and wishing she would just find the damn dress. In her mind, she was already finalising the outfit. She'd apply a light tan – a matt finish would be best. She'd call some of her bank friends and suggest a night out and make a hair appointment too but she'd do her own make-up, knowing exactly the effect she wanted to create – smouldering eyes, pouting lips and flawless foundation with just the amount of bronzer to accentuate her cheekbones. Her nights out since arriving in Toronto were practically non-existent, the bank's Christmas party a rare exception, a farce as it turned out but at least an excuse to dress in something other than severe business suits.

"Your size, madam?" asked the assistant, fingers poised over her keyboard.

"I'm not quite sure – I'm sorry," Charlotte apologised. She knew she'd lost a lot of weight, her appetite curbed by the distraction of Mia and her Facebook escapades.

The assistant swept her eyes over Charlotte's frame, obviously making a professional assessment, swiped her ID card along the register, tapped a few keys and flicked her finger along the touch screen. "You may be in luck. Our records show one in a size I believe will fit you. I'll go and check our stockroom."

Eyeing the dress critically while she waited, Charlotte planned ahead, knowing she'd be bitterly disappointed if the assistant didn't return with a dress that fitted. But the concern didn't cloud her excitement. The unworn strappy bronze stilettos sitting in a box at the bottom of her wardrobe would match perfectly. The intricate dress detail required little in the line of accessories, although the more she looked at it the more she realised her diamond watch and 24-carat chunky gold necklace with matching teardrop earrings would complement the outfit to perfection. Revisiting the compartment in her brain where she'd turned the key on her memories of Philip Lord, it seemed appropriate to expand that memory further by wearing the jewellery he'd presented her before the

Christmas break, right before he'd waved a sprig of mistletoe and refused to take no for an answer.

Painful memories flooded back, vivid in glory and cutting as deep as they had in the boardroom on South Mall, Cork city. His desire for her fuelled by an excessive amount of lunchtime liquors, he'd forced her against the wall, cornering her like an animal closing in on its defenceless prey.

"Last one," the assistant announced, brandishing the delicate piece as she approached. "Care to follow me to the dressing room?"

Charlotte shook her head, resisting the urge to handle the material, wanting to wait to savour the moment in the privacy of her apartment. "No, I'm happy to take it without trying it on. If you could wrap it, please," she instructed, opening her bag and taking out her credit card.

"You don't want to check it's your size?"

Charlotte sighed. Every time it was the same. You'd think assistants would be delighted with a quick sale, she thought, without the added delay of me oohing and aahing in the dressing room with them telling me I look fabulous – whether I do or not!

"Full credit on return?" she asked.

"Of course, madam," the assistant confirmed.

Charlotte gave a curt smile as if to say 'do your job then and bag the damn dress' but not a word left her lips until she bade her farewell. Swinging the bag as she left the store, she nodded at the security guard, refraining from waving the receipt in his face.

She hoped the exorbitantly priced dress would fit her as she envisaged.

Dropping by her favourite hair salon, she treated herself to a shampoo and blow-dry.

"Your usual, Charlotte?"

Charlotte put down her cappuccino and flicked back through the pages of the magazine she'd been reading. Pointing to a chic up-style she'd noticed on one of the models, she asked if it could be recreated.

"Hmm, perhaps a little less severe around the sides and maybe a little more body at the top. Special occasion tonight?"

Charlotte was about to shake her head but then thought better of it. Why not assume Mia's Saturday night for a change. "Drinks and dinner," she improvised.

"How nice. Dress formal?" The stylist eyed the shopping bag next to Charlotte's chair. She had refused to allow the receptionist take it when she'd passed her coat over the desk. The coat she'd live without if somebody took it by mistake – or otherwise – but not the dress. Considering the difficulty she'd had finding the perfect design in the first place, she wasn't about to lose it before she'd even had the chance to try it on.

"Yes."

Paying little heed to the stylist as she applied her expertise and technique to her hair, Charlotte enjoyed her browse through the selection of magazines, delighted to notice the promotional material the store assistant had mentioned about the new label, her exact dress featuring as part of their top buys for the season. Leaving the glossies aside for a copy of a business magazine, she was a little surprised to notice the fashion label had also made its way into the monthly publication – not as promotional material, however, but about the label's controversial background.

Reading the article with interest, Charlotte sat up

straight in her chair and gave the piece her full attention. It can't be the same person, she thought.

"I'm sorry, Charlotte, but can I ask you to hold your head still, please?"

"Oh dear, I'm a disaster for you! So sorry. I'll take full responsibility if the style loosens later." She glanced in the mirror. "Looks great. Sorry again." She lifted the magazine this time instead of moving her head.

Edward Giles Designs – Carl's brother! He's claiming credit for the label I just put on my credit card. On the verge of leaning toward the store bag to check, she felt the stylist give a gentle tug to a lock of hair she was trying to weave into her masterpiece, and thought better of it. Instead she noted the name of the magazine, pleased it was a current issue, and decided to buy a copy as well as taking a look on the Internet later to see what else was being said about the situation. Very interesting. She wondered why Beth hadn't mentioned it. And if it turned out she had just bought an Edward Giles Design she'd be looking for her money back and asking her sister to get her brother-in-law to create a speciality of Charlotte Dulhooly style dresses. She revelled in the idea of having designer couture with the cut she required.

"Charlotte, would you like it pinned back from your face?"

Studying her reflection, she was thrilled with the outcome, watching with interest as the stylist demonstrated both looks.

"Leave it hang down over one eye," she decided eventually. "It's got a sexier appeal, don't you think?"

Handing over an extra-generous tip, Charlotte left the salon, receiving admiring glances as she strolled down the street and wishing her Saturday night amounted to more than dinner for one in her apartment.

Back home, Charlotte went in search of internet stories about the fashion-designer scandal. Flicking from one report to another, she pieced together what she could, going as far as translating a French newspaper article to English, seeing as the biggest uproar involved numerous Parisian houses. Quotations and accusations filled her screen as she read libellous comments from both sides. No two reports carried the same message, journalists alternating their loyalties and breathing life into Ed's grievance for as long as they could use it to sell papers.

Charlotte was perplexed. Assessing the truth was impossible.

But one thing for sure, she thought, for the first time in an age I have found my ideal cocktail dress. Holding the dress against her body, she moved in time to the music blaring from the speakers on the wall. Pity it and so many more like it are at the root of a dying designer's heartbreak.

A young and upcoming graduate from Lyon – whose name was staring at her from the label on the dress she held in her hand – had bounced onto the platform of the fashion world during the past year. Launching a pre-Spring collection, organising fashion shows and issuing samples to stores in advance of most other designers, his sharp ideas had taken the world of haute couture by storm. Applying the same tactic to the next season, his summer pieces had been filling the European rails for weeks, vibrant colour and sassy cuts tantalising his unsuspecting public and offering a brand-new take on the original femininity of the fifties.

Reading about his key looks in one of the articles, Charlotte was interested to discover that her dress was part of his first launch in the Canadian market. Not stopping there, the collection was also being revealed in Australia and the US. She wondered whether Edward Giles, or Ed as Beth referred to him, had created the original design. From the little Beth had told her about him, his passion and pride for his work flowed through his veins. And if the reports on the net were true, he'd been defending his company's reputation, insisting the fraudster designer from Lyon had somehow managed to plagiarise months, possibly years, of his hard work, altering the tiniest detail in each piece to authenticate a brand-new label. Charlotte thought how unfair it was, and imagined that this stressful period in his life hadn't helped his progressive illness and probably played a part in its escalation. Understanding the pain of losing face and reputation, her heart went out to him. Following his stringent fight, his relentless drive to reclaim his place in a cut-throat industry, she believed his argument.

But those who made a difference didn't agree and Ed's popularity had faded before spring season even got under way. Already excited about the new arrival on the scene, stocking the newer label at keener prices, fashion houses and leading stores stripped his clothing range from their shelves and rails. Several went as far reprinting catalogues and replacing his newest look with that of the Lyon replicate.

A furious Ed had his legal team retaliate on a giant scale, his attempt to clear his name achieving little apart from ostracising him in the fashion world entirely. Reading a statement from the man himself, she sympathised at his description of their devastating response. For over twenty years, his designs had sent upper-end clients swooning and submitting pre-season orders, giving stores cutting edge style and high-society status.

Loading a video of Ed's last Paris fashion show, the cameras flashed on his face as he focused intently on the catwalk. His unbridled passion, fire and limitless imagination shone through every creation, smashing boundaries and demanding a leading spot on the major fashion publications. But the newcomer's keener price list had lost him his spot on covers of glossy fashion magazines, demoting him to the leading headline on trashy tabloids instead.

It was time to try on her own Edward Giles copy, as she thought of it. She undressed in her bedroom, keeping her back to the mirror as she'd stepped into the dress.

Ready to admire her purchase, she turned slowly toward the full-length mirror, a smile spreading across her face as she let out the breath she'd been holding. The expensive material clung to the contours of her body like a second skin as though it had been made to measure. The zip closed without effort. The fit was perfect. The halter neckline was perfect. She turned to either side, first the left, then the right, her smile broadening with every glance. Thank you, she said, offering a silent thank-you to the clever designer who'd drawn the pattern and another one to the machinist who had cut the bodice line to perfection. The bronze creation was the first sleeveless dress she'd considered wearing since her last meeting with Philip Lord.

She twirled in front of the mirror, delighted with the result. The hairstyle complemented the outfit to perfection, her naturally tawny skin glowing against the delicate bronze material. The jagged scar on her chest was completely covered. Coming to Canada and placing her trust in the hands of the best plastic surgeon Toronto had to offer had improved things slightly. But she still wasn't comfortable enough to brave scooped necklines or open-necked shirts. Now, however, thanks to Ed Giles (as that's whom she had decided to credit), her days of hiding behind shawls and shrugs were finally being left behind. She could return to the glamorous look she'd favoured, turn a corner. This dress would help restore the confidence she'd lost on that infamous evening when she and Philip Lord had their final showdown.

Excitement buzzing inside her, she changed back into a comfortable leisure suit and went in search of her Uncle Seth's phone number. She had mislaid the number Beth had given her but hoped she would find it in an old address book. No point wasting the way she was feeling now, a great time to channel her energy into something worthwhile – the perfect mood to take on her gangster uncle! I could take on the world this very moment, she thought, searching through a folder she'd brought with her from Ireland but had hardly ever opened. Spotting what she was looking for, she took out the shabby red address book and flipped it open to see her sister's neat and childish writing, *To my big sister, Lottie, Merry Xmas*. The innocence of the dedication tugged at her heart. Years had passed since she'd unwrapped the gift, yet she clearly remembered sitting around the Christmas tree with Mum hurrying them to get through the presents before they left for morning Mass – a far cry from the solitary Christmas just gone. Delighted with her sister's thoughtfulness, Charlotte had removed the matching diary and address book from its gift box, discarding the diary almost immediately, not really one for looking back, preferring instead to focus on the future and what it held in store. And her attitude hadn't changed. The address book, however, had survived, storing her contacts in the old-fashioned way, knowing they'd have been deleted or lost in upgrades if they'd been keyed into a laptop or phone.

But the number of entries in her little red book had expanded with each new phase of her life until finally it became surplus to requirements and was replaced by the contacts list in her mobile phone.

Tentatively opening the pages, Charlotte experienced mixed emotions as she scanned some of the names entered there. Her handwriting startled her. So different from what she used now, a symbol she guessed of how her personality had developed over the years. These numbers are no longer relevant, she guessed, running her finger along the page where she'd written all of her school friends' names, not bothering storing them alphabetically, lumping them together on one page instead. Remembering the tears shed on the last day of exams, she grinned at the solemn promise they'd made – vowing never to lose contact. "No matter what," she mumbled, repeating their mantra. That promise hadn't survived long after the first Christmas. Old acquaintances had been replaced with college classmates and her hectic city social life left little time for reunions.

Reading through the names now, however, she wondered what they were doing and how their lives had turned out. Better or worse than her career-wise? Married with children, she supposed for a lot of them. Strange, she thought, her face breaking into a grin as she came to Josephine's name – the girl she'd sat alongside for Leaving

Certificate Chemistry. They'd been inseparable in that final year, neither hiding anything from the other, sharing a strong passion to leave the wilds of West Cork for the bright city lights of any city as soon as they possibly could. Determination spurred them to work harder in school, studying experiments together to strive for an extra few points, jumping for joy on the results day when they achieved a higher than expected Chemistry score.

Neither friend pursued the science route, Charlotte following the financial route and Josephine leaving for Dublin to pursue a law degree. Hearing snippets through the grapevine of how well she was doing, Charlotte had no doubt but that Josephine's sharp wit had put a smile on many a face in the otherwise serious environment of the law chambers.

Her judgement clouded by nostalgia, she longed to be surrounded by people who knew her inside out, girls who'd grown up with her, sharing and understanding the embarrassment of cranky teachers and overbearing parents. Life had been so simple. If only she'd appreciated it at the time, she'd have made sure to enjoy it more.

Seth's name and number was at the top of the 'S' page, the name in neat legible writing but the number crossed out and replaced several times in accordance with the number of times her uncle had changed contact details to avoid somebody or other! Dialling his number, she waited. There hadn't been a glimmer of news or progress on the horizon since she'd last called him. And her mother's lack of contact was unusual too. All playing the waiting game, she assumed. As expected, these things moved at a snail's pace.

Her uncle's gravelly voice came on the line seconds after the first ring. "Seth's villa, how can I help you?"

Love him or hate him, it was impossible not to smile at him.

"You've downgraded since our last call," Charlotte laughed, recalling his previous welcome note of 'Seth's mansion'.

"And to what do I owe the pleasure, my dear?" Seth teased.

"Do I have to have a reason to ring you?" She stretched out on the couch and settled in for a chat with him. Gangster or not, he oozed charm by the bucketful, a loveable rogue under different circumstances.

"Your mother tells me you're thinking of coming home?"

Charlotte winced. "I've nothing decided yet, just toying around with the idea. Weather's still hot here so I may as well take full advantage. And my job's a profitable number, difficult to leave behind, especially the way the banking world is back home."

"Chip off the old block!" he laughed. "Thank God there's some Brixton blood in your genes and you appreciate a gift horse when you see one. Not enough of it around if you ask me. That sister of yours is an out-and-out Dulhooly."

"Seth," Charlotte warned, "that's my family – my nearest and dearest – you're talking about."

"My family too," he pronounced. "And speaking of them, I'm guessing I know why you're calling – I'm doing my best but these things take time. Got some documents to the solicitor too – recent geriatric assessments."

"So your claim hasn't been rejected?"

"Of course not!" he said, his tone incredulous. "I won't quit. And there's always an alternative route. That solicitor's a tough nut – a good-looking bitch into the bargain, I'm told, but too young for me now unfortunately."

She laughed at his honesty. "If it's that much trouble, why bother?"

"Mar has been good to me in the past," he said, his teasing tone turning serious. "I like to see justice done."

Charlotte wasn't privy to their brother-sister secrets but from the snippets she had overheard down the years she knew little would come between them. Regular contact always maintained, even during the periods he'd lain low and had even skipped his place at their Christmas dinner table.

"And you feel the objections you have in mind are acceptable?" She inhaled sharply. Her tone would betray her intentions if she wasn't more careful.

"I've secured medical reports from the best and . . ." He paused to cough.

Charlotte waited while her uncle tried to get his breath back. It was obvious from the seriousness of his breathlessness that he was still a heavy smoker. "Will I call you back, Seth?" she asked.

"No need, but hold on while I get a drink."

She stared into space as she waited for him to return on the line, her mind working overtime. His persistence was admirable. Nothing new there with Seth, she supposed. Knowing her uncle, he'd stop at nothing until he had turned the original will on its head, pushed Kieran out and had it renegotiated.

She brought a hand to her stomach to stop it churning. Dad will go berserk, she thought. Despite his faults, he'd been a hard-working husband and father who valued his good name and reputation more than anything. There wasn't a word in the dictionary to describe how he'd feel if the family name was dragged through the courts. As much for Frank as for Kieran's sake, she knew she had to stop this nightmare, let Polly rest in peace and allow her decisions be accepted.

Hearing Seth fumbling around, she turned back the pages of her address book until she reached her list of school pals. Looking around for a pen, she spotted her handbag and took out her ruby lip liner, circling Josephine's name with it. Though it was her West Cork phone number, she doubted Josephine's parents would object to passing on a message or better still would give her a current contact number. Having someone she could trust in the legal system (apart from her father whom she couldn't involve) could come in very useful, and having a friend she could be honest with would be an added bonus.

"Now, where were we?" Seth's voice interrupted her thoughts.

"Polly's geriatric assessments," Charlotte prompted, flipping open her laptop to type up a few bullet points so she'd be able to relate it exactly to Josephine if the opportunity arose. "What geriatricians are you using?" She kept her tone light. "One from the hospital?"

"Yes, he's an acquaintance of mine from years back. Who'd have thought Polly Dulhooly –"

"Digby," Charlotte corrected.

"I'll always remember her as Polly Dulhooly."

Quite out of character for him to sound nostalgic, Charlotte thought, but didn't comment, listening instead as he outlined his two arguments – the question over Polly's legal ownership of the property and the state of her mind as she'd made the will.

Time to get on with business, she thought, when they'd said their goodbyes. Without further deliberation, she began tracking down her old friend, Josephine, to gain her expert advice on managing objections of her own. From experience, she'd learned the merits of advance preparation. It was too late to consider consequences when the damage had already been done.

Chapter 30

Kieran left the house, the sharp breeze forcing him back inside to get a jacket. Spotting his black leather biker-style jacket, he took it from the hallstand and put it on. Locking the door behind him, he put his hands in his pockets as he walked up the road, finding a folded €20 note in one pocket and a packet of stale chewing gum in the other. Checking the inside pockets, he pulled out the small brown envelope Olivia had included in the registered envelope of documentation. He'd been so engrossed in the other package for John Kilmichael the morning it had arrived, it had totally slipped his mind and he hadn't worn the jacket since.

Slitting it open now, he withdrew a folded piece of his aunt's notepaper, watching it flap in the wind. He didn't need to check for a signature. Her handwriting was distinctive, had been calling to him in a variety of ways ever since he'd moved to Number 5.

He waited until he'd reached a park bench and sat down to read it properly.

It was dated the previous New Year's Eve.

Dearest Kieran, if you're reading this I'm no longer on this earth – can't say I'm sorry, I'd had enough of it anyway. But you, my dearest nephew, you've obviously decided to accept my offer.

Not one for showing huge emotion, Kieran had to settle himself a little before continuing. Her voice emanated from her words.

You'll be doing me a great favour to sacrifice your travels and watch over the place on Pier Road. So much has changed these last few years, my arthritic limbs making it difficult for me to get about any more or keep up with all the comings and goings.

Your friend, Jess, is back in Number 4 – a little boy with her, good-looking too, reminds me of you at that age!

Kieran couldn't help smiling. He read on.

Though she tries her best to hide it, I know Jess is miserable. That mother of hers is far too much care for a young girl. She's killing her spirit, ruining the best years of her life.

Maybe it's time you settled down, Kieran. And weren't you always your happiest in Schull? With friends who may mean more to you than you realise? Trust your instincts and follow your heart, lad.

What on earth did she mean? Was she matchmaking, trying to get him and Jess together? Again, he continued to read.

My final request appeals to your generous nature. Don't turn away my friends from the door.

Others will wonder why I chose you, Kieran. Others will be aggrieved. Greed will raise its ugly head, no doubt.

But giving everything to you is my choice. You filled a great void in my life, brought life to my home. And I want to turn that around now and bring a home to your life.

Love always
Polly

Reading it through a few times, he folded it in four and slipped it into his pocket once more. Trust my instincts? A gust kicked up, dust swirling around the ground. Kieran watched it swirl, the movement akin to the confusion he felt inside.

The only person who'd come to the door had been John Kilmichael. Was there a hidden message in there? "Why speak in riddles, Polly?" he muttered, frustrated by his aunt's cryptic messages. "Why not come straight out with whatever messages you're trying to relay?"

Jess was out of breath when she reached the top of the stairs, the heavy load she carried weighing heavily against her slight frame. Using her elbow to press down on the door handle, she opened the door to the largest bedroom and dropped the cardboard boxes she was carrying on to the floor as soon as she stepped inside. The fun she and Greg were having with Kieran had convinced her that Pier Road, despite its ghosts and bad memories, would remain their home. Fuelled by renewed enthusiasm, she'd spent hours packing her mother's belongings, carelessly boxing china and glass that she'd been forced to wash and polish by hand, receiving a lash of her mother's sharp tongue if she questioned the need to clean them when they were hardly ever used.

Eyeing the numerous bags of her mother's clothes in the corner of the room, she gave a shudder. Emptying her wardrobe and chest of drawers had resurrected an array of memories, mostly unhappy ones for Jess. I'll ask Henry to take them to the charity shop, she decided. Or they can dump them for all I care, once they get them out from under my feet.

As she stood in the doorway to catch her breath, she realised that packing her mother's belongings had given her little choice but to move in and out of the bedroom she'd been avoiding for weeks now. But emptying it had significantly reduced her discomfort there, the bare rails and drawers symbolising her mother's permanent departure. She wouldn't be returning.

Almost stripped of her mother's belongings (apart from the storage boxes and bags that would soon be moved), Jess looked at the room with a degree of objectivity. The largest room on the first floor, it boasted a magnificent view and its southerly aspect ensured ample natural light. After informing Henry and Pru of her decision to stay – not a conversation she was anticipating with any great excitement – she'd organise murals on the wall and convert it to a playroom for Greg.

Purposely leaving the bedroom door open, she accepted that her mother's appalling behaviour had been beyond her control. She'd done her best to stand up to her, noticeably stronger defending Greg than herself, normal practice for most mothers she thought wryly. Pity my mother didn't fit into the category of 'most mothers'! Shortly – once her supply of cardboard boxes and refuse bags had been replenished – all physical trace would be removed from the house. And the passing of time, Jess believed, would make the lingering dark shadows fade from her mind.

"Pru, eat your heart out," she thought, visualising her sister-in-law's fury when she arrived to find the place devoid of any trace of anyone other than her and Greg. Fuelled by a determination she wished she'd been able to show her mother, she ran downstairs to get her phone, spotting a photograph of her mother on the wall (one she'd missed) and unhooking it. Retracing her steps up the stairs, she dropped it into an overflowing storage box.

Downstairs once more, she dialled her brother's number and waited for him to answer so they could arrange a suitable time for a frank discussion. She didn't think beyond the call, refusing to contemplate anything other than a positive outcome.

The call made and a meeting set up, she flopped into a chair and let out a weary sigh, her muscles aching. She'd worked diligently, emptying wardrobes and drawers, her brain on overdrive as she'd filled box after box with her mother's belongings, feeling nothing but animosity for the deceased woman. Finalising the issue with Henry and Pru would rid her of a huge burden, clearing the way for her to combat another major hurdle, a difficult one, a huge gamble but worth the risk in her eyes. Almost there, she thought, filled with an unfamiliar sense that she might be headed exactly where she wanted to go.

Chapter 31

The shrill of the doorbell irritated Frank. He wondered who was calling. He wasn't in the mood for pushy doorstep salespeople. Attempting to peer through the frosted glass as he went through to the hallway to answer the door, he couldn't make out who it was.

"Seth!" What the hell does he want at this hour of the day, he wondered. It's been a while since he's been mooching around.

"Frank. I thought you'd be golfing?"

Obviously or you wouldn't be here, Frank thought. How often does he call for a free lunch when I'm not here? The skies suddenly darkened and hailstones bounced against the ground. He held the door open and ushered his wife's brother inside.

"Cutting back a bit, Seth," he said. What the hell am I explaining myself to this oaf for? "Marian's out," he added, hoping his guest would turn on his heel and leave. They'd given up any pretence of genuine friendship many years before.

"Oh, that's a pity? We were supposed to meet tomorrow but I was passing and . . ." he shrugged as though Frank could read his thoughts.

"Anything I can help you with?"

"She mentioned that Beth needs a bit of help with . . ." Seth's voice trailed off again.

Frank picked up on the other man's hesitancy, his instincts on alert. What was Marian cooking up with her brother? So many times over the years he'd had to intercept his brother-in-law's idea of helping, to ensure he didn't end up on the wrong side of the court room. That man couldn't lie straight in bed, never mind conduct an honest deal, he thought. And no doubt this time is no different.

"Oh yeah, she spoke to you about that?" he said cautiously, deciding to play along as though he was privy to Marian's plans.

Seth filled the kettle. "Coffee?"

Cheek of him offering me coffee in my own kitchen! "Nah, I'm steering clear of caffeine at the moment."

"On another health kick? Don't know why you bother. We're on the slippery slope now anyway. Best years behind us."

Frank winced inside. Seth had this cunning way of needling a person, getting right under their skin, probably part of the reason he'd successfully hoodwinked people and secured dodgy deals over the years.

"All depends on the value we knock out of them!" He chided himself for his childish retort as soon as the words had left his mouth, annoyed he'd risen to the other man's bait.

Seth raised an eyebrow, a mocking smirk on his face.

"Sounds interesting, Frank? Something you want to share?"

Frank felt he was looking right into his soul – and his conscience. God damn him. He'd only been in the house five minutes and already my headache's returning. The strongest painkillers wouldn't dispel the effect Seth had on him.

"I don't think Marian will be back for a while." He leaned against the doorframe, watching Seth stirring his coffee and then dropping the spoon on the counter top before going to the larder press and taking out a fruit loaf.

A few moments later, Seth was tucking into a slice of fruit loaf smeared with a thick layer of butter. "Mmm . . . tasty! Marian's larder is always well stocked. Sure you don't want some?"

Frank shook his head, finding it more and more difficult to restrain his growing anger. The liberties the man was taking, acting as though he could swan in and treat the place like a self-service restaurant. And I'm letting him! But only until I get the low-down on whatever tales Marian has run to him with this time. Though he'd put money on it that she'd roped him into lodging an objection to the will on their behalf. She'd allowed the issue to die too easily, letting him believe she was respecting his wish to allow Polly's will to stand. His wife's faith in her brother bordered on ridiculous. She considered him invincible, a man who could, and where even remotely possible *would*, make anything happen.

His chest tightened, his headache intensified, his temple throbbing in pain as he tried to dispel the anger building inside him. Watching him intently as he acted as though being related through marriage gave him a right to anything he chose, Frank tightened his fists, wishing he had the guts to smash his brother-in-law's nose and wipe the self-satisfied, smug grin from his face.

"How much has she told you about Beth then?" he blurted, needing a focus to get his anger under control.

"Enough. And it's fairly doable. You agree?"

Seth turned away from Frank, slicing another piece of loaf and sinking the knife into the butter to slather it on again.

"Depends on the approach you take, I guess. Have you made a start already?"

The natural sound of his own voice surprised Frank – no trace of animosity or intense hatred, carefully buried in the recess of his heart and mind as it had been for years. He'd made a ridiculous promise and God help him, though it had frequently come between him and sleep, he'd managed to honour his word. So far.

Munching once more, Seth swung around. "And you really don't have any issue – even though your sister had put her wishes in writing, made no secret of what she truly wanted?"

Frank stalled before replying. He was at a crossroads now. Should he admit his ignorance or merely bluff his way to see what information he could get.

"Seth! What are you doing here? We'd arranged to meet tomorrow!"

Marian's arrival halted Frank's train of thought.

"As I was saying to Frank, I was passing today and thought I'd drop by. Save me a special trip tomorrow. Great cake, Mar."

She nodded dismissively. "Yeah, yeah, eat away." Turning to her husband, she kept her tone even. "I'll take over here. I'm sure you've got more important things to be getting on with."

Wanting nothing more than to stand his ground and listen to their conversation, Frank knew Marian would steer it away from the real reason behind her meeting with Seth so it'd be a waste of his time and energy.

"See you, Seth," he said, ignoring his wife and grabbing his car keys to get the hell out of there before his head exploded.

Frank was seething. He'd missed his chance to find out the full extent of what was going on. Whatever the hell was being cooked up between brother and sister, he'd be well and truly excluded now if Marian had anything to do with it. Typical, he thought. I always let everything slip through my fingers, stalling for time until opportunity passes me by. Well, not this time. Whatever's going on between them, I'm going to find out – one way or another. And I'll bring a stop to it too.

Carl stood in line at the post office, staring without seeing at the collection of advertising posters on the wall. Frank's ultimatum was sinking in. His father-in-law wasn't a man to mince his words. He'd miss Ireland. And Beth, if he were honest with himself. Planning the activity route had been enjoyable, something he'd like to see to fruition if time permitted. Running a hand over his two-day-old beard, he felt the weight of the world on his shoulders. The heady days of adventure were behind him. His brother's mortality forced him to look at his own life and the legacy he'd carelessly cast aside. He envied his father-in-law's ability to clear Ed's name and restore the goodwill of his label. It hadn't been secured as yet but Frank's confidence when they'd discussed it had promised eventual success. As well as envying his capability, Carl was also forced to realise that Frank's devotion to his daughter filled him with jealousy. He had never been idolised by parents. And given his reckless speed and the damage he'd done to his pregnant wife, he would probably never get the opportunity to idolise a son or daughter of his own.

"Next, please."

"I'd like to make a passport application, please."

"Travelling anywhere interesting?" the assistant enquired, pushing the form underneath the glass panel.

"Anybody's guess. Can you put a stamp on this letter, please?" A ghost of a smile flickered across his face as he slipped the letter under the glass partition, hoping it would reach the recipient on time.

"We have an express service if you're in a rush for the passport," she offered.

He rubbed his eyes. The timing of his departure wasn't something he cared to think about. "No urgency today at least," he answered honestly.

He walked away from the counter with the form in his hand, wondering where on earth he'd end up. The prospect of starting over held little appeal. Making it alone held less.

Chapter 32

Driving around in circles trying to clear his head after leaving Seth and Marian, Frank came to a stop at the cemetery. He parked outside the large iron gate and sat in the car a moment to let the worst of his anger dissipate before visiting his sister's grave. Mindlessly watching people coming and going through the gates, he almost didn't recognise Beth as she stumbled through the gates, her shoulders heaving, a hand shielding her eyes.

"Beth!" he called, hurrying from the car and running towards her. "Whatever's the matter?"

"Oh, Dad, nothing I do is ever enough. I'm sinking and sinking and can't seem to do anything about it. You have to help me."

Pulling her close to him, he searched his pockets and handed her a tissue. "Come on, let's sit on the bench over here," he suggested, guiding her to the large wooden bench. "Turn that frown upside down," he whispered in her ear, a phrase he'd used to cheer her up when she'd been a little girl. If anything, his attempt at kindness upset her even more.

He slipped an arm around her shoulders and held her tight again, planting a kiss on her forehead.

"Polly got a nice surprise seeing you at the grave today?"

Of his three children, Beth was the one who traipsed from one disaster to the next and there wasn't anything he could do to change that, at least until she took it upon herself to ask his advice *before* launching into a new project instead of waiting until it was beyond repair.

"A bit late now to be visiting." She turned to look at him, her eyes filled with regret. "If I'd shown her some kindness when she'd been alive –"

"What's done is done, no point looking back. And you mightn't believe it now but things will come good again." His advice was as much for his ears as hers.

Patting her face with the tissue, she exhaled slowly to get her sobbing under control.

Watching her closely, he remembered his earlier conversation with Carl, his warning that he was to disappear from Beth's life. How would she take it? Should he allow the final choice to be hers? Should he test her feelings for him? Was this his opportunity, the two of them on neutral territory with nobody else around to either interfere or interrupt?

Reading his mind, she faced ahead, not meeting his eyes. "Why are you helping Carl and Ed?"

"What has he told you?"

"He said it was to do with keeping Ed's business afloat. Is that true?" She couldn't trust that what Carl had told her was the truth.

"Well, yes . . ."

"But, Dad, Ed's business is drowning, probably beyond saving. You're wasting your time and money."

"Let me be the judge of that," Frank insisted. Why

couldn't Carl have kept his mouth shut instead of dragging Beth into this? Probably safeguarding his back to ensure Frank didn't have a change of heart.

"But we're in as much trouble as Ed. It'll take thousands for us to try and get our heads above water. Why can't Carl get his priorities in order? Or you for that matter?"

Frank's despair deepened. "That's low, Beth. You married Carl and brought him back here, letting us know in no uncertain terms that you wanted to make your own decisions."

"But I asked you for help and you refused!"

"Buying that ridiculous house – no matter what mumbo-jumbo you listened to from the auctioneer – is the rock you two will perish on."

"I'm doing my best to turn it into a business. And we have quite a few interested clients. But I've no backing, monetary or otherwise!" She turned to look at him.

Her eyes were filled with sorrow and despondency, breaking her father's heart.

"Carl?" he asked.

She shrugged indifferently. "He's done a bit but nothing to secure finance to get it up and running. Too busy safeguarding his brother's failed empire!"

"Sometimes we need to fight our own battles and learn from our mistakes," Frank advised.

Though he'd have liked nothing better than to offer her reassurance, promise her the sun, moon and stars to make her feel better and see a brighter look in her eyes, he didn't want to jeopardise this one opportunity he had to get Carl out of her life once and for all. In Frank's opinion, he was single-handedly her biggest problem, his lack of support dragging her down. With him out of the picture, Frank would see what he could do to coax his daughter back to studying and offer her the chance to start over. Still a young woman, her options were limitless. She could do anything she pleased – even though it didn't appear like that now. The prospect of her realising her dreams and capabilities focused him on clearing Ed's name and seeing his son-in-law out of the country.

"Has he any interest in meeting debts? Does he expect the world to fall at his feet? He's certainly not cut from the same cloth as his brother."

Beth's eyes narrowed. What could she say? She agreed with everything he was suggesting but pride prevented her from admitting aloud that her choice of husband had landed her in dire straits. So instead of being honest with Frank, she attacked him.

"Did you bring that into the conversation you had with him when you and he were all cosied up in the café?"

"Not for me to tell him what to do. Is it, Beth?"

"I guess not. Men don't like speaking the truth, do they?"

Frank exhaled, finding the exchange with his daughter tough going. He ached to take his youngest child in his arms, stroke her hair and tell her everything would be okay. He watched as she stood up from the bench.

"Thanks a lot, Dad. I won't make the mistake of asking for help again! So much for putting family first!"

She walked away from her father, leaving him feeling even more fed up and frustrated than he'd been when he'd left his wife and brother-in-law to their private conversation.

Standing at Polly's graveside, an immeasurable sense of peace washed over Frank as he silently shared his problems with his sister. How he wished she hadn't died. How he wished he had appreciated her more when she'd lived. How he wished he'd realised she'd always had his best interests at heart instead of considering her an interfering older sister who hadn't always made the wisest decisions herself.

Beth's anger had upset him. Things were moving extremely slowly on Ed's case. Mags hadn't returned his call. He consoled himself that she'd changed her number. Life had been depressing enough lately without shattering any illusion he carried that she'd be pleased to hear from him. In the absence of her assistance, he was waiting for Interpol to update him on their search into copyright and patent agreements, concrete proof of plagiarism being in short supply, making it very difficult to mount further pressure on his contacts. They'd all returned requesting more evidence-based information, the case needing to be watertight before any of them would touch it.

"I didn't expect to see you here."

Frank jerked his head up at the sound of Kieran's voice. Deep in thought, he hadn't noticed him coming to stand alongside him.

"I could say the same to you."

A comfortable silence settled between them as they stood together, neither of them in a hurry to converse. The afternoon playing football with Greg had been tremendously enjoyable for both, diffusing any remaining annoyance after John Kilmichael's visit.

"Hear any more from our friend Kilmichael?" Frank asked after a while, his gaze fixed on his sister's burial place, imagining her curiosity. Harsh rain had decimated the few remaining floral tributes, petals shattered in the wind, nothing left but withered stalks and stems. The artificial wreaths, though still intact, would undoubtedly fade, the condolence messages disappearing. Yet still, despite their lack of authenticity, the plastic arrangements would survive the elements – in the same way as Polly's love for her only son did.

"Not since but I called Olivia to verify I wasn't mistaken. Their meeting is moved to next week."

"What I don't understand is why she lied to me. There shouldn't have been a reason. I never judged, barely discussed John with her. She broached the subject on every occasion, insisting he didn't know he was her son." Frank's voice caught in his throat.

Kieran shuffled his feet, his father's raw emotion making him very uncomfortable. He'd never seen his father cry. What should he do if he did? Throw an arm around his shoulders? Pat him on the back? Would that be enough? Surely he wouldn't be expected to hug him in broad daylight? His eyes darting around the grave looking for something to do and escape the awkwardness of the moment, he collected the withered flowers, bundling them in his arms and resuming his stance at the graveside next to his father – ensuring there was a safe distance between them. Even if I wanted to, I can't hug him now, he thought, not with all these dead flowers in my arms.

"Dad, you might as well fill me in on what you know. John's not a man for disappearing, it seems, and I've walked myself into enough trouble with him already."

"I rue the day she tracked him down." Frank gazed into the distance, a peculiar look in his eye. "Her life was easier without him. He's been nothing but an added complication."

"Huh? Tracked him down? That's the part I don't get.

She went to the trouble of finding him and inviting him into her life in order to lie to him!" Kieran was confused. It didn't make sense.

"She wanted to be close to him, yet was determined not to tell him the truth about his conception."

"I don't understand. I'm assuming she had him adopted? You heard me asking him but he didn't respond."

A breeze kicked up. Frank pulled the collar of his navy wax jacket around his neck, shoving his hands in his pockets.

"It's difficult to explain, Kieran. Handing him over hours after his birth devastated her. The way she described it, it was like a part of her died in that moment."

"But all I remember is her being full of life, always in good form. That can't have been an act. I couldn't be so insensitive that I didn't notice." Kieran was insistent, not wanting the warm memories of his aunt to be thwarted in any fashion. He'd have noticed if she'd been depressed. Wouldn't he?

"On the outside, maybe, but what she felt inside told a whole other story and many years had passed by the time you started staying there."

If he'd felt guilty for neglecting his aunt in recent years, he felt ten times worse now! There I was every summer, he thought, treating her home like a hostel and happy to enjoy her meals and warm welcome without giving a thought to her feelings. "I must have been blind not to notice," he admitted.

Frank turned to look at his son. "She adored you, Kieran. It was years after his birth before she confided in me. Can you imagine how I felt?" Shaking his head, he still found it difficult to believe he'd been so selfish, so caught up in his own life and career that he'd taken little notice of what she had been going through.

"She must have felt so alone." Kieran stared at the grave.

Sensing his son's anguish and unfounded guilt, Frank strived to reassure him. "I often wondered if she substituted you for him, if you somehow managed to take his place."

Kieran shook his head and groaned. This was too much to take in. "I can believe she had a son – but, of course, why not? But he doesn't seem like her at all, neither physically or in personality. Though there is something familiar about him too . . . Don't you think so?"

"Can't say. I met him by accident – just happened to be there one day when he called. After that – because I can't say I was very civil to him – Polly made sure our paths didn't cross unless it was unavoidable."

"When did she tell you about him? Was it that first time you met him?" Kieran stared at the grave again, wishing Polly could rise from the earth, sit there without hurrying him, grinning at him and answer his questions – like she'd done so many times in the past.

Frank shook his head, remembering an afternoon several years before when he'd turned up on Polly's doorstep unexpectedly. Turning the door handle, he'd been surprised to find it locked in the middle of a summer afternoon. The door to Number 5 was never locked. In fact, on a warm sunny day it was seldom even closed! Sensing something was amiss, he let himself in through the back gate, his heart skipping a beat when he found his sister curled up in a ball on the kitchen floor, her body heaving as she sobbed her heart out. Though she'd been reluctant at first to tell him what was wrong, she'd eventually relented when he'd refused to leave while she was in such a state. Sitting with her brother that afternoon, she'd disclosed every gory detail, apart from the father's identity. It was a long time before she disclosed that final nugget of information.

"Dad?"

Frank's thoughts were interrupted. He'd forgotten Kieran's original question, anxious instead to warn his son about something very important where John Kilmichael was concerned.

"I swear to you, she never told John that he was her son." Frank's expression was very serious.

"Well, he knows now!"

"So he found out in some other way!"

"But I just don't get it! If she went to the trouble of tracking him down, why didn't she tell him the truth?"

Frank kicked at some stray earth with the toe of his shoe, pushing it over the side of the grave.

"Various reasons. So she wouldn't have to look him in the eye and admit she had given him away. So she wouldn't have to disclose the identity of his father. And there was another factor – she was honouring the memory of her beloved Glen, her lost husband. She was a widow after all and he wasn't that long dead when she became pregnant. It would have been a scandal – brought disgrace on his name."

"But she denied herself . . ."

"Story of her life," Frank said. "Polly was a saint, went to her grave putting everyone else before herself."

Kieran twisted the stems of the flowers, liquid seeping from some of them as he squeezed them tightly. "Even me now, Dad? Willing me the house, she has denied her own son."

Frank continued as though he hadn't heard. "Some of those she was protecting barely gave her the time of day, didn't even attend her funeral!"

"Dad?" Frank's statement confused his son.

"Polly knew exactly what she was doing leaving her house to you, asking you to stay there for twelve months so that you wouldn't sell it first chance you got. She had high hopes for you, felt you'd been away long enough but wouldn't ever say it directly to you."

Kieran's head was melting. "Did you know what was in the will?"

Frank shook his head. "Not an inkling. But she often spoke about you, worried about you wandering the world for too long. I think in her own way she was showing you that putting down roots isn't the worst thing you could do."

"Well, it looks like John Kilmichael knew more than Polly then?" Kieran deduced.

"Your solicitor will have the answer to that," Frank said.

"Why don't we go to the city next week and wait outside Olivia's building, witness him going in and catch him red-handed?"

Father and son looked at each other, both struggling with an inherent obligation to Polly but neither wanting John Kilmichael to have the satisfaction of deceiving them.

"That's not a bad idea," Frank admitted. "We could be outside her office when he's on his way out. Then there would be no denying he's lying."

"So what *did* Polly tell John when she tracked him down?" Kieran asked.

"Pretended his birth mother had been a very good friend of hers, invented a tale about her dying, keeping a promise not to divulge any more."

"Sounds a bit loose to me. Did he fall for that?"

"He did when she handed him €10,000 and pretended his mother had left it in trust for him!"

Kieran zipped his jacket up to his neck. "And she told you this?"

"Eventually," Frank sighed. "Like you I kept questioning. Eventually she told me."

"And he never pressurised her for more information about his supposed mother or even his natural father?"

"Not that she told me," Frank replied, turning to leave the graveside with Kieran following a short distance behind.

"And John's father? Do you know who it is, Dad?"

Frank chose to ignore his son's final question, allowing the words to disappear in the wind, guarding his sister's secret as he'd promised he would.

Chapter 33

"Yes, I can hold," Charlotte said, swinging around in her office chair to take in the magnificent view from her office and savour the heat from the sun shining through the enormous windowpane.

"Olivia Jacobs speaking."

Charlotte swung her chair around once more, referring to the page of notes she'd prepared in advance of the call. "Hi, thanks for taking my call."

"How may I help you today?"

"I'm calling about Pauline Digby's will. My brother tells me you're the solicitor looking after it."

"Yes. Are you a relation of Pauline's?"

"Her niece, Charlotte Dulhooly," she replied, fiddling with her computer mouse, unable to resist opening Facebook and logging in as Mia Zepo.

"Is there something specific you'd like to discuss?"

Charlotte's response was delayed, her attention wavering as Philip Lord's profile picture appeared on the screen and his name popped up for instant chat.

I'd like to meet you?

The message was glaring, his intention even more so. Instantly she was transported to similar messages she'd received from him a couple of years before when she'd been a junior in the bank.

"Charlotte, is this a bad connection? My secretary tells me you're calling from Toronto."

"Sorry, my fault," she said. "I was distracted for a moment. I'm ringing about an objection that was lodged against my aunt's will."

Her voice trembled, Philip's suggestive message mocking her. She noticed he'd uploaded a video on his profile. Curious, she clicked on the play button and watched him come to life on the screen. His voice filled her office. She froze and dropped the receiver, clicking frantically on the mouse to try and mute the volume.

"Hello, hello, are you there?"

Charlotte disconnected as she watched in dread. Philip took a microphone and began his presentation speech. His voice, the sneer on his lips, his insincere tone – the same details that regularly tormented her as she lay in bed at night – reverberated in her office as clear as if he were standing over her. She was back in the nightmare of his attack, her flesh cut open, her mind fraught with fear.

After what was only a few seconds but felt like an age, she managed to silence him, immediately directing the cursor to the Facebook settings, her hand trembling as she frantically figured out how to deactivate the account. It was time to delete Mia Zepo, time to let her and Philip Lord back to their virtual world where their antics would no longer be a form of torment for Charlotte.

I've taunted myself enough with this insanity, she thought,

regretting her journey into the past. It had bordered on lunacy, yet had helped her realise how far from 'cured' she was.

In a strange country, she'd been coping – something she and those around her had initially believed impossible. Her determination to fight back forced her out of bed in the morning, kept her going throughout her busy days.

Still shaking, she pushed away the memories. Staring at her reflection in the glass, her Ralph Lauren turtle neck was yet another reminder. But Philip Lord had taken more than a layer of her skin. He'd stripped her outer layer of confidence and stripped her trust in the opposite sex. Seeing the deep jagged dent in her chest every time she stood naked before a mirror, she knew she'd had a lucky escape when her cries for help had brought the event manager running from the conference room further along the corridor. Due to have left the building a half hour before, a technical glitch had forced the bank's party planner to stay on – to Philip Lord's detriment, as it turned out that evening.

Hearing her burst through the door, he'd dropped the corkscrew he'd been dragging through Charlotte's skin and scurried through an alternative exit before their visitor could properly identify him. A flurry of medics and operations followed for Charlotte, rumours and speculation rife in the bank as to what happened between Philip Lord and his favourite protégée.

The bank's management had offered her the opportunity to sue and her father had pleaded with her to destroy him but Charlotte hadn't enough fight in her to either defend or deny the favours she'd been shown throughout her career. She envisaged a nasty court case, expecting him to strongly insinuate that she'd led him on, accepting promotions in return for intimate relations. Unable to face either the ordeal or the consequences, she'd booked a one-way flight to Toronto and fled once she was physically fit to travel. Her eyes wide open now, she knew she needed some form of recovery counselling, something she'd avoided until now.

She swivelled in her chair and faced the Toronto skyline once more, oblivious to the activity on Bloor Street or the intensity of rush-hour traffic below, several minutes passing before she eventually remembered that she'd cut Olivia Jacobs off.

Dialling the solicitor's number once more, she waited to be put through. This time she kept her chair turned away from her computer screen, resisting any further distraction.

"Charlotte, what happened there? I could still hear someone speaking in the background but you were gone . . ."

"I don't know. I've been trying to get though again but couldn't. Sorry about that."

"Well, in any case . . . I'm assuming you're supporting your sister's objection? The documentation I received mentioned you but doesn't appear to have your signature."

"No, I'm not supporting Beth on this occasion."

"I see."

Charlotte swung around in her chair once more, remembering her school pal's expert advice. Managing to track Josephine down, she'd enjoyed a catch-up with her old friend and shared the story of Number 5 with her in confidence.

Listening with interest, Josephine had completely ruled out Seth's attempt to question Polly's ownership. "Any solicitor worth her salt will have thoroughly looked into that," Josephine had advised. But she wasn't as confident of his fight with new medical evidence. "No doubt," she explained, "a court case will eventually see the truth come out but at what cost? At any rate, your father's the only one that can truly lodge an objection. He's her true next of kin."

"But I'm guessing the medical evidence can't be ignored either?" Charlotte had asked.

"Cripes, Lottie, your family will be torn apart if your uncle pursues things. And there'll be precious little left of the inheritance if you end up hiring barristers and the likes for both sides."

The family photograph on Charlotte's desk attracted her attention now, filling her with disbelief that her family had been reduced to such backstabbing behaviour.

"The reason I'm calling is to offer my brother support," she said to Olivia. "He's perfectly entitled to everything he has received and I for one couldn't be happier for him."

The pause that followed this statement betrayed Olivia's surprise. "In that case I'd appreciate it if you'd have your name removed from the objection."

"I know my uncle's coming up with all sorts of ridiculous notions on behalf of my sister but I'd advise close scrutiny of whatever you receive."

"So your uncle's behind this?" Olivia enquired.

"With my sister's permission, I believe. It's a mess at this stage, Olivia, but I'm officially opting out and I'd like that on record."

"I've no doubt but that your aunt would be pleased to hear it."

Charlotte muttered a few quick words of thanks and hung up, then at once dialled another Irish number – her father's this time. It was only right that he be informed of what was going on. If anybody would know how to bring this charade to a stop, he would.

"Damn," she muttered, failing to get through to her father's mobile, pressing redial every time it sounded the irritating recorded message telling her the person she was calling had their mobile switched off. But she was determined to keep trying until she finally managed to speak with him. He deserved to know the truth and she owed it to him to tell him. Without question or judgement, he'd been there for her when she'd needed him most. It was high time she stopped self-obsessing and set about taking responsibility for a change. Taking control of every aspect of her life was within her grasp. It was up to her to reach out and grab it.

Chapter 34

Ed's condition had deteriorated. Waking in the morning to find a nurse standing over him with a syringe in her hand, he knew his readings had lowered. Another notch in the wrong direction as far as he was concerned.

"Will I make it through the day?" he muttered, barely able to speak and finding it hard to swallow.

"Give over!" She gave a throaty laugh. "Looking for an excuse to put on your suit?"

He stuck out his arm, feeling like a pincushion they'd taken so much blood from him lately. Tests, tests and more tests! He often wondered why they bothered. In his own business, a piece of top-grade fabric cut into the wrong shape would be instantly discarded. He couldn't understand why they didn't do the same with him. A wasting body and a tired mind. Not much left on either count. He closed his eyes again, the effort of thinking exhausting. He'd hold on as long as he could but, short of a miracle, he felt he'd be over on the other side before he'd get to see his name in lights again.

Beth peered around the door to Ed's room, her heart

plummeting when she saw his wizened form slumped over in the chair. For the briefest moment, she thought she was too late, but then he let out some peculiar sound – a mixture between a groan and a grunt – and she let out the breath she'd been holding.

Retreating from the room and closing the door gently behind her, she took a stroll along the corridor and stopped at the tiny chapel, despite having very little faith of any description. Slipping into a pew she dropped to her knees and prayed for her brother-in-law.

Meeting Ed on occasion when she'd lived with Carl in Paris, she'd felt shy and uneasy around him. In her early twenties, she'd found it difficult to hold a lengthy conversation with a man in his forties, small talk soon running out. Carl, on the other hand, continually strived to impress him by regaling him with tales of his adventures. But his defences rose when Ed questioned him on his career plans or indeed his plans to take over the running of their parents' vineyard instead of leasing it out to complete strangers.

"That's your living, Carl," he'd advised his wayward brother, repeating it at every given opportunity. "Your income could improve tenfold if you worked the vineyard, could be a thriving business if you market it properly."

"Rental income's enough for me," the lazy Carl always argued. "I'm not going to waste my life tending grapes and irate buyers, not to mention worrying if the next crop will be a disaster."

Typical Carl, Beth thought with a sigh. Expecting the world to spin around him, pushing and pushing until there was no turning back.

Getting to her feet she turned to leave, bumping right into her father as she stepped into the narrow aisle. It was their first meeting since their heated exchange outside of the cemetery.

"Beth?"

"Dad." Mindful that she was in a chapel, she lowered her voice to a whisper. "You're here to see Ed?"

"Who else?" He followed her from the chapel without stopping to pray. "About the other day . . ."

She shook her head and raised a hand. "Let's not drag it up again. I've given a lot of thought to what you said and you're right. I shouldn't be relying on others so much." She gave him a ghost of a smile. "Time I grew up and stood on my own two feet."

Yet again, he ached to reach out and protect her but at least his words of advice had served for something. "Have you been here long? How's Ed's form today?"

"He was sleeping when I arrived so I haven't spoken to him yet. But if looks are anything to go by, he's not good." She took a closer look at her father, noticing the reduced number of dark hairs amidst the silver strands. There were shadows underneath his eyes and his jacket hung loosely on his shoulders. "Have you lost weight, Dad?" she asked.

"Not that I've noticed," he replied.

"There's a cafeteria here. Will we share a cream bun and then visit Ed together?" Her invitation surprised her as much as him. Had it been that long since she'd shown him any concern? Had her offer of a coffee come as such a great surprise? It would be good, she thought, to have company when she returned to Ed's room. She waited for his agreement.

But Frank was torn. Much as he wanted to join her, he worried that it would complicate things further. His main reason for coming had been to discuss Ed's business with him, get as much detail as he could on the circumstances surrounding the theft and plagiarism of his designs. Carl's information had lacked the attention to detail required. He'd have to hear Ed's version of events and decide for himself if there was any point in pursuing the venture.

But he couldn't do that with Beth present. It wasn't ideal death-bed conversation and she'd tell him so too! Despite her impulsive business decisions, he didn't underestimate his daughter's intelligence. And he didn't want to isolate her any further than he had already.

To hear him discussing a potential legal suit – in France at that – she'd instantly realise the cost of something so big. Taking a case to the European courts would run to tens of thousands if they lost. Naturally she would resent his decision to invest in Ed's cause over hers. And he couldn't risk explaining why he was doing it. That would lead him into further trouble. Would Beth resent him for interfering? Would she turn her back on him forever? Love was an enigma – one of the few things that had withstood the test of time.

Beth stared at him, an expectant look in her eye. He still hadn't responded to her question.

"Dad? Coffee and a cream bun before we go to see Ed?"

"Eh, I'm not sure." He pulled back the sleeve of his jumper and checked the time on his watch. "I hadn't intended staying so long. I'm watching my cholesterol – staying away from coffee and buns to be honest. What if I go and sit with him for a few minutes and then let you make your visit?" The health bit is true, he thought, remembering the last warning he'd received about his diet.

Stung by his refusal, Beth didn't argue. "Whatever,

Dad. I'm trying to build bridges here but it's obvious you're not interested."

Reaching out, he placed a hand on her arm. "That's not it, Beth. I'll always be interested."

"Just not enough to make the time to show it, Dad," she bit back at him. "Same as when we were kids and you'd rather be anywhere than spend some time at home with us." She turned away from him, hiding her disappointment.

"Beth, wait!" he called softly.

He stared after her as she walked away.

Beth sat by the cafeteria window, keeping an eye on her father's Mercedes, determined to stay away from her brother-in-law's room until Frank had left. Her feelings hurt yet again, she wasn't about to give him another opportunity to push her away.

"Bad day?"

Her head shot up. A woman of about the same age as herself stood next to her table. Shaved head, no eyebrows and a pale complexion – her story didn't require much explanation. Beth was jolted out of her self-pitying mood. *She's the one asking me how I'm doing. She's the one offering me sympathy. I'm sitting here feeling sorry for myself. There's nothing stopping me doing anything I want. I can leave anytime I want. I can jump in puddles, skip and play hopscotch, dance to my favourite tune, eat and drink what I want and yet here I am acting like a spoilt child.*

She smiled at the other lady. There wasn't any point in denying she'd been fed up. "In my head it's a bad day anyway," she admitted.

"It's all measurable," the other girl said. "I'd be so

happy if my family would relent to my cremation. You wouldn't believe the arguments they're putting up."

Beth's mouth dropped open. How could she respond to that nugget? "Would you like something to drink?" she offered instead.

Her companion giggled. "I've embarrassed you now, made you feel uncomfortable. Haven't I?"

Beth smiled. "Not exactly the conversation I'd expected," she admitted, gesturing toward the chair. "Join me?"

"For a few minutes. Got my tanning session in a few minutes."

Again, Beth's face reddened. This time, however, she didn't shrink away. "How can you make a joke out of something so serious?"

"Laugh or cry? Which would you choose? The end result's the same anyway." She shrugged. "So, are you going to get me that drink you offered?"

Beth got to her feet, hoping she had enough change in her purse. "What's your tipple?"

"Vodka and soda," she said, watching Beth's expression with interest. "Without the vodka."

Returning to the table with a can of 7UP and glass of tap water, Beth placed the can in front of the other girl.

"Who's here belonging to you?"

"Brother-in-law."

"Has he long left?"

Again, her outspokenness instilled a moment's unease. She hadn't faced up to his mortality, too busy resenting Carl and worrying about keeping the banks at bay.

"Not long," she replied. "I'm Beth. What's your name?"

"Doesn't matter," she replied. "You won't know me long enough to remember. A little while and I'm out of here."

"Going home?"

The other girl looked at her a moment, a ghost of a smile on her lips, a faraway look in her eyes.

"Oh!" said Beth. "Ah no. I'm sorry."

"Sorry? I'm not. I'm fed up of being prodded and poked, treated like a guinea pig. There has to be something better. Even if it's only sleep. Has to be an improvement. The life I want to live is no longer an option for me." She picked up the can.

Beth watched her hand shake as she brought the can to her lips, her tiny wrists appearing from beneath long pyjama sleeves. She fought back a gasp. The girl was skin and bone, taking one sip requiring a huge effort.

"Summer?"

Both girls looked up, Beth's companion slowly getting to her feet when the nurse called her name again. Before moving away, she turned to Beth, her words filled with sincerity.

"Go live your life. Live it for both of us. Don't waste it sitting around with a long face drinking tasteless coffee." She extended her hand and shook Beth's.

Watching Summer shuffle away, linking the nurse's arm for support, her chit-chat making the nurse chuckle, Beth was intrigued. So close to death, she thought, yet still in high spirits and interested in offering others the benefit of her advice.

Glancing toward the car park, Beth noticed with regret that her father's car was no longer in the spot opposite the window. Her anger had dissipated, her exchange with Summer altering her perspective. She'd acted childishly and was humbled now by the other girl's intense courage. Ridiculous behaviour at my age, she thought, planning on finding Frank and apologising as soon as she left the hospital.

Sympathising with the mixture of emotions Ed must be experiencing, she wondered why he'd summoned her for a private visit. Whatever his reasons, she was about to find out.

Chapter 35

"You should go shopping, Beth," Ed smiled when she entered the room.

"I'm not sure that's meant as a compliment?" Though her tone was severe, her lips shaped into a smile as she bent to kiss his cheek.

"That coat you're wearing is enormous. Why hide such a slight frame in something so – so – shapeless?"

Beth laughed. Ed's passion for style would obviously continue until he drew his last breath.

"You should be wearing my sculpted pieces. Designed with a figure like yours in mind."

She didn't like to tell him that she couldn't afford them at cost price, never mind purchase them off the rails. "Ah, my life's too dull. Who'd appreciate them in the local Centra when I go to buy the bread and milk?"

Ed pulled himself up in the chair, the blanket slipping from his knees.

Beth stooped to retrieve it, fixing it around him.

He grasped her hand tightly, his grip strong despite his

frailty. "Beth, I want you to promise you'll keep an eye on Carl? Make him laugh, see he's happy. For me?"

Beth swallowed hard, her hand still in the firm grip of his sinewy fingers. I can't make that promise, she thought. Not when I know I won't keep it. Do I lie to him? Or lie to myself? She recognised vulnerability in his face. She hadn't witnessed that before.

"Ed," she began, "Carl's a big boy. I'm not sure he needs protecting."

"Before you came along, he was even more reckless. You've been a stabilising influence."

"How boring does that make me sound?" she commented good-humouredly, wondering if he'd be quite so complimentary if he knew Carl's recklessness had lost him everything.

"Please. I need to know somebody's watching out for him – at least for a while after I'm gone."

This is crazy, Beth thought, overcome with a fresh bout of irritation. Carl is older than I am, yet Ed's treating him as though he were a small child who needed childcare. He certainly acts like one, she couldn't help thinking. Out of nowhere, Summer's words came back to her. I need to live my life too, she thought.

"Ed, Carl's not as defenceless as you think. You're his priority at the moment. He'll continue to be here for you. But he will be okay in time . . . after . . . I mean. Have no fear."

Ed leaned back against the multiple pillows on his chair. "There are things you don't know about our upbringing, our parents."

Oh believe me, Beth grimaced inside, there are things you don't know about your parents' legacy either. And never will if Carl has his way. He's not the innocent little brother you'd like him to be. Tempted as she was to blurt out her husband's shortcomings, she maintained her reserve. There's nothing to be gained, not even for me, she thought.

"I'm trying to make a small return on the house at the moment," she told him instead, giving him something new to focus his attention on and happy to discuss it with an experienced businessman.

"Yeah? Tell me more. Carl never said."

"It's only at teething stage so far," she explained, "but I've had quite a few enquiries." She noticed how this news relaxed him. Pity Carl didn't meet it with similar enthusiasm.

"What is it you're up to exactly? Renting a portion of the house?"

There hadn't been time to show Ed the place they'd bought, his deteriorating health in such an aggravated state at that time, though Carl had shown him photos and videos and described their original plans for the old place to distract him from his own concerns.

"Too much work required on the house for that option, Ed. It wouldn't pass a Health and Safety inspection the way it is now. No, it's a bit more creative than that. I'm, I mean *we're* trying to utilise the grounds, seeing as we can't sell them as a separate entity." She proceeded to fill him in on the ideas Charlotte had given her, explained the progress they'd made since, enjoying his input and going as far as jotting a few things as a reminder on her phone so she wouldn't forget.

"You're good at this. Business decisions come second nature to you," she said, wishing things could be different. Her brother-in-law had always been waiting in the wings to offer support, Carl's biggest mistake being that he'd neither listened nor accepted his help.

"Years of restructuring to try and keep up with changing trends," Ed replied. "The fashion industry is one of the cruellest sectors – dog eat dog."

Beth nodded. "Always need to be a step ahead, I guess?"

Ed sighed. "It can be tough trying to keep going when every door you knock on is banged firmly in your face."

"Tell me about it! And the pressure from the banks isn't helping."

Ed winced as a sharp stab of pain coursed through his body.

She jumped to her feet. "Are you okay? Will I call a nurse?"

But he shook his head. "It's nothing. It'll pass in a while."

She remained standing. "Perhaps I've tired you out. I should leave."

"Oh no, please don't. Stay another while. I'll just rest my eyes a few moments." He gestured for her to sit.

Beth waited patiently. It wasn't as if she had anything else pressing on her time. Catching up with her father could wait until the following day if necessary. No rush. Neither of them was going anywhere.

Watching Ed closely, she noticed his facial muscles twitch, the way he clenched and unclenched his fists – obviously still suffering. Taking a tissue from his bedside locker, she mopped the perspiration from his brow. "Water?"

He nodded, conserving what little energy he had left.

She held the glass to his lips and tilted it to make it easier for him to drink, concerned that her visit was wearing him out. "I'm leaving in a few minutes, Ed. You need proper rest."

He gave a ghost of a smile. "One more question?"

She placed the glass back on the locker and sat down. Not another question I can't answer, she thought.

"Why is Carl holding on to the vineyard when it's obvious the proceeds could make such a difference to you both now? He should sell it."

She stared ahead, avoiding his eye. If she ever wanted an opportunity to hurt Carl, Ed had presented it to her now on a plate. "Eh, have you discussed it with him?"

It took great effort but he leaned forward in the chair and forced her to meet his eye. "It's *nothing* whatsoever to do with me. You're his wife. What's his is yours. At least that's my understanding of how marriages work."

Not ours, Beth thought silently.

Ed mistook her silence for politeness. "I took my share from our parents long before their death. I ploughed every cent into setting up my business . . ." His voice trailed off for a moment, obviously thinking of the damage that business had suffered recently.

"Carl . . ." she began, opening and closing her mouth as she tried to think of something to say. How could she tell him that Carl had gambled heavily, lost to the croupier, chased his losses until finally he'd lost a viable South of France vineyard?

"I think I know what you're going to say," Ed interrupted. "Carl wants to help me."

"Of course he does." She nodded a little too enthusiastically. It was partly true. He did want to help his brother – but he wasn't in a position to do so financially.

"I've noticed the worry and strain in his eyes. He's protecting me from the truth, doesn't believe he can tell me what's wrong because I'm ill."

That's for sure, Beth thought. Protecting himself too.

Has been for quite some time now and will continue to do so. "He cares a lot for you, Ed," she said eventually, the lengthening pause adding to her discomfort.

"I understand that."

Beth wished Carl could be sincere and responsible like Ed. Perhaps they'd have a chance of survival then. Maybe they could even get past the loss of their baby.

But she knew she wasn't totally blameless. A voice inside her head reminded her of the heady excitement she'd felt when they'd met first. His unpredictability had made her heart thump in her chest. He'd helped her lose inhibitions, had encouraged her to push beyond boundaries of fear, joining him as they flaunted danger and mostly won. Remembering the excitement he'd exuded, she realised that he hadn't changed with maturity. He was still the same wild young man he'd always been. But life had changed her. The days of playing with fire were long gone – plenty of smouldering ashes left behind along with a hefty bill in tow.

"I care for him too . . . for both of you."

"And I for you," she said, swallowing the lump that stuck in her throat.

Beth was transported back to the first time she'd met Ed, reminded of his strong physique, his charcoal hair sleeked back from his tanned face, a red scarf wrapped loosely around his neck, brightening his dark clothing. Ed had personified haute couture, his sense of style appearing effortless, the warmth in his eyes diffusing any fear she'd had of meeting him.

"The vineyard?" Ed's energy was fading.

Beth didn't answer. She didn't want to lie. Neither did she want to tell the truth and risk the shock shortening his life even further.

"Don't feel bad . . ." He stopped to catch his breath, bringing a hand to his mouth and running his finger over his lips. "Carl's covering the cost of my case against that oaf in Lyon."

She sat up straight in her chair. "He is?" Her voice broke, stress rising inside her. Carl had already been injecting money they didn't have, attempting to maintain the utilities in Ed's design centre in Paris. Her father obviously hadn't divulged his interest to Ed or the details of his arrangement with Carl, obviously protecting the other man from further humiliation.

Her brother-in-law frowned. "If you have an objection . . . ?"

She shook her head, not trusting herself to speak. At this rate, even with Polly's inheritance if Seth manages to force it through, we'll still be bankrupt!

He visibly relaxed – almost to the point of sleeping. His eyes were closed, his breathing faint.

Could I slip out now without answering any more of his questions, she wondered? But seeing his lips move once more changed her mind.

His voice was little more than a whisper, his eyes still closed.

Beth strained to hear.

"The business, my good name, is my only legacy. I spent years building it, working perilously . . . around the clock at times . . . lost everything else."

"Don't wear yourself out, Ed. You don't have to explain."

"But I do!"

"I understand how much it means to you –" On closer inspection, she noticed tears on his cheeks.

"I sacrificed far too much for my designs, struggled to

continue improving, expecting everything – and everyone – to wait silently in the wings."

Beth didn't comment.

"You and Carl – something's wrong. What is it?"

Beth stood up and went to the window, trailing a finger along the window frame. The sky was darkening, a deluge on the way in her estimation. She turned back to face Ed, remaining where she was, not wanting him scrutinising her too closely as she responded to his last question.

"Responsibility – or lack of," she told him. "We both know it's not one of Carl's strong points."

"He'll get there," Ed defended his brother.

Beth kept her hands behind her back and gripped the window sill. "We lost a baby," she admitted, without divulging any further detail. "We've found it impossible to move beyond it."

Ed nodded slowly. "Now that makes more sense. I sensed something serious wedged between you. The loss of a child must be excruciating. Why hasn't Carl told me this?"

Beth's grip on the sill tightened. "He's not one for sharing his feelings like you."

"Counselling?"

"No." She steeled against the hurt.

"Still grieving?"

She moved back to sit opposite him, the pain in her eyes an unspoken response.

He caught her hands in his. The strength in his grip surprised her.

"I lost my one true love, took his patience for granted and expected him to wait forever," he said. "When my designs were copied, it tore through my heart, ripping it open, like a seamstress unstitching one of my favourite garments. It was as if my whole life – joy and suffering – had been for nothing, as though I'd never existed, a wasted effort." He was gasping by now. "It pains me to watch Carl going down the same route, taking you for granted. He doesn't understand the value he has in both hands. He won't appreciate it until it's gone."

Beth exhaled, disagreeing with the illusion he had about his younger brother. What she and Carl had wasn't based on a solid foundation. It lacked substance. They'd fallen at every hurdle, losing their baby the most detrimental of their disasters.

"I'm not sure there's any love left between us," she admitted eventually. "I'm not sure it existed in the first place. Lust without a doubt. Excitement too. But not the depth of love required to overcome life's cruellest blows. We struggled as two individuals, anguish dividing us as a couple."

Ed licked his lips and spoke again, the effort it took to continue obvious. "Carl is still fighting the past, and not only his immediate past. He needs to stop battling against his upbringing, the rigidity we experienced as young boys. Insist he sells the vineyard. The proceeds will go a long way in meeting your debt here. And my sculpture collection is worth a bit too . . . although it's probably a specialised market . . ."

Oh, he's let the vineyard go a long time ago, Beth thought, remembering how it had slipped through his fingers like butter sliding off piping hot toast. But what sculpture collection? It was the first she'd heard of it.

"Your collection – I thought everything had been reinvested back into your business?"

He shook his head. "Saved it by the skin of my teeth."

"Carl never mentioned this. Where is it now? Are you sure it's safe?"

"In storage in Paris." He closed his eyes again, his voice little more than a whisper.

"I'll call again soon, Ed. I promise," she said with a smile, fixing the blanket around his knees again.

"What will become of him without you?" His words came out in a rush.

A vivid image of Carl strolling down the long avenue, a bag slung over his shoulder as he set out on his new life flashed in front of Beth's eyes. "He'll make his own decisions and, knowing Carl, he will land on his feet. You'll see . . ."

"But I won't see!" Ed's voice shook with emotion. "He'll be alone, without an anchor, living an aimless life."

Beth closed her eyes a moment, guilt weighing heavily on her shoulders. Putting up face and assuming a happy marriage was a thing of yesterday as far as she was concerned. And Ed was no fool. Reassurance would be kinder.

She planted a kiss on his forehead. "Carl's stronger and more resilient than you think."

Ed shook his head, unconvinced. "He'll self-destruct on his own."

Beth laid her hands flat on his knees and looked directly at him, speaking candidly and meaning every word. "We're draining the life from each other, Ed. Neither of us have anything to give back. We'll be better apart. Perhaps, with a bit of distance, we will find a way to remain friends. Stranger things have happened. But more than anything we need to flourish as individuals."

Closing his eyes, he nodded his head, accepting her

explanation. He had tried. There was nothing else he could do. It was up to the young couple now to do what they felt was best.

"But you will stay with him until I'm gone – help him through the funeral arrangements? Otherwise God knows what he'll do with my remains!"

"I'd be happy to, Ed. You can rely on that."

He gave a weak smile. "And my ashes – you know what to do?"

"I do."

Leaving the hospice, spirits strangely higher than when she'd arrived, Beth inhaled the fresh air as she stepped into the sharp breeze, a marked contrast to the stifling building she'd left behind. Whether it brings disappointments or surprises, I've a chance of a future, she thought, turning the key and letting the jeep's engine roar to life before moving smoothly along the passageway. Left for Goleen and right to visit her parents' home in Ballydehob. Choosing to make peace with her father, she increased the radio volume and veered right as she went through the gate. Rehearsing in her mind what she would say to him, the road ahead seemed brighter than it had in a very long time.

Chapter 36

Frank drove around aimlessly, his heart heavy, his head reeling. Ed's deterioration since his last visit was stark, forcing Frank to appreciate how important it was to him to die with his reputation intact. And also minimising the timescale he had left to work on forcing Carl out of the country. He'd follow up with his acquaintances again, try and get them to appreciate the urgency of his request. He pulled into the car park of Bantry's Westlodge Hotel.

He rubbed his chest with the heel of his hand. "Damn indigestion," he muttered, deciding he'd pop into the bar and order a bowl of soup once he'd finished his calls. It'd save him making something when he got home. Marian, no doubt, would be continuing her Ice Queen act, the luxury of a dinner being handed to him a very slim chance. He began to make his calls.

Leaving Mags until last, he dialled her number, expecting it to go straight to voicemail like all his previous attempts. To his surprise, she answered on the second ring, her voice huskier than he remembered, little resemblance to the sweet flirtatious tone she'd had years before.

"Mags?"

"I'm sorry?"

He recognised her hesitancy. It had obviously been a while since her name had been shortened.

"Frank Dulhooly here, Mags. It's been quite a few years." He held his breath, hoping she'd remember him. His pride would be severely dented otherwise.

"My God! How long has it been?"

Frank sank into the driver's seat of his Mercedes, staring across at the magnificent scenery of Sheep's Head as he prepared to catch up with an old friend. Despite his wife's suspicions and accusations, they'd never shared anything other than a platonic relationship, albeit one loaded with inexplicable and undeniable chemistry, something they'd managed to resist despite a mutual attraction. He wondered what she looked like now, deciding as he caught sight of his own ghastly reflection in the mirror that he'd hold on to the image of the svelte redhead he'd carried with him since his twenties. No need to ruin it with the harsh reality of ageing.

"Before we go down the route of old times, tell me you're still a hot shot in private eye work?"

"Leader of the European pack now," she laughed. "Or so they tell me!"

Frank launched into Ed's story, explaining what he'd been told and asking if she could see a way to help.

"How much time are we talking?"

"Very little based on the seriously ill man I've just seen in the hospice," Frank admitted, opening the car window to let in some fresh air. "There's a lot riding on it, Mags. Only for that I wouldn't be wasting your valuable time."

"I'll always make time to help an old friend, Frank. I'm glad you called."

The confidence in her voice was consoling, lifting a degree of pressure from his shoulders. He wasn't naïve enough to expect miracles, but sharing the immense burden of the next-to-impossible case with Mags eased the suffocating pressure that had been descending upon him.

Kieran crawled out from underneath his aunt's bed. The old steel frame had been impossible to drag across the floor. He'd been searching through bags and boxes, delighted when he found a shoebox filled with cards he'd sent her from numerous destinations. At least I wasn't completely thoughtless, he mused, flicking through them before placing them to one side rather than adding them to the growing pile of recycling. Something to show my grandchildren, he thought with a grin.

Three suitcases were laden with every size and colour towel and set of bed linen. Glancing at them, bringing them to his nose to smell the must, he doubted they'd ever been used. Wedding gifts, perhaps? Never used in a marriage cut short before it ever had a chance to blossom, he thought sadly. Not having the heart to discard them entirely, seeing as she'd kept them for years, he placed them near the cards. But he wouldn't be putting them anywhere near his skin!

Kicking a box of towels out of his way, he cursed as the ancient cardboard disintegrated. Towels sliding onto the lino, he grabbed the top few to try and keep them together. The crinkle of plastic surprised him.

He pulled the towels aside to discover clear plastic bags with neatly folded bundles of money inside.

Laughing aloud, he counted the notes. Thousands of euro in one bag alone. Olivia's words rang in his ears: 'Any cash you find in the house is yours to spend now.'

"Finally, Polly!" he exclaimed.

He hid most of it at the back of the wardrobe before taking the stairs a few steps at a time and hurrying out the front door with a fistful of notes in his hand. He knew exactly what his first purchase would be, and once he had that necessity out of the way he planned on treating himself to a dream he'd never expected to realise. And certainly not without a bank loan.

"Kieran, so glad I caught you . . ."

He looked up to see John Kilmichael standing at the gate. Realising he still had the cash in his hand, he shoved it in the pocket of his jeans. Although not before John had spotted it. Damn, he thought.

"I'm running late, I'm afraid. Can you call back another time?" Was John one of the visitors Polly had referred to?

"I need to speak to you. It's about the parcel I had delivered here for Polly, the one you gave me last week."

"Not today," Kieran said firmly, eyeing him up and down and trying without success to believe that he was his cousin. Difficult to imagine, he thought.

"Can I call back later then?"

Unable to believe a word from his mouth, Kieran refused to engage in any further conversation until after he'd witnessed his visit to Olivia's office. "Not today, I'm afraid."

"It'll only take a moment."

"I have your number." Kieran's tone left no room for argument. "Now, if you excuse me I have an urgent appointment to keep. I'll give you a shout at a more convenient time." Like the Twelfth of Never, he thought.

Visibly unimpressed, John turned and left, his forehead etched with frown lines.

Kieran bent to tie his shoelace – at least pretended to – watching the older man out of the corner of his eye until he'd turned the corner at the end of the road. The few times they'd met, he'd given very little information about himself and suddenly Kieran was curious. He didn't even have an address for him. Dashing after him to see what direction he went, he stopped suddenly.

Kilmichael was deep in conversation. He was chatting to Seth! What on earth is he doing with him? He felt sick to his stomach. More underhanded dealings. Was there anybody he could trust? Their conversation looked serious. Kieran retreated out of sight, his head in a spin, the joy of finding the cash short-lived.

"You okay there?"

Kieran jumped out of his skin. Jess had startled him.

"Just staying out of somebody's sight," he said, somewhat shamefaced.

"Trouble follows you," she laughed, "or else you go out and find it!"

"Who, me?" He feigned innocence, giving up on his idea to follow John. What would he learn? That he lived in a two-up, two-down cottage somewhere, with a terraced garden and rusted gates? Or that he was doing some deal or other with his uncle? Too much of a coincidence, he decided, forcing a smile on his face.

He decided against mentioning it to Jess, at least not until he knew for sure what was going on in his family. Apart from his dad at this stage, he hadn't received much in the way of friendship from any of them.

"So which way are you going? Home or up town?"

"Seeing as you've asked, I was heading out to buy a car."

"Just like that? You make it sound as natural as going to get milk and bread."

He shrugged. "Polly left me a bit of money."

"Four wheels, not two? You are buying a car? Not a motorbike?"

"I'm getting a bit tired of walking everywhere and the bus service is shocking."

"I can't disagree with you there," Jess replied. "Turns me off going anywhere!"

"I'm going to have to start looking for a job soon. So, I'll need transport. That service guy up the street has a few bangers out front. I'll see if any have passed the NCT."

"And then you can teach me to drive?"

"No way! I tried teaching Beth once. A pure disaster and she's hardly spoken to me since!"

Jess picked up her pace to keep up with his long strides as they walked up the hill and turned left on to Colla Road. "Speaking of Beth. I haven't seen her around much?"

Kieran continued to walk as he responded. "Up to her eyes in debt, stuck in some old wreck in Goleen that's apparently falling down around her ears. And she's out of work."

"But wasn't she off in college doing a science degree? I remember all the awards she used to get in school – a right genius."

"Threw it all away to marry a Frog!"

Jess stared at him askance.

"A Frenchman," he explained, pulling a face.

She punched his arm. "Don't speak about your fellow-Europeans like that!"

"He's actually Irish but he lived in France for most of his life."

"So what has getting married got to do with throwing away her degree?"

"She was majoring in genetics and the only bloody gene she could catch was the love-gene! Poor bitch never finished the qualification, gave up with only a year to go."

"That's a bit unkind coming from the fellow who never bothered putting his hard-earned degree to use either." She raised a questioning eyebrow.

Kieran laughed but didn't rise to her bait. Neither did he take the opportunity to remind her that her archaeology qualification lay equally dormant.

They came to a stop outside the service garage, eyeing the used cars parked at the side.

"What do you think of that white Civic?" he asked.

She pulled a face, imagining him racing around the village. "Aren't you a bit long in the tooth for boy-racer models? Not that you act it, mind you."

"Whatever hope you had of getting driving lessons in my new car are well and truly gone," he laughed, strolling inside the gates to take a better look around.

The mechanic appeared from the garage, wiping his hands on an oily cloth. "I have a very clean black Golf if you'd like to take it for a test drive. For herself, is it?"

"She wishes!" Kieran laughed. "I'm looking for something cheap and reliable to get *me* around the place."

A car would be worth buying without doubt. He'd forgotten how crucial it was to have transport living here. But he wasn't going to blow too much money on it. Not when he had something far more interesting in mind to buy!

Meanwhile, Jess was being quizzed by the owner in typical rural Ireland style. Giving a glance in her direction,

Kieran smothered a grin before devoting his attention to the cars again.

"And your mother passed away, didn't she?"

Jess's eyes darted in Kieran's direction, signalling for him to rescue her from the interrogation. But his attention was elsewhere. "I have to go, Kieran. Greg's out early."

"Is he?" She hadn't mentioned it.

"Remember I told you?" she said, her voice rising ever so slightly.

Kieran shrugged. Had she remarked on the school finishing early? He honestly couldn't say. "Want me to go with you?"

"No, you stay and look at the cars! I'll catch up with you later."

Kieran stared after her as she hurried away.

"And yourself," the owner picked up his interrogation, "hail from around here?"

Sighing, Kieran gave a half-hearted answer. "Ballydehob." There wasn't much point in lying or refusing to answer because the other man would undoubtedly keep firing questions at him. The country way lived on, it seemed. The age-old style of neighbourhood watch. Definitely one characteristic of country-living he didn't miss!

"And who might you be there?"

"Dulhooly."

"Ah, you must be Frank's son. Heard you were back around the place. Didn't carry on the Dulhooly courtroom name then? Carry on the tradition?"

"No. Marine Engineering was more my thing." No harm to point that out, he thought.

"Let's have a look at that car we were talking about," the man said.

Kieran relaxed. Now the other man had as much information as he could get on him, he was happy to get on with business.

Test-driving the Golf along with a few others, he promised he'd call back after he'd given them a bit of thought. It felt strange – but good – to have money to spend.

"The price is negotiable," the owner said as Kieran walked away. "Give me a minute and I'll do my sums again."

"It'll have to be a good bit lower," Kieran commented as he turned around to enter into negotiations. Less than ten minutes later they had agreed a price.

No doubt it'll be in the local pub tonight that Dulhooly's son has bought a car so he must be settling down, he thought as he strolled down the hill after paying a deposit on the vehicle.

Then an ad in a shop window caught his eye. **In need of repair** – the words jumped out of him, the accompanying photograph telling a very different story. But no doubt the **in need of repair** was well hidden. What a coincidence – his heart's desire! This was fate. He patted the cash in his pocket and smiled. At least the down-payment, he thought, dialling the number listed underneath the photograph. And if these objectors – my own flesh and blood – succeed in getting me out of Number 5, at least I'll have a roof over my head!

"Just enquiring about the ad you have on the shop window here in Schull," he explained when the call was picked up.

"You're interested in viewing?"

"Yes, indeed," he agreed. "Where?"

Listening closely, he memorised the location, knowing

it fairly well and not bothering to write down the address. Ending the call, he doubled back up the hill to see if the mechanic could get the car ready for collection as soon as possible. Looked like he'd need transport sooner than he thought.

Jess was waiting for him, looking sheepish, when he got home.

"Where's Greg? I thought he was out early?"

"I invented that one. Couldn't stick his questions. Talk about an inquisition!"

"I got the same but he's harmless. Anyway, I bought the Golf. I'm picking it up tomorrow. Fancy a spin out to Mizen?"

"Once it fits around collecting Greg from school."

"Goes without saying."

"Brilliant," she said, her face falling as a car pulled up outside the wall and her sister-in-law and brother stepped out.

Kieran remained where he was, nodding at the two well-dressed people approaching.

"Henry, you remember Kieran?"

Her brother frowned, giving a cursory glance at his sister's neighbour and then back at his wife. "Vaguely," he admitted.

"How could you forget this mad fellow?" Jess accused. "We hung out together years ago. And before you say it, I know you were in boarding school but you actually came to a few beach parties with us on occasion . . ." Her voice trailed off as she waited for her brother to say something.

"I'll leave you to it, Jess," Kieran said hurriedly. "See you, Henry." He gave a courteous nod in Pru's direction.

As they hadn't been introduced he didn't think it wise to call her by her name.

The tension between the trio was palpable. He smiled as he thought of the things Jess had told him about Pru. He didn't think Pru would be quite so smug if she'd heard them. He was happier to leave them to their family meeting. He'd had enough family squabbles of his own without entertaining or getting involved in Jess's.

The house phone was ringing as he stepped inside, the first time it had done so while he'd been there, he realised. Lifting the receiver and saying hello, he waited for a response. Nothing. "Hello, can I help you?" Silence. "Who's there? Can I help you?"

He held his breath, listening as attentively as possible, convinced there was breathing on the other end. Definitely somebody there, he thought, slightly unnerved.

"Timewaster," he muttered, dropping the receiver again. "That you playing tricks, Poll?" he asked, resuming his search through her belongings with slightly less enthusiasm than earlier.

His search too was fruitless, most of it divided between charity shop and recycling bundles. He wouldn't be sorry when he'd got to the end of clearing out, repeatedly wondering why on earth she'd saved the majority of what he'd had to trawl through. Parched from the dust, he made his way to the kitchen, but was interrupted once more by the phone – his mobile this time.

"Who? I'm sorry? Oh, Amy? Nice to hear from you. What's up?" His heart skipped a beat. Hearing from his solicitor so soon could only mean one thing – trouble!

"Olivia would like you to come in and see her before the end of this week if possible."

They agreed a time and ended the call.

Washing his hands at the kitchen sink, he stared out the window, a deep sense of foreboding washing over him. The garden was still awaiting a makeover, the house partially cleared. He'd made little progress. And now, unless instinct was making a fool out of him, he felt his time at Number 5 was coming to an end. Why else would Olivia want to see him in person? What news couldn't be imparted by phone?

Chapter 37

"What's going on with you, Jess?" Henry asked his sister.

She leaned against the counter in her kitchen, her brother and sister-in-law seated at the table. She felt as though she was being interviewed. Actually, she thought, a police interrogation would be nearer the truth.

"I've had a change of heart. I'm not interested in doing a house swap anymore," she replied, working very hard to remain calm. And working even harder to remain firm about the decision.

"You can't back out now," Pru snapped. "It's what we've discussed –"

A glare from Henry prevented her saying any more, his sudden attack of loyalty to his sister surprising and irritating.

Pru's face said it all. How dare he shush her! She was his wife after all.

"Greg's happiness is my priority," Jess stated.

"I thought we'd discussed this already," Henry sighed.

She nodded, wishing with all her heart that things

could be different between her and Henry. They shouldn't have to argue like this.

"Can I get either of you anything?" she offered.

"You could give us a proper explanation," Pru scoffed.

"I've given things a lot of thought and weighed up everything you've said." She paused a moment, looking from one to the other, dreading the guaranteed onslaught once she'd finished her announcement.

"And?" Pru couldn't wait.

"Give her a chance," Henry glared at his wife.

Her brother's reaction gave Jess hope. Maybe she wasn't as alone as she'd thought. "I'm staying put. Moving to Clonakilty isn't an option for me."

"Maybe you don't believe so right now but don't knock it until you've tried it." Pru's tone was more civil, her attitude dented by Henry's remark.

"We have invested quite a bit into the place," her brother pointed out.

"Henry!" Jess cried. "Of course I'm not forgetting that! What do you take me for? And I have a proposal for you regarding paying towards it."

"No need to shout," said Pru. "Think of your little boy. Remember how miserable he was here. Why would you want to stay so close to those nightmares? Find a new address without history, baggage or bad memories. That's what you need."

Greg had been miserable. Jess couldn't disagree. But since her mother's death, his form had improved, happy now the atmosphere in the house had lightened, making little if any mention of his grandmother or her hot temper. He'd even forgotten his hatred of closed doors, his memory of his grandmother ordering him to his bedroom for the slightest naughtiness obviously fading. Insisting the bedroom door was to be kept closed was just another layer of the old woman's cruelty.

"We're not leaving here," she insisted, hating the thought of moving away from Kieran and the life she felt was slowly coming together. "Memories fade. Greg has never been happier. I don't want to put him through any more upheaval."

"There's no talking to her when she's like this!" Pru said to Henry then turned on Jess again. "You can't expect Henry to stand back and accept this! He has more right than you to be here!"

"Pru, this is Jess's home as much as mine," Henry warned, defending his sister for the second time.

Jess threw him a grateful look. "Now Greg's in school I'm going to look for morning work and, as soon as possible, I'll get a loan to pay you what you're owed for the refurbishments. It'll take another while though."

"For goodness sake, why would you get a loan when we're offering a straight swap for the house in Clonakilty?"

Jess glared at her sister-in-law, relieved when Greg burst into the kitchen and gave her an excuse to ignore her. "Hi, pet. What's the matter?"

"Kieran's out front. Can I go out to him?"

Jess felt the heat rise in her cheeks. "Not now, pet. I think he said he's busy for the evening."

"But, Mum, he's not busy. I can see him. He's sitting on the wall."

"Not now, pet," she told him. "We have guests. Want to watch a DVD instead?"

"Okay but I'm going out when *they're* gone." He pointed a finger at his aunt and uncle.

Jess didn't bother reprimanding him. She felt exactly the same herself. Taking him by the hand, she led him into the living room and set up his favourite DVD.

"Sounds very close between Greg and Kieran," Pru stated when she returned.

"Is that why you're having cold feet about moving somewhere else?" Henry added.

"This is our home and we'd like to stay," Jess reiterated. "I won't deny Greg is very fond of Kieran – and no wonder – Kieran's very kind to him." Unlike his uncle and aunt, she thought sourly, who barely acknowledge his existence.

"You're very trusting of him with your little boy, considering he's only back a few months?" Pru planted more poison in their friendship.

Jess was growing weary, Henry's support wavering between lukewarm and cold. "Look, I've known Kieran for years and, yes, I do trust him. And, yes, I do have feelings for him and I think he feels something for me too but I can't be sure."

"So I was right," Pru exclaimed, turning to give Henry a smug look.

"It isn't a very good idea to get too involved at this time, Jess," he said in a gentle tone. "You've only buried Mum. And there's no guarantee he'll stay around. You said so yourself. Do you really want Greg to get close to somebody, only to lose them again?"

Jess raised an eyebrow at her brother's advice. He'd seldom offered her any pearls of wisdom in the past. "You think I haven't already given that consideration? And Kieran mightn't be interested so I'll have to wait and see."

"Henry, tell her this isn't on. We have our hearts set on this house."

"We can always trade up to something else." Henry attempted to appease wife and sister in the one statement.

Pru snorted and took the argument back to the beginning again. "You'd agreed to move from here, Jess. Isn't it best to stick to the original plan and start a new life? There are lots of young families in our development, more convenience too."

Jess shrugged. "That was before." She looked from one to the other. "Don't you think I deserve happiness?" She turned to her brother. "Henry, I'm not side-stepping the fact you've invested money in this place but I've invested the last few years taking care of our mother while you furthered your career."

"Don't be ridiculous!" Pru scoffed.

Pru's condescending tone angered Jess. She was damned if she was dancing to her tune. "I've packed Mum's stuff. I'd like you to take it with you today please, Henry," she said to her brother.

Pru pursed her lips. "Just like that!"

Henry looked around him and shivered. "That's pretty callous, Jess. Have you stripped everything she owned?" His gaze strayed to the walls, the absence of photographs noticeable.

"Everything," she clarified. "Her clothes are in bags, the rest in boxes. Keep it, dump it. I don't want anything from it. She's left me enough mementos, none of them good. I've even packed all of her jewellery. You can have the lot."

Pru was speechless. "But they're worth –"

"A fortune? I know!"

Henry continued to stare at his sister. "Aren't you going to keep her wedding ring?"

Jess shook her head, her eyes locking with his. "I need to put the past behind me, all of it."

Pru, on the other hand, was already on her feet. "Where is the jewellery?"

"It's in her bedroom," Jess told her. "I'll show you."

Upstairs she opened one of the big cardboard boxes and took the jewellery box out.

Pru reached out eagerly for it. "Let me have that. Henry will pack the rest into the car. I can't believe you're getting rid of all of your mother's belongings. Some of her brooches and necklaces date back to her mother's generation."

Jess glared at her, hanging on to the box. "And more of it ridiculous stuff my father broke his back working to try and pay for! And she still treated him like crap!"

Henry appeared at the door. "Stop – both of you!" he said, surprising them all, his unexpected and unaccustomed outcry bringing silence to the room. "Give us a minute, Pru."

Shocked, yet relieved to hear her brother taking a little control, Jess flopped on to the floor.

Looking highly offended, Pru reluctantly exited.

There was a brief silence between brother and sister.

"Thinking of that night still gives me the shivers," Jess said then.

"She died of natural causes," Henry reminded her. "The post mortem reported as much."

"I still feel things would have been different if I hadn't left the pills beside the bed. There might have been time to call an ambulance when we got back from your house."

"Your life was hell. I didn't see it at the time, didn't want to see it if the truth were known."

"I could have left. I could have walked away," Jess argued. She'd thought it over.

"You acted in her best interests, Jess. You gave her the medication. She demanded the brandy – after she'd drawn her crutch across Greg's head and lashed out at you too."

His sister dropped the box she'd been holding, watching as pieces of her mother's jewellery rolled around the floor.

Henry came to sit on the floor beside her. "Don't think I'm not carrying guilt too. I could have intervened. Over the years I should have done so much more instead of running away – boarding school, college and marrying Pru. There was always an out and I took it."

"But you never even acknowledged how horrible she was," Jess said.

Henry shrugged. "I was afraid."

"I hated her, Henry. She terrified me. The doctor said she was manically depressed but I find that hard to believe." She stared at the paint scratches on the wall, a memory of where her mother had lashed out with the crutch, missing Jess but connecting with the wall. "I should have called the doctor before I left that evening. He might have given her stronger tranquillisers."

Henry continued stroking her hair, letting his sister talk.

"But seeing her lashing out at Greg and bringing blood to his forehead, all I wanted to do was run." She shook her head, unable to go on, unshed tears in her eyes, her lips shaping into a watery smile. "Although running was difficult when the sight of blood had me weak at the knees!"

Henry laughed. "Some things haven't changed then."

"Too much has changed," his sister responded.

"Dad left for the same reason," her brother stated.

"Did she hit him?" She'd never known for sure, had never witnessed it but guessed it had progressed to that when she'd left for Cambridge and it had only been the two of them in the house.

Henry nodded, his eyes glistening with tears as he remembered hiding in his room while she laid into her husband. "Physically and mentally, withered him with menacing looks, reduced him to nothing," he told Jess. "And again I stood by and let it happen, walking away from the atmosphere at the first opportunity."

"We should have taken it in hand years ago. If only I'd reported her assaults . . ." Her voice trailed off. It was far too late for 'if onlys'.

"Pier Road is your home, Jess, for as long as you want it to be. You'll receive no further argument from me. Or from Pru. I'll see to that," he smiled. "And if there's anything you need, big or small, just call me and I'll come running. Alone with a bit of luck!"

Eyes bright with tears, Jess nodded and pulled her brother to her, hugging him for the first time in years. "Thanks, Henry. That means more than you'll know."

Chapter 38

Marian's afternoon was ruined. She'd called around to see Seth, disgusted when he wasn't home. She rang his phone several times and he eventually answered and agreed to meet her near the Baltimore Inn in Schull. Parking nearby, she spotted Seth outside the pub talking to someone. On time for a change, she thought.

By the time she got out of the car, the man Seth had been in conversation with had disappeared.

"I'm sorry," Seth said, flopping on to the bench outside of the pub. "There's nothing concrete yet."

"But what's the delay? Surely the geriatric assessments will stand up to scrutiny?" She sat beside her brother, crossing one leg over the other.

"Don't worry," Seth sighed, pulling a cigar from his inside pocket and placing it between his lips.

"Got a cigarette?" Marian asked after she'd searched her pockets and realised she'd left hers at home.

"Afraid not. I've another cigar though if you'd care to try it?"

"No thanks!" She wrinkled her nose at the strong smell of cigar smoke. "Do you honestly think you'll pull it off?"

Seth coughed, flicking ashes onto the ground and stamping on them. "I wouldn't have taken it on if I thought it'd fail. But you'll have to be patient. This is the law we're dealing with, not a simple retail exchange at a customer-service desk!"

"No need for sarcasm," she replied, nudging him with her elbow. "Who was that guy you were speaking to when I got here?"

"John Kilmichael."

"Who?" The name didn't ring a bell.

"Frank hasn't told you?"

Marian shook her head in confusion.

"Polly's son."

"Her *what*?"

"Frank hasn't shared this information?" Seth dragged on his cigar, taking cruel delight in getting one over on his brother-in-law. "I thought he'd be bragging about his nephew!"

Marian looked dumbfounded. She uncrossed her legs, placing both feet on the ground, sick to her stomach. "No, he hasn't told me." She pursed her lips tightly, bringing her eyes up to meet Seth's. "Where Polly was concerned, Frank has always put me second. And keeping her precious baby a secret is no different. How long ago?" She looked at him. "How come you know about him?"

"*I* found him, reintroduced them," Seth told her, shocking her yet again.

"But why? You and Polly hadn't spoken for years!"

He didn't respond, simply raised an eyebrow.

She brought a hand to her lips. "Oh no, Seth! You two had a baby together? Don't tell me he's your son? No!"

Her brother gave a simple nod of his head, the faint smile on his lips a definitive response to her question and confirmation that he was indeed the father.

"You've got a son?" she repeated.

"Yes," he confirmed.

"How did you find him?"

Seth let out a long sigh. "Kilmichael is a fairly uncommon name."

"But how did you find out his adopted name?"

"Traced it through the adoption agency. There are ways and means of getting information."

She pushed her hair back from her face, shaking her head in disbelief. "But why didn't you tell me what was going on? I'm your sister! Why not introduce him to me? He's my nephew too! And I was only feet away from him just now and still you didn't even bother to introduce us," she accused, filled with a mixture of hurt and outrage.

Seth pursed his lips. "He doesn't know Polly was his mother. She wouldn't tell him, made me promise I wouldn't tell him we were his parents."

Marian seethed inside, outrage escalating to fury. Yet again, Polly had called the shots, taken the lead, dictated the direction something as important as reuniting a son with his parents should take. "And you let her away with that?"

"Yes, because that arrangement suited me perfectly. She had her reasons and I had mine."

Marian was finding it difficult to understand the picture her brother was painting. "But you were just speaking to him? You're obviously in some form of contact?"

"Not really. He knows me to see from the initial contact, knows I'm a friend of Polly's. He came along while I was waiting for you. Had called to see Kieran apparently."

"And you have no desire to develop a relationship with your son? Your only child?"

Seth shook his head. "Think of the scandal. She was a widow, her husband lost to the sea not so long before. Think how it would have affected my business dealings. How it would *still* affect my business dealings. Anyway, I'm too selfish to be a father and getting into some sort of emotional attachment with a middle-aged man offers little appeal. And I certainly don't fancy sitting a forty-something-year-old on my lap!"

"But how could *she* resist telling him? He was her only child!"

"She was ashamed – ashamed she'd been with me with her husband not too long dead – ah, you know what Polly was like, filled with morality, the romantic memory of her short marriage precious. Also, she worried her son would hate her for giving him up when she had a home to offer. But she had no choice about that. Think about it – it really would have disgraced Glen's name if his widow produced a child out of nowhere. She couldn't do that to Glen, keeping his memory untarnished the only thing left that she could do for him. Times were certainly different then but even now it would be considered a scandal. I guess guilt and loyalty overpowered compassion and love for her son." Seth paused a moment, a fleeting wistfulness crossing his face. "But not a moment went by that she didn't think of that baby, life passing her by being the price she'd paid for the difficult choice she'd made."

Marian put her face in her hands, devastated at how she had been deceived for so many years. And Seth had said the man had been with Kieran. Had Polly entrusted her secret to Kieran too? Had she insisted he keep it to himself and not tell his own mother? She wouldn't put it past her.

Marian raised her head. "Seth, I don't care what lengths you need to go to. You have to get that will overturned."

Polly Dulhooly had never shown her any respect, her brother's announcement another confirmation of that fact. Marian wouldn't stop until she'd repaid the favour.

Chapter 39

Frank was thinking of Mags as he drove back from Bantry. He had called her back again to clarify a few details – maybe just to hear her voice if he were honest with himself. Working together as junior lawyers, they'd shared a lot of cases and had lots of fun.

They had chatted a little, then touched on the "case" again.

"I'll do all I can to help, Frank. But I'm making no promises," she'd said.

"Time is of the essence, Mags."

"Well, get off the phone and let me get to work then!"

His heart felt lighter as he hung up the phone.

He rubbed his chest. Damn indigestion again. He picked up his phone from the passenger seat when it rang. He was surprised to see Charlotte's name on it. A day for surprises, nice ones at that. He pulled into the side of the road to answer.

"Charlotte!"

"Dad, can you talk?"

"Of course." He looked at his watch to figure out the time difference. "Still in the office?"

"Sure am. I won't delay but there's something I need your help with."

He pulled himself straighter in the seat, unable to get comfortable. Again he rubbed his chest with the heel of his hand.

"I'm presuming you don't know what Mum and Seth are up to?" Charlotte said.

Frank gave an involuntary groan. "This can't be good."

"Seth's falsifying some medical documents to try and oust Kieran from the original inheritance agreement and get it split three ways between Kieran, Beth and myself."

"He's what!" Frank was outraged, blood racing around his body, his face turning dark red. "How dare he disrespect my sister! I guessed he and your mother were in cahoots but I honestly believed they were following a wild-goose chase so I decided to let them walk into a trap of their own making. But producing false documentation as a means of declaring Polly mentally diminished is crossing the line and taking things to a whole new level."

"Can you get to the solicitor? Or better still, get to Mum and Seth and tell them to cop themselves on."

"They're wasting their time but they're too stupid to realise it!" Frank roared down the phone. "Even if his precious medical records were accepted, Beth wouldn't be the one to gain! As Polly's next of kin, *I* would. But aside from that, I won't let him get away with dragging my sister's sanity through the mud!" Frank started up the engine of the Mercedes. He swallowed hard, his chest burning, the pain moving towards his shoulder. "Oh God, Lot," he groaned as the pain intensified, shooting through his chest and down his arm.

"Dad, what's the matter?"

"Call an ambulance, Lot," he said, beads of sweat on his face, his body clammy. He pulled at his tie knot, finding it difficult to breathe.

Charlotte screamed at him. *"Where are you, Dad?"*

He didn't answer, everything blacking out. The engine was still running. His foot slipped and lost its grip on the brake, the car rolling very slowly down the slope, gathering speed as it moved toward the main road and oncoming traffic.

"Dad! Dad!" Charlotte's voice came down the phone, her father gone beyond hearing.

"Back it in altogether," Kieran advised the driver, opening the gates wide and guiding him into the back garden. Excited at the prospect of having money at his disposal, Kieran felt he owed a huge debt of gratitude to his aunt. He'd wanted to do something special for her, tidying the garden the best thing he could think of. He'd trawled the *Golden Pages* for a local guy with a mini-digger, delighted that the first guy he called was free.

"I want the entire area dug up," he called to the driver. "I'll be setting grass seed, so you can judge the depth yourself."

With that, Jess came running in, followed closely by Greg.

"I didn't expect an audience," the driver said with a laugh before starting up the machine.

Kieran turned to Jess. "What's up?"

"I've got the best news," she shouted over the din of the digger.

"Go inside, I'll be right in." But first he needed to give the driver his instructions. "I want that area left intact," he told him, pointing to the only surviving flowerbed in the garden, Polly's handiwork, a lasting memory of the precious hours she'd spent tending her plants. "But clear the rest. Give me a shout when you're done."

"Come inside with me," Jess instructed her son.

"No, I want to watch, Mum." Greg was indignant, refusing to join her in the kitchen, terrified he'd miss any excitement.

"We'll leave the door open, and you can stand and watch," said Kieran. "But under no circumstances are you to go anywhere near the digger. It's too dangerous and we don't want anything happening to you."

Much to Jess's amusement, Greg nodded and went and stood by the door.

"You're a good influence, Kieran," she said when he joined her inside. "I honestly believe he's better behaved when you're around."

Kieran shrugged. "You should see him when we're playing football or fishing off the pier! Then he's not so well behaved. Are you, Greg?"

The young boy giggled, his eyes fixed on the machine, watching it turn the soil over.

"So what's the big news?" Kieran asked.

"The pressure is off with Henry. I don't have to move after all. Looks like you're stuck with us next door."

He grinned and went to swing her around.

Jess confused his approach and made to hug him, their arms ending up wrapped around each other, her head tucked under his chin. She looked up at him, remaining in his arms for the briefest moment.

"Ugh! Are ye kissing?" a disgusted Greg asked.

"Don't be silly. Of course not!" Jess instantly retreated,

her cheeks flushing bright red. She'd wanted to kiss him. More than anything. Part of her was sorry she hadn't.

Kieran glanced at Jess, his lips shaping into a cheeky grin. "Excellent news, you guys, but I'm afraid my foundations here aren't quite so solid. Looks like those contesting Polly's will are producing some convincing evidence, enough to force me back to the world of wanderlust!"

An unperturbed Greg continued to stare at the digger in fascination.

The animation left Jess's face. "You can't be serious."

"Deadly serious unfortunately."

Without thinking about what she was doing, she stepped into his arms once more, raising her face to his and welcoming the feel of his lips on hers. Melting into his kiss, she was oblivious to everything around her.

Meanwhile music was blaring from the digger, the driver covering a lot of ground in a short space of time, moving over and back in rows, concentrating on the area near the garden shed.

Unable to see anything much, Greg moved outside, crouching on to his hunkers and piling the fresh earth into a mountain.

The machine approached from the back corner again.

As the kissing couple pulled apart, Jess glanced around for her son, releasing her hold of Kieran and darting to the door when she couldn't see him anywhere.

"No!" she screamed at the top of her voice, running toward the small boy who was right in the oncoming path of the digger. Too late Jess reached him. The digger had already nudged against him, knocking him face down into the earth.

"*Ooh!*" Greg cried.

"Damn, what the hell have you done?" Kieran rushed to Greg's side, waving the digger driver away when he went to help Greg to his feet. "Leave him," he growled, pulling him into his arms and waiting for his sobbing to subside before examining him.

"I can't see! Mum, I can't see. There's dirt in my eyes."

Jess tugged at Kieran's arm. "Bring him inside. We'll have to try and wash his eyes. Hush, Greg," she soothed her son.

"God, I'm so sorry about that!" The driver was shaking. "I didn't see him there."

"Accidents happen," Kieran said gruffly. "We should have been keeping an eye." Instead of eyeing each other, he thought, glancing at Jess, the taste of her lips still on his. He carried Greg inside, patting him on the back to try and soothe him.

"He'll have to get his eyes checked in the hospital for safety," Kieran advised a few moments later. "See the grit inside his lids. Very important to get all of that out."

"I'll call Henry, get him to come back and drive us to Bantry General. It's not too long since he left. He shouldn't be too far away."

"I'm sorry, Jess. I shouldn't have distracted you." He held her gaze.

She shook her head and grinned back at him. "It wasn't exactly one-sided," she responded, her words loaded, desire lingering between them.

"Raincheck?" Kieran whispered.

"Soon, I hope." She turned her attention to Greg. "Don't rub your eyes, pet. The nice doctor will clean the dirt out once we get there. Come on, we must call Uncle Henry to drive us there."

"I don't like doctors and I don't like Henry!" Greg gave another exaggerated wail, glancing slyly at Kieran to ensure he was being watched, disappointed when the shrill of Kieran's phone stole his attention once more.

Kieran recognised Charlotte's number and groaned inwardly. Another bout of long-distance complaining to come no doubt.

"Charlotte, what's up?"

Jess touched his arm and he nodded, signalling that he would follow them in a minute. He gave Greg a wave as they slipped away. Poor kid, he thought, as Greg brought a hand to his face to rub his eye and Jess slapped it away.

"Sorry, Charlotte – what's that you said?" His expression darkened as he listened to his sister. "But where is he?"

"I don't know," Charlotte was saying, "but he must have been feeling really bad. He seemed to be in great pain. He told me to call an ambulance and that was it. I stayed on the line, could hear some noises but that was it."

"And you've called the ambulance?"

"I eventually got through to the emergency services. It was a bit difficult calling from outside the country. I had no idea where Dad was. There wasn't a lot of immediate help they could offer but they promised to radio a message to the Gardaí and get them to advise as many stations as possible. Will you please find him? Before . . ."

"I'll take it from here. It's okay, Lot, don't worry. Have you called Beth?"

"No, I tried Mum but she didn't know where he was. I thought I should tell you next. You're much calmer in a crisis. You know what Beth's like, she panics at the slightest thing."

Kieran couldn't think straight. His father needed urgent

help. But first he had to find him. And with Charlotte having no idea where he was and his mother none the wiser either, where would he start? How would he track him down?

"I'll ring you later, Char. Let me see what I can do first. I'll get back on to Mum. She surely has some idea of his plans for the day."

"She told me she hasn't seen him since early this morning. And she was really off with me too – nervy and jumpy."

"Probably because it's not all about her," Kieran muttered. "Right, Charlotte. Talking won't find Dad. I'd better go."

"Thanks, Kieran. I'll ring Beth right away. Panic or not, she needs to know."

Punching his mother's number into his keypad, Kieran tried his best to try to get her to remember anything Frank had mentioned about his whereabouts for the day. With very little to go on, he called the emergency services again to report the information Marian had given him.

Chapter 40

"Will I follow the ambulance or go with him?" Marian's body trembled from head to toe.

"Best if you follow us," the ambulance driver advised. "There's only one allowed to travel with the victim and your son has already said he's travelling with us."

Kieran had been first to arrive on the scene, having run all the way up the town to the garage and collecting the Golf he'd just bought. Heading towards Bantry town, he was only a few short miles from Schull when the Gardaí rang with the news his father had been found. The remaining journey was a blur.

Marian was horrified to see her husband's body being cut from the car. Staring in disbelief, she watched as they got him into the ambulance as quickly as possible and, sirens blaring, rushed towards Cork city.

Following behind, Marian put a call through to Beth, reassuring her that her father was still alive but gravely ill.

"No! Please, Dad can't die! I didn't think it would be this serious when Charlotte called with the news. Oh, Mum, I said some terrible things to Dad earlier!"

"Charlotte couldn't have known how serious it was. And he was lucky the car veered to the side and crashed into a stone entrance. Otherwise he'd have careered straight into oncoming traffic."

"Doesn't bear thinking about," Beth blubbered through tears.

"And never mind whatever petty squabbles you had with him. You weren't to know. Nobody knew. You've had a dreadful shock, pet. Get Carl to drive you to the hospital and I'll meet you there."

"Should I call Charlotte?"

"Kieran's calling her with an update."

Hanging up, Marian was forced to do some soul-searching of her own. Beth wasn't the only one with concerns. Marian's conscience was pricking her too, recent behaviour towards her husband weighing heavily on her heart. But she'd deal with her guilt later. For now she'd be happy if he continued breathing and allow her the time she needed to make amends.

"There's a family emergency back in Ireland," Charlotte told her boss. "My father had a heart attack while driving and crashed his car. I've got to return home immediately."

"I'm sorry to hear that, Charlotte," he said, his genuine sympathy evident. "Of course you must do whatever's required. But sit there and take a moment to recover from the shock – I'll get one of the girls from Admin to bring you a coffee. Meanwhile I'll move my car around to the front of the building and, whenever you're ready, I'll drive you home so you can get organised."

"But I don't have a flight booked yet."

"Leave your flight plans to me. What Irish airport will

you be landing at? I'll organise it quickly through the company account."

"Not at all, I couldn't accept that," Charlotte waved away the generous offer, his kindness much appreciated, a powerful contrast to the pressure and discomfort she'd experienced in the workplace previously. "Dublin or Shannon – either will do. A direct flight if you can." She closed her eyes when he left the office, her thoughts a jumbled mess. But her only priority was her father's safety, other concerns unimportant by comparison.

Chapter 41

"Beth, he'll be okay. Frank's strong as an ox."

"How can you be sure?" she snapped at Carl. "He's stressed, all of us fighting and squabbling."

Carl glanced sideways at his wife, recognising her fear, understanding her reason to lash out. "I suppose so. He wants to protect his family. It's all he cares about underneath."

She snapped her head in his direction. Was her husband being sarcastic? She couldn't be sure.

"I think we should get a divorce," she told him. It was a day for truth, she felt, a day where they should all think about moving on.

His face dropped but he merely nodded. "I'm sorry, Beth."

"I know. Me too."

Their unborn baby, their lost chances, lingered in the car between them. There were some things insurmountable and both of them had known it for quite some time. Carl's reckless driving and passion for risk had caused their car to crash, leading to Beth's miscarriage and the beginning of the end of their marriage – but she wasn't without blame. She had long enabled his lifestyle and personality and had eventually paid the price. But acknowledging guilt wasn't enough to repair the damage done.

His voice was thick with emotion. "I found an old address for Ed's ex-boyfriend and sent him a letter."

"And?" She hid her surprise at this.

"He's flying in later this evening. Wants to see him apparently . . . regrets leaving but was too proud to say or return. He knew nothing of Ed's illness."

Silence fell between them for a few miles until Carl spoke again.

"Should we try again?"

"Just drive, Carl," she said, letting out a long sigh, too tired to think but not too stupid to let a bit of raw emotion cloud her judgement again.

Joining her brother and mother at Frank's bedside after running the whole way from the car park, Beth felt relief wash over her for the first time since she'd heard of what had happened to him. She had made it in time to apologise. He was still alive.

"Only two visitors at a time," a nurse advised gently.

"I'll step out and give Beth time," Kieran offered and left.

Beth moved past her mother and leaned over Frank. "Dad, I'm so sorry," she said. "Please be okay. We'll take care of you for a change."

Hearing his daughter's voice, he opened his eyes and acknowledged her with a nod of his head and the faintest of smiles.

As she kissed him, he caught her hand for the briefest of moments then released his feeble grip.

"What do the doctors say?" Beth murmured to her mother.

"They've taken some bloods but no results yet," a pale and harassed Marian explained.

"That nurse suspects his medication mightn't be suiting him. And when your father told them how many headache tablets he'd been taking . . ." She shook her head at her husband, guilt washing over her that she'd been so preoccupied with getting one over on Polly that she hadn't noticed him deteriorating in front of her eyes.

"All that stress is probably from his golf handicap," Beth made an attempt to lighten the atmosphere in the room.

"Nothing a good night's sleep won't fix," Frank said, closing his eyes again, the image of his daughter and wife sitting by his bed a better cure than any headache tablet.

Answering her phone on the first ring, Charlotte let out the breath she'd been holding when Beth told her she had just been into the ICU and talked to Frank and that he was now sleeping peacefully.

"Not out of the woods by a long shot but definitely out of immediate danger," Beth said.

"You don't have to come," she added, offering her a way out.

"Actually I do. This is a wake-up call. I'm already at the airport. Avoiding confrontation with that bastard, Philip, is cutting me off from my family and everything else I left behind."

"Carl will be waiting outside the airport for you then."

"Carl?"

"He's collecting Ed's ex anyway, so it's no trouble."

She was still amazed he'd actually written him a letter and tracked him down, the kindest thing she'd ever witnessed from him.

"Are ye getting on better?"

"We're over, Charlotte, and we both know it. Probably never begun if the truth is known. It should never have gone beyond a holiday fling. But there are more important things going on around us and it's about time I, for one, faced up to that."

After she'd finished her call to her sister, Charlotte chewed on her thumbnail as she strolled aimlessly around the airport duty-free shops, unable to sit still for even a moment and grateful for the large selection of fashion outlets to distract her. It was certainly better than sitting with her head in her hands, yet time couldn't move fast enough for her. She would be on tenterhooks until she was actually on that plane.

She spotted a dress from the label she'd bought for the party. The assistant appeared to be moving the entire rail – to the sales area with a bit of luck, Charlotte thought. She hurried to ask the girl. If there were a few more with a similar neckline to the last one in her size, she'd buy them.

"Excuse me," she said to the assistant, "are you putting those on sale?"

"I'm sorry, ma'am, this label's being removed. Designer's been arrested on suspicion of copyright theft. Huge fraud case apparently." She pointed to the TV screen overhead. "Keep an eye out for breaking news."

Charlotte opened her eyes wide. "What's the name of the designer?"

The assistant looked around her, as though she were about to divulge one of the world's greatest secrets. "Some guy from Lyon selling to Canadian fashion houses apparently. This is the second case against him according to the news but now he's made the mistake of ripping off a billionaire who's already got his lawyers kicking up a storm." Spotting her supervisor approaching, the assistant gave Charlotte a brief nod and hurried away with her rail of beautiful dresses.

Charlotte dialled her sister's number. "Beth! Wait until I tell you what I've just heard!"

But then she paused and listened, alert. "Oh God, I've got to go. My flight's just been called. Just tell Ed that his label should be safe. Greed has caught up with his opponent and this time he's copied somebody who can well afford to prove the truth to the world. Got to run to the gate now. I can't wait to see you. Give Dad a kiss for me."

Beth took out her phone and called Carl, disappointed when it went straight to voicemail. Despite their failed marriage, she could understand what it would mean to him to be able to tell Ed the news and under the circumstances the sooner he could do that the better.

"Great news for Ed," she whispered to Marian and Kieran when she re-entered the Intensive Care Unit. "That Lyon guy has gone and done the same thing to a Canadian designer and, boy, will he live to regret it! It's huge over there already apparently. And unlike Ed, this guy has the financial means to destroy him."

Marian and Kieran shrugged, neither very interested in the story.

"Dad? That's good, isn't it?" Refraining from detail so as not to upset him or divulge to her mother that Frank had been in the throes of investing large sums of cash in Ed's business, she couldn't understand the worried look on his face.

"I'm happy for Ed," Frank told the group. He sighed. "Such a pity he's not going to be here to see his good name restored."

"I'll have to ask some of you to leave," the nurse instructed sternly. "You're tiring the patient out."

"You two stay for a while," said Marian. "I'll step out for a while." And with a quick kiss dropped on Frank's forehead, she left.

Chapter 42

"Seth, I need a word," Marian said a while later, relieved she'd intercepted her brother in the hospital before he'd attempted to visit Frank. The last thing her husband needed was Seth raising his blood pressure and bringing on a second heart attack.

Just before she left him, Frank had asked her to telephone his private-eye contact, Mags, to bring her up to speed on the latest in the design-copyright theft story. Under the circumstances, she hadn't questioned him about his contact with this woman she remembered from years before, but it was something she'd ask about when he'd recovered. Turning over a new leaf was one thing, but turning a blind eye was plain ridiculous!

"How's he doing?" Seth enquired.

"How did you know he'd been brought in?"

"Charlotte. I called her. She hasn't sent her official signed objection letter yet. She told me about Frank's heart attack. You know she's changed her mind about supporting her sister? Wants Kieran to have it all now."

Marian nodded, hating the fact she still had murderous thoughts about Polly even though her husband was seriously ill a short distance away. "Just withdraw from it, Seth," she sighed. "It's useless anyway according to Charlotte. And seeing Frank as he is right now has scared me into facing my priorities and focusing on what's most important in life." Revenge, from what she'd tasted so far, was sour rather than sweet – certainly not what she'd expected.

Seth threw his eyes heavenward. "You're sure, Mar?"

"Positive."

Seth shrugged. "That's that then." He jerked his head in the direction of Frank's door. "Will I go in and say hello to himself?"

"Best not," she said, putting her husband before Seth for the first time in history. "He's resting and not able for any undue stress."

Seth laughed and walked away, leaving the Dulhoolys alone to patch things up. He, on the other hand, needed to keep an appointment in the city. Frank's heart attack didn't stop the world revolving – it simply reminded him of how quickly life can be cut short. And he had plenty to do before he had any notion of checking out of life.

Kieran came out of Intensive Care and spotted Seth as he walked down the corridor away from Marian, recognising his uncle from his familiar gait, watching as he walked along the corridor, one hand in his jacket pocket, throwing his right leg out a little. My God, he thought with a shock, that's who John Kilmichael reminded me of! But how? Polly and Seth? It didn't seem credible!

Kieran went and tapped his mother gently on the shoulder.

She swivelled around to face her son. "Has something happened?" she asked fearfully, seeing his shocked expression.

Kieran was surprised at the emotion in her voice, the dark circles under her eyes further emphasising her upset. Now was neither the time nor the place to concern himself about any relation between Seth and John, he decided. No doubt the truth would be revealed in its own good time.

"No, no – Dad's comfortable – he's fine, Mum."

Marian felt embarrassed in her son's company, surprised that he wasn't cool with her. If the situation were reversed, she knew she'd find it difficult to be quite so charitable. "I think I'll go back in to your father," she said, swinging around just as she heard a female voice calling Kieran's name.

Coming face to face with a petite and very attractive young woman, she glanced at the child at her side, gasping audibly as she stared aghast at him, shock registering on her face.

Kieran introduced them. "Mum, this is Jess. She lives next door to Polly's house. And this is Greg."

"I'm so sorry to hear about your husband," Jess said to Marian as they shook hands. "Kieran sent me a text explaining. I ended up having to bring Greg here, all the way from Bantry Hospital, to have his eye checked – he'd had an accident but the eye is fine, thank God – so I thought we'd come and say hello."

"Nice to meet you, Jess. And you too, Greg. Kieran, I'd better get back to your father." But she didn't go, instead continuing to gaze at the child, the likeness to Kieran at the same age staring her in the face. She glanced quickly at Kieran and then at Jess, both of whom were staring at her, and whereas she couldn't decipher Kieran's expression she saw the truth written in the girl's face.

Abruptly she turned and left.

She couldn't be mistaken, the likeness too pronounced. Kieran must know, she thought – he'd have to be blind not to see it. So this was another secret being kept from her! Yet another Dulhooly descendant to be introduced at some later time! This wasn't the appropriate moment to tackle Kieran, she thought, vowing to broach the subject with him in the not too distant future. But now she had bridges to build with her son and, while she knew in her heart she didn't deserve his forgiveness, she hoped he'd inherited more than a house from his aunt. She hoped on this occasion that some of her sister-in-law's kind and forgiving ways had been passed on to Kieran.

Chapter 43

Seth sat in Olivia's office, glancing at her in an admiring fashion as she peered at him over her glasses. "Thanks again for rescheduling my appointment. As I said, I was nearby and it saves me making the trip again in a few days' time."

"So, John," she said. "Just to confirm, as per your recent correspondence, you're claiming to be Pauline Digby's son? And you've brought me evidence to prove this?"

"Birth certificate is the best evidence I can offer," Seth replied smoothly, feeling her eyes on him. Polly had been a number of years older than him, but a fine-looking woman in her day, he remembered. Slipping a hand into his inside pocket, he produced a folded document and slid it across the table, hoping Olivia wouldn't scrutinise him too much and question whether his year of birth agreed with his appearance.

Unfolding it and verifying the detail, she placed it in her file. "And you were raised in a series of foster homes but never adopted, John?"

"That's correct. So that legally puts me as her next of kin."

Olivia was non-committal, declining to answer. "As you'll understand, this will all have to be supported with legal documentation."

"Of course. I can tell you all I know now if you like."

Olivia nodded, pressing the buzzer on her phone and inviting Amy to join them.

"Amy, this is John Kilmichael."

Amy's eyes narrowed, staring at the man seated opposite Olivia. She'd met him before. She was sure of it but it just wouldn't come to her. She continued to stare, realising suddenly that she was being rude. "Pleased to meet you."

"Amy, will you sit in on this meeting and take some notes for me please?"

"Sure," Amy said, taking the only other seat available. Though she tried to ignore the older man's eyes travelling the length of her legs, she felt very uncomfortable. And that's what jogged her memory, his leering stare as he looked her up and down, just as he'd done that first time she'd met him with Kieran Dulhooly. "Aren't you Kieran Dulhooly's uncle?"

Seth's jaw dropped but he recovered quickly. "His cousin to be precise."

"But he introduced you as his uncle. Seth. He introduced you as Seth," Amy insisted, looking from the man to Olivia, conscious that she'd spoken out of turn.

Olivia leaned back in her chair, intrigued by their exchange. "There's no mention of the name Seth on this documentation," she commented. Then she turned to Amy. "Can you get Kieran on the phone for me, please? I need to clarify one or two details with him before proceeding with this meeting. I need to know if he's interested in meeting this person outside of court."

Amy's eyes opened wide, Olivia's tactics interesting to say the least.

Seth got to his feet. "I can come back another time to pursue this," he told the two women. He'd been wheeling and dealing long enough to know when he was beaten.

"Can I get your signature before you leave, Mr Kilmichael?"

"Ah no need," he replied. "Don't know if I'll bother going ahead with it after all."

"Amy, perhaps you'd show Mr Kilmichael to the lift, please?" Olivia repeated his name on purpose, smiling broadly and shaking her head as he walked away at a leisurely pace. A con man, she thought, if I've ever met one.

"Well spotted, Amy," Olivia praised her secretary when she returned to her office. "So you've met Kieran outside of office hours?"

Amy blushed. "I'd best answer the phone," she said, making her escape to her desk.

"Put me through to Kieran when you've a moment," said Olivia.

Assured by the medical team that his father had stabilised, Kieran felt confident enough to leave the hospital to go and retrieve his car from where he'd abandoned it at the side of the road so he could accompany Frank in the ambulance. And now the emergency had passed, he realised he hadn't even insured the car before driving it!

"Beth, will you come with me? Then you can bring Mum's car back."

"Of course."

Kieran had called an insurance company and arranged cover on the VW Golf before leaving Cork city with his sister to make the journey to West Cork. In the absence of a hands-free kit in the car, he pulled over when his mobile rang.

"Olivia! Not more objections, I hope!" he sighed. Then he listened attentively to what she was telling him, his expression turning grave as he digested her information. "My uncle Seth attempted to impersonate John Kilmichael?" He glanced at Beth's incredulous face. "And you're sure about that?"

When she explained about Amy recognising his uncle, his face reddened. He hoped he hadn't put Amy in an awkward situation at work. He quickly veered off the subject of Amy and focused on his conniving uncle instead.

"I have to admit, it's true to form for my uncle," he said, seeing no reason to display any loyalty to Seth. It wasn't as if he'd get any thanks in return. "My family will be angry but not surprised." After that stunt, there wasn't much lower Seth could go. Dad has been spot on about him all these years, he thought, but Mum wouldn't listen.

"I'm hoping that's it then," Olivia advised, "unless you've any more relations lurking somewhere?"

"None I know of anyway," Kieran replied.

"It should only be a matter of biding your time until you've met all the terms and conditions of the will at that rate. Then you'll be able to sign on the dotted line and finally relax in the knowledge that nobody can take it from you."

"Thanks, Olivia. And tell Amy thanks too."

"Paid off going for a stroll with her then?"

"Goodbye, Olivia," he said, easing into the traffic once

more, a wry grin on his face as he imagined his mother's reaction to her brother's little stunt.

He then filled Beth in on their uncle's latest bit of skulduggery.

"I'm sorry, Kieran," a very embarrassed and remorseful Beth said. "I should never have allowed things go this far."

"Ah forget it," Kieran shrugged. "Life's too short for arguments or regrets. We've surely learned that much today."

Chapter 44

Four Weeks Later

Beth and Carl sat in the airport lounge, the urn with Ed's ashes in Carl's hand luggage.

"It's not too late if you want me to get a ticket and travel with you?" she offered, her eyes red from crying. "Ed didn't want you grieving alone."

"Best we do it this way, a clean break," he said, catching her hand in his and squeezing it tightly. "Your father's been great about things, even found some way of getting me a pardon so I can fly into Paris and on to Madrid from there."

Beth remembered the look of relief flashing over her father's face when she'd eventually found a suitable time to announce her decision to separate from Carl. "We'll have to find a way around our bank debt but I know there's no future for us," she'd said. "After Ed has passed, we'll be going our separate ways. It's for the best."

Kieran had instantly jumped in with a more-than-generous offer. "I'm happy to help in whatever way I can."

Overcome with emotion, Beth had been unable to respond.

"Unless you're still planning to disinherit me!" he added.

His sister had the grace to look ashamed. "I'm sorry, Kieran. I've been so selfish and greedy. I wouldn't blame you if you never spoke to me again."

"Don't be silly. Financial pressure brings the worst out in people."

Some of the pent up tension left her face. "If you would lend me some money to help get my plans for Goleen up and running, I promise I'll pay you back with interest as soon as ever I can."

"We'll agree some terms and conditions, I'm sure," he'd said.

She looked at her husband now, butterflies in her stomach as she contemplated managing a business alone.

"Are you going to settle in Spain?"

"I've no idea but I'll keep you posted. Isn't it great there's a collector interested in Ed's pieces?"

"Looks like he's still looking after you," she smiled.

Carl got to his feet as his flight was announced over the tannoy. "When his life assurance is sorted and his company debts are in order, I'll stretch the proceeds as far as I can to straighten out some of the French debt and hopefully ease some of the burden here too."

"You'd better go," she said, fresh tears pouring down her face as he kissed her on the lips and hugged her tightly to him. "Don't drop your brother!"

"I promised Ed I'd take charge. I won't let you down," he promised. "He'll be floating over the Seine shortly."

She smiled in return, knowing that he meant every word. His intentions were good but whether he'd manage to realise them or not would remain to be seen. In the meantime, she'd take one day at a time and see what life as a single businesswoman had in store.

New Beginnings

"Jess and Greg are at the door for you, Kieran!" Charlotte called up the stairs from the hallway. She smiled at the visitors and ushered them inside. "Come on into the kitchen."

"You're heading back to Toronto in a few days, I hear?" Jess said. "How do you feel about that?"

Charlotte smiled. "Far less scared than I was last time I flew there."

"Do you plan on settling there?"

"For another while at least. Perhaps when the banking sector improves over here again, I'll try for work. But in the meantime it makes more sense to return. I've a good job and they couldn't have been kinder when Dad was ill." Charlotte watched Greg fiddling with the cuckoo clock, his expression a mirror image of one of Kieran's.

"I wouldn't like being so far away from *my* mammy," Greg said, looking around. "Will you mind?"

Greg's question startled Charlotte. The few times she'd met her nephew he'd been shy, saying very little.

"But she'll be back for Dad's birthday in a few months, won't you, sis?" Kieran appeared beside them.

"I sure will," Charlotte responded. "Try keeping me away! I can't believe the Dulhooly family are actually risking a weekend break in a hotel together."

"If we're still speaking to each other by then," Kieran commented before turning his attention to Jess. "Are we still okay for dinner tonight? I booked a taxi earlier, thought we'd make a night of it."

Jess nodded eagerly. "I'm looking forward to the evening. And so is Greg, aren't you, pet?"

He stopped fiddling with the clock and spun around, delight visible in his face. "Henry's taking me to the cinema. And we're going for chips after. And then he's having a sleepover in my house and Mum's having a sleepover with Kieran. Aren't you, Mum?"

The adults in the room sniggered at the child's innocence, Jess blushing with embarrassment, Charlotte not knowing where to look and Kieran throwing his eyes heavenward.

"Henry said we can go to the park tomorrow," Greg added, oblivious to the unspoken innuendo around him.

"Is your sister-in-law staying over too?" Charlotte asked.

"Not a hope. Doubt she'll ever speak to me again!" Jess replied with a hearty laugh. "Not that I'm bothered once Henry's standing up to her and spending time with Greg, despite her disapproval."

"Families," Charlotte said. "Can't live with them, can't live without them."

"Bet you'll miss us all the same!" Kieran said.

Charlotte nodded her agreement. She had enjoyed her time in West Cork, but had deliberately avoided being anywhere near her old place of employment. Counselling sessions were on her agenda when she returned to Toronto but coming home had been the best form of therapy in itself, the fear of standing on the same soil as Philip Lord no longer as choking as it once had been. Instead she'd given Beth a huge amount of practical support, helping her with a lot of the administration and legalities for the activity centre.

"I'm heading off, Kieran. Are you still coming to Mum's for dinner tomorrow?"

Kieran nodded. "Wouldn't miss your Last Supper," he laughed.

Kieran's announcement had come as a huge shock to at least some members of the family – a shock of the nicest type however.

"I still can't believe it myself," Kieran had repeated when he'd broken the news to his unsurprised parents and shocked sisters. "I wake up every morning and imagine I've dreamt it!" But in his heart he knew it was the truth, would never forget the moment Jess had blurted it out, without preamble or lengthy explanation.

Once he'd told her the good news about him being able to stay on in Pier Road, she'd burst into tears, shocking both of them when she'd buried her head in his chest and came out with words he knew he'd never forget for the rest of his life: "Greg is yours, Kieran. He's your son." At first he'd thought he'd misheard but then she had wiped her face with the sleeve of her cardigan and looked up at him, her eyes holding his as she repeated the words slowly and distinctly: "He's yours, Kieran. He's your son. I should have told you, but you were away and I didn't know if –"

"Greg is my son? You're sure? But we were only together once . . ."

"That's all it takes," Jess said in a very meek voice, eyeing him warily, fear visible in her eyes. "Don't you want him to be yours?" She stepped back, increasing the distance between them.

Kieran had been speechless. "I'm in shock, Jess. Hurt you felt you couldn't tell me before now. And feeling many more emotions I can neither name nor fathom right now. But not wanting Greg isn't one of them. Get that thought out of your head."

Marian had hugged him when he'd confirmed her suspicions, Frank clapping him on the back, both insisting he bring Greg and Jess to Ballydehob so they could be properly introduced.

"I've had the heart attack, and I'm in recuperation," he said, "so I reckon I fit the perfect pipe-and-slippers type of granddad."

"In time, Dad. But Jess hasn't told Greg yet – not until we've had more time to discuss the best way to go about it. And then I sincerely hope you'll remember your perfect granddad role when he's nagging you with millions of questions about golf and anything else he can think of!"

"I'll have to get a silver rinse in my hair and look the part of the granddad's wife," Marian added with a laugh, placing a hand on her husband's shoulder and giving it a gentle squeeze.

Kieran noticed Beth and Charlotte exchanging a look. Their mother's gesture hadn't gone unnoticed and neither had the relaxed atmosphere in their parents' home. It made a refreshing change, however long it lasted.

Their father's health scare, despite the initial fear it had instilled in his wife and children, had catapulted the family into a zone they hadn't experienced in many years – a semblance of normality.

Kieran came back into the kitchen after showing Charlotte out.

"I can't wait to tell Greg," he whispered in Jess's ear, resisting the urge to kiss her.

"We agreed, remember?" she warned, her twinkling eyes belying her stern tone.

They'd agreed to give Greg time to get used to Jess having a boyfriend before launching into the news that his friend next door had not only become his mum's boyfriend but also his daddy.

Kieran laughed, tossing Greg's hair instead and punching him playfully on the arm. "Yes, bossy boots! Isn't your mammy a right old boss, Greg? What do you say to a game of ball and we'll leave her here?"

"Suits me perfectly," she returned. "I've a hot date to prepare for anyway!"

"Well, don't let us stop you. I'm sure the effort will be appreciated! Come on, Greg, let's go before she changes her mind!"

Jess laughed. "Hang on a sec. I have a bit of good news! Beth came to see me yesterday. Did she tell you?"

He raised an eyebrow. "No, she didn't. What did she have to say?"

"She asked me to do a tourist-friendly archaeological write-up on her property! I'm so excited, you've no idea!"

Kieran smiled. "I'm glad, Ms Indiana Jones. Finally you're getting some practice in. You might make an honest living yet!"

"So might you! Putting your marine engineering to some use at last!"

Kieran laughed. "I'll never forget Dad's face when I told him! I really thought he would get a relapse. Well, it's only for a few months and will be a shock to the system no doubt. God forbid I'd commit to anything more long term! But it'll be great to get back to boats again."

Buying the boat in Mizen and putting it right had given Kieran a taste for engines again. And now he'd decided to stay in one place, he'd figured he'd have to be occupied or risk getting into all sorts of trouble. He'd noticed a few jobs on websites and was lucky enough to be offered a trial period with one company.

"Greg!" Jess reached Greg in the nick of time, right before he dropped what looked to be an ancient china plate on the floor.

"Leave him, Jess, he's fine."

"Are you going to be working in the sea? Catching fish?" Greg's face was animated.

"Fixing engines on boats, buddy."

"You might see my daddy!"

Kieran and Jess exchanged a look.

He dropped to his knees and looked the little boy in the eye. "I'll be sure to tell him he should be proud of the job you're doing looking after your mum."

"And that I'm a good footballer?"

"The best," Kieran laughed. "And speaking of football, let's go!"

He swung the small boy onto his shoulders as soon as they'd parted from Jess outside, tapping the football ahead of him and listening to his son's chatter as they made their way to the park.

"Can we go on your boat again soon?" a delighted Greg bounced up and down on Kieran's shoulders, his fingers messing with his father's gelled hair.

Reminded of John Kilmichael's unexpected visit a few days previously, Kieran glanced back at Number 5, the little model boat on his bedroom window sill just about visible from the road but in any case something that would be forever etched in his memory.

"The same model Polly's husband left the shore on – a story she told repeatedly," John had explained as he'd handed Kieran the boat. "Pity the kit hadn't arrived sooner. I'd have liked her to have seen the finished result." He'd explained how she's got him to source and order an identical model, intending that he would assemble it for her at her house on his next visit, a task which he'd now attended to painstakingly as a memento of a kind friend.

"I've a feeling she knows," Kieran had said, accepting the boat from John. And for a moment he'd been sorely tempted to go upstairs and bring down the heartfelt letter Polly had addressed to her son. Later, watching John walk away from Polly's house, he'd had a strong feeling that the time would come when he would do just that.

"Mum said you're going to give the boat a name," Greg said, wriggling to get Kieran's attention.

"I'm going to name it *Aunt Polly*!"

"That's a funny name for a boat," the small boy argued.

"Funny or not, that's what it will be," he said, breaking into a run. "What better way to remember an amazing woman than have her bobbing in the water nearby, still keeping a close eye on us all?"

Kieran's final words were little more than a whisper, his face breaking into a smile as an unexpected burst of sunshine broke through the clouds and the sound of a ship's horn could be heard in the distance. And somehow he knew she was okay, content in the knowledge that where there's a will, there's a way . . .

If you enjoyed *Where There's A Will*
by Mary Malone, why not try
Love is the Reason also published by Poolbeg?
Here's a sneak preview of chapters one and two.

Love is the Reason

Mary Malone

POOLBEG

Chapter 1

In a studio apartment in New York City, Matt Ardle stretched his full six feet five inches on the double bed, one muscular, tanned arm behind his head, the other loosely around Heidi's shoulders.

"Happy?" he asked, flipping on to his side to face her.

Her response was prefaced with a breathtaking kiss. "Ecstatic! I can't believe we're actually living in The Big Apple, a ten-minute walk from Times Square! It's everything I imagined it would be."

Jumping from the bed, she ran to the window, pushed up the lower sash with all her might and stuck her head out into the chilly New York air. Allowing the noise from nearby 57th Street to filter into their modest 7th Avenue studio apartment, she stretched as far as she could, excitement fizzing inside as she looked to her left toward Central Park and then at the opera lovers queuing for tickets outside Carnegie Hall on the opposite side of the street – the Box Office opened mid-morning.

"Have you called home yet?" Matt asked tentatively, getting up and crossing the floor to join her.

She shook her head, her long mane of auburn hair shielding her face and masking her expression. A silent response that spoke multitudes.

"Don't leave it too long, Heid. You don't want your parents putting out an SOS for you." He held his breath, watching for a signal to indicate she'd heard him. And hoping more than anything that she would heed his words.

Calm before a storm. The whispered words arrived uninvited in Matt's head, forcing him to contemplate the inevitable, pouring cold water on his short-lived escape from reality. He hated being the responsible one, ironic as it seemed under their circumstances. But Matt wasn't one to shirk doing the right thing. Probably down to his mum's ability to instil a conscience in her sons, he thought, a warm feeling flooding through him as his mother's sound words of advice rang loudly in his ears. His pulse quickened as an unexpected rush of heat surged along his neck and into his cheeks. Secrets – he hated secrets, hated not being able to share this important event with his parents. Or anybody else for that matter. Instantly, he qualified his latest actions by convincing himself he was saving his family from worry and what they didn't know couldn't harm them. His pulse slowed in pace but his nagging conscience refused to be placated.

He leaned his shoulder against the wall, tracing the old-fashioned floral wallpaper-pattern with his index finger, reminded of the time he'd scribbled on the walls of his grandmother's hallway. Gloria had scolded him at the time, yet many years later he'd heard her bragging that she'd been the first to discover his artistic talents. Comical really, seeing as his graffiti efforts on the wall of the basketball court got him a severe reprimand from the local gardaí at the time. His granny, of course, found a positive amidst the shame of having the gardaí ringing on the doorbell. She had pointed out the quality of his drawing to anyone prepared to ignore the fact that he'd been defacing public property!

Would Heidi's parents be so forgiving when they discovered she'd absconded to New York without saying a word, he wondered. With him? Matt didn't think so and in the absence of any response from Heidi on the matter, he tried again to get her to rethink her decision and at least let her family know she was safe.

"It'll only take a moment to make contact, Heidi. Tell them you have a new number. Even a one-line email to put their minds at ease. You won't have to disclose where you are unless you want to. What if they've been trying to call your mobile? Or they need to get in touch with you urgently?"

Not for the first time, he fretted about the consequences of Heidi's decision to follow him, fearful of the determined lengths she was capable of going to (and not only in geographical distance), hating the distasteful fact that he too was party to her deceit.

Packing his things with his mum, he'd been really careful to continue the charade that he was setting out on a big adventure alone. Well, the big adventure part was true. But alone? He'd barely spent a moment alone since he'd met Heidi at JFK airport.

When he'd accepted the offer as a gym teacher and basketball coach at NYC College, Heidi had instantly conjured up plans of her own. Back home, he'd been caught up in the fizz of her excitement. Extricating himself from arrangements he'd made with college friends, he'd welcomed her suggestion with open arms and a big smile on his face. But now that they'd arrived and their web of lies was spinning wider and wider, he had serious reservations about the wisdom of their decision.

Heidi half-turned towards him, raising an eyebrow and shrugging her shoulders. "In another few days, I'll call them and give them my new number. It's no biggie, Matt!"

His persistence matched her obstinacy: "But what's the worst thing they can say, eh?"

He watched as she slowly withdrew from the window, tugging on the frame to get it back into place. Once she'd secured the old-fashioned latch, she drew the heavy velvet drapes together, shutting out the city and isolating them from the rest of the world.

"Stop fussing, Matt. I'm not expected back from Cyprus for another few days so they won't be even thinking about me yet. Anyway, in case you haven't noticed, I *am* a consenting adult!"

"Oh, I'd noticed," he deadpanned, looking deep into her eyes, then slowly allowing his gaze to rove the length of her svelte body, the deep physical attraction he felt for her causing his breath to quicken.

Heidi's soft, seductive voice cut into his fantasy.

"Don't you want to be alone with me?"

Matt moved a step closer and nodded, drinking in the outline of her firm breasts, her tiny waist and legs that went on forever.

She ran her tongue over her lips. "Can't we savour where we are for now? Being away from it all without having to hide from interfering and disapproving families? We deserve this bliss. Allow us to enjoy it. Please?"

Her words hung in the stuffy room, the mood between them intensifying, their anonymity paramount and their location immaterial once they were together.

Unable to resist her tantalising, Matt reached out and pulled her into his arms. He inhaled the lingering scent of the latest YSL fragrance she'd sprayed from a sample bottle in Macy's, his tongue flicking gently against her earlobe, his body tingling with lustful anticipation.

"Cold?" she asked when he shivered in her arms. "Maybe it's time you put on more than your boxers." She tilted her head as she looked up at him, her bright blue eyes twinkling mischievously, her finger trailing over his chest, circling his belly button, her hips swaying gently against his thighs. She was expert at distracting him and expert at getting her own way, making it impossible for him to refuse her anything.

"Or maybe it's time you took off yours, you little minx," he said, feeling her warm breath on his ear, submitting to her advances and entwining his fingers in hers. Guiding her towards the wall, childhood scribbles and family issues were the furthest things from his mind as their lips met. Their rented space in Midtown Manhattan was a safe haven from the world's demands and the chain of events about to unfold. At least for now.

Chapter 2

Lucy Ardle curled up on the couch in her sister Delia's conservatory, oblivious to the magnificent sea view, the uncertainty of her future stretching before her, a brand-new chapter in her life about to begin.

Earlier that afternoon she'd been fraught and distracted, her mind on the other side of the Atlantic with her son, Matt. He'd left for New York a few days previously, excited and apprehensive. Watching him walk through the departure gates of Shannon Airport reminded her of his very first day at nursery school when he'd clutched his teacher's hand and waved Lucy a solemn goodbye. This time his wave had been cheery, his bright eyes holding hers until he'd disappeared beyond the security gates. The lump in her throat threatened to choke her long after he'd disappeared from view, a dark cloud of loneliness slipping around her.

Danny didn't understand. But husbands seldom did, Lucy thought, fiddling with the collection of bronze figurines on the table beside her, remembering Danny's sorry attempt at comforting her when she'd tried to explain how she felt. She wasn't a fool and had known full well he'd been watching the Sports Channel over her shoulder while she poured her heart out. Irritated by his nonchalance, she'd stormed from the house, telling him in no uncertain terms how inconsiderate he was being.

She drove furiously to their entrance gate where she braked sharply, scattering gravel. Then she nosed out onto the narrow byroad, glancing up the road to her neighbour Carol Black's lavish house, Hillcrest, wondering if she was there. But a chat and a coffee with a neighbour wouldn't remedy this situation. Only a heart-to-heart with a sister would do.

As per usual, Delia was on hand in a crisis, her home not far from Lucy's by car, living as they did on opposite sides of the seaside village of Crosshaven in County Cork.

Lucy's lips shaped into a sudden smile as she remembered her younger sister's shock when she'd arrived on her doorstep, babbling incoherently, tears rolling down her cheeks.

"Anyone would think there was a death in the family and not a bit of upheaval over a graduate leaving home!" Delia had blurted out, ushering Lucy inside Bracken, her split-level home on Strand Hill.

Once Lucy's sobbing had subsided, Delia went to the kitchen to make coffee.

"It's a lot tougher than you expected, eh?" she said as she returned with a laden tray: steaming coffee, a bowl of whipped cream, a plateful of the chunkiest chocolate-chip cookies Lucy had ever seen and two enormous mugs.

"The emptiness is surreal, Del, not to mention the dread of endless boring days with nothing to do. As for the stillness in the house . . ." Lucy shuddered. "I find it impossible to stay there any length of time. And I know I was forever shouting at him to lower the volume on his rock music but I'd do anything now to hear the thudding bass guitar bringing the house back to life."

"Come on, this isn't like you. I thought you were delighted for Matt to spread his wings?" Delia went for reinforcements, returning a moment later with a large box of chocolates – an essential accessory in any crisis. Unwrapping the cellophane, she took the lid from the box and gave Lucy all four of her favourite Turkish delights from the top layer.

Popping one in her mouth, Lucy lined the others up like soldiers on the table in front of her. Thinking hard about Delia's question, she sucked on the mixture of milk chocolate and soft gelatine, enjoying the rich taste as it slid down her throat, reaching for the second one before she'd even finished the first. "Of course I'm happy for *him*. It's me I feel sorry for."

"You weren't nearly this bad when Stephen left for Oz, Luce," Delia reminded her, filling both of their mugs.

"I know but this is totally different, a complete wrench. I missed Stephen like crazy. But at least Matt was still at home then. And I was busy. It's so damn orderly in the house now. No sports gear lying around, no mess in the kitchen and nobody clearing all the nice stuff from the fridge in record time."

"Surely that's not all bad?" Delia ventured carefully, scooping a generous helping of cream into her coffee and pulling her feet under her as she made herself comfortable on the couch for a marathon sisterly chat.

Lucy shook her head. "For the first time in years, I can hear myself think. And I can honestly tell you I don't like one word of what I'm hearing." Loneliness expanded inside her like an inflating balloon, overwhelming her with its severity, making it impossible for her to look forward.

Delia reached out and took a truffle from the box, nibbling at it as she outlined her sister's predicament aloud. "So the boys are settling into new lives, Danny's happy to leave them to it and that leaves you where exactly? Disgruntled? Lost? Bored? As far as I can see, Luce, it's time to give yourself a kick up the backside, step out of your comfort zone and take your spare time in a new direction."

Lucy's eyes misted. "Look at the state of me. I'm pathetic. I can't even think straight, never mind anything else. Being a mother and wife, organising school runs and PTA meetings are all I've known for the last twenty years."

"That's the most ridiculous thing I've ever heard," Delia shot back, popping two chocolate hazelnuts in her mouth, her patience and tolerance wearing thin, annoyance speeding up her chocolate consumption. "It's a hell of a long time since you've done a school run! For God's sake, Matt is twenty-one! It's not like he was hanging around your feet every day. He was barely ever home. Get a grip, sis!" She crunched the chocolates loudly, running her tongue around her teeth to extricate tiny pieces of hazelnut, refusing to indulge Lucy's self-pity.

This time her sister couldn't disagree. "Maybe not, but he was always coming and going, generally with a few others in tow."

"To pick up his laundry and get fed no doubt," Delia muttered under her breath, instantly remorseful when her sister's face crumpled. "Ah, I didn't mean it like that,

Luce, but he's a grown man and he wouldn't want you pining after him. Give yourself some time to get used to things. You'll soon find your feet again."

"I hope so, Del. I really do. But, right now, it's a shock to my system."

Munching on chocolate after chocolate, they managed to eat their way through to the second layer, discussing Lucy's dilemma in great detail and coming up with a few suggestions to ease her into the next phase of her life. Surprise November sunshine filtered into the conservatory as the sisters chatted amicably, the unexpected warmth – along with Delia's reassuring words – brightening Lucy's spirits and encouraging her to look forward once more.

"Next week, Del," she promised her sister determinedly, allowing herself another day or two to wallow, "next week will be the start of something new, a time to find myself again. And who knows what adventures will come my way?"

Carol Black breezed in the front door of her luxury three-storey home, more than satisfied with her Saturday afternoon. Eric was due back from his business trip the following day and had promised they'd have reason to celebrate. And knowing how her husband liked to do things in style and have her looking her best, Carol hadn't left anything to chance. Her platinum bob gleamed after her trip to the hair salon and the dress she'd spotted in Lily & Clara's boutique window in Ballincollig was now safely wrapped in tissue paper and rightfully hers.

Flicking through the post sitting in the box since the previous day, she soon realised it was all bank stuff and dropped the envelopes on the hall table for Eric to deal with. He'd made it clear from the early days of their marriage that he didn't like her opening his post so now she never dreamt of doing so, in any case finding his wheeling and dealing complex and impossible to follow, something she'd have lived quite happily without. But the rewards were fruitful, and the lavish lifestyle something she'd become accustomed to, so she was happy to turn a blind eye to the intricate and possibly suspect detail.

Feeling suddenly weary and pleased at the thought of having their large sleigh bed to herself, she craved an early night with the plasma TV and her fashion magazines for company, but unfortunately her daughter Isobel would need a lift to the airport in a while.

At present Isobel was locked away in the study on the third floor, knee-deep in prep work for yet another project she was co-ordinating for her high-level IT position. Amazed by her daughter's hunger to succeed in such a male-dominated environment, Carol often worried that one day Isobel would look back and weep, regretting spending her Saturday nights wrapped up in the latest software development instead of a handsome man's arms. A stickler for perfection, she had a flight to Dublin that evening, adamant she'd need Sunday to set up her conference room and get everything exactly right (including burning mood-sticks to induce the exact atmosphere she wanted to prevail) so the first of her presentations, on Monday morning, would go without a hitch. Isobel left nothing to chance.

Definitely inherited the ambitious gene from her father, Carol thought with a smile, grabbing her Lily & Clara bag and her bundle of glossies, anticipating a perfect end to her day once she'd dropped Isobel to the airport.

If you enjoyed these chapters from
Love is the Reason by Mary Malone
why not order the full book online
@ www.poolbeg.com

POOLBEG WISHES TO

THANK YOU

for buying a Poolbeg book.

If you enjoyed this why not visit our website:
www.poolbeg.com

and get another book delivered straight to your home or to a friend's home!

All books despatched within 24 hours.

POOLBEG

WHY NOT JOIN OUR MAILING LIST
@ www.poolbeg.com and get some fantastic offers on Poolbeg books